MID-
NIGHT
SHER
-BET

MID NIGHT SHER BET

MIDNIGHT SHERBET

ISBN – 9798363055614

emmasmithbooks.com

for the people in my life
who taught me friends
can be soulmates too…

carmel

The boy is looking at me.

I thought he was as I boarded the bus back in the city centre, energy drink in hand. He was lurking under the shelter, hidden beneath a baggy hoodie and chunky trainers, then stepped from the shadows to hurry up the steps behind me. I sat down first, on one of the long, inward-facing benches that line the centre of the bus. The boy slouched opposite, all swagger and lazy inattention.

I thought we locked eyes when the driver brought us to an abrupt stop at a red light, halting just in time to avoid smashing into the car in front. It almost sent me hurtling forward into the aisle, but I grabbed hold of the rail and managed to pull myself back up, catching his eye as I went.

They were brown, almost black against the white of his face. And they were staring straight at me.

I thought he smiled when I pulled out my phone to check the time, betraying myself with a glance in his direction.

I thought he smiled when I reached across to push the button, so that the bus would stop for me next, but now – as we draw to another red, the city flashing all around us – it's unmistakable.

He's looking at me.

Staring at me.

It's not as if I don't like being looked at. I don't usually care what other people think of me, not really. People stare all the time, whether they like what they see or not.

But what I hate is being looked at like *that*.

Like I'm a toy in a shop window, an animal in the zoo, something to lust over, tongue out and drool dripping down their faux-designer shirt.

He smiles, one of those half-conscious, all-eyes-and-no-mouth smiles, then lifts a hand in what could be a wave. It could also just be a stretch of the fingers, given the lack of effort.

"Hey," he says, as the bus starts off again. Lights dance on the seats around us, red and blue and green and yellow, all shades of jewel. My hands are patterned in colour. I push them beneath me and first gaze out of the window, watching as the city dances by. McDonald's, some supermarket or other, Kevin's Fish and Chips, Andrew's Kebab Truck…

And the boy's reflection, staring back at me in the glass.

I glance down at my lap in order to avoid meeting his eyes, but that only seems to make things worse.

"Hey," he repeats, louder this time. An old lady sat by the driver jerks her head to look at us, the scowl on her face clear. We're the only other people on the bus, and we're making too much noise. "I'm Finn."

Again, I don't respond. Maybe not a method proven to actually work, but replying will only give him hope. He has messy black hair and a face attributed only to soap stars or models for supermarket clothes, freckle-studded and sharp, too many white teeth and a pointed nose. He's good-looking, and I'm sure he knows it. But that isn't the point.

I pull out my phone, pretending to be deep in conversation with the blank screen, and hear him let out a sigh.

"I'm just being friendly."

And I'm not reciprocating – take the hint.

But I don't say that.

It feels too much like giving in.

The bus is approaching my stop, where a couple of kids are messing about on the bench. The streetlight above has long been out of use, so one of them has set up a phone torch on the rafter, casting blue light over their faces. We pull to a stop, pipes exhaling.

"Let me walk you home!" the boy insists. He's behind me as I make my way to the door, nodding to the driver and pushing earphones in. There's no music playing, and the silence is deafening. The kids from the bus stop push past me as we step into the cold night's air.

My house is about four streets away, the city dark and empty. Semi-detached houses with dying lawns, flaky-painted doors and broken bicycles loom up and down the main street, the odd car roaring past in a blur of light and fumes.

The boy still hasn't left my side.

"You live round here?" he asks. When I don't reply, he pulls his hood up further to hide his hair, then reaches out to me, in a way that's so subtle that I don't notice until it's too late. The bus pulls past us, the old lady still watching through the window as he grabs my hand.

"Woah!" he exclaims. I try to move away, heart pounding and anger pulsing through my veins, but I can't pull free of him. He's strong, far too strong, nails digging into my palm as I attempt tug my hand away. "What are you doing?"

"Bugger off!" I hiss. "Just leave me alone!

He pulls back, wounded. I wait for a moment, hoping he'll take the hint, but his grip only tightens and sharp pain ricochets through my hand and up my wrist.

"You're *feisty*!" he continues. "You do realise that's a major turn off, right?"

Of course it is. Guys like girls who are submissive, who give in to their attention and are flattered by their desperate attempts. Guys like girls they can exert their power over with minimum pushback, fluttering lashes and blushes.

I'm not one of those girls.

We're nearing the end of the street now, where the traffic lights blink and the crossroads open. The boy is clearly intent on following whichever path I head down.

Shit.

I don't know what to do. I know he won't try anything while we're still in public, but any of the three streets head into unknown territory, where houses are set deeper on silent lawns and bushes make the perfect spot for malpractice. If I head down my own street, he'll find out where I live.

The thought alone makes my belly ache.

"Please just leave me alone," I say. I sound more confident than I actually feel, and the boy cocks his head in surprise. "I'm not interested, okay?"

But it's not okay, not really.

Boys like Finn aren't used to being told "no" – not even when it really matters.

We've crossed the road. I don't know how, but the boy has somehow led me through the red lights down the street that leads to my own, which I hope is a coincidence. Wind blows up my jeans and the heavy thud of our trainers on the concrete is the only sound audible above rustling trees and the occasional car. The road is growing quieter, houses further apart and set down long green drives. We stop before a hedge, thick with leaves and just-turning foliage.

Before I can run, his hands are on my waist, squeezing

tight. I can't breathe, can't *think*, frozen under his gaze.

"You're beautiful," he says in that low, sleezy tone. I suck in a breath, wriggling to get away, but he only moves in closer, arms tightening around me. "Girls like you shouldn't be left to walk home alone, you know? Anything could happen…"

"Get *off* me!" I tell him, but is sounds more like a whisper, voice struggling.

"Don't play hard to get," he murmurs, leaning in closer. His breath reeks of gum with an undertone of Monster; there's a tiny, glistening ball of snot on the end of his nose, watching me. I hold my breath, so that my lips are turned in away from him, as he leans towards me –

"What are you doing?" comes a voice from behind us. The boy spins round, eyes wide, and loosens his grip on my waist in frenzied panic.

"None of your –" he begins, then stops when he sees the culprit. "Who do you think you are? *Superman?*"

It's a boy about our age, stood on the curb in a puffer-jacket with a fluffy hood. He has his hands on his hips and feet planted heavy on the ground, expression etched into a frown. He's tubby, all blue eyes and fluffy brown hair, spots laced across his skin and stubble poking through his chin.

"She said *get off*," he says, while my attacker rolls his eyes and turns to face him, letting go of me at last.

I don't need to think twice.

"Hey, stop!" he yells, as I begin to hurtle down the street. My trainers hit the pavement hard and I can't hear him following me, so I keep going, faster and faster, until I reach the corner, where I stop to glance behind me.

Finn is still in the same position, staring at me in fury, but doesn't make an attempt to come after me. Heartrate slowing,

I turn my head to the other boy.

Superman – or Superboy – has his phone out, held up so that I can just make out what he's doing. He has typed in three numbers and has his finger poised to dial.

"Turn around and walk the other way," he says, voice level. "Go on!"

I watch as the boy reluctantly slopes off, hood up, back towards the crossroads. Superboy slips his phone into his pocket and glances back up to where I'm standing, face illuminated by the streetlight.

He holds his hand up to wave, but I don't wave back. Instead, I stare at him, hoping he knows exactly what I'm trying to say.

Thank you.

Superboy smiles.

remy

I watch as the girl hurries round the corner and disappears from sight, hair tucked under her hat. If this were a romcom, I'd chase after her in my nice not-work-stained clothes, not a bead of sweat in sight, and fold her into my arms as a true hero should. She'd laugh – maybe even cry with relief – and allow herself to sink into me, all soft and appreciative, finally finding The One.

But this isn't a romcom, and I'm no hero.

I'm just Remy Evans.

I turn in the other direction before I can change my mind, padding down the road towards the bus stop. I've missed my bus. I watched it escape down the road and out of the city, smoke burbling from its fat exhaust. But it was worth it to save the girl… so I keep telling myself. If I hadn't spotted her trying to tug her hand away, *anything* could have happened.

The shelter is in darkness. A car flies past every few minutes, aiming to bypass the red lights and escape the city, scurrying into the countryside away from the chaos. Even at night-time, something about Hull seems to scare people off, unappreciative of its dirt-scattered walls and graffiti.

But not me.

I pull out my phone and plug in my headphones, waiting out for the familiar click which tells me they're connected. Coldplay: the ultimate definition of happiness. I listen for music to flood my ears as another car roars past, headlights flashing…

Maybe I should've chased after her?

The bus takes another half hour to arrive, finally pulling up the street in a haze of maroon. I glance up from my lap just as it comes to a stop. The final few takeaway shops and one electrical store selling half-price appliances still have their windows lit up, blue and red and green, like boiled sweets in a line above the road, and a flash of movement catches my eye as I go to stand.

An old man is curled up in a duvet outside the kebab shop, eyes wide. They're filled with that hollow, hungry look, the look of someone who hasn't eaten for far too long, who just wants something, *anything*, to fill the void.

"Two minutes?" I yell, catching the eye of the bus driver as the door opens with a hiss. He nods, holding up a hand to wave. And – with barely a second thought – I dash across the road.

The kebab shop is just about to close, cashier pulling down the blinds as I push through the door, bell tinkling. I buy one chicken kebab, a portion of cheesy chips, then grab two lemonade cans from the fridge as an afterthought. There are six sausage rolls in a packet on the side, only a pound, and so I pay for those too, grinning at the cashier and throwing him a wave as I leave.

The old man has an unopened bottle of something murky tucked into his duvet, hip flask by his side. He gazes up at me as I hand him the goods, face open in surprise.

"God bless you, lad!"

It's enough to make everything feel worthwhile.

Back on the bus, I pick a seat by the front, tucking my bag beside me and settling into the cushions.

It's moments like this that I live for. Moments of open, genuine happiness, of shocked delight and gratefulness, humanity at its best. The look of the girl when she got away from that boy, even though I didn't do nearly as much as I should have; the look of the old man when I passed him the food, hot and warm and cheese-covered.

Maybe I'm selfish. Maybe – just maybe – I spread joy because it makes me feel good, creating a shot of euphoria from causing someone just a little happiness.

But, in a world where you can be anything, there's no reason not to be kind.

***

The house is silent, hall in darkness. Light creeps under the living room door as I dump my bag and shoes, socks shuffling on the floorboards as I push through into the dim.

"Hey," I say softly. Mum is curled up on the sofa with baby Angelique tucked into her breast. Her lips are suctioned onto a nipple, illuminated by the white lamp above.

"Good day, love?" she murmurs. She beckons for me to come over, and kisses me on the forehead. Lingering, she breathes in deeply, then gestures for me to sit. "How was work?"

I started working at a corner shop in Hull a few weeks back, right on the outskirts, in one of the poorer areas. It's a quaint building, painted cobalt blue and lemon yellow, with wooden boxes set atop turf on the street outside, filled with produce. The owner, Ravi, is the heart of the community; no one would ever steal from him, so the fruit remains outside in all weathers, sheltered beneath a little green canopy. He opens day and night, too many hours, heading back to his empty house and tabby cat each night before going again.

Ravi is one of the best people I know, the kind of man I aspire to be one day. Truly selfless.

"It was wonderful," I tell her, settling into the cushion. "I made a deal with this independent trader – she makes her own pickles, chutneys, that sort of thing – and Ravi is going to stock her produce from now on! He said it was a good call… he's been looking for more locally sourced products."

"That's wonderful, love," Mum says, but she clearly hasn't taken in a word of what I've said. "Your dad will be back soon. I think he's been at the office, they had a big mix-up or something…"

"I think I'm just going to finish some homework. I got extra English today. Mr O'Flannel thinks it'll boost my application if I have a stronger knowledge of Milton, and…"

But she definitely isn't listening now, gazing down at Angelique as I continue to talk to a deaf ear.

"He's set me a list of poems from a similar period to analyse, and let me borrow this book of critical theories about Milton's life and influences. It looks pretty interesting –"

"Shhh, baby." At first, I think she's talking to me. Then I notice her hand on Angelique's cheek, stroking the space between her nose and little blue eyes, and stand to leave.

There's a space on the other side of her breast, where one nipple lies untouched. Her shirt is laid over the arm of the chair and one hand caresses the air, fingers moving up and down like she's playing an invisible harp. She's been losing weight recently, the doctors say. It's a normal part of grief, but, if it gets worse, we should call them again before things spiral out of control.

"Shhh, Toby," Mum whispers again, this time not focusing on Angelique at all, but running her hand over her breast, eyes glassy. "Shhh, Toby…"

The space where my baby brother should be stays empty, untouched, as Mum tries to reach him, tries to stroke his little blonde head and encourage him to feed.

"I love you, Mum."

But she's lost in another world.

I drag my bag upstairs, to where my bedroom sits at the top of the landing. It's only a small house, just big enough for the four of us, but Angelique still sleeps in my parents' room. She'll have my room once I leave for university, Dad says. And when I come back to visit, I'll have the sofa.

It's a decent size, painted deep blue with the occasional bubble of white from where I ripped off childhood stickers during puberty. I've since covered the gaps with Sharpie-scrawled quotes, from Shakespeare and Keats and my favourite Seamus Heaney, but there's something beautiful about those holes still, something haunting. I collapse onto my bed and tug the Milton book from my bag, dog-eared and library-stamped.

I open it to page eleven, where Mr O'Flannel left a bookmark, and start to read…

Only I can't. One thought – one image, one mental photograph – goes tumbling through my mind, over and over and over.

The girl.

The girl, with her brown eyes and slouchy hat, pulled fast

over her earphones. Turning the corner after staring at me with that long, concentrated glance, mouth unsmiling.

I try to find my place on the page again, but my eyes won't stop wandering. The words blur together and music dances across my mind, Coldplay and Oasis and The Beatles, black and blue and pink and orange and –

The girl, again, clearer than ever. Tugging her hand away from the boy's, expression full of fire, teeth ground together in a decisive line –

I snap the book shut, face burning. There's no way I can concentrate on the words of Milton tonight, not even for the sake of my Oxford application.

"Screw you, beautiful girl," I mutter, then I flush even more, whole body burning. "Screw you."

Should I have chased after her? It wouldn't have made a difference if I did. Girls like her don't like guys like me – that's a fact. For all my optimism, I've had those same words drilled into me since I was eleven years old and asked Carlotta Stevens to the school dance in front of our entire French class, only for her to squash the chocolate cake I'd made her down hard on my head.

Big guys, guys with acne and lacking facial hair and chubby fingers… we don't get the girl. It's the kind of thing I'd say is a rumour, if it wasn't so true. At eighteen, having never so much as pecked a girl's lips, you start to wonder whether there's really no hope.

I hop off my bed, floorboards creaking as I land too heavily. There's a mirror opposite my bed, one Mum hung up so that I could try on my prom suits in privacy when I was sixteen and going through "the phase". I pull off my shirt first. It's a *Mario Kart* number Matt bought me at a gaming convention, one of my favourites. The sticker is starting to peel. Then I tug off the vest I wear to keep my stomach tucked in and my body as inconspicuous as possible.

There he is. The real Remy Evans.

Worse than the guy who hides behind puffer-jackets and hoodies is this guy, this… monster. A guy who's pale and can only grow a smattering of thin, pale hairs across his chest and underarms, whose stomach sticks out over his jeans when he forgets to wear a vest. The guy who's never had a girlfriend, who was rejected three times before finally giving up, resigning himself to the fact that he may end up a bachelor with seven cats. I don't even *like* cats.

Sighing, I glare at the body before me, watching it transform into a pale lump. Tremulous white skin, a smattering of off-coloured moles, twin nipples set on a heavy chest.

ugly

fat

disgusting

Maybe I was right. I spread joy because it makes me feel good, gives me a shot of euphoria I don't deserve.

I'm selfish.

I act like everything is so great, like the world is so beautiful, like I'm so excited to live this life.

I love everything…

But, at the heart of it all, I hate myself.

carmel

I don't look back.

Perhaps he deserves a second glance – he did save me from that boy, after all – but I just can't do it. I'm already late, and Mum will be wanting her tea.

I dash onto my road, tearing round the corner under the light of Mrs Dichre's porch. It's late now, past eleven. Half of the streetlights are out, meaning my street is cast in darkness. Our house is halfway down the row of run-down terraces, a solitary lamp still flickering in the living room window.

Mum is curled up on the sofa as I let myself in, blanket tucked under her chin. Mrs Dichre pops in most nights to check on her whilst I'm out; she's left a bunch of flowers in our vase (an old yoghurt pot) on the coffee table. The wrapper from a microwave meal lies next to it.

"Evening, chuck," Mum whispers, lifting her chin to smile at me. She looks tired, dark circles round her eyes and cheeks tinged grey. "Get yourself something to eat, then go straight to bed. It's almost twelve."

"You've already eaten?" Guilt writhes in the pit of my stomach, though the evidence is clear as she nods. I notice the sweet-and-sour stains around her mouth, where new wrinkles seem to form each day. She hates "ding-dong" food as she calls it, but Mrs Dichre was only trying to help.

"Don't worry about me," she insists. "I think Mrs Dichre

left some onions and a slice of cake on the kitchen side, but I think you'll have to go shopping tomorrow, Carmel…"

Shopping. Like I have time for that.

I smile, nodding and backing out of the door, but my heart is already pulsing with dread for the following day. Even if I didn't have enough to do, whirling round the supermarket with a shopping trolley looking for half-price veg isn't something I usually enjoy.

"I'll be back in a minute," I tell her. She nestles further into the blanket, smiles weakly, then nods a sad, almost unnoticeable nod.

She was right; the kitchen is almost bare. Mrs Dichre has left a bag of onions on the table, a slice of her daughter's birthday cake wrapped in a tissue beside it, but apart from that, there's nothing in the cupboards. They've even been left open as if to emphasise the fact, so she might as well have left a sign on the door reading, *This is an embarrassment, Carmel – you need to go shopping!*

Two pots of spice shiver under a layer of mould, and the salt-and-pepper shakers are covered in damp from where the upstairs bathroom sometimes leaks. The backs of the cupboards have been turning green, worse by the stove where the humidity from the kettle breeds unspeakable things.

I try to chop the worst parts off the onion, and find that the centre is fairly fresh, crunchy and white and fleshy. With some of the paprika from the cupboard, they almost taste good, if a little spicy. The chocolate cake is going hard but the icing tastes okay, and there are three skittles stuck to the top.

I finish eating before I go back through, licking my lips and throwing the knife in the sink to wash tomorrow. I know she can sense it anyway, but part of me still wants to shield Mum from how bad our situation really is.

In the living room, the lamp is flickering even worse than before, on and off and on and off like the light of an ambulance. It must be giving her a headache, but she isn't complaining. I don't think she has the effort to do so. Instead she just... lies there, eyes partly closed, pale lips pursed. Her disease is spelt out in big, black letters, all over her body.

Mum isn't like a lot of people. She rarely makes a fuss, never lets the cancer affect her mood, our relationship. Sometimes she can't help but fret, but I don't mind that. It's just how she is; a fighter, a survivor. She never wants people to see that she's suffering, not if they don't have to.

She didn't stop working until she collapsed in the corridor and they forced her to leave, and even then, she tried her best to pick up extra cleaning jobs to pay for my college transport. She worked long hours, fitting them around hospital appointments and scans, skimping on her own food to make sure I always had enough. Now that she's mostly bedbound, she transfers the benefits she receives after bills into my account without a word.

Even though it's different now, she's still my mum, my confidant, the one person in the world I love. She's the person I can ask anything, tell anything to, gossip with, cry on. She's more than just my mother, in fact. She's my best friend.

But not tonight.

She's been looking worse recently, since the chemo stopped. It's like she's sunk into the person she was before, cowering inside the shell and trying to hold her exterior together. We don't talk about the ratty wig she refuses to take off, or the unfinished sleeve of tattoos on her arm. She keeps her makeup bag by the sofa and applies it each morning, no fail. She never tells me how bad she's feeling, but it's clear on her face as she slips in and out of herself, morphing into a version of my mother I don't think I recognise.

Her blue eyes are still open a crack, but it's obvious she just needs to sleep. I lean forward to place a kiss on her forehead, lips meeting cakey, foundation-crusted skin. Phlegm rises in my throat.

Hold it together.

"Night, Mum," I whisper, squeezing her thin fingers. My mother murmurs in reply.

My bedroom is on the first floor, next to the room she once slept in, which hasn't been touched in months. It's a tiny room, and Mr and Mrs Acharya from next door keep me up most nights with their creaking bed and banging headboard. The walls of the terrace houses on our street are paper thin; Mr and Mrs Acharya are trying for their fourth child, says Mrs Dichre. I'd move into Mum's double room if it didn't mean admitting to myself that she'll never be well enough to sleep there again.

I dump my bag by the door, floorboards creaking. My sketchbook takes up most of the bulk. When I pull it out, a sense of calm ripples through me.

Art is always like that. It can solve anything.

I carry it over to the bed, careful not to crease the sheet of tracing paper I tucked in the edge. I started the art foundation at college just under a month ago, and so far, the best part has been the free materials. I ransack the draws before I leave each day, which are filled with paints and brushes and paper of all colours and thickness, from card to tracing to creamy watercolour. We're still in the introductory phase of our course, and this week's project was focused on figure drawing, which is right down my street.

I start to draw my mum first, a feature in almost every page of my sketchbook. I know the curve of her cheekbones instinctively, know the wayward direction of the hair in her wig, know each and every tattoo on her pale arms. I scribble around the edges with an orange highlighter I stole from college, creating the warm glow of the lamp, scattered over her blanket. Her eyes watch me through the page, shadowed blue.

I finish the piece before I've even taken a breath, heart racing and eyes filled with unshed tears. I can't even look at it. I turn the page, fingers trembling, and push the drawing well out of sight, before I take up my pen and start again.

I draw the boy from the bus this time. Finn, he said his name was. Finn, with his dark eyes and boy-band good looks, and the kind of tacky expression you see on cartoon characters. The bus is always a feature of my sketchbook in some way. It's different every day, which is one of the reasons I hate it.

I finish the piece and stick the tracing paper over the top, so that his face just shows through in an eery fashion, partly translucent.

Then I start again.

There are always a few hours missing of each day, in my sketchbook. I draw the bus journey in the morning, draw my day at college, draw my few "friends" and lunch at the canteen. I draw in my art classes, draw the teacher and room and other students, sketch the still life compositions they set up on the central table. I draw the two and a half hours spent in the college library after most people have gone home, tucked in between stressed year thirteens and year twelve nerds. I draw the journey away from college, the changing leaves and frantic shoppers, the kids hurrying to after-school clubs.

Then I skip three hours exactly, from the minute I arrive at work to the moment I catch the bus again, at half ten. No one, not even the privacy of my sketchbook pages, needs to see what happens during that time. Sometimes I participate in the other classes, do some quick sketches, but nothing… nothing that compares.

I find myself flipping onto a third spare page, however. My pen hovers over a patch where I've previously stuck a square of brown paper, hoping to try working onto a different, more textured background, and presses down in a thick, black starting point.

The face which forms before me isn't one I was expecting. It's rounded, chubby, with blue eyes and fluff dotted across his acne-covered cheeks. The figure is dressed in a puffer-jacket with a fluffy hood and a *Mario Kart* t-shirt. I draw that smile, open and friendly, before snapping my sketchbook shut and sending it hurtling across the floor, where it lands with a clunk against the skirting board.

That's enough for today.

remy

I can't stop thinking about the girl.

I'm still thinking about her when I wake up the next morning, duvet thrown off in a frenzy and body covered in sheen of sweat.

I'm still thinking about her when I drag myself out of bed and into the bathroom, where I stand in front of the mirror for five minutes, debating what to do with my hair. Those brown eyes, the earphones dangling from under her hat, the messy curls and pale, almost translucent skin under the lamplight… Should I just brush it out as normal, or try to gel the front bit up, like some of the guys at school do?

I'm still thinking about her as I choose my outfit, pulling out all the drawers from my wardrobe in order to decide. Light blue denim, dark blue, black, grey, a nice top, perhaps one of my birthday presents from Matt, the space landing one, or the one with *Shrek* badges pinned to the rim. I pick the space landing in the end, the astronaut's little face peeking out from under helmet in exactly the same way the girl's face did.

I'm still thinking about her when I go down for breakfast. Pancakes, microwaved and smeared with chocolate spread, with a glass of bitty orange juice, even though it makes me feel faintly sick. I'm still thinking about her as Mum slips me my packed lunch, in the Disney container I've had since I was seven, filled with a fig roll, egg and cress sandwich, leftover coleslaw. My bag's crammed full of books as I go to leave, but it's so fat I know I'll look like a tortoise if I lug it round all day. In the end, I leave Mr O'Flannel's book on Milton at the back door. He can have it back another time.

"Have a good day, love!" Mum calls, waving from the kitchen. Angelique waves a fist, gurgling her goodbye. "Are you at work later?"

I nod, slamming the door behind me. It's a simple lie, and she probably won't notice if I'm late back, either. She doesn't need to know the real reason I'm travelling into Hull tonight.

Matt is waiting for me at the corner of the road at quarter to nine, as usual. He's on his phone, eyes fixed on the tiny yellow Pac-Man as he navigates the maze, tipping it left and right to avoid being swallowed up. He barely glances up as we start walking, but my best friend has never been one for small talk.

"You 'kay?" he asks. "Your hair looks different."

I roll my eyes, because that's just so *Matt*. He might not say much, but, after being friends for fifteen years and never once wavering, he knows me better than I know myself.

"You've done something different… which means there's a girl," he continues. "That's it, isn't it? Is it Lily?"

"What?" I almost splutter with indignation, but Matt's face is all-knowing. It's like we have some sixth sense shared between us, a telepathic cord connecting our brains. He finally switches off his phone and pushes it into his pocket, expression serious.

"Because you know she's off-limits, right? I called dibs the Halloween she dressed as Shaun the Sheep. Just because she likes you, doesn't mean –"

"Lily doesn't like *me*," I insist.

Matt shakes his head in pity.

It's true, though. Lily and I have been friends forever, and the thought of ever being anything more is just *wrong*. Which is why it took me so long to accept that Matt liked her, to accept there was ever a possibility of me becoming a third wheel. I don't know if Lily likes him back. I don't know if Lily really likes *anyone*.

But Matt's long-time crush on our honorary third-best-friend only got worse when he decided she was, in fact, infatuated with me. It's nonsense, obviously. The three of us are better off as friends.

I roll my eyes at him now, and say, "Like I've told you a billion times, you need to just tell her how you feel!"

Not that I actually want him to do that. Like I said… we're best friends, the three of us. Adding something else to the mix would disrupt the balance, tip the scales.

"Whatever." Matt switches back to his laid-back self, picking a half-chewed piece of gum from his pocket and throwing it into his mouth. "Who is it, then? Who's the girl? Or boy… I won't judge."

"Won't you?"

For a second, I debate not telling him. It's not as though it would help. She's still *way* too good for me, and I don't even know her name. But, as he watches me with his eyes narrowed and mouth sucked into a thin line, I know that I can't *not* tell him… nor can I keep it in for any longer.

"Course I won't."

"I don't believe you."

"Remy…"

I suddenly can't keep it in any longer.

"It's a girl," I burst. "I don't know her name. All I know is that's she's beautiful and lives in Hull and gets off the bus at around eleven on McKing Street, about a five minute walk from where I work. She had a blue rucksack and a black beanie and all of this dark curly hair, and I swear I'm in love with her."

Matt stares at me for a moment. We're approaching the school gates now, and the pavement around us is filling up with people. One year seven kid is watching us with a disgusted expression, and the year eleven smokers blast fumes at us as we pass them with our breaths held.

"That was a *lot* of information in a *very* short space of time." Matt raises his eyebrows. "God, Remy."

My heart is racing and my palms are all sweaty, but I'm quiet as I wait for him to elaborate, watching a response ticking through his mind.

"You want to see her again, I guess?"

I nod. I *have* to see her again. That's non-negotiable.

"Okay," Matt says. He's clearly still thinking, thoughts revolving round and round his head as we start up the main path towards the sixth form block. "Okay, Remy. Let's do this!"

"What do you mean?" I ask, eyeing my best friend sceptically. "Is this another one of your bright ideas?"

"Maybe." Matt's lip quirks, eyes sparkling. "Would you object?"

"I just want to see her again."

Matt grins, nodding once, twice. "Then leave it up to me, Remy. Leave it up to me…"

***

The common room is mostly empty, save for a few straggling year twelves crammed into a booth with bacon sarnies and cartons of strawberry milk. On a high table in one corner, lounging on stools with books and sketchbooks and stationery scattered across the surface, are the rest of our friends.

"Good morning, Remykins," Lily exclaims, reaching out to fist bump me. She leans a little too far and almost topples off her stool in her overalls, but Matt grabs her from behind as she steadies herself, flinching at his touch. "Have you done something different to your hair?"

I roll my eyes again as I take the seat next to Nima. Perhaps I shouldn't have used any gel, because it's clearly not working. She doesn't look up from her maths homework, scribbling over the page in pastel pink fineliner, washi tape clutched tight in her hand, but that's not unusual. At the other end of the table, Mike and Steph are engaged in a serious set of D&D planning, sketching out characters and filling out profile sheets while they share their daily bag of sausage rolls.

It's the same every morning. Since we started at sixth form a year ago, this has been our table, which no one else dares sit at. That may be because Darcie Carlton started a rumour about Mike and Steph fingering each other on one of the stools, but, as Matt insists, could also be because we're *incredibly* intimidating.

We've been good friends for most of secondary school, a bunch of misfits brought together through our love of video games and nerdy films. Matt, Lily and I met Nima in year nine, when Nima started up a 'Save the Pandas' club we joined to improve our social lives, and Mike and Steph are always just *there*, a duo no one is really sure what to think of. We may not be the coolest kids in school – or even anywhere near socially acceptable – but we've grown into a tight circle, a gang of losers bound for life.

If anyone can help me find the girl, it's them.

"Okay, everyone!" Matt claps his hands together to get everyone's attention. Mike and Steph look up in surprise, like they didn't realised we were here. Nima doesn't move from her maths, although her hand goes slack on the pen she's holding and she stops writing for a second. "We have a problem, and we're gonna need all of you to help."

"Can it be after period one?" Lily cuts in, pulling a face. "I need to finish my personal statement before lunch, or I'll never get Mr Roberts to read it in time for the Oxford deadline."

Like me, Lily hopes to apply to Oxford this year, only to study classics instead of literature. It's been our dream ever since I met her in English class on the first day of secondary school. I know how important this is to her. The thought has barely left my mind over the last few years, always hovering on the outskirts, tempting me closer. We visited over the summer, with Lily's parents. The golden sunlight and architecture and beautiful green campus, churros from a stall on the side of the road and trips around the vast dining halls…

It only made me even more desperate to get in.

Finding the girl, however, is a matter *slightly* more pressing.

"Shut up and listen, *then* you can continue!" Matt ignores her mock-hurt expression and thumps the table in indignation. "Remy needs our help!"

"Is everything okay?" Steph asks, pushing her glasses up further on her nose. There are sausage roll crumbs stuck to the peach fuzz on her chin, and her hand is twisted into Mike's across the table in some sort of Gordian knot. I grimace and nod, before Matt takes over again.

"There is a female," he states dramatically, "a female, who gets off the bus at eleven o'clock in Hull on McKing Road –"

"It's McKing *Street*," I cut in, but he brushes me away with his hand.

"– on McKing Street, who owns a blue rucksack and a black beanie. Our good friend Remy, here, is in love with her. We don't know her name, age, sexuality, relationship status, nationality, whether she speaks English –"

"She definitely speaks English."

"– but we need to find her." Matt stops, gazing round the table as everyone stares at him. Nima is with us now, forehead creased as she tries to read my expression, fineliner clutched in her hand.

"So we need to stake out her bus stop?" she asks.

I hate to admit that that was my idea, too, but it's the only thing I thought could possibly work.

She echoes my thoughts exactly, adding, "That's the only way we can find her, right?"

"Right." Matt grins, bringing his fist down on the table with a loud thump. He looks incredibly proud of himself, and Mike and Steph are nodding curiously, exchanging glances.

But Lily is frowning, cheeks flushed pink.

"Count me out," she says. "I have so much to do for my Oxford application, and it sounds too much like stalking to me…"

"Don't be daft!" Matt insists. "It's just called… I don't know, helping a friend!"

She still looks disapproving, so he sighs and adds, "And I'll buy you gummy bears. Those blackcurrant ones they only sell at Colin's Sweet Shop. Your favourite."

Everyone's watching her now. I don't know why, but

something inside of me *needs* her to say yes. I want my friends in on this, fully approving… it's important, somehow. Something about tonight feels *right*, like it has the power to change everything.

"Fine," she says at last, exasperated. "But you better keep your promise, Matthew. I don't know if I trust you."

"Of course I will, Lily dearest," he says, beaming. "It's on, then. Tonight, we're getting Remy a girlfriend!"

carmel

Mum always feels worse in the mornings.

She sleeps through most of the day, so at night, it's a struggle. It's always too hot or too cold, too noisy, the man squatting in the house next door playing music too loud and rattling the floorboards with his druggie friends. To our other side, Mr and Mrs Acharya's baby-making sessions can shake the whole wall, so badly that their youngest, little Arjun, wakes up and starts screaming, bawling through our three floors and into the street beyond.

Mum will be no doubt writhing and crying by the time I go downstairs, hungry and yet not hungry enough to eat, covered in sweat. I try to make her breakfast before I leave, setting her up the best I can for a good day, but this morning, there's still nothing in the cupboards.

"Wait there," I tell her, pulling my hoodie over my head and reaching to grab the front door keys. "I'll go grab you something from the shop, okay?"

It's getting colder in the mornings now, as October takes a hold and the sky is a permanent shade of ashen grey. The nearest store is only a five minute walk from our street, yet I still need a shower and to finish my assignment for college today, and the bus leaves in half an hour – and if I'm late for that, the next one won't arrive for another thirty minutes.

Ravi is just opening up when I reach the shop, pulling the

shutters from the window and reeling out the canopy. He waves as I approach, smile wide.

"Carmel!" he exclaims. "You're out early!"

The store front is blue, letters above spelling "Ravi's Shop" – simple, but catchy – in bright yellow paint, wobbly gold outlining each. The bell tinkles as he pushes through the door.

Ravi's Shop really is as simple as that. A corner shop come grocers, come random jam and chutney supplier… it stocks all kinds of cultural and international foods and essentials, open too many hours, poor Ravi surviving on coffee and good spirits alone.

"There's nothing in for Mum's breakfast." I'm too tired to think of an excuse, too drained to act composed. Ravi has known my mum since the early stages of her diagnosis, when she'd stop by to buy fruit for my packed lunches or jam for my toast at suppertime. His face drops as he notes my bedraggled curls and the bags under my eyes, and he gestures for me to come inside, waving an arm in enthusiasm.

"I have microwavable porridge pots in the back, ones I use for my own lunch. They're wonderful – just a splash of milk and five minutes, and they're ready to go!"

"I don't have any milk." It's more than just a little embarrassing to admit that I can't even keep the essentials stocked up for my terminally ill mother. Ravi frowns. This is a corner shop, and everything has to be a set price in order for Ravi to make any money. Despite selling other local products at the back for discounted prices, essentials like milk and bread are expensive, and sell quick. "I… I just need some apples, or something, I don't know…"

"How about a selection of fruit? Then you can make her a fruit salad!"

I try for a smile, but my lips tremble and I know that if I say too much, my voice will shatter completely. "I don't have time. I'll just get some bananas and leave, I'm in a bit of a rush…"

But Ravi has just the thing.

He leads me to the back of the store, where two bookshelves are stacked with homemade items and packets branded with the familiar Yorkshire rose. There, he finds me a packet of crispbreads, made from wheat grown nearby (of course), and pops a jar of rhubarb jam in the bag with them, tied with brown string and topped with gingham. He gives me a discount, and takes my money with an accompanying hug.

"I won't rip you off, Carmel, not when the food is for your lovely mother!" He glances around his shop again, eyebrows knitted, and his face lights up when he spots the bucket by the counter. "Ah! These are last weeks' apples – half price. Take them, Carmel, and tell your mother I'll pop by later this week to say hello!"

Mum has drifted back to sleep by the time I arrive home. I leave the food on the coffee table as I head for my shower, laid out in a little circle on one of her nice plates, ones we never usually use anymore.

It'll be a nice treat when she wakes up, at least.

The bus is about to set off by the time I get there, sprinting down the road with my hair flying out behind me. The driver stops getting ready to leave when he sees me, rolling his eyes and holding out a hand to take my money.

"Never on time, are you, young lady?"

"Sorry, sorry, I just…"

He doesn't know the half of it.

College is buzzing with life when I arrive, hurtling past frantic year twelves and thirteens in my hurry to reach the art block. The teacher who leads the art foundation course – an extra year of art after finishing A-levels but before starting university – hates tardiness, and I need to stay on his good side if I want a distinction.

He makes us call him "Gareth", though he's still Mr Leam in my head, and taught my graphics class for the second half of year thirteen.

I like him, I think. So far, he seems to like me too.

Mr Leam is already at his desk when I arrive, ticking off names. He checks the clock as I enter, eyes narrowing as though he really wants to catch someone out.

"Carmel?"

"Yes, Gareth?"

"You're almost late."

"Isn't almost late just… on time?"

"Sit down."

I sit.

When I first started the course at the beginning of September, everyone else seemed to know people already. There were a few girls I recognised from A-levels, along with a number of artsy types I'd seen hanging round the library, and two boys with dyed hair and chains who seemed friendly enough. I sat with them, hoping they'd more or less leave me alone, and they have so far. We eat lunch together and walk to and from the buildings side by side, but I'm not even sure of their names.

We nod at each other now as I find a stool, enough that it doesn't feel awkward, but in a way that's distant enough not to prompt further conversation. It's like that every day. Boy 1 – the one with green hair and a nose piercing – passes me today's assignment without a word, and Boy 2, who has black hair and a pale, watery complexion, drops a roll of masking tape before me. I pull out my sketchbook and push my curls back into a bun, frowning at the blank page.

There's an imprint in the middle, where my pen scribbled over the previous page, marking a figure. I make out the fur of a hood, two eyes, a round nose against circular cheeks.

Superboy watches me, just a shadow in the daylit art studio.

"Today, we're painting cityscapes based on our humble city," Mr Leam begins, standing and approaching the whiteboard with a black pen and large, angular stick, jaw set. "Right angles, curves, civilians, windows, rubbish, scroungers, the lot. Be as stereotypical and offensive as you'd like; I want to see the landscape around us channelled into your piece in as much gory detail as possible. Collage, scribble, smudge, splatter… whatever your heart feels will get the image across."

I take in a deep breath, pencil already poised over my sketchbook as I ready myself to begin. I have a cheap gouache set I bought online in my bag, pastels and coloured pencils in the front pocket. Once I've drawn my outline, I pull them out and grin to myself, watching my materials go rolling across the table.

This is *exactly* my kind of painting.

remy

The day won't pass quickly enough.

My lessons drag, even more than usual. Despite my love of learning, constricted environments have never been good for me. I can't concentrate, can't breathe, can't *think* in stuffy classrooms, especially when there are other things on my mind.

"Are you joining us today, Remy?" Mr O'Flannel asks, raising an eyebrow.

Mr O'Flannel has been my favourite teacher since I started at Vibbington Secondary as an eager year seven; he was the only teacher who actively encouraged me to read, not caring that I should be attending PE lessons rather than hiding in the library with a book, unlike the other teachers, who assumed I was lazy (which wasn't exactly false). He'd lend me books after class, *Holes* and *The Maze Runner* and *The Catcher in the Rye*, passing them under the desk if I finished my work early.

One thing he doesn't stand for, however, is lacking concentration.

I straighten up and try for a smile, but my eyes won't leave the clock. It goes tick, tock, tick, tock as I gaze at it, the big hand moving towards the six in what feels like slow motion.

Twenty-five minutes past three, twenty-six minutes past

three, twenty-seven minutes past three, twenty-eight minutes past three, twenty-nine minutes past three…

The bell goes at last, bursting through the open door and blasting the room in its shrill cry. Mr O'Flannel lets out a sigh as the class begins to pack away and I rush from my seat towards the door, bag half open and hair in disarray. He raises his hand in farewell, but I don't have time to reciprocate.

I'm a man on a mission.

I hurry out of the English block, heavy on my feet. Lily skipped this afternoon's lesson to send in her Oxford application, but she's stood outside the common room with Matt already, Nima walking up from the opposite direction, engrossed in the path before her. Mike and Steph emerge from the sliding doors as we come to a halt in front of our meeting spot.

"Ready?" Matt asks.

"Ready."

The train station is about a twenty minute walk from the school, a better bet than catching the bus. There isn't another until five, the one I usually catch for work, and it's a forty-five minute drive into Hull's centre. Trains from Vibbington are pretty regular for a small town, and only cost ten pounds for the round journey, worth every penny.

We hurry amid the school crowds as the town writhes around us, tepid and stifling, buzzing with activity. It's market day, something we probably should've considered before we set off. Nima pushes ahead in her short skirt and biker boots, stomping her way through pensioners and tracksuit-clad mothers, as the rest of us follow.

"Come on!" she shouts, gesturing to us. "We'll be late for the train!"

The station is small, just big enough for our town, yet the

platform is already filling up. Nima makes her way to the front of the crowd and stands on the yellow line with her hands on her hips, gazing determinedly into the distance as if to catch sight of the train. Lily is close on her heel, frowning.

"When are you finally passing your driving test, Matthew?" she asks, exasperation thick in her voice. "I *cannot* be doing with public transport any longer, I feel like my head's going to explode –"

"Blackcurrant gummy bears," he cuts in, pushing the bag under her nose. "I went during fifth period. They're all for you, Lil."

She can't help but smile as she plucks one from the bag.

The train is two minutes late, but we're right at the doors when it pulls to a stop, clambering aboard. We grab a table by the window and Mike and Steph sit just across from us with a frail old man who's eating an egg sandwich with a knife and fork, head bobbing to the low rhythm of his radio. We cram our bags under us as the ticket collector bustles around, taking our money and eyeing Lily's gummy bears jealously, and then we're off, pulling out of Vibbington and into the countryside with a long-winded, satisfied *pffftp*.

"In a few hours' time, you'll be meeting your future girlfriend, Remy," Matt says, settling back into his chair and grinning at me. There's a lot more to that grin than is spoken aloud, but I just smile back. Fifteen years of friendship has so far resulted in us both nearing eighteen and never having kissed a girl, and so tonight is monumental for more reasons than one. I notice Matt's hand hovering a little too close to Lily's on the seat between them, fingertips just touching, and another look passes between us.

"I have a feeling," I say, "that tonight will be a *very* important night."

Lily and Nima glance up then. I think we can all feel it; the rush of emotion, the tingling sensation beneath us, a tinge of possibility hanging over the horizon. We're not spontaneous, not exciting or in any way cool… but this, this evening of change, of adventure, will no doubt be the start of something awesome.

"And even if we don't see the girl," Lily says, cutting through the silence. "No matter what happens, let's just have fun, okay? Then tomorrow, it's back to school as normal, back to revision and uni applications and greasy bacon sarnies…"

"Agreed," Matt says. "But we are going to find the girl, Remy. We are."

I nod, though my fingers are crossed beneath the table.

We are going to find her.

We *are.*

***

The train pulls into Hull just twenty minutes later, coming to a stop beneath the grand station roof and ejecting passengers before it turns around. We go to buy a coffee each, though Mike and Steph decide to share a hot chocolate and Nima only takes miniscule sips at her acai refresher, lost in another world. The station leads into the city centre and cool October air floods its platforms.

"We have approximately," Matt checks his watch, "*seven hours* to kill until we find her."

"That can't be right," Mike objects. "That means we'll miss the last train home."

That's when, for the first time, we start to re-evaluate our supposedly marvellous plan.

"My curfew is eleven anyway," Lily says. "What time did

you say she gets off the bus, Remy?"

I flush, the look on my face telling them that the answer isn't one they want to hear.

"*This* is why we plan things," she continues, shaking her head and glaring at Matt in despair. "This was your idea, Matthew. We've travelled all the way to Hull to see a girl, but we won't make it back to the train in time to make the last one – and break my curfew!"

"Don't blame me!" Matt says, but Nima cuts in before he can argue back.

"Can everybody please just chill?" Exasperated, she shakes her head and takes another sip of her refresher, nails baby blue against the white of the straw. "We just need to re-evaluate the plan, okay? If we want to see the girl – which we might as well, seeing as we've come all this way – we'll just catch the bus back, get refunds on our returns. You can all crash at mine, tell your parents you're gonna be home tomorrow instead."

I can see my best friend's brain ticking over as she says this. Group sleepovers are always a big deal to Matt. He sees them as a chance to finally get Lily to fall for him, in whatever way is possible. Despite her sleeping in Nima's bed and us on the floor (and despite his awful morning breath and terrible bed hair), he still thinks they're an opportunity for something to finally happen between them.

"That sounds good," he says, careful to keep his voice light, though it still wavers on high-pitched. "Your parents won't mind that, will they, Lil?"

"I suppose not." She shifts a little on her feet as a group of tourists come bustling into the station through the wide doors, and we're propelled to the side away from them. "Maybe I should go home. I could spend the evening with you, then get the train back whilst you find the girl. I'm not that bothered about seeing her, if I'm honest."

"You can't go back early," Matt objects. "It'll be fun!"

"I'm not sure." She frowns and glances at me, cheeks turned pink as she adds, "I don't think Remy needs me there, anyway."

I don't get what she means. We all just stand there for a moment, frozen in time, as Lily shuffles a few steps away from us, hands locked in front of her.

"I want you to be there, Lil," I tell her. "This is kind of a huge deal, and I want you to be a part of it."

We stay staring at each other, breaths held. The tension is awkward, stilted. I'm not exactly sure why. Everything feels wrong, like there's something unsaid between us, an elephant in the room.

Then Matt cuts in again, bounding up to her and throwing his arm around her back, all big eyes and eager smile and puppy-like pawing.

"This is an adventure, Lily!" he announces. "This is going to be *the night*!"

She looks back at me, eyes searching, expression unsure.

"Fine," she says, after the longest of pauses. "I'll stay."

Matt punches the air, grinning and letting out a ridiculous whoop.

Lily, however, still has her eyes fixed on me.

"But I'm only doing this for Remy."

carmel

The day won't pass quickly enough.

To start with, the hours are sucked away into a vat of artwork. They drip into my paint water, the pencil I use to sketch out city shapes as I collage them together, the pieces of netting I use as paving stones. They float away with the grey clouds I hang over my cityscape, Hull's drab Humber the exact same shade as my eyes, a kind of murky brown I've mixed up hundreds of times in order to paint self-portraits.

But, after the piece is done and my sketchbook closes over its double page spread, the clock's start moving slower and slower. It's like they're stuck, glued onto the face and determined not to budge.

I buy a panini for my lunch. It's chicken and bacon, the lettuce limp and lukewarm, the bacon fatty. Boy 1 and Boy 2 share a large salad bought from the college's "healthier" canteen, digging in with spoons and chattering amiably about Pokémon. I'd usually listen to their conversation with relative enthusiasm, but today, every word seems to drag. By the time the bell goes for fourth period, I'm convinced that if I hear "Pikachu" one more time, I'll scream so loud that the protective glass on the fire alarms shatters.

I won't, of course.

But still.

There's a graphic design workshop afterwards, one that's

compulsory, and Mr Leam has invited us down to the computer suite to take part. Graphics isn't my strong point. I only achieved a B at A-level compared to the A* I received for my fine art course, and I miss the freedom of pen and paper, can never afford to buy the fancy equipment they want us to use at home, software good enough to handle the horrific amount of coursework.

It's safe to say I'm dreading it now.

We start off by creating basic cityscapes, adding blocks and spheres and slightly less-than-realistic triangles to a canvas of royal blue, blocking out shapes and adding contrasting ones over the top, watching the city form on the screen. We have to do it bit by bit, no copying, each window drawn onto its wall and each door a different shape and design. Monotony isn't something I can cope with; it allows me to think too much, to procrastinate the day ahead and all the chores I still have left to do, the shopping and the cleaning and work after school… I make squares and rectangles with my mouse, eyes trained on the palette in the upper corner, mind whirring as I try to block out everything else.

Mr Leam makes his way around the classroom as we work, watching, chastising anyone who so much as coughs. We have to work in silence, feeling the city leak from beneath our fingertips, settle over the screen in a cluttered blob of grey and blue and brown.

"That's a unique take on a city, Carmel," he comments, stopping just behind me. I note his eyes roaming over the intense blue sky, the darkening buildings, the streets lit with flickering streetlamps.

Boy 1 has recreated New York, with its fancy skyline and Central Park amid streets of gainsboro. Boy 2 has gone with a similar theme, presenting Paris against a baby pink background, all glittering balconies and fluffy clouds, the Eiffel Tower standing tall in the hazy backdrop.

Mine's nothing similar.

"There are no trees in your city," Mr Leam continues, eyes still crossing my computer screen. "No life, no people, no cars, even. Just buildings. Dark, angular buildings."

I'm silent as he watches me add a single red umbrella onto the street at the bottom of the drawing, stark against its surroundings.

"Is that someone you know?" he asks, frowning. "The red holds some significance, of course. It adds passion to a place where things go to die."

"It's me," I say. Boy 1 and Boy 2 turn to look at me then, eyebrows lifted in surprise.

"It's you," Mr Leam repeats. "A single figure, masked by an umbrella, in a city of darkness."

"All alone," Boy 1 echoes, and Boy 2 nods along, eyes fixed on my screen.

A girl, all alone in a city of thousands, hidden beneath an umbrella. It's red, the colour of love, passion, exuberance. No life can flourish between its grey walls, no lights on in its apartments, no safety available from its cold, uninviting streets.

The illustration is a perfect depiction of my life.

remy

Hull city centre is a hive of activity on Thursday nights. Despite it being cold and significantly cloudy, people have come out in force, clutching cans of Monster in tattooed hands and shaking their badly-dyed heads, tracksuits a little too big and trainers fluorescent against the paving. Shops are starting to close as we wander along the streets, the city towering above us.

"Shall we get McDonald's?" Nima suggests, finally finishing her drink and pushing it into a bin. "I could do with the energy if we're going to be up late."

The McDonald's in question is teeming with customers, and the queue snakes out the door. It's on the main street, and kids with bikes hover outside with burgers and cokes, hoods up and cigarettes hung from lips.

It takes ten minutes to get inside and find a table, right at the front by the window, looking out into the city. We order six meals and extra fries, splitting the bill between the notes and coins we pile onto the table, doling out the change into equal piles. Nima and Lily get chicken burgers, while the rest of us plump for triple cheeseburgers and milkshakes, Mike ordering nine mozzarella dippers for him and Steph to share.

"One hour down, six to go," Matt announces, through a mouthful of burger. Time is dragging my nerves by the nailbeds. "I think we need to start talking strategy, Remy. We still don't know what you're going to say to the girl!"

That's just one of the things I've artfully avoided thinking about today. If I don't overthink it, it can't come back to hurt me when I'm ready to freak out, moments before we meet.

"I'll just wing it," I say, taking a sip of my milkshake. "Sense the… vibe."

Lily raises an eyebrow at me, so I hide behind her ice cream in an attempt to save myself from her watchful gaze. It's not as if she has any more idea than me about how to approach this, but Lily is never unprepared.

"And what if she finds this behaviour… I don't know, stalkerish?" Steph pipes up.

Again, that's something I've tried my best not to think about over the last twenty-four hours. It's the main thing which would probably debunk my plan. But hearing it come from Steph – perhaps the most experienced of us all, her and Mike being the only ones who aren't still virgins and who, according to Mike, have done *way* more than just sex – I can't help but wonder whether it'll be more of an issue than I first worried.

"She won't," Matt answers for me, rolling his eyes. "Girls like this stuff. It's cute to be pursued, isn't it?"

Lily doesn't even acknowledge that he's spoken.

"Why if she just… doesn't like you?" she continues.

That, however, is the one thought I find impossible to ignore.

It's entirely feasible, almost inevitable, even more so than her finding my behaviour stalkerish. I'm Remy Evans, overweight and acne-spotted, pale and jelly-like, with too much fuzz on my cheeks and chin and not enough anywhere else. I'm disgusting, unattractive, so much so that I was on Darcie Carlton's list of *The Ugliest Guys at Vibbington Sixth*

Form last year, barely a week into year twelve. Even *Matt* didn't make the cut.

Last night, in the dark, I thought I'd shared something special with the girl. Something new, something I'd never experienced before. It didn't matter that she was beautiful, ethereal, that I was dressed in a *Mario Kart* shirt and puffer-jacket. Something clicked.

But now, in the cold light of day, it feels like I'm viewing the situation through a completely different lens.

"Don't be ridiculous," Matt cuts in, scowling at Lily. "Remy's a catch!"

"I never said he *wasn't*," she replies, though her face is tinged with pink now. "He'd be great for some girls, but nobody is perfect for everyone. What if he's just not her type?"

"Then why did they share a moment last night?" Matt retorts, turning to look back at me. "You *did* share a moment, didn't you, Remy?"

That's the thing. What felt like a moment, a meet-cute, a love-at-first-sight kind of thing, now feels like a single glance. She didn't even smile at me as we stood there, metres away from one another, dark eyes staring into mine.

She didn't even *wave back*.

It wasn't a moment, not really. She probably thought I looked hideous, a complete nerd, stood there in a t-shirt intended for twelve-year-old boys fresh out of primary school. I saved her from that dick of a guy, but even so, she most likely found him more attractive than me. Who wouldn't?

"So we're going on a wild goose chase to find a girl who might not even remember you? You have no idea what to say to her, or how to make it not seem stalkerish, and you don't even know her name, yet we're following her to her bus stop late at night to ambush her?" Lily pauses, glancing round expectantly.

Mike and Steph raise their eyebrows at each other in subtle exasperation, and Nima swallows the last of her burger to break the silence. Matt's face is flushed as he tries to think of an answer, hands clutched around his lemonade.

"This is my fault," he says, but when he turns to me again, there's still a flicker of hope on his face. "This may be the dumbest thing we ever do, but Remy deserves it. We spend day after day sat at that same table in the common room, eating chicken wraps and soggy bacon sarnies, and only *half* of us have even kissed someone before. Even if tonight goes tits up, it's like you said, Lily – we're making the most of it. We're having an adventure."

"Thanks for the speech." Her voice is dry, but I can tell from the look on her face that she agrees with him, even if she doesn't want to admit it. "The chicken burger was pretty good, I'll give you that."

"Exactly," Nima adds. "And you don't get anywhere in life by not taking risks."

Taking risks isn't exactly part of my daily routine. Normally, I'd rather sit inside my comfort zone and watch the rest of the world unfold before me like a movie, remaining safe on the sidelines. Taking risks can be painful, terrifying, things you avoid at all costs.

Taking risks can hurt – hurt *bad.*

"Even if it goes wrong," Nima continues, "you'll know you had a go."

It's true. With all good things comes heartache; I know that better than most.

When Mum got pregnant with the twins, it cut her into pieces to lose one of them, Toby. I know there've been times when she regrets getting pregnant, having to go through all that pain. But through losing Toby we were still gifted Angelique, and we count her as a blessing every single day.

"I'm being ridiculous, aren't I?" I say. "She's never going to like me back. She'll probably freak out about seeing me again, thinking I'm following her or something."

But my friends shake their heads back at me.

"Maybe," Lily answers, but I can tell she's only joking. "But even if she does, you've lost nothing."

"Except a chunk of my pride." I don't mean that though, not really.

"If you get rejected tonight, I have a ton of Ben and Jerry's in the freezer, and I've only worked my way through half of it this week." Nima's grinning when she says that, though I can tell there's a whole lot of pain behind her expression, a litre of tears and regret. "I promise it's the only cure for heartbreak, Remy."

She would know, of course. Her ex-girlfriend – if you could call her that – committed suicide a few weeks ago, sending the entire sixth form into a state of shock.

If anyone knows heartache, it's Nima.

"And then we can watch *54 Pigs and Counting*," Matt continues. "Your favourite film!"

"I'll even give you one of my blackcurrant gummy bears," Lily offers. "You'll be okay, Remy."

"I know I will," I admit. "I have you guys."

And although they all roll their eyes and Matt starts to fake-gag in ridiculously elaborate way, I can tell they don't really mind.

It's the truth.

carmel

When the bell signifying the end of fifth period finally rings, I'm the first to shut down my computer and evacuate the room. The bus which takes you to the retail park on the outskirts of the city leaves in ten minutes, and I have no time to lose if I want to make it there and back before work starts at six.

"Goodbye, Carmel!" Mr Leam shouts, pointing out how rude I'm being by leaving unannounced. I'm forced to wave as I hurry out of the door and down the corridor, into the yard and out of the gates, trainers pouncing on the tarmac.

The bus is just pulling up as I arrive at the stop, pink and breathless, stuck at the back of a queue of twenty. It's mainly pensioners, as it takes you directly to the shops and picks you up an hour later. They're slow to find their bus passes and coins, burrowing in handbags and purses beneath the grey sky.

It's warmer on the bus today, but I pull my hat over my head regardless. After yesterday's fiasco, I'll do anything to hide myself from the wavering glances of Hull's undesirables.

The bus pulls up to the shops in a clatter of dropped shopping bags and eager mules, as the pensioners ready themselves to shop. If they don't get everything in an hour before it picks them up again, there's no other bus here until the next day – which would be disastrous if they forgot their pickles or digestives, of course.

"You go first, love," one old lady tells me, as we get stuck trying to leave our seats at the exact same time. "With my bunions, it might take me twenty minutes to even get down the steps!"

I take a trolley at the entrance, entering the store through its sliding doors. It's dark, lights flickering down the main stretch, but the bakery is lit up by tiny white bulbs. Doughnuts, baguettes, tiger bread, sourdough... The loaves are too expensive for me, of course, though it all smells delicious, fresh from the oven and kept warm behind glass doors. Mum makes me buy sliced bread to keep in the freezer, and we defrost pieces one at a time over several weeks, so nothing ever goes to waste.

I pick up the fruit and veg next, though most of that is cheaper frozen, too. Diced onions, peas and sweetcorn, along with broccoli and cauliflower florets, and a bag of broad beans which appear to be on offer. There's a woman watching me as I load the trolley with oven chips and tinned tomatoes, stood a little way off with a toddler in hand and two deluxe steaks in the other. It's all right for some, I suppose.

I choose BBQ Pringles, since they're half price. We always buy at least one treat item a week, though I prefer sour cream. Next is meat, though most of that is found in the freezer section, too. I can't remember the last time we bought a whole chicken or rashers of bacon. Mum's cousin Steve usually brings a turkey for Christmas – when he remembers, that is. Breaded chicken, cheap scampi and frozen sausages all go in the trolley, icy beneath my numb fingers.

I still get nervous going up to the counter, though I'm used to it by now. I've been shopping on and off for Mum since I was thirteen and she started working nights, picking food from the lists she'd text to me and paying using her credit card. The women at the checkout always tutted at me and asked if I was okay, if I needed help packing, where my parents were and why they weren't helping.

It's been five years now, and the disapproving looks have ceased, the fake sympathy waning. I pay with my own money, my own card, from an account made up of savings and my wages and various swigs of benefits money.

"Afternoon," I say, swiping my card across the machine. The cashier grunts in response as she hands me my receipt, spittle erupting from her mouth as she thanks me.

"Have a good day."

The bus is already piling up when I arrive with my five carrier bags of frozen goods, hands aching under the weight of it all. I push them onto the window seat, checking my watch. I should be on time now, as long as I leg it home and unpack the shopping in under twenty minutes – which should *just* be achievable.

I change buses at the stop, heading to my side of Hull with my bags and card tucked against me. I watch, eyes fixed out the window, as the scenery changes around me, from large estates and office buildings to run-down terraces and semi-detached houses with overgrown lawns. I watch gangs of teenage boys traipse past with scooters and stolen sweets, couples sharing a vape beneath shop canopies and middle-aged men drinking cider from large bottles in pub gardens.

We finally turn onto the main street near my house, and I hurry to get off the bus with all my bags, barely having time to thank the driver.

My twenty minutes begins now.

Mum is asleep when I arrive home, which makes things so much easier. I leave the bags on the kitchen table as I start to unpack them, shoving things into the empty freezer willy-nilly, dumping the pringles beside the toaster and placing bottles of off-brand pop in the cupboard above the oven. And then I'm off again, rushing out of the door and locking it behind me, waving to Mrs Dichre through the window and landing with a flying jump on my fourth bus of the day.

"Where to?" the driver asks, scanning my bus pass.

"The arts centre," I say. There's a stop two streets from there, which is on this route, and he always knows where I mean.

"You have a class?" he asks, feigning interest.

I shrug. "Something like that."

This bus is almost empty, the seats scattered in crumbs and lollipop sticks after a day of misuse. I reach the back and sink into the padded cushions, rucksack to one side and hat still squashed firmly onto my head.

I watch, heart still pounding, as my side of the city is left behind. We pull away from the grime and filth of Hull's backstreets and into its heart, away from Mrs Dichre and her wax fruit ornaments, away from Mr and Mrs Acharya's rapid baby-making, away from where my mother lies dying on the sofa in our front room. We drive past kebab shops and multicultural supermarkets, and bakeries selling half-price croissants filled with Nutella. My sketchbook writhes in my bag as I take it all in, hands itching for my pen, but I take a mental picture instead, swallowing each detail, each colour and piece of litter, each side of faded graffiti.

I watch the city's homeless, the chavs and the middle-class bankers, the dads buying pizza on their way home from the office, little children shoplifting sweets coming back from school. A mismatched lottery draw of strangers, all milling to the same place, along the same streets, blind to the world around them.

I want more than this.

I want more than *Hull*.

The arts centre is by the station in the centre of the city, and the bus pulls to a stop just by St. Stephen's, the main shopping hub. I hop out, rucksack slung over one shoulder, and thank the driver with a slight wave. There's enough money left over from shopping to buy a latte from McDonald's, although the queue is far too long and I'm forced to wait, tip-tapping one foot as I watch Hull wriggle to life around me. No one seems to be alone tonight, hurrying to meals out and to catch the last of the shops, drinking pitchers of alcohol and while waiting for nightclubs to open, gazing out of the grease-smeared windows.

There are kids my age exploring for the first time, after moving to Hull's university over the last few weeks. I always pictured I'd be like that one day, an innocent fresher in a new city, paint on my fingers and sketchbook tucked under one arm.

But that was before Mum got ill, of course, and my best bet was enrolling in the foundation course at my local college to buy me some time.

I grab myself a coffee and drink it on the way to the centre, hurrying when I notice the time, trainers padding over the cobbles. It's set down a backstreet in a large, terraced building, and only half the windows face out into the light. I dump the cup and push through the door just as my watch ticks to five to, and the receptionist looks up from her desk with a scowl.

"You're just on time," she says, passing me a twenty-pound-note under the Perspex screen. "Sign, and I'll ring upstairs to Johnno."

I write my name in neat capitals on the dotted line, scrawling my signature beneath.

CARMEL REEVES

A syllable from caramel, but not so sweet.

"They're in the third floor studio," the receptionist continues, pulling the book back and inspecting my name with a bitter-faced glare. "The sunset was screwing with the lighting in your normal room, apparently. Do you want to leave your bag with me, just in case?"

I've only had my stuff stolen once, and it wasn't my bag anyway. The people here aren't so bothered about valuables, not least my sketchbook or ratty purse. I hand my rucksack over anyway, watching as she twists to lock it into one of the many safes she keeps behind the front desk, each with a rainbow-coordinated key.

I take the steps two at a time, slowing as I approach the top. The third floor studio is the one with the skylight; it no doubt has the best lighting, with bright, whitewashed walls and rows of black easels. The door is propped open, the room already filled with students.

"Carmel!" Johnno exclaims, plucking his brush behind his ear as I enter, barely flinching when paint runs down his cheek and into the crease of his mouth. "Great to see you again!"

I smile, though it takes everything I can to stop my teeth from grinding.

"We're starting in two minutes, so if you just want to pop behind the screen…"

I nod. There are thirty pairs of eyes fixed on my back as I approach the bamboo screen, a stretch of twigs loosely held together with string. I pull off my hat, leaving it on the floor beside me as I reach to unlace my trainers, placing them in a neat line beside me.

There's a rush of cold air as I pull my hoodie over my head, unclasping my bra and shrugging it off. The skylight is open and a breeze dances towards me, turning my pale stomach goose-pimpled and tickling my arms, my chest, my breasts. I struggle to undo the knot on my joggers and wrestle them down my legs and over my feet. Then I just stand there, in my underwear, waiting one final minute before taking off my pants.

"We're ready when you are, Carmel!" Johnno calls. I can hear that he's stood behind his easel now, paintbrush once again poised to begin.

I suck in a breath of cool air, hands intertwined before me.

And then I step out from behind the screen.

remy

The girl's bus, we discover, pulls onto her street roughly every half hour. As Matt points out, it's possible she could've been forced to take a late one last night and might usually come home earlier… which is how we end up squashed into the bus shelter two hours early, a portion of cheesy chips between us and Mike and Steph sat straddling each other at our feet.

"Do you not think we should move, just in case she gets off the bus and sees us all sat here?"

Lily has a point, but it's freezing now, dark clouds descending on the city. We're all too cold to get up.

The kebab shop opposite is still open. It doesn't feel like a day since I bought that poor man some food, dropping it onto his duvet before running to catch the bus home, mere seconds after meeting the girl. A couple emerge with a polystyrene tub of onion rings, slathered in ketchup.

"It's kind of scary here," Lily continues, shuffling closer towards me. Matt is to my other side, head on my shoulder and coat zipped up to his chin, and Nima's bare legs are dotted with goose bumps. "All the houses are so… run-down."

It might not be the nicest area of Hull, but to call it scary is a *little* over the top. Back in Vibbington, my own street is almost identical to this. Crumbling semi-detached homes with overgrown lawns and rusting cars, and a corner shop protected by iron bars. Most of the houses once belonged to the council, but they were bought out by private owners, most of whom now rent them to families like us. It might not be as clean and tidy as Lily's new-build estate, but it's ours.

"It's just so *cold*," she adds, as though the temperature is exclusive to Hull's outskirts. "And windy. I can still feel a breeze under this shelter."

"Have some more gummy bears," Matt murmurs. "That'll help."

I hear her rustling in her bag for them again, and they're passed round as we continue to huddle there, beneath the darkening sky.

Minutes seem to last hours as we sit there, the chips going cold, cheese all rubbery and trembling in grease. People come and go via the kebab shop on their way home, and I try with everything inside me to picture the world through their eyes, to see the beauty of their routine, of Hull's dimly lit streets and peeling paintwork, but anxiety eats away at my insides and takes over my mind completely.

"Gum?" Matt offers, passing me the packet. "Might take your mind off things."

It doesn't. Silence wraps itself around us, broken by Mike's heavy breathing as he slobbers over Steph, the crumbs from his mozzarella dippers still stuck to his lips.

Buses come and go. They pull up and invite us to get on board, but no one hops off at our stop. Passengers watch us through steamed-up windows as we gesture for the driver to carry on, we don't need a ride. Two homeless women ask us for spare change as the headlights illuminate us briefly, and we give them the rest of the chips and all of our coins from the earlier trip to McDonald's. The city drifts to sleep around us, the Humber lulling it gently at a distance. Its murky depths groan in the moonlight.

"I'm going to sleep so well tonight," Lily whispers, and Nima smiles in response. She tucks an arm around her best friend and nestles closer, so that the four of us are cuddled together in a mismatch of winter coats and scarves, big boots and trainers, tights and jeans and Lily's thick overalls, bags clumped at our feet.

It turns half ten eventually, the alarm Matt set going off in his pocket. It's the Wii music, beeping away beneath him as he pulls out his phone and swipes it away.

"Only half an hour until her bus comes in," he says, stifling a yawn. "I think we need to think of somewhere to hide, so she doesn't see us the moment she gets off."

Which makes sense. Now that it's so close, I'm more nervous than ever about seeing her again, and I don't want to bombard her by unleashing my entire friendship group. Waiting for the girl in the dark, huddled on a bench in her local bus shelter, suddenly feels so stupid. If she doesn't find this endearing, she'll no doubt find it creepy, and I'll have blown my chance completely.

"Maybe this is a bad idea," I say, standing and pushing away from the bench. My friends stare back at me with incredulous expressions.

"Remy," Lily says, shaking her head. "I one hundred percent agree with that statement, but you've just got cold feet, okay? We didn't just wait around in a mouldy bus stop for seven hours for nothing."

"I *partially* agree with what she just said," Matt chimes in. "You might as well see her, Remy, now that we're here. You've got nothing to lose!"

Only I have.

I've been rejected too many times in my short life, but this is the first time I've been old enough to really *care*. This isn't like when was I eleven years old and asked Carlotta Stevens to the school dance in front of our entire French class, only for her to dump the chocolate cake I'd made her all over my head (and smear the icing over my cheeks to spell out "loser"). I might not know this girl, but it feels so much more *real*, like there's something huge riding on the next half hour.

I'm Remy Evans. I've come to the conclusion that I'm a massive nerd, always have been and always will be, like wearing geeky t-shirts, love English literature, for my sins. I have an eclectic taste in music and I'm a little on the chubby side. Girls, as a rule, don't like me.

But this is the first time in a long while that I've put that to the test.

"We've had a good night either way," Nima pipes up. "Don't feel pressured to do anything, okay, Remy?"

"What she said," Matt adds. "But… I think you should just go for it. Take a risk. You'll just regret it, otherwise."

I know he's right.

If I don't, there'll always be that voice in the back of my head…

A voice wondering what would've happened if I took a chance and put myself out there, just this once.

"Fine," I say, after a pause. "But you guys need to wait up there, well out of sight!"

They oblige, scuttling up the road with ten minutes to spare, the opposite direction to which the girl took last night. I watch their waving hands as they disappear, heart pounding beneath my shirt.

You're going to be fine, absolutely fine.

And so I wait.

I wait, hands latched on my lap and goosebumps dancing

all over my body.

I wait, watching as the kebab shop prepares to close, the last stragglers hurrying up and down the streets with takeaway pizzas and cans of energy drink to their warm, safe beds.

I wait as eleven ticks by, and the bus pulls up before me.

I wait, breath bated, as passengers begin to disembark. There's an old man with a walking stick, and two teenage girls with a lemon cheesecake held between them in a clear plastic bag.

I wait as the driver glances behind him to check there's no one else wanting to get off, then the doors close and it shuffles off down the road, leaving me in darkness.

She never

got off

the bus.

I feel a lump rising in my throat and swallow hard. It's fine. She'll probably get off the next one.

she hasn't shown – waiting for the half eleven

I wait until my hands are freezing cold on my lap, barely able to move them across the screen to reply to the others. The owner of the kebab shop drives off in his van, leaving the shop in darkness, and bushes wriggle around me in the night-time breeze. I wait, shivering vigorously, as the next bus pulls up and stops.

I watch the door as it opens, eyes fixed on its plastic steps.

She doesn't get off this one, either.

"You need a lift, son?" the driver calls, gesturing to me. "I can't wait all day."

I nod, a single movement which says it all. The driver

leans back as I stand, lifting my phone to my ear and waiting for Matt's voice to flood through it, tears prickling behind my eyes.

"Remy!" he exclaims, sounding all crackly. "Did she show?"

"No." I hesitate by the doors of the bus, then grab the pole and pull myself onto the first step. "She didn't show, Matt. We're going home."

remy

We pile into Nima's hall an hour later. Her parents are out of town at some business conference, as usual, and the house is silent around us. We take our shoes and coats off and head into the kitchen after her, bodies heavy, minds wide awake.

Nima makes us all coffee – the real deal, from a machine and everything, not just the instant stuff Mum buys from the supermarket – while we gather around the island. She flicks a switch to turn on the central heating, then places the steaming mugs before us on leather coasters. Even the mugs match. They're matte black, and have the tiny John Lewis logo printed at the bottom in white.

"Get those down you," she says, pulling up a stool to sit opposite. "I'll get the ice cream."

We don't bother with bowls. Nima and I share cookie dough, while Mike and Steph plump for chocolate, and Matt and Lily use straws to suck the melty bits from both.

"I'm sorry, mate." Mike's expression is apologetic as he reaches out to thump my shoulder. "At least we had a go."

But that's just it. I didn't "have a go", especially since I'm no better off now than I was yesterday. I still haven't spoken to the girl, haven't tested my luck, haven't waited to see if she's into me or not, even a little. I haven't proved anything, just that my stalking skills are decidedly lacking and I most likely won't ever see her again.

"Nothing ventured, nothing gained," Lily continues. "There'll be other girls, Remykins. There *are* other girls."

That's not really the point.

We take the ice cream upstairs, along with two bags of popcorn, the fluffy blanket from the sofa, and six cans of cream soda. Nima's bedroom is a paradise of pink and fluffy, painted roses climbing the walls and ornaments on every surface, but it's a tip right now; clothes festering in a sweaty pile on the floor, and crumbs littering the carpet. She pushes things aside to make room for us atop her bed, then closes the door with a definitive click.

"Movie?"

"*54 Pigs and Counting*." Matt smiles at me, and I can't help but return one.

We huddle up at the headboard, blanket spread over our legs. The film begins on Nima's laptop, but I've seen it so many times I don't need to watch the screen to know what's going on. Tears blur my eyes, unshed, as a lump in my throat begins to swell.

Don't cry, don't cry! You're not a baby –

I feel a hand reach for mine under the blanket, cautious. It's small and slight, tucking itself gently around my fingers, so gently that I can barely feel it.

I turn my head, just an inch. Lily's eyes meet mine.

"You okay?" she mouths. I nod back, the lump in my throat restricting even the smallest of movements.

I feel her fingers harder then, forefinger and thumb making circles on my palm, faster and faster, round and round. I can scarcely breathe. Lily is soft as she squeezes my hand in hers, the motions hidden beneath the blanket, invisible to everyone but us.

"Thank you," I mouth back.

After the movie ends, we start to prepare the beds. Nima and Lily have the double, Mike and Steph take the single airbed outside in the corridor, and Matt and I create makeshift mattresses from the living room's sofa cushions. I note Matt watching Lily wistfully as she pulls on a hoodie over her overalls and clambers into bed without getting undressed, eyes heavy.

"You okay down there?" Nima asks us, hovering before turning down the lights. "If you need any extra sheets, just go into the cupboard on the landing below."

"I'm good. Night, Ni."

The room descends into darkness.

There's always a certain order of which we go to sleep on sleepovers, one which never really varies. It's been contested by each of us at some point, depending on who stays up the longest, but the official list has been verified and cross-referenced over thirty times, and is currently stuck above Matt's bed at home.

Lily goes first. She gets tired easily, drifting off throughout the movie, eyes drooping once midnight has passed. She doesn't snore, just breathes heavily, a sure sign that we won't be seeing her until something loud rocks her awake.

Next are Nima and Matt, around the same time. Nima tosses and turns, trying to get comfortable, even more tonight than usual. She snores – like a foghorn. She also drools, which Lily has *plenty* of video evidence of.

Matt's a light sleeper, awoken by the smallest of sounds, but he always drifts off peacefully when Lily's around. It's like he feels safe, comfortable, mirroring her breaths as he lies there. I listen to him now, breathing matched right up to hers, as we lay in the dark of Nima's bedroom.

Mike and Steph go last. Neither of their parents are keen

on them sleeping together at home, so sleepovers are the only chance they get for any private time.

They're loud. They're louder tonight, especially, because we've been out in public for so long that they're eager to be intimate again, just the two of them, out in the corridor. I can hear Steph's moans, Mike stifling his breaths, phlegm rising in my throat.

I don't often fall asleep last.

I don't have a sleep schedule, or any particular pattern. If I'm settled, I sleep, and that's it.

Tonight, I can't sleep. I can't stop thinking about that girl, about myself, about how ugly and pathetic and weak I am, about how I'll end up alone, even when everybody else is married with three kids and a dog and is happy –

I stay awake the whole night, listening to Matt and Lily's synchronised breathing, to Nima's gentle snores.

I just lie there, completely still, as Mike and Steph's bodies convulse together beneath the blanket, to the sound of their rhythmic, loved-up moans.

carmel

I started modelling for Johnno's class when I turned eighteen. We were struggling for money, Mum couldn't work, and now – as a legal adult – I'd found a way to earn cash every single night, without moving a muscle.

On paper, it sounded like the perfect plan.

My first class was in December, on one of the coldest days that year so far. There were no requirements for models, Johnno told me. No specific sizes, shapes, hair removal, nothing. I just had to be makeup and clothes free, he explained. That way, we'd get the most authentic pose possible.

It wasn't as though I felt *shy* about modelling. The students were all strangers, a lot older than me; they'd taken the class with dozens of completely different models for years before. They weren't the type to judge, to mock, or even to care about what my body looked like. They were drawing from life, sketching the energy and emotion, the tension between my eyebrows and the ink splattered over my fingers. They didn't care about beauty standards, whatever society deemed acceptable. They just wanted someone to draw.

There was one night I had my clothes stolen, taken by some lurid old men who'd paid double to see a "younger model", then dumped in the gutter outside the arts centre and pissed all over them. Johnno and the receptionist lent me an old smock and some black leggings to take the bus home in, but I never wore the jumper again, couldn't rinse the urine stench from my favourite pair of jeans.

Aside from that, it's almost been... fun. It's freeing, standing in front of a barrage of strangers and letting them judge you, pick apart your flaws and turn them into something beautiful, something they can call "art".

They don't care about my flabby stomach, the stretch marks on my thighs, my unruly curls or unshaved legs. They don't exaggerate the parts of me which aren't "aesthetically pleasing", but capture them so realistically, so wonderfully, that I almost look... good. Even if I don't, I look like *me*, and that seems like enough.

Tonight's session is two hours long. It's chilly but I'm mostly fine, stood on the table with one leg outstretched and my arms held tight behind my back. It's a younger audience. They're probably university students or around that age, drawing in sketchbooks and painting on canvases pulled from rucksacks and tote bags. Johnno stands by the edge for the most part, snapping his fingers every time my pose alters even a little, and walks around each piece of work with an eagle's eye, the silence speaking volumes.

There's a break an hour in, as usual. The students go for coffee downstairs and Johnno snaps a single photograph of my pose from behind, to make sure we can recreate it later.

I wait until they've all left the room to move. Johnno helps me down from the tabletop and offers me one of his biscuits, but I decline, grabbing my coat and dropping into an empty chair. It's cold on my bum, like ice, as Johnno hoists himself onto a stool opposite.

"You're doing well today," he says, nodding. "You barely moved, and your posture is improving. You should try doing this professionally, Carmel. You have quite the temperament for it."

I try to see what's flattering about the statement. There's nothing artistic about standing still for two hours straight, nothing skilled about picking a pose and sticking to it, day after day after day. If life modelling professionally is a career path, it's not something I see a future in. Not for me, anyway.

"Thanks," I tell him. "That… means a lot."

"I mean it." He reaches behind him, pulling a leaflet off his desk. It's for an agency – a proper agency – one which distributes life models across the country for all the best art classes. It's glossy and printed with an embossed gold logo, and feels heavy in my hands, luxurious. "The pay is pretty decent, too. You'll be wanting to move to uni, I assume? It could be a steady part-time job to nab while you're there."

"I'm… not sure." The leaflet is professional, the kind of company which would provide me with a proper wage and income while I study. But… it's a lot. I flip it over to view the contact details, mind whirring.

If I do go to university, perhaps it's something to consider.

"Don't close any doors just yet, Carmel." Johnno watches as I stand and cross the room to place the leaflet by my clothes. "You never know what the future might hold…"

The next hour passes even more quickly. I sink back into the pose and let it flood through me, hold my body still, into a perfect shape. The class is silent, concentrating entirely on me, as the sun fades outside and the room descends into shadows, Johnno too paranoid about changing the mood to switch on a light. It's almost black by the time we finish, LEDs flooding the room.

Stretching, I climb down from the table and disappear behind the screen to get my clothes. I pull them back on as the class disappears and Johnno wipes the surfaces. He spritzes air freshener and pushes the lid firmly onto the biscuit barrel, leaving a custard cream on the table for later.

"You staying for the next session? It's Dolores."

I don't have to think twice.

One of the perks of my job is the free life drawing classes I get to take, two or three times a week. Dolores is perhaps my favourite model, my biggest inspiration when it comes to art. She's sixty-three, but acts like she's almost my age.

Filled with self-confidence, Dolores is always brimming with certainty that everything in this world, no matter what it looks like, is beautiful.

It's how I try to be, too, but it's not always that simple.

I take a seat right at the front, with a piece of plain paper and a biro. Sometimes, the best artwork is created from the simplest of tools. The next students enter the room, a significantly smaller amount this time, as the centre's latest life drawing class begins in the city's heart.

Dolores is early. She decides to pose sat down today, as her back has been playing up, but sits on her stool with no care for the rest of the room. She winks from opposite me and puts a hand behind her head in mock flamboyancy, and I grin back, poising my pencil to begin.

It's a beautiful thing, capturing a scene from life. I observe every hair, every wrinkle, the slight angle of her toenails, her sagging breasts. I draw her face and those bright, beady eyes, and her hooked nose and smiling mouth, naturally cherry red and glistening.

I sketch the arch of her bent knees, her ribcage and folded stomach, her thin eyebrows and the warts dotting her hands. It's so late now that Johnno will most likely have to take me home, like he often does when I stay behind for a class, but I don't care. All my worries slip away, disintegrating from my memory as I work on the piece. My mum, the shopping, Mr Leam's class, my impending applications for uni…

Dolores eats biscuits with us in the break. She chooses gingerbread as she sits there, laughing away with Johnno, barely conscious of her bare body. She asks me about my art foundation, and about my mother, and how Mrs Dichre is coping with her arthritis.

The class finishes later than anything else in Hull on a Thursday night.

The last few stragglers are darting out of nightclubs in order to wake up for their early morning lectures, and couples wander hand in hand by the river. Johnno walks me to his car and I get in the passenger seat, waving to Dolores as we pull away from the curb.

I almost fall asleep as we drive. Johnno lives about ten minutes from my house and pulls down the same old streets, past Ravi's closed shop and the bus stop, where someone has left a half-eaten polystyrene tub of cheesy chips. He drops me right outside my front door. Mum must've turned the flickering lamp off in the window, for the house is shrouded in darkness.

"Thanks for the lift," I tell him, climbing out. "See you tomorrow night, yeah?"

The door isn't locked, but Mrs Dichre has left a note by the knocker. I don't bother reading it. It's always the same sort of thing, about how I'm an awful daughter, leaving my mum like that for hours. Hypocritical, really, given she's left the house unlocked, but it doesn't matter; she doesn't have a clue. I scrunch it up and throw it down the hall, just as a groan comes from the living room.

"Carmel!"

She's awake.

"What's up?" I whisper, placing a hand on her forehead as I crouch next to her. "Do you feel under the weather again?"

She doesn't seem to have a temperature, and her skin is dry and cold beneath my hand. But she shakes her head vigorously and gestures towards the lamp, expression distraught.

"The bloody bulb's gone," she tells me. "It went out just after Mrs Dichre left. You'll have to buy a new one, Carmel, you know I can't cope without the light on!"

I try to soothe her by pushing the hair from her wig behind her ears, but she just writhes beneath me, still groaning.

"Carmel, you need to buy a new one, I need the light for tomorrow night!"

"I'll get one," I insist, though the thoughts are already closing in and everything's becoming dark, dark, dark. "I promise."

"I love you," she whispers, finally pushing back against the cushions and closing her eyes.

"I love you too, Mum."

remy

I can barely get out of bed the next day. Nima brings up toast to prepare us for school, and the rest of my friends begin to pull on yesterday's clothes and do their hair, eyes heavy.

My whole body hurts. It's an agonising, bone-aching pain, built from a sleepless night of overthinking and regrets, churning through my stomach and rippling across my limbs.

"You okay, Remy?" Lily is watching me, eyes concerned.

I shrug it off and smile back, doing my best to act unperturbed. "Just didn't sleep great."

It's an understatement at best.

We eat the toast in a hurry, barely bothering with toppings and spread. Nima's house is a ten minute walk from the school, and we all have lessons period one; it's the last day of the week, and our timetables are crammed with meetings and revision sessions and UCAS updates before the weekend swallows us whole. We grab our bags and books and folders from the hall and hurry into the street, practically jogging all the way to Vibbington Secondary School and Sixth Form, arriving just on the bell.

"See you at break, Remy!"

Matt has sociology. Nima has maths, followed by a stint in the art studio to catch up on some coursework. Nobody is entirely sure what subjects Mike and Steph do, and Lily and I have English.

We don't speak as we walk to Mr O'Flannel's classroom. Lily pretends to be deep inside a Jane Austen novel, and I walk beside her, unsure of what to say.

We've barely spoken since last night, when Lily's hand found mine beneath the blanket. It didn't feel so wrong at the time, so treacherous to our friendship. But now, in the cold light of day, the memory is stilted, awkward.

The lesson is another on Milton. Mr O'Flannel's book is still in my porch, but he doesn't ask for it back. The class passes in a blur of silence and empty hands, blank pages. I don't contribute answers, and Lily barely looks up from her book, scribbling away.

Mr O'Flannel catches me at the end, beckoning me over to his desk. Lily doesn't wait for me, scuttling out of the door at the first possible chance to her politics class, giving a little flick of her wrist by way of goodbye.

"Remy?" Mr O'Flannel waits until the last few stragglers have left before continuing, shuffling papers on his desk to fill the silence. When the door finally clicks, he turns to me with a straight face and latches his fingers over his lap. "We need to talk about your Oxford application."

My stomach drops as he sighs, shaking his head.

"You're leaving it *very* late, Remy," he continues. "Lily submitted hers yesterday afternoon, and the other students across subjects have been sending their applications for the last week. You don't want to be rushing."

I still don't respond.

Up until yesterday, I thought I had my application under control. I was up to the exact same point as Lily, had redrafted my personal statement six times in order to perfect it. But now, stood opposite Mr O'Flannel and his unfamiliar serious expression, the reality of it all comes crashing down on me. I have less than a week left to submit the application on UCAS and decide on my four backup options, and there's no way what I have currently is enough to get me an interview.

"If you want me to proofread your statement again, I'll need it for this weekend," he adds. "Have you got a copy to hand, or saved on the school system?"

I shake my head. The only drafts of my personal statement are saved onto my laptop at home, which Dad and I share for work.

"Right." Mr O'Flannel sighs, though this time despairingly. "I really do want to help you, Remy. You're one of the smartest lads I've ever taught at A-level, and you'd be an asset to Oxford. But… I really need to see more enthusiasm from you. You've been in a trance these last two days."

"I'm sorry." I'm not sure what else to say to that. I haven't been myself recently, not really. I've been a version of me, one who overthinks and gets in his head about a girl, about my looks, my failures. That's not the Remy who first aspired to go to Oxford all those years ago. "I've just been… distracted."

"These are the most important years of your life, Remy. No matter what happens once you reach university, doing well in your A-levels sets you up to go there in the first place. Don't lose focus now."

It's easier said than done.

"Send me your personal statement once you get home, okay? I'll email my suggestions over the weekend."

I nod, resisting the urge to bite my lip.

I can do that.

It'll be fine.

"Keep your head down, Remy," Mr O'Flannel finishes, going back to shuffling bits of paper, one hand moving absently on the mouse. "This is the final sprint. The finishing line is fast approaching."

**

The rest of the day passes in a whirlwind of grey. I'm exhausted, going through the motions, with too much on my mind. Everything else is invisible to me.

Firstly, I can't stop thinking about the girl. It gnaws at my insides, the regret and embarrassment, my failure clear. Her face, her hair, her eyes, the way she hurried off down the road and stared at me, for two long minutes, face saying nothing. Looking back at last night makes me cringe, filled with embarrassment and hatred for the person I thought I was.

It's confusing, too much to think about on top of everything else. I don't know whether I'm more mad at the fact I didn't see her, or the fact I turned up to find her at all.

Neither makes me feel wonderful about myself.

Lily won't stop creeping into my thoughts, either. We still don't say a word to one another at break or lunch, which nobody else seems to notice. Mike and Steph are preoccupied with another extensive game of Dungeons and Dragons, and Nima is swatching highlighter shades, tongue poking out from the corner of her mouth. Matt and I make small talk about the latest Marvel movie, and Lily continues with essay planning for her history coursework, surrounded by notes and files and research.

All the while, Oxford hovers at the back of my mind. I can sense my personal statement, lying unread on my laptop at home, waiting for me to work on it.

You're going to blow your chance! You'll never get an interview if you don't start putting in effort!

I shudder, taking a cautious bite from my panini.

The voice in my head is right, of course. I won't get an offer from Oxford if I can't even apply on time.

You won't get in anyway, not if you're this slack! Look how proactive Lily's being – she'll definitely get a place, she spent weeks on her application and has already submitted it!

Sometimes, I wonder why I'm even bothering.

***

The bus leaving Vibbington that night is almost empty.

Not many people travel to Hull at four on a Friday, not least when the journey is forty-five minutes by bus, even slower in the rush of homecoming traffic. I watch the familiar countryside blur into a kaleidoscope of green and yellow and brown as we trundle along the main road into the city.

Ravi's shop is open when I arrive, his last member of staff just going off duty. He raises a hand in cheerful solidarity as I push through the door, bell tinkling.

"Remy!" he exclaims, grinning at me from behind the counter. "It's great to see you again. It always feels far too long!"

"It's good to see you too, Ravi." I put down my bag by the door to the storeroom. We're pretty well stocked for the end of the week, and there's a new box sat by one of the end-shelves, waiting to be opened.

"Go on," Ravi says, smiling. "You know what it is."

It's the produce from the deal I struck with a local independent trader. Jars of pickle, chutneys, jams and jellies fill the box to its brim, each labelled and sealed with chequered material, red and blue and green and lilac.

"This is awesome," I breathe, pulling out one of the jars. "Shall I start moving it all onto the shelves, deciding prices, that sort of thing?"

"They're all yours, Remy," he replies. "You display them, you price them, you make the signs." He wanders over to join me, picking up a jar of rhubarb and ginger jam and shaking his head. "You have a very good eye for things. You'd make a wonderful tradesperson one day."

And even though I don't want to be a tradesperson – even though this is only a part-time job to me, nothing more and nothing less – it's the only positive thing anyone has said to me all day, and my insides glow at the compliment.

"Thanks." I start to take the jars from the box, separating them into their different categories and colours, ready to arrange and create signs for on Ravi's chalkboard plaques. "That… means a lot."

carmel

Mum is still going on about the lightbulb when I get up the next morning. How she barely slept without knowing she could switch on the lamp, how she worried all night that robbers would think our house was empty and break in on account of there being no lights on, how it was cold and dark and lonely. She's sweaty and boiling hot, writhing under her blanket and wig in a disarray, eyes watering as I reach down to hug her.

"Shall I give your hair a wash today, Mum?" I suggest.

There's about twenty minutes to spare before I have to catch the bus, but that's not enough time to rush to the shop – I'll have to hurry after college, before work.

Mum nods. She tugs off her wig and hands it to me, the synthetic hairs rustling in my hands. It must have been too warm for her last night, because she's refused to take it off these last few weeks, on account of it being the only shred of decency she has left. There are a few bugs clumped at one side, and a bald patch is appearing by the parting.

When Mum first lost her hair, we signed her onto a waiting list with a charity which provided wigs made from real, donated strands. I'd been tempted to brave the shave myself, but Mum wouldn't let me. It was bad enough losing her own hair, let alone mine.

The waiting list grew and grew and grew, but since Mum

is mainly bedbound and not likely to get better, her case was never seen as a high priority.

Her head is pale and grey-tinged in the pale light peering in through the front room's windows. It's all lumpy, tufts of fluffy hair sat here and there, freckles lacing her forehead.

I take the wig into the kitchen, fill a bowl with steaming water from the kettle. I have some conditioner upstairs, along with some cheap shampoo I won in a raffle last Christmas, and dump the contents into the bowl. The wig goes in next. Dirt rises to the surface almost straight away, like dots of black vanilla in one of those posh deserts.

"Carmel?" It's Mum. Her voice sounds strained and I can tell she's getting worked up, so I drop the wig for a moment to listen, the slish-sloshing of the water coming to a stop.

"Mum?" I shout back. "Is everything okay?"

"I need my wig!"

She needs her wig.

It's sopping wet now, but the water left behind is murky and filled with spots of grime. I run the hair under the tap to rinse it off, slapping on a little more conditioner in hopes that it'll help, until the whole thing smells wonderfully fresh and summery, with only an undertone of fusty.

"Coming!" I yell again, hurrying over to the tea towel hung by the oven. I try to dry off the wig the best I can, rubbing it free of the soapy water and suds, until it gleams under my hands. "Two minutes!"

I got a bottle of dry shampoo from Mrs Dichre for my birthday last year, and it's almost empty now. Dry shampoo comes in handy when the hot water's always on the blink and the shower is full of black mould. I spritz it twice, then carry it through to the living room, where Mum is still curled up under a blanket on the sofa.

I push the wig back onto her head. It's shinier now, almost like new, and the fringe dips over her pale eyes.

"You look lovely," I say. "Shall I get you some porridge?"

"Toast," she insists. "Please, beans on toast."

"I don't know if I have time for beans," I start, but her expression is so desperate that I can't say no. "Fine. Beans on toast it is."

"You'll remember to get that blooming lightbulb tonight, won't you?"

I've already turned my back on her, ready to disappear into the kitchen, but I nod again. If she wants a lightbulb, that needs to be on the top of my list of priorities. Otherwise she won't sleep, won't eat, won't be able to spend the day without fussing and fretting to Mrs Dichre about how desperate she is to have her lamp back.

She's not often like this. Usually she's patient, and forgiving, and puts my needs first.

But when she's unwell – and I mean *really* unwell – she gets agitated, restless, achy. That's when she takes it out on me. She can't help it.

"Of course," I say. "I'll remember to get a lightbulb."

"You know which one you're getting, don't you?" she checks. "If it doesn't fit, I won't have any light…"

"I know," I tell her. There are two tins of beans in the cupboard from my shopping trip yesterday, so I empty one into a glass bowl and move it to the microwave. I pull two slices of bread from the freezer and place them on top to defrost, watching the food go round and round in circles, head spinning. "I know."

I toast the bread for two minutes each, buttering them lightly with own-brand margarine. Then I pour half the beans on top, the other half going into a plastic Tupperware with a spoon.

I pass the plate to Mum on my way out, and she smiles appreciatively. She doesn't need to see my own breakfast. I keep it hidden behind my back as I give her a gentle kiss on the forehead and evacuate the room, shouting goodbye before pulling the door shut behind me.

I eat the beans on the bus to college, though they're already going cold.

A day of lessons, and a lightbulb.

I think I can manage that.

The shop is pretty empty that night. A few mothers pop by on the way home, trailing kids from afterschool clubs to buy fresh fruit and vegetables and locally produced biscuits, creating the image of an ultimately good parent. They ask if our items are organic or vegan, insisting that their children eat a banana each *straight* away – "We'll pay at the till!"

I sell three jars of chutney to an older woman who claims it tastes best with marmite and gherkins, and buys a bucketful of oranges to make into marmalade. Another lady buys a jar with a fancy purple label – she's been craving cheese and pickle sandwiches all day, she says – while her husband picks out veg for their casserole. The products I bought from the independent trader seem to be going down a treat with the residents of outer-Hull, and Ravi is more than impressed.

"You can have a cut of any profit made!" he claims, beaming. "You're truly making a huge success of these jars, Remy."

It's true – perhaps I have an eye for this sort of thing after all. If Oxford doesn't work out, working in an area like this could be kind of… fun. Selling local produce, striking deals with family businesses, people like this woman, who makes all the products in her kitchen at home. It's a job with meaning, purpose. Keeping alive tradition and trade, helping people out, seeing it go directly to the customers.

I can see why Ravi loves it so much. He's a pillar of the community here, selling good quality food, giving free items to the kiddies and making conversation with their parents, making sure they feel listened to, respected. There's a level of trust evident here, knowledge that anything you say will be kept within the shop walls. Everyone trusts Ravi.

It's strange, but I think you see more in a place like this. Different types of people, ways of life, cultures and classes and backgrounds.

It's not hard to find beauty when everything's so *rich*, so saturated. Jewel-bright oranges and purple saris, the laughter of a little boy as he bites into a maroon gooseberry, soft Hindustani music playing through Ravi's speakers.

I usually work until ten, when Ravi shuts up shop. There's always half an hour or so afterwards spent tidying up and chatting behind the counter before I get the half ten bus back, eleven at the latest. I still need to send Mr O'Flannel my personal statement. It floats around my mind as I continue to write the slate signs, over and over…

"Jam and rhubarb chutney," I murmur, scribbling away at the slate with my stick of chalk. It doesn't look right. Why doesn't it look right? "No, apple and rhubarb chutney, stupid. Then it's rhubarb and ginger *jam*."

I don't look up as the bell tinkles. I hear the door click shut behind the next customer, hitting the frame with a crunch. It's most likely another mother, or perhaps an older lady, buying her weeks' worth of veg before trotting home to her husband. I scrub out the chalk and try again, attempting to make my writing perfectly circular, rounded –

"You don't happen to have a spare lightbulb, do you?"

My ears prick up then. A lightbulb, in a corner shop? There's a sign above the door stating our area of expertise, and electrical appliances isn't one of Ravi's many (slightly random) lines. I can't see the speaker, head hidden behind a stack of potato crates, but I roll my eyes anyway.

There are always the odd few people who come in expecting to find something we most certainly *don't* sell. Ravi usually sends them off with a list of local shops and recommendations, forever the gentleman.

This time, however, I don't hear him reach for his stack of shopping advice… nor do I hear the bell tinkle behind the leaving customer.

Instead, Ravi goes, "Of course! I have a few in the back, just in case my desk lamp goes."

Then he proceeds to name the exact model and size, and I hear the door to the storeroom open and close as they disappear inside.

APPLE AND RHUBARB CHUTNEY
£3.59 or TWO FOR £6.00

I manage to tack the slate to the edge of the shelf. It looks good, professional, my writing neat and rounded in all the right places. It's clear, and the pricing isn't too bad. I state at the top of the cabinet that all produce is handmade locally, because things like that always sell well.

"Thanks, Ravi," I hear the voice of the customer again, the storeroom door opening. "Mum will be so pleased with this. She really struggles without the light on…"

I glance up from behind the potato crates. There's a lightbulb suspended in someone's hand, and Ravi appears to be following them out of the storeroom. He closes the door behind him, just as the customer turns around –

It's the girl.

It's the *girl*.

It's.

The.

Girl.

Every muscle in my body freezes.

I just stare at her, gobsmacked. Because this can't be real. Because I must be hallucinating –

She's even more beautiful in daylight than she was when I first saw her on Wednesday, dark eyes sparkling and cheeks rosy from hurrying here, curls in disarray beneath her hat. She's wearing clunky trainers and baggy jeans, a raincoat thrown over her shirt in bright yellow…

She hasn't seen me yet. She'll no doubt spot me as soon as she turns around, and I'm just sat here on the floor, writing signs. I leap to my feet, so fast that the floorboards thud beneath me, and both Ravi and the girl pivot towards me in a flash.

She's facing me.

She opens her mouth.

She speaks.

"It's you."

I nod. It's like I'm frozen, unable to make any other movement. Our eyes are locked, the room completely still between us.

"You know each other?" Ravi is the first one to break the silence. He seems amused, mouth curved into a smile as his eyes flit between us, back and forth. "I wasn't aware you had many friends in Hull, Remy."

"We're not friends." She says this far too fast, like the idea of us being linked offends her. "I mean, only in passing. I've never spoken to him before."

Quiet descends again, so Ravi twists on his feet and pushes open the door to the storeroom again. Taking the hint, he says, "I think I'll go get some more kombucha for the racks by the door. It was nice seeing you – tell your mum I'll be dropping by over the weekend!"

And then we're alone.

Completely alone.

"I never actually said thank you." The girl speaks first, eyes narrowed. She's looking right at me but doesn't seem at all flustered – not like me. Her voice is level, hands clutching the counter behind her. "So... thanks, I guess. That guy was a creep."

"I... I..."

This is the part where I should say something. What do people usually do in response to gratefulness? Do I shake her hand, give her a hug?

Am I supposed to... kiss her?

She continues to watch me, waiting for a response, but it's like all the words in my head have merged into one and my tongue is thick in my mouth.

"Anyway, I'm in a rush, so..." She makes for the door, bell tinkling as she pulls it open. "It was nice to meet you."

"You too!" I blurt out the words in my desperation, as she takes her first step out of the door.

I can't let her get away. Not like this, not when I've been so eager to meet her. I follow her, aware of the sound my feet make on the floorboards, out into the street. "I'm Remy, by the way. Remy Evans."

It's a completely pointless statement. Ravi already said my name.

But the girl nods, replying, "I'm Carmel."

Carmel.

Just a syllable away from caramel, but *so* much sweeter.

"Carmel." The word practically drips from my tongue. It suits her. It really suits her. "I'll remember that."

She nods again, but I can tell she wants to leave. Her feet are facing down the street in the same direction I know she disappeared last time.

Yet I don't want her to go. Not until I've made a move, like I planned all along.

"Um… Carmel?"

She's already started to walk away, and turns upon hearing her name.

"Remy?"

There's a hint of annoyance in her voice.

Shit.

I need to move faster.

"Can I have your number?"

Carmel blinks at me. "My number?"

"Yes."

"Why?"

"I… in case you ever need a lightbulb."

carmel

I stare at Superboy – whose name is Remy, apparently – with my mouth open wide. A lightbulb? He wants my number in case I ever need a… lightbulb?

"Okay," I say after a moment's pause, cocking my head. "Do you want me to write it down for you?"

There's a pen in the pocket of my coat, of course, so I pull it out and reach for his hand. He's a little chubby, like I first noticed, and his hand is soft in mine.

"There you are," I tell him, raising an eyebrow. "If you text me later, I'll save your number. In case I need a lightbulb, you know?"

"Lightbulbs are always useful." His voice is breathy, slightly higher than I was expecting. He's staring at his hand in shock, like I've given him a tattoo. "You can't see without them."

I don't know how to respond to that. Should I laugh? It doesn't really feel like a *joke*.

"Anyway," I continue. "I really do have to go now. Thanks again, Remy."

And then I turn and walk away, resisting the urge to look back.

***

I don't need another lightbulb. The one Ravi gave me works perfectly as I twist it into place and flick the switch, watching Mum's face light up and her eyes glow blue.

"It's perfect," she says, pulling me in for a hug. "You thanked Ravi for me, didn't you?"

My mum has always had a sweet spot for our shopkeeper. Before she got ill, she'd stop by his store each night to buy a few apples or pears for our pudding, though the locally sourced produce was much more expensive than in the supermarket. She always looks forward to his visits now, and a grin spills over her face as I tell her of his intentions this weekend.

"It's a good job you washed my wig." She frowns, mind ticking as she goes over everything else she needs to do to prepare for him, tongue sticking out. I do the same when we're concentrating. A Reeves' trait, Mum calls it. "The nurse comes later, doesn't she?"

Once a week, we get a visit from one of the hospital's many nurses, Patrice. She gives Mum a bath and checks her progress, monitoring her temperature, checking for infections, insisting she changes her clothes more often and doesn't wear the wig. She's far too bossy, obsessed with cleanliness and doing everything "right". It's also clear she doesn't rate my own care skills.

"Thank goodness I'll be out," I reply.

Patrice isn't exactly my favourite person, so I always make sure I'm working at the time she arrives. I've bumped into her on more than one occasion, and it's always tense.

"She'll call me if she needs to update me on anything, won't she? And you'll ring me if you need help?"

Mum nods.

You see... being a carer is more complicated than just

looking after Mum, making sure she's in the right hands. It's reading between the lines, making sure you don't miss a beat. Mrs Dichre lives just down the road, but Patrice notices things about the cancer we sometimes don't see. If she needs new tablets or another stint in hospital, I have to be there to discuss it with her. Mum can't always do those things herself.

"It'll be fine," I tell her, pulling away at last. I wander through to the kitchen, leaving the door open so that the sound will carry. "You're doing great."

There's no reply as I start to prepare her tea. Microwavable rice and some boiled peas, nice and healthy. Patrice will no doubt ask what she's eaten today, and it needs to be the simplest of dishes to pass her approval, packed with fibre. I pile it onto a plate and carry it through to her, grabbing myself a banana on the way.

"Here you are, madam!" I announce, placing it on her lap. "Your food is served."

But there are black, tear-filled streaks running down her face.

"Mum?"

As a rule, my mum cries a lot. She cries when she's agitated, frustrated, when she wakes up in the night and can't get back to sleep without me. She cries when she thinks about not being here for my future, when she remembers that two years ago she was given six months to live, however hard she tries to remember that she's already surpassed that, that she's doing great, so great.

This is different. Her face is pale and unmoving, and she doesn't look *upset*. The sadness is calm, tears leaking from a still expression as though she can't seem to stop them.

"Mum?" I repeat. She hasn't touched her plate yet. The steam rising off the peas is evaporating into nothing. "Your tea's going cold."

But Mum is unresponsive.

"Just have a bit, okay? Patrice will only complain otherwise, and you won't sleep if you're hungry."

There's a knock on the door, then, making Mum jump. I stand, eyes still on her until I'm out into the corridor.

It's Patrice.

"Hey," I say, stepping backwards to let her in.

"Afternoon!" Patrice replies. She's a large woman, on the pale side, with tattoos just like Mum's up her arms and bulbous calves. She walks around me, but she doesn't go through to the living room yet. Instead, she smiles at me and starts tut-tutting.

I stare back, waiting for her to speak. Patrice isn't known for her sympathy, not least towards me, and the look on her face is making me feel... uncomfortable. She genuinely looks sorry for me, and I don't know why.

"I'm kind of in a rush," I say eventually, after a moment of silence. "I have to get to work."

Patrice shakes her head then, looking even *more* sorry for me. Mum has picked up her fork now and I can hear it clanking against the plate as she takes mouthfuls.

"Bye!" I shout down the corridor. "I love you!"

I'm sure I don't imagine the tears in Patrice's eyes as I turn away, shutting the door behind me with a loud, final click. There's an uneasy feeling in my stomach as I make my way to the bus stop, churning round and round and round and round.

Something is wrong.

I know that.

Mum knows that.

Patrice knows that.

Something is very, very wrong, and it's not just the fact my mum has terminal cancer and is going to die some time in the somewhat… ambiguous future.

It's something else.

Something which tells me that maybe they know more about the future than I do.

remy

"Matt?"

The call finally goes through, and I hear the familiar *Mario Kart* theme tune down the line. I'm on an empty bus pulling out of Hull, nestled by the window beneath a black night sky, phone pressed firmly against one ear.

"Remy Evans," he replies, disinterested as usual. "You know what time it is, right? I have a sociology test tomorrow, and I need to get some sleep!"

"You're still on your Switch, mate," I respond. "I have big news!"

"Big enough for a group call?" he suggests. "Lil and Nima will probably still be awake…"

He's right, but now isn't the time. Things were too weird between Lily and I today for me to tell her all about Carmel, and I know *exactly* what her advice would be. This is a problem for Matt and I to solve – just us two, like the old days.

"I did it," I say, ignoring his offer. "I got the girl's number!"

He's silent for a moment, crossing the finishing line as Yoshi gives a cry of exuberance.

"You what?"

"I got the girl's number!"

It sounds much more impressive when I say it out loud,

echoed by the empty bus. We pull out onto the main road and I watch as cars pull past in a blur of colour and lights, heart swelling.

I got the girl's number.

Am I dreaming?

"The girl as in… *the girl*?"

I roll my eyes at no one in particular. I don't know why it's so difficult for Matt to comprehend… though I too am filled with disbelief, so I can see where he's coming from.

"Yes, dumbo. Her name's *Carmel*, like Caramel, but without the 'ra'. I have her number written on my hand!" I glance back down at it then. Her handwriting is all messy, the opposite of mine; it reminds me of a twelve-year-old boy's. It's kind of cute, endearing. "I don't know how to text her. I've never done this before."

"And you're asking me because…?"

I'm a little exasperated then. I want Matt's help because he's my best friend, because we've gone through all of this together. Me getting a girl's number feels like hope for both of us, after years and years of staying single, of being completely undesirable to pretty much every female ever.

"I just need help, okay? I have no idea what to say to her!"

That's not *strictly* true. I've spent the last few hours at work completely distracted, trying to think of something witty and charming to send to her, something which will make her sit up and reply almost instantly. I don't know if it's possible to make someone fall in love with you using just a sentence, but I'm sure going to try.

"Just say hi," Matt tells me. I can hear him starting another race, Yoshi's bike revving at the start line. "Then you can get to know her. You know, like a normal person."

But I don't want to do normal.

I want to make a great first impression, sweep her off her feet from the get-go.

"Come on," I say. "Do you want me to get her, or not?"

Matt sighs, and I know then that he's about to say yes. He still has that weird complex about Lily and I becoming a thing, and if I start dating Carmel, any chance of that happening will go out of the window. I listen to him think, before he finally lets out a grunt of agreement and I punch the air.

"Thank you!" I put my phone on speaker, then click onto the messenger app. I type in the girl's number, focusing carefully on each digit, pushing them into the keypad. "I need to send something funny, okay? Something to blow her mind."

"How about a fact?" Matt suggests.

A fact? I haven't even considered that. We love facts in our friendship group, forever sending them to the group chat and competing for the very best, since we're not very good at actual sports.

Carmel *must* like facts. All the best people do.

"Or a pun," Matt continues. "They're more clever, subtle."

Puns, too, are my speciality.

There's no way a pun won't work on her.

"Like what?" I ask. "God, Matt. There's so much pressure riding on this."

Matt's silent for another moment as he wins the race once more, Yoshi's cry echoing across the bus.

"Okay, no puns," he concludes. "Princess Peach says that's too cheesy."

Typical.

"I honestly think you should just go simple, Remy," he continues. "You don't need to impress her; you've already got her number. How did you do that, anyway? And where did you see her?"

So I tell him how she came into Ravi's shop, how she spun around and saw me, how she was the most beautiful girl I'd ever seen. I tell him how I followed her outside, and how she said thank you for saving her the other night, at least twice.

"Then I asked for her number, in case she ever needed another lightbulb," I explain. "And she gave it to me!"

"In case… she ever needed another lightbulb?"

"I don't know how it worked, either, but it did."

"You're one of a kind, Remy. You're one of a fucking *kind*."

The bus is pulling into Vibbington now, trundling down the high street and stopping with an exaggerated sigh at the stop. I thank the driver as I disembark, *Mario Kart* still blaring from Matt's end of the phone as I start up my own street and push open the garden gate. The living room light is on, and I can just see Dad's silhouette in the window.

"I'll have to call you back," I say, clicking off speakerphone. "I'm home now."

"Let me know what you send," Matt says. Then he hangs up, leaving me in silence.

I pop my head round the living room door on my way upstairs. Angelique seems to have already gone to bed, and Mum and Dad are catching up on the news, eyes bleary and fixed on the screen. They don't notice me for a moment, until I tap gently on the wood and they turn to look at me.

"Oh, Remy," Mum murmurs, holding out her arms for a hug. "I didn't hear you come in, love."

They never do, nowadays. I let her surround me, her soft scent filling the air with familiar, comforting vanilla.

"Did you have fun at Nima's yesterday?" she asks. Most

parents might be suspicious of opposite-sex sleepovers, but lately, Mum hasn't had the energy to care. I nod as I pull away, backing up to the door. "That's good. Sleep well, Remy."

I practically run up the stairs, phone still clutched in my hand. Once in my bedroom, I save the number in case it deletes itself, then click "compose". I stare at the empty conversation for a moment, before beginning to type.

hi, it's remy. i don't have any lightbulbs.

I've clicked send before I can think twice about it.

There. It's gone. I can't do anything about it now. It was straight, simple, to the point. It was a little witty, too, I think – depending on the tone of which she reads it.

Or does it just sound blunt?

It sounds weird, of course it does. Who even says that?

I push my phone away from me across the bed, shuddering. There's nothing left to do now but wait for a reply.

I try to read the book of critical theories about Milton's life Mr O'Flannel let me borrow, but the words blur on the page into an incomprehensible blob, and I can't understand half the things it says. My back grows sore against the headboard and the book is heavy in my lap, and my phone won't stop staring at me from the other end of my duvet.

"Stay there," I tell it. "I'm going for a shower."

I don't dare stay under the water for too long in case I miss her reply, but at least it distracts me for a little while. I dump my clothes by the door and dash under the spray, running the shampoo briefly through my hair, slathering my body in shower gel and soap. There's no time for modesty as I stumble out and wrap the towel round my waist.

I make my way across the landing and back to my bedroom, heart thudding.

There's. One. New. Message.

How can you see if you have no lightbulbs?

I just stare at the screen, eyes wide.

She replied.

She replied.

She *replied*.

i can see in the dark.

There. Sent. Another line to hopefully make her chuckle, even just a little bit. I watch the conversation glow white in the dim light of my bedroom, breath caught in my throat.

Wow. You really are Superboy.

Superboy. What does that mean? I'm not super, not really. I'm just ordinary Remy Evans, living a dream.

how did you know?

carmel

I click send before I can think twice.

I don't really care if he knows I call him Superboy; he's just some random guy who works for Ravi, after all. I most likely won't see him again, but even if I do, he seems a bit of a weirdo, all nerdy slogan t-shirts and semi-witty remarks, the kind of guy to make a meme page on Instagram and watch YouTube videos about physics.

how did you know?

The message comes instantly, phone lighting up in my hand. He's a quick replier, I'll give him that. Whenever I text Boy 1 and Boy 2 regarding our art homework, they're always slow to respond, sometimes waiting twenty-four hours before supplying me with an answer, albeit short.

In contrast, Remy seems ultra-keen to continue our conversation.

Pushing my phone into my pocket, I let out a sigh. Because I've run out of effort, bored of being friendly. The bus comes to a stop opposite the kebab shop and I leap off it, waving to the driver and pulling my hat hard over my curls, huddling under my coat all the way home.

The new lightbulb is bright in the window as I walk up, turning the key and pushing through the door. Patrice always leaves a chemical smell lingering after her infamous bed baths and check-ups, and today's no different. She's been using banana soap, as usual. Mum hates it.

"I'm home!" I call, kicking off my shoes. "I'll just make myself some tea!"

I can still recall Patrice's face as I make my way to the kitchen. She looked like she was about to cry, eyes full of sympathy, like she knew something I didn't. Something felt wrong – very wrong. I'm almost scared to find out what.

I turn on the oven, preparing frozen hash browns and fishfingers on a tray. While it heats up, I place mixed veg in the microwave and watch through the murky window as it thaws, condensation dripping down the glass sides and forming a puddle of stodgy water on the ring.

I take my meal through to the front room. Mum is watching TV, volume low. It's some celebrity chef, and his gourmet pasta dish looks a lot more appetising than my own.

"Evening, love," she whispers, trying to smile. "Did you have a good time at work?"

It was just the average two hour session, to a class of university students. One of the boys tried to chat me up afterwards, but I told him I wasn't interested and hoped he'd stop watching me as I got changed – which he didn't, obviously. His eyes lingered even as I was pulling on my scarf and gloves, smirking one last time as I ran down the stairs.

"It was fine," I say. "Kinda quiet, you know?"

Talking about work is easier than asking Mum what's really going on, in a way. It's easier than asking why Patrice was acting so oddly earlier… and it's safer than knowing the truth.

The last time Mum's illness got worse, she'd developed pneumonia. It was a few months ago, when I was in year thirteen, and the heating bill hadn't been paid because of a fault in her account. Although it was summer and the nights were warm, a few rainy spells caused damp to develop along the windows and by the front door, and the whole room was fusty, cold. She had to go into hospital, where they told her another episode like that might finish her off.

We're more careful now, paying our bills on time and borrowing blankets where we can from the nurse and Mrs Dichre, checking our bank accounts each month to see the money leave, to see the numbers rise and fall.

I'm still terrified that she'll get sick again, that her body won't fight it. We always knew she'd get worse, that the disease was untreatable, but I'm not ready for her to go just yet.

"I'm glad," she says, closing her eyes. "I'm so bloody proud of you, Carmel."

The hash brown is still frozen in the middle, the vegetables slimy and covered in sludgy water. It's a struggle to swallow, my mouth clogged up with food.

"So…" I hesitate, frowning at Mum. I really, really don't want to know what happened with Patrice, but I need to. I'm Mum's carer, her daughter, the person who's supposed to help her through the disease. I can't do that if I have no idea what's wrong, or how bad it's become. "What did Patrice say?"

I sense Mum's sharp inhale.

That means something must have happened, that she heard something she didn't want to. I wait, hands clutching my knife and fork tight, as she breathes out again.

"She…" Mum pauses, opening her eyes to look at me. Her skin is pale, wig slipped sidewards.

It's getting worse, I know it is.

I've known that for weeks, but haven't wanted to admit it.

"She said there's little change," she finishes. Her cheeks are pink, just filled with enough colour to qualify as a flush. "There's nothing to update you on."

She's lying. She's lying, and we both know it.

I take another mouthful of fishfinger and carrot, the outer part of the hash brown. The chef is still staring at us through the screen, chopping up a warm salad, frying courgette and "pak choi" in cumin and chilli powder –

"That's good."

Mum nods, trying to smile again. Her teeth are yellow from years of smoking ciggies and her tongue is rough and ulcer-spotted, eyes glassy. She has a little toothbrush and pot of water I refresh each night, but her dental hygiene isn't what it once was – the same goes for the rest of her body. The cancer has her in its grips and isn't willing to let go.

"I think I'll go to bed now," I say, standing and taking my last bite of hash brown. "Night, Mum."

Mum reaches up to hug me, body fragile. She's always been on the plump side, but her bones are tiny and weak beneath her skin, which sags against me. I pull back, leaving the room as quickly as I can to avoid her seeing the tears in my eyes.

Upstairs, my room is in darkness. I drop my bag and sketchbook onto the floor and kick them into the corner, pulling off my coat and jeans and jumper. I climb into bed in my knickers and t-shirt, phone clutched in one hand, duvet squeezed tight in the other.

I turn it on. The reply from Remy is still lit up in blue, marked as unread.

how did you know?

I don't want to reply. I'm exhausted, mentally drained, and this conversation – a jokey, nothing-filled collection of awkward blabber – isn't something I have the energy to partake in.

But I can't leave him on read.

You seem special.

I'm kidding, of course. Remy *does* seem special, in a fragile, geeky sort of way, and I'm sure he's a great person. He's different to a lot of guys. Kind, genuine, like he just wants to help people and doesn't care about the reward, his personal gain. He doesn't seem like the type of person to care what others think of him, which is something I admire. It takes guts, courage, more than most people contain.

I turn off my phone, placing it face down at the end of my bed. I push the charger in and wait for it to buzz, before leaning back against my pillow and closing my eyes, heart pounding.

I love you, Mum.

I should've told her that before I went to sleep, I know that. But at least there's always tomorrow…

For now, anyway.

"She likes you."

Nima puts down her pen and stares at me across the table, brown eyes wide. The others are staring at my phone in shock, and Lily's mouth is open in a perfect "o".

"She called you special," she reads out. "Who does that if they don't like the person?"

"Someone who likes the person." Matt rolls his eyes, taking a sip from his coke. "Mmm, this is *good.*"

Only Matt would agree to come for a coffee and order a diet coke with double ice, watching the rest of us sip our lattes with a wrinkled nose.

We're sat in a café on Saturday morning, just the four of us, after an emergency meeting was called. Matt insisted the girls help us on The Carmel Issue, but now that we're here, I'm starting to wish he hadn't.

"Go on, Remy, send something back! She's clearly into you."

She can't be, though. It makes no sense. Ever since I saw her again last night, I've been turning it over and over in my mind, trying to understand why she gave me her number, why the lightbulb thing seemed to work. I made a complete fool of myself, acting all awkward and embarrassed and Remy-like, and there's no way she'd find that attractive. Because it isn't. It isn't even a little bit.

"I don't know what to say." I pick my phone up and pocket it again, just in case. When Nima liked Lisa Cotton in year ten, we all took it in turns to steal her phone and send her daft messages, ultimately ruining her chances. Lisa Cotton made a huge fuss in maths about how Nima was a "lesbian freak", which thankfully landed her detention for the next month.

I can't risk that happening with Carmel.

"Ask her to see you," Nima says, as if it's that simple. "Then you can get to know her in person, rather than over message."

But that sounds even more impossible. I'm a disaster in real life, so much so that I can't even talk to a girl I like without seeming completely off my head. At least the Remy I can be over the phone is calm, calculated, controlled.

"I'll just make a fool of myself," I insist. "She's probably just being friendly."

Which is the only thing that makes any sense.

"Then meet her as a friend," Matt continues. "Try get to know her, let her get to know you. Then you can start the seduction, ooo."

Lily has been quiet throughout, a frown on her face. I don't know how she feels about the situation, what with how weird things have been between us since the sleepover, but her nose wrinkles every time someone says Carmel's name. Her hands are tucked into the sleeves of her jumper as she takes another sip of her milkshake and leans back against the booth.

"I agree with Remy," she says. "The girl's probably just being friendly. You can't like someone after saying, like, three words to each other."

Matt glances back and forth between us, brow creased.

"Remy does," he says. "He liked her the moment he first saw her."

"Yes, well. That's stupid. It's just… attraction, hence why *Romeo and Juliet* is the worst Shakespeare play. You don't even know what she's like, Remy!"

Lily's right, of course she is. I don't know Carmel, not really.

But I feel like I do.

There was something about her from the moment I saw her, something real, something raw. The person she is, the way she dresses and walks and acts, the way she speaks… it makes sense to me.

The moment I saw her, she just felt *right*.

"I can't explain it," I say, eyes fixed on the table. "I like her, I don't know why. She's special."

Nima reaches out to pat my hand. She felt the same about her last girlfriend, no doubt. We'd all been sceptical; the blonde bimbo Macey Collins was part of our year's popular group, an acquaintance of Darcie Carlton and Co., but Nima saw something different in her. They met after the populars pushed Macey out, took her ex-boyfriend's side after a messy breakup, and Nima saw an opportunity to befriend the girl she'd been crushing on since the start of the year.

Sometimes, you know someone is right before you even properly get to know them. That's how it is with Carmel. Something about her draws me to her, makes me question everything.

"Fine," Lily says, rolling her eyes. "But don't come crying to me when she breaks your heart."

The table lapses into silence as we order lunch. Lily's attitude towards Carmel has been cynical from the start, but this is a new level of pessimistic. Is our love story really that doomed?

My eyes skim the menu for something light, too caught up in Carmel to have much of an appetite. I go for the chicken salad sandwich in the end. It comes with extra mayo and chips which defeats the purpose slightly, but the minute the plate is placed in front of me, the scent alone makes me salivate. The others choose tuna melts and the café's infamous quesadillas, and we order second drinks to come with our food, diet cokes and water and a J2O.

We finish our food in record time, Matt and Lily making small talk about the movies and nonsense, Nima painting on her napkin with a half-empty bottle of nail polish she had in her pocket.

I take out my phone, placing it on the table before me.

I need to do something, say something. I can't waste any more time staring at an empty screen.

"I'm doing it," I say suddenly. "I'm asking her to go on a date with me."

The others glance up to meet my expression, and Matt slaps me on the back in congratulations. Nima's nodding her encouragement, but Lily's face has paled.

I start to type.

this might seem random, but... i really wanted to try out this new american pudding place in the centre, and i wondered if you wanted to go with me? i don't know anybody else in hull and it's supposed to be pretty cool!

Do I send kisses?

I don't, pressing send before I can reconsider. My friends are all watching me.

"I asked her to Paula's Puddings, that new café they've just opened in Hull," I inform them, flushing. "I thought it would make a cute first date, but… I don't know, is it too much? I'm going to have to make conversation with her the whole time, and eat in front of her, and probably get food everywhere, and just –"

Nima puts up a hand to stop me. She's shaking her head, the expression on her face scolding me.

"Remy, it sounds *perfect*. If she doesn't say yes, she's stupid."

"I didn't even specify a time," I say, groaning and dropping my head into my hands. I didn't read it through before sending, didn't even *think*. I was so conscious of me most likely backing out of sending it that I probably fluffed up the only chance I'll get to ask her out, by being so ridiculously dumb –

"It's fine. If she says yes, she'll give a time." But Matt sounds so confident, so sure that this is all going to plan, that I have to protest.

"What makes you the expert? You've never even *had* a girlfriend."

"I just *know*." He's gone bright red, which makes me feel guilty. He's only trying to help, after all. But as much as he *thinks* he knows, I need to be certain I'm doing this right. Matt isn't likely to meet anyone while Lily's around, so this time, we're focusing on me.

We order dessert to prolong our stay, perusing the menu for ages before deciding. I get a fruit salad with vanilla ice cream, and the others all get chocolate brownies with clotted cream and caramel sauce – which instantly makes us all go "Carmel!" – and more milkshakes, though my stomach is churning too much for something so sickly.

The café lets us stay half an hour after we've finished

eating, since it's the afternoon now and they're emptier than usual, the October sun outside shining bright in the sky. A middle-aged couple are sharing a slice of lemon drizzle across the room from us, and a family of four are nursing coffees and discussing something on a sheet of paper before them, expressions serious. Matt is playing a game on his phone again, and Lily has her history exam notes out in front of her.

"Have you sent your application off yet?" she asks, glancing up from her work.

That's when it hits me.

I still haven't sent my personal statement to Mr O'Flannel. There's less than a week left until it's too late.

When I don't reply, Lily's eyes widen and she taps the table hard with her pen. "Remy! Do you want an interview, or not? You're going to miss the deadline!"

It's been the last thing on my mind the last few days, as much as I hate to admit it. Going to Oxford has been my dream for as long as I can remember, but now, new Remy is too preoccupied thinking about a girl to even apply.

"I have five days left," I say, though it sounds pathetic even in my head. "I just need Mr O'Flannel to read over my personal statement."

"I can do that," she says, rolling her eyes. "I've read enough stupid samples to know what's what. Send it to me, okay? As soon as you get home."

I nod, trying for a smile. I'll remember that. This afternoon, I've got nothing better to do other than revise and catch up on some homework, so I can easily email my draft to Lily. And to Mr O'Flannel, though he won't check his inbox until Monday anyway now…

"Promise me?" Lily says, eyes fixed on mine. "This is serious, Remy."

My phone buzzes.

"She's replied."

carmel

I stare at the invitation. Remy – or Superboy, as my head still insists on calling him – is asking me to go and get *pudding* with him.

I've seen Paula's Puddings a few times on my way to work. It's a new café that's only just opened in the city centre, American-style, selling ice cream sundaes and pies and buckets of different flavoured cookie dough. It's reasonably priced, too, though the outside is greasy and outdated, in need of a good scrub.

I don't often go out to places like that. College, work, the odd drink from McDonald's now and then… I don't like spending money on something I can find cheaper alternatives for. Meals out, and even trips around and out of the city, are a complete waste, in my opinion. And yet I'm sat on my bed, art coursework spread out in front of me, debating what to say to him.

I should say no. I don't really know this boy, and the only reason he's asking me is because I'm the only person in Hull he's mildly acquainted with. Does he not have friends from wherever he comes from, friends he could take instead? I don't get why he's asking *me*.

Although I'd probably decline anyway, I don't get invited places by people, ever. I can't remember the last time I even got an invitation to a kiddie birthday party, an outing to the bowling alley arranged between mums. I don't have a group, a special friend I've had since primary school, acquaintances from college. I don't have *people* in general.

I'm not that likeable, not the kind of person others want to take out for meals or to the cinema. People have pointed out my coldness before, my abrupt nature. It's off-putting, apparently.

But… this boy is asking me to go out with him.

And something inside me, something I didn't know *existed*, is making me want to say yes.

I'm bored anyway, stuck in a pile of drawings and testing sheets, swatches of watercolour and biro and ink. I have the whole of tomorrow to finish this off before I go into college on Monday. Mum is asleep, and I have nothing else to do this afternoon.

Besides… it might be fun. He seems like a nice guy. The food isn't too expensive, either, compared to other places. They do a lot of special deals, since they've just opened.

It's nice to feel wanted.

It's nice to even be *considered*.

Okay. I'll meet you there at three.

I hit send.

I run downstairs to tell Mum at once, knocking on the door and pushing through without waiting for a reply. She's facing the TV, but it's not switched on. I thought she'd be asleep but her eyes are focused on the blank screen, body still.

"Mum?" I say, gently tapping her foot. "Mum, I'm going out for a bit, okay?"

Today is one of those days, clearly. Sometimes, when she's not doing so good, she gets all unresponsive, trapped in her own head. She doesn't want to talk to anyone, doesn't want to move, doesn't want to *think*, just stare and wait until it passes.

If she wasn't in this mood, she'd probably be happy to see me going out, making friends. Mum has always felt bad that I don't do much with my spare time, but we're very different people in that sense. She's sociable in nature, and was always out with different guys and a gaggle of girlfriends before she got too ill to drink. I think it makes her sad that I'm the opposite, like I'm missing out on life experiences. I'm not fun-loving, not up for adventures.

I see beauty in all the little things in life, but not the big things, the exciting things.

Not anymore, anyway. There's no point.

"Mrs Dichre will be round later. And Ravi is popping by, remember?"

Mum is silent as I close the door behind me, tiptoeing back to my room.

Upstairs, I tug open the doors to my wardrobe. Most of my clothes are Primark finds, or thrifted – I like bright colours and designs, clothes that make a statement, bring life to a scene. I pick a pair of baggy jeans, some socks covered in avocados, a bubble-gum pink jumper. My yellow coat is hung on a hook by the front door, trainers sat with their familiar hole-in-the-toe and fading optimism.

can't wait!

Remy's reply is so innocent, so *nice*.

He's excited to see me, Carmel Reeves, and I don't understand *why*. He doesn't know me, doesn't know how terrible I am at making or keeping friends, at being a normal human. He doesn't know how boring I am, how girls don't seem to ever like me, how the only guys who've ever shown mild interest in me are the lurid old men at the arts centre.

I know it's only because he doesn't know many people in Hull, but my heart is racing as I board the bus, passing him a handful of coins and taking a seat at the very back.

I don't need friends.

But maybe – just maybe – it'd be nice to have just one.

Lily takes another sip of her milkshake, cheeks stained pink. Nima and Matt are gobsmacked, staring at my phone with almost as much shock as me.

Carmel said *yes*.

She wants to go on a date with me, meaning she's interested and doesn't think I'm a total flop and actually wants to get to know Remy Evans, beyond my fat exterior and awkwardness and weird talk of lightbulbs.

"We're meeting at three," I say, checking the time in the corner of the screen. "Shit. That's less than an hour away. I need to catch the train, quick!"

"We'll come with you," Nima says, standing and pulling on her coat. "We can do some shopping, get McDonald's, then meet you after."

Matt nods, jumping to his feet and grabbing his bag.

Lily, however, stays seated.

"I'll be fine here," she says. The straw is still stuck between her teeth. "You go. Have a good afternoon, yeah? I need to revise for my history test."

I don't want to just *leave* her there, but her expression is set. Perhaps it'll be easier this way, anyway. Less awkward, less tense. She doesn't seem to like Carmel or support my pursuit of her, and I don't think we're going to change her mind.

Nodding, the three of us say our goodbyes and leg it out of

the café, hurtling down Vibbington's main street to the train station, pushing through the Saturday hubbub in order to reach the platform in time.

Weekends are always a terrible time to try and get into Hull. Everyone and their great aunt seems to be out, bustling across the platform with bags and cases and umbrellas, and the ticket machine is hidden behind a gaggle of bodies. Nima is slight enough to make her way through the gaggle and pay for three tickets, and we're on the train and settled in three minutes flat, waiting with breaths held to set off.

"You're shaking," Matt notes, grinning at me. "Nervous?"

Nervous doesn't even *begin* to cover how I feel.

I'm a wreck when it comes to girls, awkward at the best of times. I'm not even dressed for the occasion, wearing yesterday's sweaty shirt and a pair of old jeans, trainers mud-encrusted and palms moist. I've done nothing with my hair, and there are at least three spots on my forehead which have appeared overnight.

"I haven't shaved," I say, rubbing my face in my hands. "God, I look like a… a…"

A gremlin? An ogre? An ogre who hasn't been on a date before, who hasn't even kissed a girl, let alone had one like me back.

I'm a complete disaster.

Carmel seems… different to me. More experienced, somehow, like she's done things like this already. She's beautiful, stylish, independent, the kind of girl who *must* have had a boyfriend before. Right?

I'm just lucky that she doesn't have one right now. One ready to fight me as I try to get with his girl, to pull me behind Paula's Puddings and beat me black and blue. The thought makes me shudder, and my friends notice the grimace as we pull away from Vibbington.

"Hey! You've got this." Nima reaches across to grab my hand, squeezing it encouragingly. Matt pats my shoulder, though it doesn't really help. "She said yes, okay? Which means she's into you."

"I know," I say, nodding. "I know."

She must be, or else she wouldn't have agreed to go on a date with me. There was no pressure to, no reason other than the fact we shared that moment on Wednesday night, brought together by fate in Ravi's shop forty-eight hours later.

I *know* she must like me, though the thought seems stark in my head. Girls don't just go out with strangers for the fun of it, especially not pretty girls, girls who could have anyone they want, girls who are stylish and have a thousand corkscrew curls, and probably have heaps of friends.

Girls like Carmel.

The train pulls into Hull's station twenty minutes later, dragging itself along the track to a stop and hissing as we arrive. We sidle off one at a time, checking the station clock. We have fifteen minutes to spare, which is a relief. I'm not going to be late.

"Let's find a bench to sit on, yeah? That way we can wait for her, watch her arrive."

Matt and I nod at Nima and follow her through the crush.

There's seating all around the city centre, and a few concrete planters are placed opposite Paula's Puddings. We sit a little beneath a tree, semi-disguised, so that we'll see her walking up to the red and white striped door. The café is grimier than I was expecting, the prices pretty low. The plaque outside is already chipping.

"Great place for a first date!" Matt says, but I can't seem to find a trace of sarcasm in his voice.

The tension is high. We wait in silence, Nima's foot tapping up and down, up and down, as shoppers come and go; little children run riot, grandparents chasing them and trying to find ice creams, parents trailing sticky toddlers and whining teens. There's a homeless man laid in a doorway opposite, but I don't have cash on me, and the queues to the takeout places are winding down the street.

I watch each teenage girl as they pass by, making absolutely sure they're not Carmel, that we don't miss her. Girls with straight hair, wavy hair, blue eyes, green eyes… but none with her trademark curls, those big dark eyes, her colourful clothes. None of them compare, not even a little.

"What does she look like?" Nima asks, leaning over Matt to talk to me. "So that I can look out for her."

What *does* she look like? I don't even know how to answer that. Carmel is unique, different to any other girl. She's indescribable.

Three o'clock ticks by, and there's still no Carmel to be seen. Matt has long disappeared into a bakery to buy a sausage roll, returning with four to share with Nima, but another five minutes pass and there's still no sign of her. It's cold, a wind picking up and brushing my jeans, and my friends are shivering beside me as they munch on the pastries and observe the street.

"Her bus was probably held up," Matt says, scrunching up the bag and throwing it into the bin with an artful curve. "You can't trust public transport these days."

But when ten minutes have passed and she still hasn't arrived, I think we all start to fear the worst.

Maybe it was a dream too good to be true. Maybe she was joking, messing with me, sat with her friends in a booth at McDonald's, watching us through the window. Maybe this is all just an elaborate prank. Maybe I'm being filmed for a documentary on lonely, desperate teens…

That's when I see her.

She's wandering down the street, sketchbook under one arm, eyes fixed on the page. She's sketching something, baggy jeans trailing on the ground behind her, yellow coat zipped up tight. I almost can't breathe for a moment, frozen, until Matt prods my arm and whispers, "Is that her?"

I nod, lost for words. She hasn't seen me yet, hasn't even looked up from her sketchbook, too engrossed in whatever she's drawing.

"She's so cute!" Nima squeals, clapping her hands and gesturing for me to get up. "Go on, Remy, go talk to her! She's almost at the restaurant!"

But I can't even stand, legs like jelly beneath me. Carmel is approaching Paula's Puddings fast, finally putting away the book and zipping up her bag, about to turn around and skim the area in three, two, one…

Matt grabs hold of me and pushes me forward, watching as I stumble towards her. We catch eyes as she straightens and hoists her bag further onto her shoulders, my friends dispersing in the background, hurrying off to waste the next few hours in the shops while I completely humiliate myself –

Carmel gives me a strange smile, clearly taking in my flushed face and odd, stilted walk. I can't seem to act normally, body malfunctioning, feet turned inwards, knees wobbling. I come to a stop in front of her, tucking my shaking hands into my pockets and trying to smile back.

She looks even more beautiful today, in the cold light of the city centre. I don't want to stare, but it's hard not to.

"Hey," she says, raising an eyebrow. "Are you okay?"

She thinks there's something wrong with me already.

Blushing an even deeper shade of red, I nod vigorously and try for a handshake, which she greets with caution.

Her hand is warm in mine, so slender and smooth and perfect. A jolt of electricity runs up my back, and I drop it at once.

"Shall we go inside?" she says.

I nod again, still completely lost for words.

The restaurant is only moderately busy. Customers fill the booths closest to the window and filter onto the tables behind, checking out the new food, the discounts, the specials. The carpet hasn't been changed since the room was an arcade a few months back, and the walls are painted a tacky red, lights clinging to the paintwork and giving way to posters of vintage pudding recipes, advertisements and feminist slogans.

"Paula is definitely a middle-aged woman who's always wanted to be cool," Carmel whispers to me, and I can't help but smile, though I manage to supress the gurgle of startled laughter.

We take a seat right at the back, in the left corner. It's sour and dingy, the tables made of dark wood and still sticky from the last customer's order, but Carmel isn't bothered. She takes a seat on one of the plastic chairs without a fuss and so I try to do the same, though I can't help but wince as my back touches the stained exterior.

"Not to your standards?" she asks, raising an eyebrow.

Great. Now she thinks I'm a snob, too.

We're silent for a moment, unsure of what to say. I'm terrible at this, terrible of making conversation, especially when she's so bloody *gorgeous*. Her skin is smooth and brown, save for one spot by her jaw, dark eyes large and framed by long lashes. She twists a curl around her finger and tries to distract herself by looking at the menu, as if the action will fill the awkward silence.

"What are you ordering?" She glances up as she asks this, noticing me staring. Her cheeks flood with pink and I have to bite back a strangled cry, instantly embarrassed. I glance at my own menu, the words jumbling before me as I try to pick one, my hand moving down it, finger picking out words, words, words…

"I think… a peanut butter sundae." I clap my hand over my mouth as soon as I've said it, shaking my head. I *hate* peanut butter. I don't know why I said that, not when there are so many options to choose from.

But Carmel's eyes have lit up and she's nodding as vigorously as I'm shaking, stabbing the page with her finger.

"Yes, I love peanut butter! All the best people do." She grins, looking a little more relaxed now, like I'm not as strange as she originally thought. "Let's both get peanut butter sundaes, then. That's one thing we have in common."

Shit, shit, shit. I've already lied to her, and we're *five minutes* into the date. How is it even possible to be this awful at… being a human?

Carmel does all the talking when the waiter comes over, so I just sit back and stew. I can feel sweat patches forming on my t-shirt and so can't take off my coat, though I'm so, so warm, and as the waiter takes the menus away, I don't even have that to hide behind.

"So," Carmel says, waiting for me to say something.

So.

carmel

I regret my decision to meet the guy almost instantly. Someone I thought could be a friend is rapidly turning into someone who can't make conversation, who can't properly shake hands, who can't even order his own sundae without sweating up a storm. So far, the only thing we have in common is the fact we love peanut butter, and I only said that to kill the awkwardness. I don't like it, not really. It's one of the only requests I refuse to buy for Mum, on account of it tasting like literal wallpaper paste.

"What year are you in?" I ask, hoping this will be an icebreaker. He can't be much older than sixteen, surely, with his nerdy t-shirts and puffer jacket, fuzzy cheeks and acne.

But he replies with, "Year thirteen." He pauses, before asking, "How about you?"

He's in year thirteen, meaning he's seventeen, eighteen at a push, almost the same age as me.

I wasn't expecting that.

"I'm doing a foundation year at college," I tell him. "I finished year thirteen back in May, so I'm in the year above you, technically."

"A foundation year?" This seems to pique his interest, awkwardness slowly evaporating, words flowing more freely. "What in?"

"Art." It's a little more complicated than that, but I'm sure he doesn't really care – he's just being polite. It's the standard question, the thing people always ask. The education conversation is one I'm well versed in, so much so that I don't wait for him to ask the next question. "Hoping to study it at uni next year."

Again, it's way more complicated than that. I have the grades to go to any art uni across the country, the foundation year to cement my place, but my ties to Hull could well mean I can't leave. They don't do art degrees here, don't do illustration or design or painting, and the daily train journey would cost a bomb even with a railcard. The other kids on my course have already started applying, but I'm stuck at step one, unsure whether I'll ever leave Mum.

"I want to study English," Remy pipes up, voice more excited now, more engaged.

Of course he does. English is the kind of thing posh kids study, flicking through all those fancy novels and clothbound classics, writing essays on pretentious topics, lacking any awareness for the *real* issues of the world.

"I'm applying to Oxford."

Right. So he's smart, too. I don't know anyone clever enough to apply to *Oxford*, one of the most prestigious universities in the country, in the whole *world*. Most of the people I knew last year went to smaller unis, ones which offer art courses, courses in digital media and graphics and drama. The cost of living alone is high in fancy cities, without factoring in equipment, food, boring stuff like plates and cheese graters and mattress protectors.

I've definitely made a huge mistake agreeing to see this guy. It's not as though we have any chance of becoming friends, even in passing.

What did I think we could have in common?

For all he seems nice, he lives in a completely different world to me. It's a world where applying to top universities doesn't feel like a big deal, a world in which he's uncomfortable sitting down on restaurant chairs because they're a bit grimy and he doesn't want to dirty his jeans.

I'm biting my tongue, but I already want to leave. I just have to get through the peanut butter sundae, swallow some of the ice cream beneath it, and I'll be fine. I can go home and get on with my coursework, and pretend this never even happened.

The sundaes arrive just minutes later, in tall glasses topped with chopped nuts and swirly straws, long spoons delving right to the bottom. There's peanut butter everywhere, dripping into the vanilla ice cream and mixing with the chocolate sauce they've hidden at the crux of the glass.

Remy is sceptical as he takes his first mouthful, swallowing hard. He tries for a smile, but it's pretty obvious the sundae isn't up to his standards.

"Mmm," he says, licking his lips. I cringe at how awkward he is, how desperately he's trying to act as though he likes it. "I sure do love peanut butter."

Get. Me. Out. Of. Here.

I lift a spoonful of peanut butter to my lips, but it's like eating sandpaper.

"So…" I try to think of something else to say, *anything* to say. There must be something else to talk about, something to help fix how awkward this feels, how painfully difficult it is to make conversation. "Where do you live?"

Remy puts down his spoon. "I live in Vibbington. It's a market town about half an hour away – do you know it?"

"I have an aunt from Vibbington. But she doesn't talk to us anymore."

"How come?" Remy has abandoned his sundae altogether now, and moves it into the middle of the table. I don't like it any more that he does, but I'd never just waste five pounds of my hard-earned cash like that, not on something that's still *reasonably* edible.

I ignore it, however, and focus on trying to answer his question. "She disapproved of the man my mum was dating, and said she'd disown us if it continued."

Remy crinkles his forehead, adding, "Your dad?"

"No," I say, though my voice is a little harder now, patience wearing thin. "Just some guy she was with."

Whenever I talk about my mum's previous boyfriends, people always try to guess which was my dad, or assume "the guy she was dating" *has* to mean my biological father. It's ludicrous to think she could've been with more than one guy, apparently.

When they know the truth, I've heard the s-word more than once.

"Oh." Remy gives me that look then, the one people always do when they find out my parents aren't together. It's one of sympathy, but also of thinking I'm broken, assuming I'm devastated and in need of their pity. It's not true. I don't need anyone's pity, least of all his. "Are your parents divorced?"

"No." I watch him struggle to understand, before adding, "He was just some guy she was seeing. They never married or anything, didn't even take a photo together. I don't know his name, just vaguely what he looked like – I'm mixed, if you couldn't tell. Mum doesn't know much else, either. That, or she can't remember. Or doesn't want to." I tug on one of my curls, biting back a grimace.

Remy writhes in his seat, unsure whether I'm joking or

not.

Poor, poor guy. He's clearly never heard a life story like mine before.

"I… oh."

Is there anything else you can say to that?

I get it, of course. People like Remy – people who are smart, who hope to go to prestigious universities, who have nice little jobs at nice little local stores – will never understand how the other half lives. He probably has a perfect little family, loving parents and younger siblings who adore him, a warm house and a place in a private school.

He shouldn't be sat here with me, in Paula's Puddings, clinging onto an acquaintanceship doomed to crash and burn.

"Anyway." I push the mostly-eaten sundae away from me, so that it clinks against his. There are just a few nuts and the dregs of the chocolate sauce left in the bottom, but I'm not desperate enough to try and finish. I pull away from the table and go to stand, trying to find the words to tell him that this has been nice, that I'm super busy and need to go home, get on with my day. "This has been lovely, but… I really do need to get going."

His face falls. "You do? We've barely been here half an hour."

"I… I have stuff to do."

Stuff, to me, involves heating some scampi in the oven and boiling some frozen peas, sticking bits of painted paper into my sketchbook to prove I've tried different techniques, before moving onto my final project for the half term.

Remy doesn't need to know that, though.

I go to leave, lifting a hand to wave goodbye, when he jumps from the table and shouts, "Stop!"

The people from the booths by the window turn round to stare as I pause, glancing behind me at his urgent expression.

He's bright red and his upper lip is trembling, and I frown at him as we stare at one another.

"Yes?"

"Don't go."

Don't... go?

Did I mishear him?

I don't want to stay for another minute, not if I can help it, and surely he feels the same? It's been nothing but awkward so far.

"Just wait, let me tell you something." He's breathless, gesturing for me to sit down again. I do, reluctantly, and he pushes the sundae glasses aside to face me properly. "I'm sorry I'm so awkward. I've probably fluffed this, haven't I?"

It feels cruel to agree, so I shake my head in sympathy, and he gives the smallest of smiles.

"I'm just really shy. I *do* want to get to know you, even if you do think I'm a snob, or a nerd, or just really weird..."

"Or all of those things." He clearly thinks I'm joking, because he lets out a little snort of laughter as he nods.

"Or all of those things." He takes a deep breath, hands knitted on the table in front of him. "The truth is... I've never done this before. I'm not very good at conversation, or meeting new people, or doing any of this stuff. But I really want to try, if you'll give me another chance."

I can't say no, not when he's looking at me like that, eyes wide and face full of hope. He must be really desperate for a friend, because even though today's been a flop, he still wants to make this work... still wants to make this work with *me*, of all people.

"Fine," I say, after a moment of silence. Remy's face lights up with a beam, but I'm not done yet. "On one condition."

"Anything," he agrees, thumping his fist down with surprising vigour. "Anything you want, I'm your man."

I raise an eyebrow, but his expression is serious.

"Okay…" I pause. "*I* choose where we're going next."

remy

Carmel seems to know where she's going, footsteps decisive as we hurry along the pavement. I follow behind, forever the lovesick puppy, eager to keep up. Her brown eyes are crinkled and her curls fly out behind her as we hurry, trainers pouncing and city milling about us in a blur of Saturday shoppers and chavs.

"Have you ever seen Hull properly, Remy?" she asks, over her shoulder. I have to speed up in order to match her pace, but she walks faster every time I do. "I call this place 'A Hull with a View'. It's sick."

I have no idea what she means by that. I've seen most of Hull before, know all the best spots. I used to come with my parents when I was younger, to walk along the Humber or explore the backstreets. Dad was an amateur photographer back in the day, and he found the rugged buildings, foreign supermarkets and cheap graffiti the perfect subject for his pieces, very Philip Larkin-esque. We've tried out every food place on Humber Street, seen every building in the old town, spent many an afternoon in Hull Minster.

He stopped taking photos when Toby died, but my memories of the city are still vivid, beauty spots ingrained in my memory.

I wonder, briefly, what kind of art Carmel does, what she was sketching on her way to the café. Maybe it's something she'd have in common with my dad. Maybe…

"I love it here," I tell her, though I'm out of breath. "It's one of those cities which always just feels *alive*."

I can tell she knows what I mean. She's an artist, someone who captures and finds beauty in even the ugliest of places, who can turn the dullest of corners into an aesthetic, a perfect frame. She's smiling, nodding her head, as she turns to me and holds up her hand to high-five mine.

We're out of the city centre in a heartbeat, hurrying down a street lined with bricks and litter-filled gutters, the buildings on either side blocking out most of the light. It smells fusty, damp, like old sewage or infected water, and something darts back inside a pipe as we pass it, a couple of tracksuit-adorned teens sidling past with cigarettes jammed between their lips. Carmel is insistent on leading the way still, but grabs my hand all of a sudden and tugs me down another alleyway, one which cuts a line of terrace houses in half.

"Come on!" she hisses. "We're taking the back route, because to get to the fire escape from the front of the building requires you to run past reception, and if they see me, I'm *dead*."

The alley is dark, almost pitch-black, the walls on either side painted with thick, peeling paint in a shade of midnight. Carmel still has hold of my hand as we hurry, but there's no time for tingly-sensations or to sit back and enjoy the feeling of her skin on mine. I'm focused only on following and not showing how slow I am, how weak and unfit and pathetically chubby, not when she's barely broken a sweat.

The building at the end is at least four or five storeys high, with windows set on the back wall streaming light into the dank space. There's just enough sunlight peeking through the gaps now, but Carmel doesn't stop to admire it. She drops my hand and starts pacing over to where the fire escape juts out of the building's edge, all black metal and slippery steps, climbing right up to the sky. It doesn't look safe, clinging temperamentally off the edge of the building by a few puny screws.

"You ready, Remy?" she asks, grinning. "It's pretty tall."

"I've seen taller!" I haven't seen taller.

I haven't seen taller at all.

Oh, bloody *hell.*

My biggest fear is heights. My knees go weak even gazing out of my bedroom window sometimes, imagining how awful it would be to plummet to the ground.

I had a panic attack on a zipwire on the year eight trip to a forest camp thing, and always sit facing the aisle on aeroplanes.

But Carmel doesn't need to know that.

"You sure?"

"Absolutely. I'm ready!" I exclaim, painting on my brightest smile.

Carmel is slow at first, conscious of her feet slipping on the wet metal as we start to progress up the fire escape. I'm close behind, just in case she falls, but she seems to have so much more control than me, trainers gripping the footholds as she climbs. I clutch the railing so hard that my knuckles go white, and try my very hardest to follow her advice.

Don't. Look. Down.

The building is taller than I thought it was, reaching right up into the clouds, at least a million, billion metres above the city's skyline.

My breathing is all heavy and I daren't look at my feet for fear of seeing through the slats. I focus on moving one foot first, then the other, the exact distance between each step. It's fine. I can do this. I've done things like this before, once went up the Shard in London, albeit using the lift. It's fine. I can do this. I can. One, two, one, two, one, two…

One

two

one

t

w

o –

My gaze slips, and suddenly I'm staring down at the pavement, which we seem to have left behind by a mile. The bins are just green blobs at the edge of the alleyway, first steps practically miniscule, the space below us just a tiny square of grey.

"I told you not to look down!" Carmel calls, from where she's progressed onto the next landing, and is staring down at me with an expression of exasperation. "Remy, look at me. You're absolutely fine. You just need to keep your eyes on me, and take each step one at a time."

I nod, swallowing.

I *can* do this. It's just a fire escape.

"I can do this," I repeat, this time out loud, and Carmel lets out a snort of laughter above me.

I lift one foot, placing it heavily onto the next step. I don't let go of Carmel's gaze. Her eyes are fixed on mine, dark brown and chocolatey, but I can't focus on that. *Think about the fire escape.* Phlegm rises in my throat as I plunge my foot into a puddle on the next step, where the dented metal has been gathering water overnight. It seeps slowly through the toe of my trainer.

It's just a fire escape. It's just a fire escape, and if Carmel can do it, I can too.

Once I reach the landing, Carmel gives me another high five and beams, swivelling to face the next two flights of stairs.

"Just two more, then we've done it," she says. "I promise you're okay, Remy. Just follow me, and we'll go super slow."

It's embarrassing enough that she can clearly now tell I'm terrified of heights, but the next sets of steps look so long and black and slippery and terrifying, and the gaps between each seem even greater than they did before. *Don't look down, and you'll be okay…*

But my throat is closing in and I don't think I can do it, don't have the strength to force myself not to look at my feet.

"Look, I'll hold your hand, okay?" A pair of warm fingers slip over mine, and Carmel's face appears in my peripheral vision. She has one eyebrow raised and doesn't look as though she's filled with the most sympathy ever, but she clearly wants to help and I'm grateful for that. "Just keep your eyes on the next landing."

It seems so far away, so distant. But with every step, we get a little closer. Carmel is patient as we swivel atop it and embark on our final flight of steps, brows knitted and expression serious. I swallow again, but this time it doesn't seem so impossible, and I can already sense the fact that it's almost over, that I'm almost there, that I'm not dead yet –

The final step onto the concrete roof feels like the greatest achievement ever known to man. One small step for man, one giant fucking leap for Remy Evans.

"You did it!" Carmel says, though she still looks a little despairing, and gives me a final, weaker high five as we step away from the edge and further onto the roof. "Welcome to 'A Hull with a View, Remy."

Smiling, I turn to gaze at the skyline stretching out before me.

My *God* does it have a view.

The rooftop must be at least two or three storeys above the buildings around it, above the terrace houses and lines of shops, above the Paragon Interchange with its fancy 20th century latticework, above the few brick-lined streets with stalls and carriages lined against the prettiest buildings. The whole of Hull folds out before us in a mismatch of brown, grey and blackened buildings, graffiti-strewn and covered in litter, the city pulsing with life.

Shoppers and cars dash here and there, hurrying to and from the centre and disappearing out of the station into the crowds, pink lemonade in hand and Primark bags hanging from fingers. Teenage girls rush to cafés and designer shops to spend their pocket money on overpriced coffee and clothes, and pensioners purchase woollen jumpers and expensive gifts from the shops in St Stephen's, finishing their day with a walk by water, to spot fish and have a bite to eat.

I turn to glance at Carmel, who too is staring out at the view. Her curls are all mussed up by the wind, and her expression is soft as she observes her city, her home, folding out before her in all its chaos.

I thought I loved her at first glance, but now – sat here, gazing out over Hull together – I *know* that I love her. It feels insane that there was ever a moment in my life where I wasn't aware of that fact.

I love Carmel.

carmel

Coming up here has always been calming for me. When I first started modelling at the arts centre, money was so tight and Mum was so ill that I constantly felt like I was being chased, whether by worries or the disease or schoolwork or the fact I was running out of time… that one day I might go home to find Mum had passed and she never even got to spend her final days with me, that I lost out on the chance to ever say goodbye.

I found the back entrance when it was getting dark and the receptionist had gone for her coffee break. I darted down the side of the building and clambered up the fire escape, which was luckily bone dry, and landed at the very top before I even thought to look down.

The city stretched out before me in a mess of sunset-orange and warm brown, pockets of black drowning in the midst of it all. I had a set of watercolours in my bag, but the painting I produced was more than just me capturing what I could see before me. It became an expression of how I was feeling, thinking, the way I viewed the city around me whilst my mum lay dying in our damp house on the other side of town. It was messy and complex and real, so full of colour and emotion and thick, vibrant strokes. I have it stuck on my bedroom wall still, right above my bed.

The rooftop became a place I'd go whenever I felt down,

whenever I needed grounding, whenever I fell out of love with life and the city which has become so much more than just a home to me. It's a reminder, now, of better things to come and of leaving things behind, things which might be painful or damaging, things I just want to forget.

It's easy to pretend you're any one of the people down there, hurrying about, living an ordinary life, a life which is beautiful in its mundanity. It's easy to get lost in the way the light catches the river by Princes Quay, the water of which is eight metres deep and surrounded by high concrete walls, the water of which no one has explored for years and holds the city's darkest secrets. It's easy to close your eyes and feel the breeze on your face and know you could be anywhere, absolutely *anywhere*, just for one moment.

I take my sketchbook out now, even though Remy is watching and I can feel his eyes boring into the back of my skull. I pick a page I've already covered in sky blue paint, and take out a 4B pencil and cotton bud. Starting to draw, I block in buildings and shapes and movement, scribbling figures at the bottom of the page, the Paragon Interchange sat next to St Stephen's in all its glory.

I draw a few clouds, smudging them together with the cotton bud, creating a sky filled with depth and honesty and the reality of living in a city like Hull, a city where the only fumes come from cars and frying kebabs, a city with more dark spots than a petri dish. I scribble logos and business names, adding in the many takeaway places and high street clothing brands, a book shop and the hobby shop, tacky as ever. Remy's breathing heavily as he watches me draw, but there's no time to feel self-conscious. The water is black, almost completely so, filled with eels and shopping trollies and a single rotting body, the corpse of someone I imagine to have topped himself in the dead of night, never to be seen again.

I snap my sketchbook shut, encasing the drawing in its depths. Remy lets out a sigh as I push it back into my bag.

"I can see why you're studying art," he says. "You're… incredible."

"It's easy," I say, though it's not really. My skills have taken years of practise, of scribbling and shading and working hard, and although now it seems easy, it doesn't just come naturally. It takes desire, passion and thought and love and attention. It takes your whole mind, flows through your entire body.

"My friend Nima does art at A-level," he continues. "She has to put in so many hours, but she loves it. You should meet her. She's coming to see me afterwards to get the train home, with my mate Matt."

I smile, but inside I'm cringing. I don't particularly desire to meet his nerdy little friends, even though Remy seems all right for a rich year thirteen dweeb. He's wimpy, a little ridiculous, but seems… nice. Kind, good, like doing the right thing is just in his nature.

"What are your friends like?" he asks, shuffling a little closer. I'm right by the edge, where a thin metal railing separates me from the sky, but he's further in, away from danger. "I bet they're all arty types, like you."

"I don't have any friends."

We're silent for a moment too long. I only said that to make him uncomfortable, but it's true. I have Ravi, and I have Boy 1 and Boy 2, but that's as far as my social life extends.

My mum is my best friend. She's the only person I really care about.

"You don't have any friends?" Remy's mouth is open wide in horror. "You must have *some*."

"No."

"Not even one?"

"No."

"But… why?"

I shrug. It's not that hard to believe. I've never needed other people to be okay, never needed to socialise in order to be happy. I'm at my very best when I'm on my own, modelling or drawing or just existing, by myself, doing my own thing. "I like being on my own."

He frowns, shaking his head. "Don't you get lonely?"

Loneliness isn't something I think about. Even as a kid, I thrived off of being on my own, skipping out on partnering up in class or in PE lessons, playing throw and catch with the wall and figuring out maths problems in my own time. Mum worked a lot, so I got used to learning to play my own games or take a book to Mrs Dichre's to read, or sit in the corner of kids' club with my sketchbook and a pen, scribbling away.

I sigh. "You can be my first real friend, if you like?"

I'm only joking, obviously, but Remy's face lights up and he nods vigorously, grinning at me.

"That's fine by me, Carmel. Here's to being your first real friend."

We both raise imaginary wine glasses to toast, and I make the chinking noise as they hit. I take the first sip, and Remy makes accurate slurping sounds as I down the whole thing in one gulp. A lorry backs out of the narrow street below us, and the beeping interrupts our feast.

"That was delicious," Remy says, grinning once again. "I almost feel like a proper adult now."

"Do you drink?" I don't expect him to say yes, so I'm

surprised when he nods, cheeks flushing sheepishly.

"Nima gets hold of stuff for us sometimes, and Matt's older brother always bought us big crates of cider when we had D&D meets last year, before he went off to uni. He worked at a pub, then dropped out midway through first term to do an accounting apprenticeship back home."

"Wow." I nod, impressed. "I had you down for a good boy, Remy. Seems like I was wrong."

"Oh, I'm still good," he says. "I've only ever had one detention in my life, and I never swear in front of my parents... and I've never had a girlfriend before."

None of those things surprise me, but he's gazing expectantly at me for a response. Remy doesn't seem like the type to skip out on homework – not with hopes of attending Oxford, anyway – and the upper class probably aren't as accustomed to cursing as we are. I'm not surprised he hasn't had a girlfriend, either, as awful as that sounds. He's awkward, shy, the kind of boy who probably struggles talking to girls he likes.

"I don't drink much," I say, which is definitely an overstatement, "and I used to get heaps of detentions for not doing my homework in secondary school. I used to swear like a trooper in front of my mum, and... I've never had a boyfriend before, either."

Or a crush, or even anyone I've even found vaguely cute, but Remy doesn't need to know that. It sounds so much starker when I say it out loud. Not being attracted to people comes with the territory of having no friends. It's not something I've ever cared much about, and doesn't take up much of my headspace. I don't even know what it would feel like to... experience that. Everybody looks the same to me.

He blushes even deeper pink when I say the word

"boyfriend" – as though I've just broken some sacred code – and cocks his head to one side, trying to pinpoint the rest of my sentence.

"You *used* to swear in front of your mum?" he observes, scrunching up his nose. "Why don't you now?"

Shit. Wrong tense.

When talking about my mum to teachers or acquaintances, I'm always careful to use the present tense, acting as though she still works as a cleaner, still makes my meals, has a hectic social life, is still my best friend in the whole world.

Only the latter is true.

"She's… ill. I don't really have cause to swear in front of her at the moment."

Saying she's ill means nothing. It doesn't mean terminal, or deadly, or that she's going to die and leave me all alone. It just means she's ill, perhaps with a curable disease or a bad bout of flu, or a virus, a cancer that is being treated and could, one day have a cure.

"I get that," Remy says. "My mum's ill too, and I feel like I always have to be on tenterhooks around her, just in case I say the wrong thing."

My ears prick up upon hearing that.

Remy's mum is ill, too? That surprises me. He comes across as though his life is perfect, as though he lives in a little house with working central heating and loving parents and siblings, hence his good education and awkward disposition.

"What's wrong with her?" I ask, though it comes out more rudely than I meant it to.

"How about we swap?" he suggests. "I tell you, and you tell me about your family in return."

That seems fair. I wouldn't usually just tell people about

my mum, not unless absolutely necessary, and have them feeling all sorry for me. It feels too much like asking for sympathy.

But Remy and I are on even playing fields now.

"Cancer," I say. Then the dreaded sentence, the phrase I try so hard to avoid. "Terminal cancer. She won't get better."

His face breaks into the classic sympathetic expression then, all big eyes and drooping mouth and, "Oh, Carmel, I'm so sorry –"

"And yours?"

He pauses, wincing. "My... my younger brother died when he was a few days old, in his cot. He just stopped breathing. There were two of them, twins, and his sister lived, and Mum – I don't know, the doctors say it's PTSD, and she's grieving badly, not coping well. It was a good six months ago, but she still won't let Angelique out of her sight, and... yeah. It sucks."

I'm silent for a moment, breath held. I'm not used to being the one giving sympathy. I'm usually the one *receiving* it, however awkward it may be.

"That's... awful," is what I eventually say.

Remy nods, muttering, "Yeah."

"What was his name?" It seems like the right thing to say, to put a name to the little baby who died in his cot, to the one Remy is clearly used to dubbing "my younger brother".

"Toby," Remy whispers, after a moment. "His name was Toby."

I've blocked out most of my memories of Toby, from those awful few days. Seventy-two hours of waiting, of breaths held and hands clutched tight, of making sure nothing happened to Angelique, that she was safe at home with my grandparents.

It's not as simple as saying he *died*. It's true that he stopped breathing in his cot… but that was just the beginning.

I remember the day Mum brought Angelique and Toby home for the first time, in a double carrier they'd spent hundreds of pounds on. I was sat at the kitchen table doing English homework for Mr O'Flannel, engrossed in the world of *Tess of the D'Urbervilles*, highlighters splayed out around me. The door opened and my dad's worn face appeared around the edge, eyes shadowed and forehead lined in the mere twenty-four hours since they first left for hospital.

"We're home, son," he said, face splitting into a smile as he pushed the door open further for Mum to drag the carrier through. "We're home."

The twins were almost identical at birth, just tiny, bald babies with starfish hands and big blue eyes. Angelique was always bigger, louder, the one who ate more, who cried more, who opened her eyes and stared at us as we peered into the carrier, entranced by the two newest members of our family.

Toby was different.

He didn't cry much, not really. Even at night, it was Angelique who woke us up at all hours, needing food, attention, always thirsty for more. She'd reach out and cling to our fingers, hand wrapped tight around them, while Toby just… existed. He took his food slowly, carefully, and slept through most of Angelique's fits. He was so small, so fragile, that as I held him to my chest and rocked him back and forth, back and forth, I was terrified of breaking him, of causing his tiny head damage.

Those first few days were full of visits from family, friends, Mum's university housemates, Dad's "mates" from down the pub. All I remember from that week is the love and warmth which surrounded us; the love and warmth the twins brought us, brought the whole town. Everyone wanted to stop by and see them, drop knitted cardigans and jumpsuits through the door, pass tiny socks through the letterbox, pass us cake and biscuits and extra nappies. We had a garden party for our street, though it ended up spilling over both our front and back yards and disappearing down the entire road, tables and camp chairs and sofas pulled out of front doors and littered in front of each house.

There's a picture in my room of Matt, Lily, Nima and I sat on the couch downstairs, cradling both babies. Matt has Angelique, Lily with her hand on his shoulder, and Nima and I have Toby between us. Angelique is smiling, almost, in that impossible way only new-born babies can achieve.

Toby's eyes are closed.

They were both at home that night, tucked in the corner of my parents' room, in their expensive double cot. We had double everything at that point. Matching bottles, matching outfits, a double pram, double blankets and matching coats and hats. We didn't have much money, but they spent a fortune making sure everything was equal, that neither twin ever went without.

Having them completely changed our family. It had always just been the three of us in our damp ex-council house, with our caravan holidays in Skegness and our sci-fi obsession, our movie nights and Friday takeaways. Now there were two more lives to consider, two extra beings amongst us.

It was a Friday night, when it happened. I remember that much. I'd just got in from school and was cooking chili con carne with my dad, using a packet mix from the cupboard. I added extra spices to browned mince – paprika, chilli powder, a little cayenne pepper – when a high-pitched scream echoed through the kitchen. We both jumped.

"She's probably seen a spider," Dad said, rolling his eyes and taking the wooden spoon from me. "Your turn to hoover the bugger, Remy!"

I hated hoovering spiders because I felt so guilty about it afterwards, but it was the only method Mum would accept. She was terrified of them, of their pincer-like legs and beady eyes, their hairs and claws and invisible fangs. I grabbed the thing from under the stairs, tugging its wires so that I wouldn't trip, and began to progress upwards, lugging the hoover step by step.

"Mum?" I called, reaching the landing. "Which room are you in?"

I plugged the hoover into the wall, stepping over the wires and grabbing hold of the tube. The room to my parents' room was ajar, so I pushed forwards and into it, dragging it behind me.

I froze.

Mum was knelt on the floor by the double cot, face

streaked with tears, head bowed. Angelique was laid safely on her side, gurgling and holding up her tiny hand to meet mine, but Toby was crushed between my mum's arms, eyes closed, body still.

"It's Toby." Mum gasped, barely able to get out her words. "He – he – he's stopped breathing."

***

The next few hours were a blur. I don't recall phoning the ambulance, but it's there in my logbook, the emergency 999 minutes after finding Mum and Toby in a huddle on the floor.

My grandparents rushed in from down the road to keep an eye on Angelique while the three of us travelled with Toby. It was a female paramedic, I remember, who took my baby brother to her breast and examined him, checking his legs and arms and tiny chest, before pushing him down onto the table with surprising force. They just needed to get him breathing, she insisted. That was all they could do.

They found a pulse half an hour after we arrived at the hospital. He was alive, they told us, but only just. He wasn't fighting, wasn't trying to keep his heart going, his body moving. They were doing all the work for him.

We weren't allowed to see him, not at first. Mum and Dad sat either side of a fish tank in the hospital waiting room, me across the room, buried in *Tess of the D'Urbervilles* again. I don't know how I managed to concentrate, not when my baby brother lay dying just a door away, struggling for his life. It makes me feel sick, thinking about it now.

We ate jelly and underdone toast from the canteen, with packets of Wotsits and crumbly cream crackers. There was a full meal on offer, apparently – roast beef and all the trimmings – but the smell of instant gravy and Yorkshire puddings turned our stomachs.

"You can have a free meal for the boy, if you'd like," the server offered, gesturing to me. "You look like a hungry young man."

It was just another way to say I was fat, so we shook our heads politely and backed out of the canteen with our crisps and jelly pots, back to the waiting room, to our chairs covered in blankets and duvets and bags, the remnants of a family on the edge.

It was a good few hours before they finally let us into his room. One at a time, they said, in case too many voices and movements overwhelmed him. They'd only just gotten him stabilised – he was breathing by himself, in his own time, lungs opening and closing instinctively.

Mum went first, followed by Dad. I was last. I waited by the fish tank, huddled up against my parents' belongings, as a series of coos and strangled sobs drifted from the open door. I waited, breath held, as my dad stood at the threshold and watched his wife cling to their new-born son's tiny hand, tears streaked down her face. I waited as they backed towards me, Mum gesturing for me to go next.

"Try and be as quiet as possible, Remy," she whispered. "He's very peaceful in there."

It was a white room, specifically painted for children, the blank walls covered in rainbows and bugs and farmyard animals, coloured bunting decorating the cables and wires. Toby lay inside a cot, surrounded by metal, tiny eyes closed and lips pursed.

"Hey, bro," I murmured, advancing towards him and reaching out to grab his tiny fist, heart pounding inside my own chest. "How you doing?"

But he swung his arm away from me and placed it straight across his stomach.

I stood there for a few seconds longer, waiting for him to do something, for him to hold out his hand or open his eyes or give me a sign, any sign. But he didn't. He was still, completely still, unresponsive as I said my last, "Goodbye, bro."

We sat in the waiting room for three days in total, visiting him every couple of hours, buying balloons and teddies from the gift shop, delivering cards from various relatives and friends. Matt, Lily and Nima visited on the second day, and Mike and Steph insisted on video calling me, both clamouring to be right in the centre of the camera. Angelique was even allowed to see him, my grandparents carrying her in so that she could gurgle at him and touch his tiny fists to hers, rewarded with the opening of his baby blue eyes and a gentle hiccup.

The third day arrived, and Quavers were bought from the canteen. Mum went one step further and purchased a pot of mac'n'cheese, eating it with a plastic fork, letting Dad and I each try one bite of the cheesy goodness.

Toby took his last breath at three pm, before the monitor started beep-beep-beeping and the nurses all came rushing, thundering down the corridor and filling his little room.

"What's going on?" Mum asked, waking up from her nap and glancing around groggily. "What's happening?"

They wouldn't let us into the room, not while it was so full of nurses and doctors, hurrying back and forth and fetching equipment and more wires. We were trapped in the waiting room, unable to do anything, completely helpless.

Eventually, a nurse emerged from the room with a sombre

expression, mouth turned downwards and eyes filled with something I couldn't quite pinpoint.

"I'm so sorry," was all she said. "I'm so, so sorry."

carmel

I'm silent as Remy speaks, unsure whether it's appropriate to butt in and give my two cents. His voice is an octave lower than usual, eyes downcast as he tells me all about his brother, the baby who died, who just one day stopped breathing, stopped trying to survive.

"It's funny, but I think I was prepared for it, in a way," he finishes, fingernail latched between his teeth as he speaks. "He died in his cot, really. Those days in the hospital, he was just… hanging on."

Hanging on. I wonder if that's how Mum feels, sometimes. As though she died the minute she was diagnosed with cancer, and is now simply just "hanging on". Hanging on like Toby, laid in the cot with all those wires and cables and electronic connections, there's no quality of life, no purpose, nothing to cling onto.

"Do you think Angelique misses him?"

Remy has to think about that for a moment. He's still chewing on his nail, eyes narrowed, as he formulates his response.

"I think she does, yeah. She just doesn't know it yet." He stops, eyes flitting over to the view, where they wander across the skyline absently. It's reflected in the blue of his eyes, those tall, anger shapes jutting across his pupils. "She never really seems content, so Mum struggles with that. She cries a lot, wakes up more than a regular baby, can refuse milk, refuse to be held or cuddled. Or sometimes she just lies there and stares at the empty space. They still have the double cot, the double pram, matching bottles, cups, outfits. Mum can't bear to part with them."

It's like my mum and her wig, in a way. She can't bear to be separated from the only thing that makes her feel normal, like there's nothing wrong, like she's completely, one hundred percent fine.

"I get what you mean." Remy glances back at me as I say that, frowning. "Obviously not in the same way, but... it's easier to cling onto things sometimes, rather than accept change."

We fall into silence again, but it's a comfortable silence, an amicable one. It's one of whirring traffic and beeping lights, of hearing the train pull into the station and another slowly chug out, of shoppers hurrying to and from St Stephen's beneath us. It's a silence filled with honesty, with the knowledge that both of us have shared more than we expected to, and that that knowledge has brought us closer, closer than I've ever really been to anyone.

We start down the fire escape ten minutes later, Remy first. He's being brave now, no doubt finding it easier to go down than up, and barely whimpers as he almost slips on the wet metal. I follow behind, close at his heels, as we near the bottom and arrive in the alleyway.

"You'll have to lead. I can't remember where to go."

And so I do, weaving through backstreets and little cut-throughs, careful not to step on rat droppings or dog poo, avoiding the chavs and making my way round a gaggle of homeless men asleep on a piece of old carpet, one cigarette shared between four. I'm Carmel, inhabitant of these streets, of this city, and I know where I'm heading, where I'll end up. I'm in control.

Remy doesn't say another word until we're back in the city centre, where the light is beginning to fade and the city is almost lapsed in golden rays, sunset beginning on the horizon.

"Will you wait for Nima and Matt with me?" he asks, voice hopeful.

I shrug.

We sit on one of the benches outside the station, a coffee each and a doughnut on the table before us. We split it in half, so that Remy gets more jam and I get more doughnut, then sit and wait as the city bustles around us with busy Saturday shoppers and men rushing home from work. The coffee is too hot and the doughnut is too cakey, but there's something nice about this feeling, something real, something raw. Something about sitting beside Remy and watching the world go by and feeling accompanied, content, like I don't need to be anywhere or do anything except exist.

Maybe I don't exist often enough.

Things are fine, calm, peaceful, until he says, "Can I see you again?"

My body freezes.

Remy wants to see me again. One afternoon together wasn't enough. Something about me, about this new friendship, has left him wanting more, and I have no idea what.

"When?" I ask cautiously. Then I voice my query out loud, before I even realise what I'm saying. "And… why?"

It seems barmy to me, still, that he'd want to see me again. I'm just an ordinary girl, with nothing in common with him, and he's… he's everything I'm not. He seems happy, friendly, comfortable in his own skin, smart and ambitious and *settled*. For all his grief, Remy's life isn't half as messed-up as mine is, not in the slightest.

"Because you're fun," he says simply. His eyes are latched on me, all blue and warm and soft, and I resist the urge to look away. "How about one night this week?"

I work each evening during the week, and only have a few hours to spare before each class. I don't want to tell Remy about my job though. Not yet. It's too personal, too intimate, to share at this point. Maybe one day – if this friendship goes on much longer, like he clearly intends it to – but not while I don't have to.

"I'm busy," I say, before realising it sounds too much like a weak excuse. "But I'm free next weekend, if that's okay?"

I watch carefully as Remy's eyes light up, and his head begins to nod.

"That's great!" he says. "I'll do all the planning, just you wait and see. I have the *best* idea."

"I can't afford anything too flash," I reply, frowning at him. "Whatever it is, it has to be done on a budget."

But Remy grins, holding out a hand to shake mine in a solemn promise. "I promise you, Carmel," he says. "You won't have to pay a thing."

remy

Matt and Nima approach us from across the street, dodging traffic and waving enthusiastically at the girl beside me. Carmel's cheeks are pink as she shakes hands with both of them.

"I'm Nima," says Nima, grinning and hopping from foot to foot. "How was Paula?"

It takes me a second to realise she's talking about Paula's Puddings, but Carmel gets there first anyway. She seems off-hand, talking in a way that sounds jerky, forced, but that's just the way she is. Nima and Matt are nodding back with relative enthusiasm. I can tell from Matt's face that he's relieved it went well, that I'm one step closer to Carmel than I was on Wednesday.

"That's great!" Nima replies, pulling her hand back. "We'll have to do something soon, Carmel – all of us. The others can't wait to meet you!"

I'm inwardly cringing, but Carmel doesn't react. She just smiles another plastic, awkward smile, says her goodbyes, and leaves us standing by Café Nero with our half-eaten doughnut and her empty coffee.

We're silent for a moment as she leaves, unsure of what to say next.

"Well," Nima starts, glancing at me. "I think we have a *lot* of catching up to do."

The train leaves in ten minutes, and there's not another for at least a half hour after. My friends grab drinks as we're leaving, and we make it onto a table in no time, the two of them sat opposite, me by myself on the double seat. My legs are aching after all those steps and legging it through the city, but I feel… good. Content, almost like – for the first time in my life – everything is going my way.

I've always been the one witnessing my friends' successes, congratulating them when boys ask them out, when girls give them their first hugs, send kisses, hint – just slyly – that they may want to be more than just friends. I've watched from the sidelines my entire life, doubting whether those things would ever actually happen, or whether I was destined to be alone.

Not now.

I've been on my first date, at last, and it feels good, feels right, like everything I've been waiting for has finally arrived.

"So." Nima places her hot chocolate on the table with a splash, as the train pulls out of Hull and starts to travel through its outskirts, a sight I'm slowly becoming accustomed to. Tacky high-rise blocks and colourful factories skim past us in a whirl of concrete and scaffolding, trees and bushes turned grey from fumes, grass deadened and leaves fading to orange from sickly yellow. The sky is grey, but what more should I expect? It doesn't detract from the beauty of the world. Nothing does. "You need to tell us *everything*."

Everything would take too long to unfold, at least to Matt and Nima. The colour of her eyes, the way she walks, hair bouncing, the curve of her hand as she holds a pencil, a spoon… I could gaze at her all day, at her heart-shaped face and almond eyes, at her brown skin with barely a spot out of place, at the few freckles along her nose, her jaw. Her lips, like perfect pillows against the smooth expanse of her cheeks and chin, and her long, delicate lashes, just lightly scattered with mascara…

If they actually cared, I'd spend the next half hour describing every inch of Carmel in excruciating detail. There's nothing I didn't notice.

But I don't say all that, obviously. It feels personal, private to Carmel and I, to our blossoming relationship.

"We both love peanut butter," is what I start with. Nima and Matt raise their eyebrows in simultaneous surprise, as I add, "We had peanut butter sundaes."

It wasn't even that bad, really. The peanut butter was scratchy against the roof of my mouth, ice cream spoilt by the slightly-off taste, but the chocolate sauce at the bottom was good, and I enjoyed some of the plain ice cream, the scoops which hadn't been affected by the drizzle.

"But you *hate* peanut butter," Matt says, after a moment's pause. "You always argue with Lily about it, because you think it tastes like fly faeces."

"That is… well, true." I flush, while my friends roll their eyes at each other and Nima takes an exaggerated sip of her hot chocolate. "But Carmel doesn't know that."

"Is there anything you *actually* had in common?" Nima asks. "Or did you just lie your way through the date to please her?"

"You make it sound a lot worse than it was." I didn't just do that, did I? No, of course I didn't. I was honest with her. I told her about Oxford, about my A-levels, about my friends and interests and general life.

I told her about Toby.

The train rushes through the countryside, the world around us turned moss green, everything saturated and yellowed as October moves on, travelling towards November at surprising speed. Each stop is a breather, as my friends turn away from me to watch the platform, to people-watch and protect our part of the carriage with glares and shaking heads.

"So did you ask to see her again?" Nima checks, eyes narrowed, as we move away from the station second-to-home. "Because I wasn't sure if I put my foot in it, saying we should do something sometime, all six – *seven* – of us."

"Of course I asked. I'm not a complete idiot."

"And what did she say?"

"She said yes."

Matt and Nima high five each other as I flush.

"And where are you taking her?"

I don't say anything for a moment, hesitating. I wait for realisation to dawn on their faces before nodding, faster and faster, identical smiles breaking out across both of their faces.

"Remy," Matt says, shaking his head. "You have *so* got this in the bag."

***

My parents are cooking enchiladas for tea. Angelique is already in bed, but Dad is in the kitchen sprinkling cheddar over the neatly wrapped bundles, and Mum is laying the table with knives and forks and a bottle of expensive red wine.

"Evening, love," she says, as I push through the door and dump my coat on the rack. The smell of Dad's cooking fills the whole room, warm spices and cheese and sour cream dip wafting in from the kitchen. "Would you like a glass?"

My parents aren't funny about me drinking, not since my eighteenth, but they rarely let me drink wine at tea, especially not on a random Saturday evening. I nod as she begins to pour, watching the red liquid lap the edges and drip onto the table. It's a proper branded bottle, not the just cheap kind we usually get from the supermarket.

"What's this in aid of?" I take my first sip. I'm not the biggest wine fan – it tastes pretentious to me, alcohol pretending to be better than it actually is – but even *I* can tell the difference. "Dad hasn't cooked like this in… ages."

My parents used to love cooking, before the twins. They loved food in general. It's probably why I was so chubby as a child, a trait which definitely transpired into my teenage years. We'd get takeaways each Friday, an Indian or Chinese or Bert's Fish and Chips down the road, and Dad would make Mexican food during the week, putting together tacos and burritos and salsa and chili con carne.

Mum hesitates, taking a sip of her own wine. I can hear Dad opening the oven, and the door from the kitchen opens as he pushes through with the steaming tray.

"Would you like to tell him, or should I?" she asks, eyeing him carefully. Dad shrugs, placing down the enchiladas in the centre of the table, so she continues as he heads back for the rest of the food. "You see… we had our first proper therapy session today, as a couple. It's called relationship counselling, I think. Something of the sort."

"Relationship counselling?" I pause, trying to take it in, to understand the term. "But… isn't that for couples getting a divorce?"

The kitchen door reopens, and Dad is stood there with a pot of sour cream and another of grated cheese. He takes his seat at the head of the table, opposite me, as Mum reaches for her enchilada and slips it onto her plate with a thump.

"Typically, yes," she says. "But… it can also be for couples drifting apart through grief, or for couples struggling through childbirth, especially when the mother has postpartum depression."

"Baby blues?"

"In other words, yeah." My parents share a smile then, and my stomach twists uncomfortably. I reach for an enchilada next, going for the one with extra cheese. I knew my parents were going through a lot, but I always just assumed it was because of Toby, not their relationship. They love each other, love each other unconditionally. They don't fight, don't even scrap, and to discover they're having problems makes me feel... funny. Like maybe I haven't been noticing as much as I should, too wrapped up in my own problems.

"You're not getting a divorce, are you?" I check. "Because I know it's been tough, but you have to think of Angelique, and me, and... you know. It's probably just a blip –"

"We're not getting a divorce, Remy." My dad raises an eyebrow at me, signalling for me to stop talking. "We're just getting help, that's all. It's nothing drastic."

"It's counselling," I repeat, still trying to process what that means, "for *couples*."

"Yes," Mum says. "In fact, it was Marion and Martin Walton who suggested it to me – they said it helped them for a while, so we thought it wouldn't do any harm to give it a try."

Mr and Mrs Walton are Lily's parents, some of Mum's oldest friends. Although I didn't meet Lily until year seven, Mum knew Marion through anti-natal classes way back, and they kept in touch throughout my childhood. To know they too have problems feels invasive, like I know too much about their relationship.

"And did it help?" I don't really want to ask that question. There's fear curdling in the pit of my stomach, and my defences are up as I wait for them to reply.

"Yes," Dad says, and there's a sparkle in his eye as he glances at Mum, who, for the first time in a long while, gives a big, genuine smile. "It did."

The meal passes quickly after that, filled with small talk and questions about the sessions, about my day, about where I've been and with who, which I artfully lie about, of course. And then I'm done, placing my knife and fork together on the plate and getting ready to leave, taking my last mouthful of enchilada, which, just as it did all those months ago, tastes absolutely bloody amazing.

"Night," I say, pushing back in my chair. "I have a lot of homework to be getting on with."

"Night, love," my mum says, leaning forwards for me to kiss her cheek. "See you in the morning."

I rush upstairs, the taste of chillies and grated cheese still on my tongue. Once I'm in my bedroom, I shut the door with a click and drop onto my bed. My heart is racing. My phone has been buzzing all evening but I've resisted the urge to check it, and so I switch it on now with my eyes firmly shut and open them, bit by bit, to check the barrage of notifications.

Carmel's text comes through first.

Thank you for today. Free Saturday and Sunday. Just let me know when.

It's simple, blunt, but it means she's actually eager to see me again, not just being polite. I send back a quick reply, equally eager to play it cool.

I skip through the messages in our group chat next. There are various snaps of Matt and Nima trying on hats around Hull, of me on the train, of Carmel's approaching figure on the busy street. I don't listen to the voice notes and click off with no desire to read more, moving onto the next notification.

It's Lily.

i hope you had a good time in hull with carmel. she's really lucky to have you. think i might move to the front in english – need to focus on my grades this year, can't be getting distracted x

I read the message several times over, then backwards, then slowly, word by word.

Think I might move to the front in English – need to focus on my grades this year, can't be getting distracted.

She wants to move to the front in English.

She wants to *move*.

We've sat next to each other in every English class since we were eleven years old, even when there's a seating plan. It's our thing, our common ground, the thing which cements our status as best friends. English is our joint passion, the thing we've both wanted so, so badly since the day we first met.

okay – no worries. good luck with oxford.

I press send, waiting for the two ticks to turn blue. They do in a heartbeat.

you too, remykins x

There's nothing else to say to that. I lie back against my pillow, closing my eyes, and drop my phone down beside me with a thump. She needs to work on her grades and everything, on her Oxford dream. I get that. I get that, because it's what I want too, a dream I've lost sight of since Carmel, the only thing I've wanted since…

I sit up straight, heart pounding.

Shit.

My Oxford application.

carmel

I draw Remy that night. His blue eyes and fluffy brown hair, head full of dreams, the hands of a baby reaching down to greet him. I draw him telling me all about his brother Toby as I scribble buildings and spires and fading weeping willows, our moment on the rooftop captured on the page forever. Because no matter how hard I try, I can't get him out of my mind. The way he made me feel, how natural and easy the friendship was feeling by the time we left.

And how odd that ultimately feels to me.

He seems nice. A little sensitive, perhaps slightly childish for a boy his age, but… nice.

It's not *that* that bothers me. I'm not one to shit on toxic masculinity; it's a real issue, something I wrote a whole essay on in my year eleven English class when studying *Macbeth*. I understand as much as the next person that there's nothing wrong with being vulnerable, with being shy or a little distant, awkward. It just makes you human.

But something about Remy disarms me. He's almost too nice, too good to be trusted. And because of that, I'm positive I can't – and shouldn't – trust him.

Despite all that, I can't stop thinking about him.

Thinking about how nervous he was to go up the fire escape, and how proud he seemed when he'd done it, no injuries obtained. How shocked he was by my artwork, the pieces snobs in my class would walk past without batting an eyelash, thinking it not "obscure" enough, lacking pretention. I think about his blue eyes gazing into mine as we spoke intently about his younger brother, uncovering that perhaps his life isn't as perfect as I thought.

I contemplate the conundrum of Remy Evans all the way home. I walk – it's long, forty-five minutes or so, and requires Google Maps to navigate some of the city's streets – but it gives me time to process the day, to recharge my social battery before I go back home to Mum and work and all my problems.

The city is still buzzing with life as Saturday night creeps over the day, seeping into Hull's crevices. Lights illuminate the doors of nightclubs and bars, and boards announcing special offers spring up here and there, covered in tacky Hawaiian leis and plastic grapes. There are coach parties entering from all over the county, tugging in theatre goers and birthday boys and university students hoping for a "decent sesh".

I stop off at one of the many international supermarkets before I reach home. I pick one just a few streets away, conscious of lugging heavy bags all the way down our road and past Mrs Dichre's nosy viewpoint. The sign over the door announces Ye-Jun's Bargain Buys, and the bell tinkles as I enter.

I've always loved international supermarkets. They're so much richer than the average British chain, so much more vibrant in colour and flavour and variety. The smell of spice and soy hits my nose immediately.

"*Annyeong haseyo!*" The shopkeeper greets me in cheerful Korean, and I lift a hand in response.

I go to the fruit and veg aisle first. I love wandering past the dimly-lit shelves and crates and spying all the exotic fruits and misshaped carrots, the pak choi and fist-sized oranges, taking photos on my phone to later convert into artwork, make into prints and gouache illustrations. I pick a handful of earth-covered beetroots and two parsnips and throw them into my basket, before heading down the cereal aisle towards the snacks.

International crisps are so much better than the British equivalent; that's just a fact. I pick up some sort of Chinese-spiced potato puffs and some sour cream pea-shoot snacks I know Mum loves, then spend a good few minutes deliberating over drinks, over the different flavours of this Japanese canned pop. I grab two pot-noodle type things from the bottom shelf and tuck them beside my beetroot and packets of crisps.

I stand, lugging the now heavy basket up with me, but pause as I hear footsteps on the tiles.

They stop right behind me.

"Well, well," comes a voice, filled with mocking. "It's you again."

I turn.

And stood before me is the boy from the bus.

He looks much less frightening in the daylight, much less intimidating than when he grabbed hold of me and tried to kiss me on the dark street.

Finn, he said his name was.

Finn, with his messy fringe and angular face, his freckles and his too-white teeth.

I twist backwards, already starting to walk away. All the words I want to muster are stuck inside my head. Dried noodles, pasta shapes, and barbecue beans – that's all I need. He doesn't deserve another glance.

And yet the feet are still behind me, sloppy trainers shuffling along the floor as I turn onto the next aisle and head straight for the tins section, heart thudding in my chest.

"Wait up!" he calls. "I just wanted to apologise."

Apologise, my arse. Although I know nothing's going to happen, that we're in the middle of a supermarket with the owner nearby and another customer just metres away in one of the fridges, sifting through packets of prawns, something about seeing the boy again unnerves me. If it hadn't been for Remy, I never would've gotten away from him that night. I can't even allow myself to ponder what could have happened.

"Hey, bitch!"

I flinch. Does he realise how patronising that sounds, that women are so much less likely to respond to such a horrible term? I stop, eyes still fixed on the rows of beans before me, and Finn pauses behind me to catch his breath.

"I think I gave you the wrong impression the other night," he says, reaching out to put a hand on my shoulder. I shake it off as I go to pick the correct tin, but he perseveres, and the breath catches in my throat as he latches his hand around my wrist.

"*Czy ten mężczyzna ci przeszkadza?*"

I blink as the man sifting through refrigerated shellfish calls over to me in what I'm pretty sure I recognise as Polish, and Finn abruptly drops my arm. I have no idea what he's saying so I shrug my shoulders, cheeks flushing red. I want to thank him, but I just need to get out, *get out*. The boy won't try anything in public, and I don't need anyone to fight my battles for me, not this time.

"Please, just fuck off," I say, though my voice wavers and I sound like I'm going to cry, which I absolutely am *not*.

Finn raises an eyebrow and takes a step back with his

hands raised in surrender. "Hey, chill. It's just a bit of fun."

"A bit of fun", however, is not the phrase I'd use to describe it. The noodles and rice are just a little way off, so I try to make my way over to them as confidently as possible, though my hands are shaking and the basket feels unsteady in my sweaty palms.

Pull yourself together, Carmel! He's just a dumb teenage boy!

My heart is racing and my tongue feels thick in my mouth, and my fingers fumble as I try to pick up a bag of long-grain rice.

"You're being rude, aren't you?" Finn continues. I can hear the amusement in his voice, like acid against his cold immaturity. "It's a good job that fat guy came to your rescue the other night, because I don't think I really like you that much."

I stop, unsure of whether I heard him correctly.

"What did you just say?" I ask, spinning round. Finn's expression hasn't changed, but there's a nasty gleam in his eye. We stare at each other for a moment, unspeaking.

"I said, it's a good job that fat guy came your rescue the other night." He draws out each word, speaking in a deliberately slow voice, as though I'm thick. "Because I really don't fucking like you."

My heartrate's up again, though this time it isn't because I'm scared. My blood is boiling and I have to steady myself for fear of toppling right over as I tremble on the very balls of my feet.

"Never say that again." The tin of beans is still in my hand, and I'm holding them up by the ring. Slowly, as Finn rolls his eyes and crosses his arms across his chest, I begin to pull back the ring, hearing it tear. There's a plop as a single droplet of bean juice hits the floor, but the boy doesn't notice, doesn't care, as he continues to stare me down with that same look of amusement.

"Right," he says, as though stifling a laugh. "Are you going to set the chubster on me?"

"No," I reply, through gritted teeth. "Though I'm sure it'd be his pleasure."

And then I tip the can upwards and flick it forwards, watching – eyes wide, heart surging – as a torrent of barbecue beans comes raining down on his face, all gooey sauce and pellet-like beans and tiny flecks of paprika.

"You bitch!" he exclaims, leaping backwards and reaching up to scrape the beans away, though they've already dripped down his chin and into the neck of his designer shirt, staining the white fabric a horrible shade of tomato-orange. "Bitch!"

He's still dripping in barbecue beans as I turn on my feet, leaving my basket behind in the aisle and legging it out of the door.

**

The front door is open. I can see that from right at the end of the street, where a crack of light from the hallway lamp casts its glow onto the pavement before the house.

My fingers are sticky and I'm still clutching the tin between my fingers. I don't regret throwing the beans, though, not even a little bit.

Fat guy. Chubster. Bitch.

My hands tremble as I think about Finn and his vulgar insults, nasty comments. Who does he think he is? What right does he have to treat me with such disrespect, to be so utterly vile towards Remy, who's too nice, too naïve, to ever fight back?

Fat guy.

Chubster.

Bitch.

I swallow, launching the tin into a nearby bin. It lands with a clatter.

The front door has most certainly been left open, I can see that now. Mum was in no fit state to talk to anybody when I left her this morning, staring forwards with that blank expression, unable to even speak, to form words. Mrs Dichre doesn't call at the weekend, and neither does the home nurse.

"Mum?" I call, stepping over the threshold. I hesitate before going further, pushing my bag off and dropping it by the telephone table with a too-loud thud. My heart is in my mouth, shuddering with every step. "Mum?"

I move towards the living room door, tiptoeing on the hardwood, and poke my head around gingerly. There, sat on the coffee table with a steaming mug of tea in one hand and a copy of Mum's favourite gossip magazine in the other, is Ravi.

"Carmel!" he announces, and I sag in relief. Mum is sat opposite him with her legs stretched right out in front of her, two biscuits on her lap and wig properly brushed out and positioned on the centre of her head. "Make yourself a cuppa and join us!"

But seeing Mum so happy, so content, makes me shake my head.

"It's okay. I have homework to be getting on with," I explain. "But it was nice seeing you, Ravi."

I leave them to it, nursing their cups of tea and eating their biscuits, flicking through the magazine and talking ten to the dozen. I'm not new, not exciting… not a man. I never make her *that* happy, so I might as well leave them to it.

My body feels heavy as I make my way upstairs, the past day still rampant in my mind. Remy, Finn, the peanut butter sundae, all of my shopping still sat on the floor of Ye-Jun's Bargain Buys… I push through my bedroom door, and a pile of cut-outs and paint samples and sketches and tiny printed letters greet me, jumbled up in one incomprehensible mess on my bed.

I sag onto the floor, pulling my knees up to my chest and burying my head deep inside of them.

And then I cry.

I drop my personal statement at Mr O'Flannel's door on Monday morning. He's sat at his desk with a mug of coffee and a pile of marking before him, and grins as I knock, gesturing for me to enter.

"Remy!" he announces, swivelling round on his chair. "You never sent me your statement."

"I have it here now." When I hand him the USB, my hand is surprisingly steady.

I spent all day yesterday redrafting it, perfecting each line, guaranteeing there's nothing he'll want me to remove, that isn't quality, won't back my chances. The final draft is sophisticated, elegant, written by a student who deserves an Oxbridge place.

Mr O'Flannel plugs the USB into his computer, waiting for it to load. He clicks on the file and it opens in Microsoft Word, so he pulls his glasses from around his neck and pushes them onto the bridge of his nose to read.

We're completely silent for five minutes or so as his eyes skim my statement. It's impossible to read his expression, to gage what he thinks of this masterpiece, my life's work. The piece is 3870 characters long at present, an expression of myself, of Remy Evans at his finest. I discuss my job, my previous work experience with a local newspaper, my career goals, my love for Milton's *Paradise Lost.* Not a single detail is left unanalysed.

Finally, Mr O'Flannel stops reading. He hesitates, then removes his glasses once again and turns to look at me.

"Well," he says. "That was certainly *interesting*, Remy."

"Was it okay?"

Without sounding *too* full of myself, I was expecting more of a reaction than that. Part of me was hoping he'd would turn around with a huge grin and shake my hand, congratulating me on such an innovative personal statement, one which would almost certainly get me an interview with Oxford, if not bypass that step altogether. But his expression is still unreadable, face contorting into something which almost resembles a frown.

"It was… different," he says, eventually. "It sounded a lot like all of the samples you see online, the ones by pretentious private school pupils boasting about their all-expenses-paid gap years and work experience with the BBC. It sounds very… typical. It reads like the kind of thing you'd *assume* you have to write, in order to get into Oxford."

"Is that good?" I don't really understand what he's saying. If it sounds like the personal statements I've read online, the ones by people who were offered an interview on the spot, then surely that's a… positive thing?

I was aiming to sound impressive, well-read, the kind of upper-class boy they'd want to welcome into their institution.

And I achieved that, right?

"It depends," Mr O'Flannel continues, "on whether this is really *you*."

I'm the one frowning now. My English teacher watches me as he tip-taps the desk with his fingertips, glasses swinging from side to side on the chain around his neck.

"Of course it's me," I say, shuffling a little closer so that I can point at parts of the screen. "I talk about my work experience, my hobbies, my favourite authors. It's just a more sophisticated version of myself."

"That's the point," he continues. "It feels unauthentic, Remy. Like you're trying to be something you're not."

Unauthentic? Since when did authenticity get you anywhere? There's no way Oxford would want to offer a place to the real Remy Evans, the shy, overweight mess of a boy who can't talk properly in front of girls, who's so cripplingly insecure, who secretly thinks most classics are pretentious and overly-analysed, despite my love for English and desire to study it further.

"Oxford won't just offer places to the same clones, Remy," Mr O'Flannel continues. "It doesn't matter if you make yourself sound more posh, or like a typical English snob. They get enough applicants like that from the private schools."

I don't know what to say. My personal statement is still sat in front of us, waiting, in all its 3870 character glory.

"How do I change it, then?" I ask. "How do I make it more me?"

"I wouldn't try and change it, Remy," he says, pulling the USB out from his computer. "In fact, I'll keep this for now. I want you to rewrite the entire thing. But this time, write it from the heart."

***

Write it from the heart…

What does that even mean?

I ponder his request all afternoon as I sit in the library and dwell, a frown etched across my face.

"What makes you passionate about this subject?" one prompt asks, glaring up at me from my phone screen. "Why English? Why not something else?"

"Where would you like to take this subject?" queries another. "How will you use the skills from this degree to further your life and career prospects?"

The prompt questions all offer up the same answers, the ones I'd written into my first draft, the one I thought had been perfect. Shivering, I give up and click onto the next website, which has an even more extensive list of example statements and advice from top university admissions teams.

"Don't be too informal," one warns, while another reads, "Be careful to not sound too professional, to the point of coming across in a way that seems fake."

Which is it to be? There are so many rules, so many requirements, that my mind boggles just trying to interpret it.

I wish Lily was here to help me. She flew through the application process, scribbling draft after draft and eventually sending off her UCAS form a week before the Oxbridge deadline. I won't be surprised if she gets in straight away, for all her speed and hard work, her dedication to the course.

We didn't sit together in English this morning. She'd already moved by the time I got there, sat at the front next to a quiet girl named Soraya, who was showing her how to make origami hearts.

She barely even glanced at me as I walked by.

I click onto another website. This one is easier to follow. It gives you a rough structure, then underneath reads, "Don't get hung up on the dos and don'ts of writing a personal statement. Your university will want to see that you're unique, and so you want your statement to stand out. Before reading any more, go away and write your statement all in one go, then come back here for tips on how to edit it correctly, and make it desirable for universities. The base, however, needs to come directly from you, and needs to be as authentic as possible."

I glance down at the piece of paper before me, at the pen in my hand. *Go away and write your statement all in one go; it needs to come directly from you.*

I shut down the computer, staring at the blank sheet.

And then I start to write.

I've always loved literature. As an avid reader, discovering literature and its analysis once reaching secondary school opened up a new world of ideas and interpretations. I believe that studying literature and its impact on society throughout the centuries is extremely important in understanding humanity and the world. Literature bridges the gap between decades, cultures and religions, helping people to understand new concepts and shift mindsets.

I won't bore you with the details of my taste in books, or my so-called passion for poetry. My literature A-level has fuelled my passion for the subject, as I'm sure is the case for most students hoping to pursue the subject. I could tell you all about my love of Milton, about how influential the work of Shakespeare and the likes have been on my own life, but I'd be lying. I'm not the greatest fan of classic literature, of the canon as a whole and its involvement with female erasure, but I don't think that detracts from my love of the subject. Contemporary fiction is so important, especially when considering society today and the impact certain books can have on the minds of the impressionable. The kind of novels being released today are, in my opinion, far more important than classic literature in shaping the views of the next generation and getting ideas out there, promoting huge social change and bringing light to issues which - in the current climate - need to be put under the microscope far more than those of the past.

Despite this, my history A-level has certainly complimented my study of literature. Books and poetry can show so much about a time period, and teach an audience about how the world has changed. Reflecting on the mistakes of the past is important in learning and improving our own lives, but can also help us to appreciate the world we live in now - something I'm highly passionate about. I want to make a difference. Reading Malala Yousafzai's 'I Am Malala' can only get us so far, as I truly do believe in taking inspiration from those who stood up against their oppressors in times so much different to now, such as the suffragettes and Edelweiss Pirates. A well-rounded study of literature is what I aim for. I don't believe simply focusing on exploring the canon can do much good, in the same way only reading contemporary fiction can be limiting.

Work experience with my local newspaper has really given me a taste of what it can be like to work in an industry focused solely on spreading ideas and messages through the written word. It really highlighted the importance of articles and creative pieces in influencing people's ideas and spreading messages; I'm a keen writer, and this is something I wish to pursue at your institution. I think it would be incredibly interesting to focus on the audience and to always keep in mind the impact words can have, because the power of the written word isn't something which can be exaggerated. It truly is one of the greatest achievements of mankind.

Going forward, I'm desperate to learn more about literature and its place in society in order to take the correct steps towards being influential in my own way. Studying the written word in such a way isn't simply looking at language and form, but analysing society as a whole, and the importance of new ideas and concepts. I'd love to go into working for a charity of some kind, and have previously volunteered at soup kitchens and charity shops to give me a greater idea of what it can be like to be at the receiving end of such services. It's given me the empathy needed to understand the issues I've studied in my A-level classes when reading books such as 'Oliver Twist' or Hosseini's 'The Kite Runner', and has provided me with skills I can now transfer into the real world.

There's no reason you should offer me a place at your institution over any other applicant, as I'm sure they're all fine students and have an equal passion for the subject. But, should you choose to give me a chance, I can promise I won't let the skills I'll pick up from studying your course go to waste. I intend to use every privilege I have to make a difference in the world, in any way I can.

I want to make a change, and in order to do that, I need to BE the change.

carmel

Remy tells me to meet him at ten o'clock on Saturday night at the Paragon Interchange, no questions asked. It's only Wednesday, but I'm buzzing with excitement at the thought of seeing him again, of having another day of adventure. There's still a part of me which feels sceptical, aware of how much he knows about me, how overly nice he seems, so much so that it's almost unbelievable… yet something inside me *wants* to like him, *wants* to be his friend.

I've never felt that way before, not about anyone. There were a few girls in primary school I thought were cool, the kind of girls who made each other loomband bracelets and shared Frubes in the playground, but I was always too scared to speak to them, worried I'd be labelled a freak. When I did make acquaintances, my social battery was too low for those relationships to ever develop into anything further, fizzled out like sparklers on bonfire night. Boy 1 and Boy 2 are barely even that to me, yet Remy – awkward, gentle-giant Remy – has so far surpassed my expectations.

Mum never asked where I went on Saturday, and, if I'm honest, I don't think she even noticed I was gone. Ravi seems to have worked miracles on her. She's so much chirpier as we move through the week, and on Tuesday morning, I even awake to hear her rattling around the kitchen, putting some beans on the heat.

It's the first time she's stood up in weeks.

I try not to mind too much. I should be happy that she's getting better, that she isn't letting the cancer get her down in the same way it has done previously, yet there's a sharp hint of jealousy in my heart each time I think about Ravi's success with her. I can't even get her to eat, some days, yet here he is, working his shopkeeper magic and managing to completely shift her mood, her mindset, *everything*.

I'm on my way to the arts centre now. Mrs Dichre was coming round tonight, and I didn't feel like being around while they gossiped, so I spent a good three hours in Starbucks while I waited for my class. My sketchbook is in hand, pencil moving over the page at a rate of knots, trying to capture as much detail as I can.

The centre towers over me. I push through into reception, instantly at home. I hide my sketchbook away and pass my bag to the receptionist, but she doesn't even make eye contact today. She's eating a chickpea salad, face like soured milk, and waves me away with barely a smile. It isn't Dolores' day, so I won't be staying for the later class. All I need is my body, nothing else.

The class isn't yet full, and Johnno greets me from across the room. He waves me over, pulling the pencil from behind his ear and grinning as I jump up onto the desk.

"How's my star model today?" he asks, one eyebrow raised. "You never told me your answer about the professional modelling jobs I told you about, Carmel. Did you give them another thought?"

In all honesty, I haven't even *thought* about the jobs over the last week. I've been so preoccupied with Remy and my mum that the possibility of taking up a proper life model job was the least of my concerns.

"I don't know," I say, shrugging. "I don't know if I'll even go to university. I could just continue working here."

As awful as it is to think about, Mum's sudden recovery over the last few days has made it so much more unlikely that I'll ever leave Hull. As long as Mum is alive, I have a duty to stay and care for her; I can't go galivanting off to university in a whole other city, miles away from her. I'd much rather have my mum alive than get a degree, of course, but the thought of staying in Hull for the next ten, twenty years makes me feel… small. Trapped. Like I'll never escape the dingey streets or our damp house, the graffitied side streets and tacky city centre.

"Just… keep it in mind, Carmel," Johnno says, turning back to his computer. "Whenever you're ready, I can send off photos to the agencies as examples, write you a reference, pass your number onto bigger companies. If you do go to uni, what cities are you looking at?"

Secretly, I've browsed the fine art courses at both Newcastle and Leeds, though both universities are Russel Group and the requirements are way too high. I've also looked at Falmouth, which has incredible facilities and great opportunities, but just seems so *far*.

"I don't really know," I lie, shrugging. "I haven't given it much thought yet."

Johnno raises his other eyebrow, frowning. "You'll have to start applying soon, won't you? You're a talented girl, Carmel – you'd easily get a place somewhere, if you sent off your portfolio. Even if you get accepted and eventually decide to defer a year, it's better to apply now and decide whether you actually want to go later on."

He's right, of course.

But the thought is still terrifying.

The class is slowly filling up. It's a group of pensioners

from one of the local art groups, the kind who tour old country houses to paint statues and garden walls. They book sessions like this to fill the empty evenings, and they're never very good, painting too politely, skipping the details and drawing my body in an idealistic, slightly false way.

I slip behind the screen. It's common practise now, and I know exactly how to walk out, how to pose, how to act like I'm not at all self-conscious, like I don't care what they're thinking. I don't care, not really, but the first steps always take a different kind of blasé attitude. A body is just a body, nothing more, nothing less, but it's the connotations of bare skin that – at first – made me so uncomfortable, aware that what I was doing was unusual.

I make my way over to the table, careful not to make eye contact with any of the students. I climb up using the stool on one side, and stand, hand on my hip, as light streams in through the skylight and dots my skin with speckles of gold.

Slowly, everything else melts away, and it's just me, my body and the sky, at one.

I send off my personal statement on Thursday morning, under the watchful eye of the head of sixth form, Mr Roberts, Mr O'Flannel by his side. It's the last day before the deadline and my hands are shaking as I submit it, watching the icon load before the screen is submerged in red.

"There you go, Remy!" Mr Roberts beams and slaps me on the back with surprising vigour. "All done. Now, you wait!"

Some people hate that part. They hate the pressure, the not knowing, the weeks of pondering and stressing and wondering, hoping, about that interview place. I don't mind too much. This has been almost seven years in the making, and I'm not exactly looking forward to getting my result.

Rejection from girls is one thing, but rejection from the institution I've put my whole entire heart into trying to get a place at is another. It's a huge deal, something which has the power to change my life.

Oxford can take six years getting back to me, if it wants. I'll have no complaints.

"You'll get in," Matt says, nodding confidently. "Your personal statement was *great*."

Mr O'Flannel liked it, too, which was a bonus. He thought it was very me, very real, and that if Oxford rejected me based on that, at least I'd know I'd given it my all. Somehow, that's even more daunting. If they've received a tiny piece of my soul and still decide they don't want me, why should anyone give me a chance?

But my statement is gone, lost into the depths of the UCAS website, irretrievable, impossible to amend.

My fate is entirely in their hands.

It's one less thing to worry about, at least. But my impending date with Carmel on Saturday is already creeping up, filling too much of my mind, and I'm so nervous – so utterly, ridiculously scared, convinced I'll completely mess it up – that I've resorted to full-scale planning mode, filling mindmaps and graphs and huge A4 sheets with terrified jottings-down and notes.

We're sat in the common room, the aftermath of sending off my Oxford application still reeling, as I show my friends the plan. Lily isn't really listening – she's preoccupied with a book she's reading, though she hasn't actually turned the page for the last ten minutes – and the others are all leaning over my notes, tracing my rounded handwriting and frowning.

"It's a bit *much*," Mike says, the first one to speak. I can tell the others are trying to spare my feelings.

I sigh, snatching back the main mindmap. I wrote "Carmel and Remy's Second Date" in curly capitals in the centre of the page, underlined in pink. There are fish floating all around it, two little penguins sketched in the corner of the paper.

"For a start, they look like puffins," Steph adds, pointing to my poor birds. "But I agree with Mike, Remy. You're going to scare the poor girl off."

That's the last thing I want to do, of course. Paula's Puddings was relatively understated, but since that went so well, I want to blow her mind. The date idea is something we and Matt have theorised about ever since we first started crushing on girls, and it feels monumental to be finally putting it into place.

I've already messaged my cousin to set up the venue, to get the go-ahead. Saturday night, she said, would be perfect.

"But I've sorted everything, it's all booked," I say, pouting. "She'll love it, I know she will…"

"The place is fine," Mike cuts in, shaking his head. "But you don't need to make it so… romantic. I mean, rose petals and champagne? Just go casual, get a pizza and some coke, see what happens, watch a movie, take some blankets."

He has a point, but doing it like that just seems so… unexciting. I've been waiting my whole life for the chance to do something romantic, a huge gesture for a girl, and to switch rose petals for pizza and champagne for coke seems almost *blasphemous*.

"I'd have to agree," Matt pipes up, pulling a face. "I think most girls would prefer something a little more understated anyway." He turns to Lily then, and I can tell his cheeks turn pink as he jabs her arm and asks, "What do you think, Lily?"

"I don't know," she says, slamming the book shut and glaring at him. "Does it matter? I'm not Carmel."

Matt flushes even deeper red, turning to Nima. "What about you, Ni?"

"I like casual. I agree with the others, Remy… You're so cute, but tone it down a bit, yeah?"

They're probably right. Carmel doesn't seem like the kind of girl who cares about flashy gestures or expensive things, and maybe going straight in with the romance might come across wrong, like I'm trying too hard, like I don't actually care about her – just about the way things look and what I might get in return.

"You really think I should be more casual?" I check, and my friends roll their eyes, every one of them, in simultaneous exaggeration.

"Fine." I take my plan and scrunch it up into a ball, throwing it in a gentle arc to the nearby bin. It misses and bounces under a table, but my point is still clear. "Here's another piece of paper. You're planning it for me."

remy

Saturday rolls around far too fast. School drips away in an amalgamation of bad food, too much homework and essays on *Tess of the D'Urbervilles* and Shakespeare's *Othello*. My friends have been formulating a plan and gathering supplies all week, but they haven't given it to me until now, as I stand at my front door on Saturday morning and take the mindmap from Nima.

"It's complete," she says, grinning. "Can I come in and show you? Even Lily helped…"

Mum and Dad are at the zoo for the day with Angelique. I told them I'd be out when they got home, and probably wouldn't be back until tomorrow. I said I was staying at Matt's, of course. They don't need to know what my actual plans are, or they'd probably try and stop me.

Ever since they admitted to their relationship counselling thing, they've been much more present, attentive. It's like something's switched, and they've finally remembered they have three children to think about – not just the twins, but me, Remy, their son.

I thought it'd be nice to see my parents happy again, but they're returning to their old, over-protective ways, it's somehow now easier just to lie than face their questions.

I invite Nima up to my room, kicking aside old socks and pants in an attempt to get the place looking presentable.

There's a funny smell coming from somewhere and she wrinkles her nose as I reach for the Febreze, gesturing for her to sit down.

"Get it out, then," I instruct her, impatience taking over. I squash myself beside her on the bed so that I'm gazing over her shoulder as she pulls out the plan, unfolding it carefully and placing it over both of our laps.

It's very messy, and everyone looks as though they've added some contribution to my second date. There are five different coloured pens and a load of scribbles and doodles and little notes, arrows flying here and there in what I can only describe as mindmap hell.

"Remy's Second Date Extravaganza," she says, beaming. "You said you have the place from half-ten onwards, right? That's sort of how we've planned it, and there are snacks and supplies in the bag…"

I reach down for it, pulling out a packet of tortilla chips and some cheese and chive dip. There's another pot filled with salsa and a box of breadsticks, and – hidden beneath what looks like a proper projector, DVDs and all – a box of condoms.

"I won't be needing these," I assure her, face promptly flushing, but Nima waves it off with a smirk.

I recognise Lily's handwriting at points across the plan, which only proves what Nima was saying about her helping with it. She's added movie suggestions and my favourite chocolate, and all her notes are in teal – my favourite colour. She's even sketched a tiny turtle in green and brown fineliner, because she knows how much I love them.

"I don't get it," I say, stabbing it with my finger. "You know she's moved away from me in English? To sit with *Soraya*, of all people. They don't even like each other, you know what that group is like."

Nima does know, of course. Her ex-girlfriend was part of their clique, one of the cogs assuring its popularity. She understands better than most why it's so ludicrous that Lily should choose to make origami hearts with Soraya than sit with me at the back of the classroom, discussing movies and scribbling Kings of Leon lyrics over the spare pages of our notepads.

"You're so clueless, Remy," Nima says, rolling her eyes. "Go on, throw them back in the bag with the crisps."

I look down to see that I'm still holding the condoms.

"What do you mean?" I ask, swiftly changing the subject with a frown. "Why am I clueless? She's being so hot and cold with me over Carmel, it's no wonder I don't get it –"

"Why do you think she'd feel odd about you liking a girl, Remy?" Nima raises an eyebrow. "It's not rocket science. You're the only one who hasn't noticed."

"I don't know what you mean."

"Come on, Remy. Think."

But I don't want to think. Things have been weird between us since we held hands that night at Nima's, *54 Pigs and Counting* on the television. I don't want to examine the cracks in our friendship, because deep down, I don't want to admit to myself that there are any.

"She's liked you for years." Nima speaks slowly, spelling it out for me. "She has a massive crush on you, and you've picked up *zero* of the signs."

I blink back at Nima, mouth falling open.

She's liked you for years.

No, not Lily. Matt jokes about it, but she's my best friend, my platonic soulmate, my partner in literary crime. We used to write plays about broken marriages in year nine drama classes, took breakdance classes together as a dare in year eight, taught each other to sing on the playground when we found out a round of BTEC X-Factor judges were coming to Hull over the summer.

She has a massive crush on you.

You've picked up zero of the signs.

I love Lily more than is possible to put into words, but she's my *friend*.

There's no way she could actually like me.

"You're overreacting," I say, trying to laugh, but it gets stuck in my throat. "She doesn't like me. As a friend, yeah, but she doesn't have a *crush*."

"That's why this Carmel situation has been hurting her so much," Nima continues. "She's trying to distance herself from you so she doesn't get hurt."

That can't be right. Nima must be joking. Lily is strong, doesn't let anything affect her, least of all a *guy*. She rarely even gets crushes, and even if she does, she approaches them like she would a maths problem, pragmatic and calculated, not willing to waste her chance.

Real things hurt Lily… deep things. Not this, never this. She can't like me, not really. She just *can't*.

But Nima's expression is dead serious, mouth a straight line and eyebrows slightly raised.

She's not joking.

"I think you need to speak to her, Remy, try to smooth things over." She stands, pushing the mindmap back onto my lap and stepping over various pairs of boxers and odd socks to get to the door. "But if she decides this is too painful and just wants to distance herself from you, that's her choice to make."

No. Lily wouldn't do that, would she? Even if she does have a little crush, whyever that may be, it wouldn't ruin our friendship. We're too strong for that.

"I can't just… bring it up with her," I say, shaking my head at Nima. She's still stood in the doorway, about to leave, but there's still so much I want to ask her, want to check. "How am I supposed to do that? Nima?"

"Just talk to her. Tell her that although you like Carmel, your friendship with Lily is more important than her."

Your friendship with Lily is more important than her.

She's right, isn't she? My relationship with my best friend of seven years means so much more to me than a crush on a girl I barely know.

I don't understand why my heart is saying differently.

"You'll be okay," Nima says. She taps the doorframe twice as we stare at one another. "Do the right thing, Remy. Don't let that girl consume you."

***

I send Lily a text as soon as Nima is gone, alongside a photo of the Hamlet figurines she bought me for my birthday, arranged in funny positions acting out act two, scene one.

can we talk sometime?

She doesn't reply.

I can't stop thinking about her as I get dressed, pulling on a swanky dress shirt and my old school trousers, smoothing my hair until it looks dark and slick and professional, very Elvis-esque. I sit in front of the mirror as I do it, dabbing Sudocrem on my spots, trying to slick my eyebrows so that they stay flat.

I look okay, I think. Not Carmel-okay, but… Remy-okay.

I wonder why Lily likes me, when I look like this? I'm nothing like Charlie Boxton, the guy she was head over heels for in year nine, a football player and elite mathematician. I'm not much to look at. I'm goofy, the "funny" one, the one girls don't take too seriously. I'm the nice guy, her friend… I'm not crush material.

And if she *does* like me, I don't get why it's taken so long for others to like me, too.

I glance back at my reflection, teeth gritted. It's just… awful. Still, with my acne semi-disguised and my face de-fuzzed, I look like a blob. A rounded, wobbly blob of white flesh and red patches, of off-coloured moles and pale blue eyes, twitchy.

I pinch my stomach so hard through my shirt that it actually hurts, but the jolt of searing pain through my skin is exhilarating. Two nail-prints of blood appear on the underside of the white.

I'm hideous. Fat. Ugly. A complete mess of a human.

Even if Carmel is interested, by some miracle, there's no way she'll like me for longer than a week. She'll realise what's hidden beneath my nerdy t-shirts and floppy fringe, realise I'm a freak – a chubby, twelve-year-old freak, trapped in the body of an eighteen-year-old disaster.

I swallow, trying to focus on my reflection. It's not all bad… but it mostly is.

My phone buzzes beside me, and I grab it at once. My mind immediately goes to Carmel, but that's not what the name reads as I switch it on and swipe across the screen.

i'd love to talk, but i don't think that's a good idea. need to focus on my studies and stuff. think i'm going to distance myself a bit from you guys. i love you all, but it doesn't feel right and i can't be getting

**distracted. good luck with oxford. you'll have to tell me
how it goes. x**

The phone falls from my hands, landing with a clatter atop
the Sudocrem tub.

*I love you all, but it doesn't feel right and I can't be
getting distracted.*

Lily – my best friend – doesn't think it feels right. She
doesn't think *we* feel right.

Our friendship, all seven years of it, *doesn't feel right*.

I don't even notice the tears until my hands are wet and
my nose is running and my head is throbbing, and all I'm
really aware of is this awful, hollow, aching pain, which
wracks through my body as I cry.

carmel

Remy is late. Very late. He hasn't messaged me, either, and I'm just about to give up.

I've been looking forward to this day all week. Unable to focus on anything, excited for another adventure, craving the chance to just leave the house and talk to someone and do something *different*, something which isn't cooking or cleaning or homework or standing, naked, on a table in the middle of an art studio.

Remy can't even be bothered to turn up.

Maybe I was wrong about him after all? I thought he was *too* nicey-nicey, didn't have enough backbone, yet here he is, letting me down. I check my phone for the six hundredth time, but there's nothing. The next train is due to come into the station in five minutes, and if he isn't on it, I'll lose hope completely.

When I told Mum I was going out for the evening and wouldn't be back until tomorrow, she was ecstatic. I was finally meeting people, going out and having the kind of life she led at my age, as a teen rampaging the streets of eighties Hull…

I lied about where I was going, of course, said I was having a sleepover with some girls on my art foundation. I don't know how she believed that I'd suddenly met these girls after knowing them for three years and never giving them the time of day, but she was way too happy to properly question it. Maybe it doesn't matter who I'm with, anyway... It's enough that I'm being sociable, having a life, doing something different.

If I go home tonight and tell her he cancelled on me, she'll be devastated, probably more so than me.

"Hurry up, Remy," I mutter, checking my phone once again. I'm sat on an unoccupied bench in the middle of the platform, staring at the tracks, tip-tapping my foot. Two minutes, then the next train is here.

If he's on it, we're good.

If he's not, I'm *royally* screwed.

It pulls into the station eventually, and I hold my breath as the doors open. I don't have much hope. He should've been on the last train, and surely would've told me if he'd just missed it. He's probably decided not to come after all. He didn't think it necessary to tell me, thought I wasn't worth a message to apologise.

A businessman with a large suitcase and a second briefcase steps onto the platform, winking at me. I shudder, settling my shoulders further into myself. A couple, covered in the coolest tattoos I've ever seen – butterflies and leaves and brightly-coloured flowers, tumbling over their arms and legs – are next, but they don't even glance at me as I stare. A gaggle of teenage girls dressed in skimpy dress, heels and too-long hair extensions; a granny, clutching a bright-red handbag and struggling down the steps; a family of three, two parents and a screaming baby, all with huge bags and cases, like they've decided to relocate to Hull at half ten on a Saturday night.

I'm about to turn away, the doors empty. I pick up my lukewarm coffee cup and bag, preparing myself to leave as I stand and wipe myself down to get rid of the crumbs from my cookie. There's a sick feeling creeping over me, a feeling of disappointment and betrayal, and of disbelief, almost, that Remy – kind, good-hearted Remy – would stand me up.

"Carmel!"

I stop, heart pounding. There are footsteps on the tarmac behind me as I spin around.

It's Remy.

"Carmel!" he repeats, as relief floods through me. He's here. He's all dressed up in a proper white shirt, cuff-links and all, and smart black trousers, and he's clearly attempted to shave because there's a rash spread over his cheeks and chin, and a few spots of Sudocrem are visible where he hasn't properly rubbed it in.

"I'm sorry I'm late," he says, completely out of breath from chugging towards me. "I… I had a rough day, I kind of fell asleep and had to run to catch the train, I'm so sorry –"

"It's okay." And it is okay. I'm just happy he's here, and alive, and I don't have to go home and tell Mum my new friends are unreliable and completely let me down. "Shall we go?"

**

Remy seems to know where we're going, but it's a long trek and I'm not dressed for the occasion. I'm wearing the only "nice" clothes I own… a pair of slip-on pumps I bought from the supermarket for a family funeral, and a charity-shop flowery wrap dress. I haven't tied up my curls and they blow around my face as we walk, obscuring my view. The city is dark and we're heading in the direction of the Humber, the slick body of brown water which snakes through Hull and beyond.

"Can you guess where we're going yet?" Remy asks, grinning. "It's a landmark, that's your clue."

A landmark? Despite being the UK's City of Culture a couple of years ago, Hull isn't known for its *landmarks*. It's a grotty port city with a history of fish and grime and brutal accents. The closest thing we have to a beauty spot is the parkland in the centre, which is always littered with crisp packets and pigeon mess.

"I need more than that," I insist, but Remy just shakes his head.

We've been walking for a good fifteen minutes now, and the landscape has shifted. The shops are long gone, giving way to huge office blocks and industrial buildings, to car parks and cranes. The Humber is like a pulsing monster at Hull's heart, breathing foul air across its banks. I can sense we're close. The surrounding area is beginning to reek of fish and stale eggs, and there's a weird thumping noise coming from the end of the road.

"I don't get it," I say, frowning. "Are we just going to the riverside, or…"

I don't particularly think visiting the River Humber is really worth an evening of my time. It's known for being dirty, filled with mud and grime and silt, the water never even a little bit clear. It's the type of water you'd never go for a dip in, not even on a sunny day. The banks are the perfect place for dirty teens to dwell, covered in rocks and dead grass. Especially in the dark, when no light finds the expanse, it's pretty much just a swirling mass of black – terrifying to even think about.

"Not just the riverside," Remy says, tapping the side of his nose. "Come on, just down here…"

And suddenly I realise where we're going.

The aquarium.

The aquarium, built over the banks of the river staring out over the brown expanse of water. It towers over us like a huge pyramid turned on its side, the point jutting out over the Humber's edge like the jaws of a shark. It's so much more imposing in the dark than it is in daylight; so much more eery, so much more terrifying to stand under and take in, like it's about to tip right over and squash you whole.

"Isn't it closed?" I ask, but Remy just smiles back mysteriously.

The aquarium is, perhaps, Hull's only tourist attraction. It's a ridiculously impressive piece of architecture I've drawn at least four times in my life; a huge creation built right on the river's edge, seven storeys high and built with two underwater elevators, housing jellyfish and penguins and turtles and stingrays, soaring through roof-high tanks and tunnels made entirely of glass. It's maybe one of my very favourite places in the entire city… and Remy, for some reason, has brought me right here, at eleven o'clock at night, just like that.

"What the hell?" I say, though I lower my voice, conscious of how loud I sound. The car park is empty and Remy is leading me past the main entrance to one of the side doors.

"We have to be quiet, just in case anyone's still inside," he murmurs. He presses down on the handle and it opens inwards easily. "Everyone should be gone by now, but just in case…"

"Are we *breaking into* the aquarium?" I ask, beginning to panic now. "What the hell, Remy? We could get into serious trouble for this!"

But Remy shakes his head and gestures for me to follow him inside, a smile still tugging at his lips. "We're good, I promise."

He shuts the door behind us once we're inside, enclosing us in what looks like a staff corridor. There's a room opposite with the door still open, where a kettle, microwave and round table are sat amid yellowed walls and many safety posters, and pipes cover the ceiling.

"My cousin works here, in security. She always promised I could use the building whenever I wanted, as long as I'm responsible or whatever." He turns behind him to lock the door, then pockets the key. He's clutching a carrier bag of what looks like food and a metal contraption, and beckons to me as we start down the corridor. "They let the building out for group sleepovers, so we're not really breaking any rules… apart from not paying, but let's just overlook that."

I'm dreaming, I must be. There's no way I'm actually *here*, breaking into the city's huge aquarium at eleven o'clock at night with a boy I barely know.

"What the hell?" is all I can repeat.

Remy leads me through a door and up some stairs, both of us careful to tread lightly. It isn't so glamorous from this angle, but through the windows set in the double doors up ahead, I can make out a dark room filled with blue lights. Remy takes my hand, and it's cold and clammy in mine, and squeezes gently as he presses a palm against the door.

All the breath in my body escapes me at once, leaving me lost for words.

We've entered the aquarium.

remy

When I woke up from my nap, brought on by an exhausting crying fit after I received Lily's message, I was convinced I'd screwed everything with Carmel up. I glanced at the clock and my whole heart stopped beating.

I'd been asleep all afternoon, all evening, even – and I only had five minutes to make it to the train.

I ran all the way to the station, working up such a sweat that I'm pretty sure I now reek. I missed the train by at least three minutes. The next one would make me half an hour late, but I had faith in Carmel. She'd be there; she had to be. And if not, I'd take this whole day as a sign that maybe my friendship with Lily wasn't worth sacrificing.

I didn't think to message Carmel as the train sped along. I was so stressed it never crossed my mind.

She was leaving as I leapt off the train, the last one there. I didn't care about making a fool of myself, in that moment. I just gave my absolute all in shouting her name and jogging up to her, face probably bright red and steam erupting from both ears and nose.

It felt like a scene from a rom-com, where the main character chases after the love of his life, determined not to let her go.

It was romantic, no doubt.

The comedy was all me.

She looked incredible, of course, all flyaway curls and long legs and brown skin, doe eyes disappointed with my being late. I managed to speak, but I'm not sure how. It was like every coherent thought had evaporated from my mind, and all I knew was that she was stood in front of me and I'd almost ruined everything, and I had one more chance to make tonight go smoothly and make Carmel mine –

"Shall we go?" was what she asked.

And so we did.

I led her to the aquarium, set on the banks of the River Humber, deep in the heart of the city. My cousin Rachel works there as part of the security team. She's been promising Matt and I free reigns of the building ever since we were old enough to understand what that meant, but only once, for a really, really special occasion. We'd been planning to hold our first dates here since we were thirteen, plotting to completely sweep our crushes off their feet. Carlotta Stevens missed a trick, there.

The side door was open, as she'd instructed. I was to lock it, then follow the corridor up to the centre of the attraction.

We'd have the whole place to ourselves.

Now, Carmel is just seconds behind me as we climb the steps to the very top, her hand clutched tight in mine. I'm nervous, terrified that I'll screw it up and she'll end up hating the whole experience, but Carmel has this awe-struck expression on her face, like this was the last thing she was expecting from me.

I'm rubbish at romantic gestures, but this feels different. It's special, not simply buying roses from the supermarket or a Valentine's meal deal. I'm doing something unique, something we'll both remember for the rest of our lives.

The last time I saw Carmel, we were sat on the roof of a

building overlooking Hull, watching the city unfold beneath us. She told me all about her Mum's cancer, and I told her about Toby, my little brother, Toby. Things felt real, in that moment, like both of us had shared a part of themself in order to become one.

This, however, feels like the *true* start of something. I press my other palm flat against the door, and she sucks in a breath.

Pushing forwards, we step into the aquarium.

A huge glass wall rises above us, blue and dark and never-ending, soaring towards the ceiling. The room is silent, like the clear-water tanks have absorbed any sound. Before us, a turtle blinks. It's resting against a bed of silt-like sand, eyes unstaring.

"Wow," Carmel breathes, letting go of my hand and taking a step away from me. "Shit. Can I take photos?"

I nod, watching as she pulls out her phone and approaches the glass. She ducks under the barrier to get closer, and crouches to snap some shots of the turtle, resting with his face pressed up against the tank wall. The lighting in the room is blue and electric, the floor pitch-black and walls sloping gently away from us.

"This is crazy," she says, shaking her head and standing again. "I've only actually been inside a few times, because it's *so* bloody expensive. Are you sure your cousin said this was okay?"

The aquarium have to up their prices because they do so much conservation work, but I know Carmel isn't interested in hearing that. She doesn't even wait for a reply before she bounds off the take photos within the next tanks, eyes ablaze with excitement as fish and algae and anemones burst across her screen in all the colours of the ocean.

We don't travel through the aquarium in the traditional

way, instead taking every corridor as we find it, squeezing under barriers and tripping upstairs, eager to see everything, to spot each creature, everything I can remember browsing on the website. We find clownfish, with their funny markings and gormless expressions, and a seahorse, like the kind which decorate Angelique's raincoat back home. We spot a variety of tropical species in the big, open-top tank in an entirely turquoise room, and Carmel presses her lens right up against the glass to take the photographs, tongue stuck out with concentration. It's just another thing I've learnt about her, one more thing I love. She's so lost in the moment that we don't say a word as we head around the aquarium, unspeaking, in perfect harmony.

We enter the jellyfish room, where the ramp curves down into the "cool sea". Species erupt from boat-holes in the wall. Brightly coloured jellyfish, like luminous bursts of candyfloss, swirl through the circular windows and glow incessantly as we watch, mesmerised. All the while Carmel snaps away, a small smile tugging at her lips.

Next are the starfish, the huge anemones, the gross slugs trundling across branches. Spiders, with their spindly legs and stilted, bowed way of walking; insects, camouflaged inside their glass cages; frogs in all colours of the Amazon rainforest, hopping up and down, up and down, as we gaze through the window at their tiny lives.

There are more fish, of course, with their funny names and backstories told on plaques beside each tank, and mimics of skeletons, giant, deep-sea creatures hung from the ceiling. The underwater lift, perhaps the aquarium's star attraction, obviously isn't in use at this time, but it doesn't matter – the rest is good enough for us.

There's a vending machine outside the café, and Carmel

insists on buying a Twix, though I inform her we have snacks for later. She gets chocolate all round her mouth but I don't have the confidence to tell her to wipe it away… and besides, she looks cute like that, like a little kid who's been secretly tearing chunks out of the chocolate cake in the fridge. She gets me a packet of Skittles and I thank my lucky stars that I remembered to pack gum, because I don't want my breath to reek of sour candy when we get settled down later.

We end up by the penguins, our final attraction. They're still swimming, even at this late hour, zooming through the water and hopping onto the mock-icy sides to huddle by the window. The tank has been built so you can sit at the side and stare beneath the water, at the penguins gliding through it, like perfectly-designed submarines, completely streamlined against the salty pull.

"I love penguins," Carmel says, holding up her phone to record them. "I'd love to do some really expressionistic pieces of them moving through water and how it surrounds them, the bubbles and colours and rush, all of it."

We're sat side by side with our knees pulled up to our chests, fabric straining over my knees where my old school trousers are far too small. Carmel is only a breath away. Her curls tickle my cheek as we watch them in stunned silence.

"They say penguins mate for life," I say, voice barely above a whisper. "They do this thing that's like proposing, and then stick with the same partner forever."

"That's nice," Carmel says.

Then I lean over, and I kiss her.

carmel

When Remy kisses me, it's like every thought inside my head turns to panic. Panic that this shouldn't be happening, that I don't know how to react, that his lips are pressed against mine and I can't move, frozen, unable to push him off or lean out of it. Panic that it feels wrong and yet somehow unoffensive, like it doesn't make a difference whether he kisses me or not, because it just doesn't feel like… anything.

I've never kissed anyone before, unless you count a quick peck from Steve Short in year two, behind the adventure playground on our primary school field. I've never *wanted* to kiss anyone, not really. The thought doesn't repulse me, but it doesn't fill me with joy either.

Remy clings on for far too long, suctioned against me. As I sit there and let him kiss me, face pressed up against mine, I can't help but liken him to the starfish we saw in one of the earlier tanks. It was stuck to the side of the glass, grips facing us, hanging on for dear life in some kind of weird, watery limbo.

That's exactly what this feels like.

He finally pulls back, cheeks flushed pink, and turns back to the penguins. I open my mouth to say something but no words come out.

What are you supposed to say after that happens?

Thank you?

That was… nice?

A penguin soars past the glass, rocket-like body and neat flippers tucked against its belly, the blue lights from the corridor making patterns all around. They each have names, apparently, though I don't know how to tell them apart. The world fascinates me, but I've never been much of an animal lover. I can admire something through a glass tank as art, a wonderful creation, but nothing more.

Penguins mate for life, Remy told me. Is that what he was getting at? Trying to perform some penguin proposal ritual in order to seduce me?

It feels awkward to be touching knees now, to have our shoes resting against one another. I thought we were friends, but friends don't… kiss. Not like that, anyway.

Have I been misreading all the signs?

The Twix wrapper crinkles in my pocket. I reach down to squeeze it, just for something to do. It must've been a mistake on Remy's behalf, too; that's why he hasn't said anything. I don't know how guys' brains work, but maybe it was the heat of the moment, the mention of penguin true love and the dark, atmospheric lighting that compelled him to reach across and kiss me, pressing his lips against mine and holding, hard, the moment wilting around us.

I don't watch much TV, don't listen to much music. I don't have the same fascination with love as the other girls always did in school, never wanted sex the way guys joked about in year ten DT lessons, making crude gestures with the table clamp.

Maybe Remy does like me… and maybe I like him back. Maybe that was why the kiss didn't repulse me. Maybe that's just what kissing feels like.

I swallow, mouth now dry. I drop the wrapper into my

pocket and bring my hand out again. I lean forward and press my forehead against the glass, feeling cool air rush through my body. It's icy cold. With my eyes flush against the tank, I can see right into the watery world and beyond... like I'm a penguin, one of them.

I don't think I like Remy. I want to be around him, want to spend time with him, but doing anything else just makes me feel numb. Moments like this, moments where you can feel the cold biting at your skin, are aware of every movement the penguins in front of you make... those are the moments which strike deep inside of you, offering pleasure. Remy's kiss didn't do that to me. It was like pressing my lips against a lamppost, feeling the soft metal beneath me. It didn't make me feel, didn't tarnish my soul in any way.

Next to me, I feel Remy do the same. Reach forward and press his cheek against the glass, so I can sense that his head is turned in my direction, staring straight at me.

Slowly, I do the same. I turn my head so that we're both gazing at one another, his blue eyes staring straight at mine. They're even more electric now, as the aquarium's aquamarine lighting reflects off of him and causes shadows to dance across his acne-scarred face, the pores on his nose.

Remy isn't repulsive, not in any way. He's raw and real and honest-looking, the rash on his cheeks spelling out the fact that he shaved earlier, his bushy brows hiding the fact that he doesn't ever tweak them, that he isn't that kind of guy. He isn't repulsive, but he just isn't... beautiful.

Not to me, anyway.

I can see something different in Mum's eyes when she talks about Ravi, like she's filled with the greatest happiness, like he has the power to cure her of all ailments. He speaks to her soul in a way I can't imagine, feels for her in a way I'm yet to experience, that's for sure. There's a chemistry between them, something I thought was always exaggerated in books, a sensation too other-worldly to actually occur.

Now, gazing into Remy's eyes, I understand completely. There's a difference between liking and loving, a difference between the two feelings. He has this far-off, dreamy expression, like he's not really seeing me, like he's gazing at a piece of artwork, a song playing through his head.

I like him. I like him a lot. I'm not a people person, but Remy is honest, kind, funny – the kind of person who'd take you to an aquarium on a Saturday night, just because. He sees the world the way I do, finds beauty in all the little things, has found pockets of wonder in our city, a city which, from the outside, looks like one of the ugliest. He could be an artist for all he can see, for all he feels.

I like him, but I like him the same way I like Ravi, Mrs Dichre, my relatives, some of Mum's old school friends who'd take care of me when I was younger. I like him more than those people, in fact, because there's something special about Remy, something different, something which pulls me in closer.

I like him, but I'll never *love* him.

Not like that.

remy

Kissing Carmel is like taking a deep breath and leaping off the edge of a cliff, into the unknown. Gravity doesn't exist, and all I'm aware of is the feel of her lips against mine, warm and gentle and soft, like when you melt sugar and butter together in a pan and create a sticky mass of goodness, swirling around a wooden spoon. She truly does taste like caramel from the Twix she just ate, only sweeter, warmer, molten.

I can't pull away, stuck to her like glue, heart pounding beneath my chest. My eyes are closed yet I see her through my lids; the curve of her heart-shaped face and those almond eyes, her brown skin with barely a spot out of place, the freckles along her nose, her jaw. Mascara dusted eyelashes against her cheeks as I imagine she closes her eyes to kiss me back, those pillow-like lips edging against mine, promising more.

I've never kissed anyone, but I've read enough poetry to understand that when you find The One, the person you're destined to be with, the being your soul shares a home with, everything shifts. The universe sends light tumbling through clouds to scatter you with stardust, and your heart beats faster, faster, faster, like it's about to burst out of your chest.

Carmel is The One, and kissing her is everything I've ever dreamt of.

I pull back eventually, and turn straight towards the glass. My cheeks are burning and I feel a little dizzy, so I focus on the water before me, at the penguin soaring past me, little flippers stuck to its body. Penguins, I remember, mate for life. They find a partner and propose, then stick with that same little bird until death they do part.

That kiss felt very much like my penguin proposal.

Carmel doesn't say anything, and I'm too awkward to speak, unable to make the next move. I hear her fiddling with the Twix wrapper in her pocket, the crinkling foil making indentations on my eardrums against the silence of the aquarium's corridors. It's dark all around us, barely lit by the turquoise lighting, and the penguins look ready for bed, curling together on the icy side with their heads tucked down and flippers flush to their sides.

Every touch feels electric, every nudge of her knee against mine, of her slip-on pump against my own, slightly-too-small school shoes from year eleven, crushing my toes bit by bit. I wonder if she shifts her foots intentionally, each movement a sign.

I wonder if she wants me to kiss her again.

But then she surges forward, pressing her face against the glass. Her forehead touches the tank's outer wall and her eyes, huge and brown and fierce, gaze into the depths, taking in the swift glides of the penguin still swimming through the water, completely enraptured.

She's beautiful. Each dark curl catches the aqua lighting and glints as she stares, eyes wide, breath steaming up the glass just a little. She presses her hand against the wall and I watch as it leaves a mark, a mark as tiny as her hands themselves, and lets out a little sigh, just a gentle one, barely audible.

I lean forward to press my own face against the glass, but my cheek hits instead. I can't take my eyes off her. It's cold, like ice beneath my skin, but it's refreshing too… not that I feel it much. My whole body is hot, surging with desire and love and passion for the girl before me, longing to reach out and curl my arm around her, feeling her body fold into me.

Slowly, she twists her head so that her own cheek is resting against the tank, forehead now slick with condensation.

We just stare at one another, eyes fixed, gaze held steady. Dark brown against bright blue, unmoving, stuck in place.

I want to kiss her again.

I want to kiss her, to lean forward and press my lips against hers without thinking twice about it, no second thoughts or regrets, just me and her, together in what feels harmonious, like it's meant to be.

I can't read her mind, but something special is darting between us, something right. She's barely breathing, but there's something electric surging through the air, and I can hear my heart thumping in my eardrums like the steady tick-tock of a bomb, ready to go off at any moment.

I love you, I think, willing the words to travel through the air and hit Carmel, surround her with my love and protection and happiness, keeping her safe, always. *I love you so much.*

Because I do love her. I love her huge eyes, like a puppy's, gazing at mine through the aquarium's dark corridors, reflecting the light like spinning marbles. I love her heart-shaped face and brown skin, the way she works a pencil, the way she walks, like she's in a trance, only aware of everything around her, finding beauty in the city she loves, her hometown. I love the way she says what she thinks and can be sharp, almost hurtful, when I deserve it most. I love her honesty, the way her personality stands stark against her body, clear for everyone to see.

I love her.

I love her, and, in this moment, I think she might feel the same.

carmel

We stay with the penguins for a while longer, before I claim to be hungry and Remy stands to help me to my feet. He's planned out the rest of the evening to the nth degree, he claims. I'm going to *love* it.

He leads me through the aquarium's corridors, past tanks of fish and bugs and creatures, past signs we've already glimpsed over, the vending machines and open-tanks of tropical wonders. I'm pretty sure we take the long way round because he doesn't seem to know where we're going, passing the same collection of blobby anemones at least three times, clustered together against the glass.

"I'm not lost," he protests.

We eventually make it to our destination, and Remy grins at me sheepishly. I don't know why I wasn't expecting this; it's clearly the most beautiful spot in the whole of the aquarium, the most impressive architecturally, and my heart swells a little as he tugs a blanket from his carrier bag and drops it onto the floor.

"It might not be very comfy, but at least we have a good view."

We're inside a tunnel made entirely of glass, a tank of fish arching over our heads. Sharks and stingrays glide steadily through the blue, as the endless ocean stretches on and on above us, as far as the eye can see. Remy gestures for me to lay down with him. I drop to my knees, falling onto the blanket as his arm stretched around me. I lean into him, feeling his warm body beneath mine, as we watch the tank above us.

The sharks are just as beautiful as they are in nature documentaries, and I pull out my phone to snap some photos. They're sleek and grey and not *that* big, but they slide through the water effortlessly, like there's no weight against them. The stingrays are just as impressive, flaps warbling as they soar overhead, like planes in a deep blue sky.

"It's so peaceful," Remy says, voice an octave lower than usual. "I feel like I could lie here forever and watch them move, feel them all around me. It's like we're in the water, too, if you get me."

And I do get him. Lying beneath the glass tunnel, feeling it all around us, is truly like we're at one with the ocean, swimming through it like mermaids.

Remy starts to set up our movie night, pulling out the projector and reading the instructions once over with knitted brows, finger following the words. I pull out the snacks. There are dips, breadsticks, tortilla chips… and a box of condoms, which I hold up to him with furiously red cheeks, shaking my head back and forth.

"What the hell did you bring these for?"

Remy holds up a hand in protest and says, "My friends packed the bag, not me!"

I can see that he's embarrassed, but anger is surging through my veins, faster and faster. "And why would *they* pack these? You know nothing's going to happen, right?"

"It was probably their idea of a joke," he says, and I can tell he just wants to disappear into the ground at this moment in time, face burning. "Honestly, I'm so sorry, you can just bin them if you want."

I do – not that it makes me feel much better.

Remy sets up the projector so that it casts a picture onto the lower wall, just before the glass tunnel begins. It's not the biggest screen ever as the wall is only short, but it means we can rest against the other edge of the tunnel against the concrete floor, blanket wrapped around us, as the tank arches above the screen and right over our heads, into the abyss.

The film is *54 Pigs and Counting*, which I've never actually seen. Growing up, I was never a huge fan of cartoons. I always found them cringey, too kid-like for me, the graphics basic and stilted. The only animated movies I did enjoy were the princess-y ones, though. I loved the aesthetics, the moonlit night of the ball and the cottage in the woods, creatures scurrying off to mine gemstones, the forest lying in wait to snatch the princess up.

This movie isn't terrible, apart from the fact there are a lot of pigs and three yappy dogs. I'm more of a cat person.

We share the snacks between us, the cheese and chive dip in the centre of the blanket, the crisps on either side. I'm relieved he's bought original tortilla chips, the breadsticks filled with herbs and encrusted with salt. That's perhaps the best part of the evening, aquarium aside. We rarely buy food like this at home anymore, unless it's for Mum, as a treat. Eating it now feels like cause to celebrate.

Remy's close to me, snuggled up with his chin right by my shoulder. I can hear every mouthful, his jaw crunching down on the tortilla chips, dip moving round his jaws.

It makes me feel faintly sick.

We don't speak as the film rolls on, though I'm not really following it anyway. There are lots of animals, and a bad woman trying to find them all, and terrible backdrops; you can tell it's old. My eyes keep drifting up to the sharks and stingrays up above, following them as they drift over the glass ceiling, transfixed to their smooth, effortless bodies, their sneaky expressions, the way they move, each jolt of a fin or swift bash of a tail.

When the movie's over, Remy stands to switch off the projector. I take the opportunity to shift away from him in our blanket cocoon, moving closer to the tunnel's entrance and curling up on my side, the concrete floor hard beneath me. Remy climbs back in and hesitates, as though considering whether he should kiss me or not, eventually deciding against it. He plumps for a swift stroke of my back instead, and I feel his hand move down my spine like a slippery fish, making me jolt forward.

He settles into the blanket, facing away from me, so that the bases of our backs are just touching. I shuffle away as far as I can, pulling it further around me.

I'm not used to sleeping with someone, not even Mum on one of her bad nights. Being so close to someone, having them in my personal space as I think about sleep, makes my skin crawl and my hands shake beneath me.

I don't know why I'm so abnormal. I'm almost nineteen-years-old and can't even sleep next to a boy without twisting and writhing and wanting to get out, to move around, to disappear.

Most girls my age would take advantage of the situation. They'd cuddle into the guy, especially if they knew he was interested, and maybe "spoon", something people used to talk about all the time in secondary school as though it was the most romantic thing ever. They'd kiss, maybe even go further. Remy's friends were clearly expecting something more than this. That's why they packed the condoms.

But I'm not like most girls. I'm a freak, a freak who can't

stand physical contact or being in the same vicinity as a boy, who felt nothing from a kiss, who just felt numb, emotionless.

I've known this my entire life, known that I just... don't like people. But I'd also never had an opportunity like this before.

Remy is lovely, so kind and caring and friendly, the kind of guy any girl would be lucky to have. He may not be typically attractive, but he has warm blue eyes and a face you can trust, the kind of face you'd recognise anywhere as just being good, so unbelievably *good*.

If I was normal, I'd like him. I'd want to be with him, romantically. I'd have kissed him back, wouldn't be huddled up as far as possible away from him right now, the very thought of him touching me making my skin crawl.

Even if I'm not attracted to Remy, in particular... I should feel like that about *someone*.

It's not too dark in the tunnel, the blue from the tank still dancing across the floor and over Remy's sleeping body. I can hear him breathing in and out, in and out. He must be completely out of it. I wait another few minutes, lying still so as not to wake him, before pushing the blanket off me and standing, as quietly as possible.

The tunnels of the aquarium seem darker, eery, without Remy by my side. I pass the same attractions I've seen a hundred times this evening, barely giving them a second glance. There's a café which looks out over the Humber and beyond, which has a shelf for you to sit on and observe the footbridge and car park below, lit up by streetlights.

My bare feet make no sound as I enter, phone clutched in my hand. There's a coffee machine by the till. There doesn't appear to be any milk left, so I take it black, pouring dark liquid into its little cardboard holder.

I carry the coffee over to the window, where I pull my feet up above the ledge and gaze out onto the car park.

Then I pull out my phone.

My hands are quick and fast as I type. I pour my feelings into the search bar, Googling everything that comes to mind, every phrase which could, in some way, explain how I feel, put a name to whatever lives inside me. I don't want to kiss him. I don't want to be close to a boy. I can't see myself ever wanting those things, either. It's deeper than simply not having met the right person, when my brain judders just thinking about the possibility.

I don't want a relationship. I don't want to wait and see, daydreaming about the possibility in the meantime. I don't want to be *touched*. I don't want to be in love, to have all these things expected of me.

And then: I don't think I *can* love.

Asexual.

The word stares back at me, in bold, harsh lettering. It's too cold, too obvious, too honest. I've heard the word before in science lessons, when talking about organisms which don't need sex to reproduce, who can just pop out offspring like there's no tomorrow. Asexual. That's not what I am.

Asexual: a person who has little to no sexual feelings or desires, or who is not sexually attracted to anyone.

All the blood in my body runs cold.

I *can't* be asexual. I'm normal, just an ordinary girl, an ordinary girl with feelings which… aren't so ordinary. I'm not this, not this word, this anomaly, this obscurity of nature.

I can't be.

I just *can't* be.

I try to shift the words around in the search bar, looking for another explanation.

The one it throws back is even more terrifying.

Aromantic: a person who has little to no interest in or desire for romantic relationships.

No… These weird labels, these complicated jumbles of letters, they can't be me. I'm Carmel Reeves, a normal girl, just an ordinary, simple person, someone who isn't complex, who's easy to understand. I'm an artist, a daughter, a loner… nothing else, not aromantic, not asexual.

A person who has little to no sexual feelings or desires, or who is not sexually attracted to anyone. A person who has little to no interest in or desire for romantic relationships.

Shit.

Shit, shit, *shit*.

remy

I wake up to a collection of soft curls in my mouth, and my alarm blaring. I set it to go off at six am so we could get out on time, but – as the little LED sign on my clock reads as I fumble to pick it up, clicking the button on the side – it's already half past, and it must have snoozed at least three times already before I finally registered the beeping through my sleep.

"Shit," I murmur, extracting one of Carmel's curls from my mouth and wiping my lips with the back of my hand, suddenly tasting dry shampoo and something which smells like perfume. "Carmel? Carmel, the staff will be here soon, cleaners and stuff. Carmel, we need to get out!"

To my side, a sleepy Carmel whirs to life. Her eyes are bleary and her cheeks are pink, and there are globs of yellow in each corner, encrusted dribble by her mouth.

It's weird, but even seeing her like this – all mussed up and still exhausted, nose red from where she's laid on it all night – makes me want to kiss her more than anything.

"Come on," I repeat, standing and tugging the blanket off her. "We need to… shit, I'm so sorry –"

Her dress has ridden up overnight, and pulling the blanket has only exposed her knickers. I throw it back down, blushing furiously, as I proceed to pack the crisp packets and breadstick box and projector back into the carrier bag. Carmel makes herself decent, then we push the blanket down over the rest of our belongings, putting our shoes on and hurrying out of the tunnel.

The aquarium is lighter at this time, though some of the corridors are still entombed in darkness. We make our way back to the door which leads to the staff quarters, then down the stairs and into the corridor we first arrived in. I fumble to find the key and we step out into the weak sunlight, locking the door behind us.

The car park is empty, the Humber moving steadily beside us. We stand on the concrete embankment as it churns beneath us. It's murky brown and dense, like coffee, frothy bits foaming at the banks. It's an overcast day so far, and the sky opposite is pale blue, just a sprinkling of yellow set above the horizon. Carmel wipes her eyes to get the sleep away and smudges her mascara, but it was already messed-up anyway, and she still looks perfect.

"Can I treat you to a McDonald's?" I ask, and she nods without saying a word.

We're exhausted by the time we reach the nearest one, with the help of Google maps. We don't say a word as we walk through the quiet streets of Hull, past the cranes and office blocks and towering warehouses of the night before, everything so much cleaner in the daylight, so much whiter, brighter. The yellow "M" is visible from right down the road. Carmel traipses after me like her feet are ready to crumble.

She orders a coffee, no sugar, and an egg McMuffin with two extra hash browns. I pick orange juice, grateful that I still have some gum left over, and a sausage and egg McMuffin – with four hash browns, of course. The waitress looks as tired as us when she brings our order over. People just shouldn't be awake at seven am on a Sunday.

"Are you doing anything today?" I ask. I'm eager not to let her go home yet, and Carmel shakes her head.

"I'm not – just homework – but I'll have to go home soon, make Mum her breakfast."

Of course. Carmel's the sole carer of her mother, who has cancer. She's given no indication as to how ill she is, whether it's in the later stages or is still being treated, but the fact Carmel has to make her mum's breakfast says everything.

"I can help, if you'd like," I suggest. I think the early morning has given me confidence, because we're both sleep-deprived and the words come out much more smoothly than I was expecting, just like that. "I'd love to meet her."

"No, don't bother yourself." Carmel doesn't meet my eyes, taking a huge bite out of her egg McMuffin. "Wow. This one has three yolks."

We don't speak much as we finish our meals, just the odd complaint about how tired we are, how good the food is, how elite hash browns are. Carmel finishes her coffee way before me and goes up to the counter to order another, and I sip my orange juice as I stare out of the window at a Hull slowly burbling to life. The only people out this early on a Sunday morning are builders and workmen on their way to service offices and new-builds, decked in high-vis clothes and hardhats, tools stowed away in their vans.

Carmel walks me to the train station, which is apparently on her way home. Most of the shops are closed in the centre. It's weird to see it looking so dead, silent, like a ghost town. I check the arrival of the next train and it isn't for another two hours, but Carmel has to go home – in fact, she insists. I can't help but feel wounded as she emphasises the importance of cooking her mother a proper Sunday breakfast, beans with two sausages and a few fried mushrooms. I get it, obviously…

I just wish I could spend more of the day with her.

"Thank you, though," she says, as we reach the Paragon Interchange. The architecture of the building soars above us, and I smile, shaking my head, like it's no big deal.

"I've really enjoyed myself," I say. "It's been… nice."

"It has." Carmel smiles then, a real, proper smile, and tilts her head to one side. "I really like spending time with you, Remy. The aquarium was sick – I'll never forget that."

"Can I see you again?" It's the second time I've asked her that. I wonder when it'll get old.

But Carmel nods, giving me another little smile and waving as she starts to back away, still stumbling on sleepy legs.

"Just… just message me." She turns fully then, shouting over her shoulder, "Bye, Remy!"

I watch as she disappears down the road, into the centre of Hull. I don't let my eyes leave her until she turns the corner and is out of sight, curls lost amid the buildings, body enveloped by her city.

Then I force myself to move, to leave her behind and accept the fact that I can't be with her forever, that just a day feels like a blessing, and that hopefully – fingers and toes crossed – I'll be able to see her next week, to plan an even more extravagant date for the two of us.

The train station is empty.

Not even coffee chains have opened their doors, and the only people there are two homeless men, huddled together under a duvet. I have two hours to kill. I might as well trundle back to McDonald's to get them some breakfast.

I pick two sausage and egg McMuffins in the end, from the one just down the street. I order six hash browns between them and two orange juices, because nobody wants cold tea.

Neither man awakes as I leave the food by their feet, hurrying off in the opposite direction and sitting down on the platform, opposite the wall.

I still have the projector in my bag, so I switch it on and face the bricks.

I rewatch *54 Pigs and Counting.*

And all the while, I can't stop thinking about Carmel.

remy

On Monday morning, for the first time since we started sixth form all those months ago, Lily doesn't sit with us.

Matt and I get our bacon sarnies from the till, trundling over to where Mike, Steph and Nima are huddled on our usual table, but Lily is nowhere to be seen. Her usual seat is empty; our overalled best friend has completely disappeared.

"I didn't think she was serious," Matt says, face pale, as he takes his seat atop one of the stools. "I don't get it. Just because of a stupid crush…"

Since I informed Matt that Lily liked me over the phone last night, he's been… cold. Although it's not my fault, I can understand why he's hurt. He's had a huge crush on her for years, would do anything to make her happy, but she only finds him mildly irritating. It doesn't make sense to either of us that she would like me, not when Matt's fairly okay-looking and always tries to please her, but that's not the point.

He thought me and Carmel getting together would solve the problem, take me off the market. Instead, it's driven Lily further away from us, completely severing any chance he had to get with her.

I know how crushed I'd be if Carmel rejected me, or if she even just refused to see me once. I can't imagine how much pain Matt is in right now, however hard he's trying to hide it.

"She's in the library," Nima says, hearing our conversation. She's trying to work on her maths homework, like most mornings, but the common room isn't exactly the best place to concentrate. "It's only Remy she doesn't want to see right now, Matt. You should go talk to her."

But Matt just shakes his head. "No point. I don't have a chance with her, do I?"

None of us have the heart to say no.

"Anyway," Nima says, twisting away from him and focusing on me. "Come on, Remy – tell us what's happening with you and Carmel. Did the condoms get used?"

That seems to get everyone's attention, as my friends all peer at me excitedly, waiting for my answer. I roll my eyes, shaking my head as I say, "No… but I did kiss her!"

Nima promptly cheers at that, reaching over to whack me on the back, but Matt just looks annoyed. He cocks his head to the side and takes a bite out of his bacon sarnie.

"Well done, Remy!" Nima exclaims, grinning. "Was it good? Was it a proper kiss, or just a peck? And did she kiss you back?"

"Now Matt's the only kiss virgin!" Mike adds, to which Matt frowns and buries his head further into the sarnie. "And Lily… But go on, Remy, tell us about it! Was it a twenty second stonker? Or an I'm-pecking-myself-in-the-mirror… chonker?"

I blink, bombarded with too many questions at once, too many to process. "I don't know. Kisses are just kisses, aren't they?"

"Kisses are *not* just kisses," Steph pipes up, rolling her eyes. Her and Mike have their hands locked together across the table, and are currently in the process of making sandwiches for their lunch. They often do this in the morning if they don't think they'll have time later on during the day, slicing pickles and pressing plastic-wrapped cheese slices onto white bread. They like to eat the same, perform these rituals, and often stop off at the supermarket before school to prepare for a picnic-making sesh in the common room.

I feel faintly nauseous looking at the slimy pickles slithering across the table, and ignore Steph's comment.

"Anyway, kissing aside… I need advice about our next date, Ni. I'm all out of ideas. The aquarium was supposed to be the date to end all dates, so I kind of forgot that I'd need to plan more."

It's true. We built up that date so much in our minds that I kind of forgot I'd need another plan. I've set the bar high now, raised Carmel's expectations beyond what I think I can deliver.

But Nima is grinning wickedly, and I know from the look on her face that this idea is a good idea. A very, very good idea.

"I know what we can do," she says, tapping the side of her nose with her finger. "Have you forgotten what week it is, Remy?"

I frown, trying to wrack my brain. "Clearly."

"Hull fair, Remy." Nima rolls her eyes, jabbing me right in the chest. "Hull. Fair."

Shit.

It's *Hull Fair*.

Every year since the four of us became friends, we've been to Hull Fair. My mum took us the first time, standing with Lily while Nima, Matt and I tried every ride possible, swooping over the city into the night, spinning so hard Nima was sick all over her *Hello Kitty* t-shirt and pink brogues. It's become a tradition, something we do each October when the huge funfair drops its anchor in Hull, spilling out over the city and sprinkling it with festival cheer.

Mike and Steph came with us last year, and this time, the six of us had been planning to try almost every ride there. It was a risk – we might be ride connoisseurs, but even we get queasy from time to time – but we're all for taking risks, except maybe Lily.

Only she won't be coming with us this year, of course.

Which sucks.

"We should invite Carmel!" Nima exclaims. "Then you can spend the evening with her, and she can meet all of us!"

"Invite Carmel?" I echo. Invite Carmel, my crush, the girl I'm trying to impress, to meet my friends? She seemed wary of Matt and Nima last weekend, to say the least, but spending the night at the funfair with them, eating fried onions and brandy snaps and root beer from overpriced vans, hurling her body around the city sky on rides is a completely different thing.

"I like that idea," Matt says, nodding. "I want to meet her properly."

Which, in Matt code, could mean a number of things, but certainly not *that*.

"I think she'd be too shy," I object, trying to get out of it, but my friends are shaking their heads at me. "Besides, it's expensive, and short notice, and she'd probably say no anyway."

"Don't be daft!" Nima says, rolling her eyes. "It'll be night-time, we'll be too preoccupied to make small talk with her. It'll be fun! Besides, she didn't seem very shy last time we met her."

That's true. Carmel isn't *shy*, exactly. Maybe just… distant. She told me she doesn't have many friends, and that's probably because she's so cold, so spiky, until you get to know her properly. Then she's the perfect combination of soft and complex, intrigue and understanding.

"Come on, Remy. Message her and see." Nima is persistent. She keeps jabbing me in the chest as she speaks, like that's going to spur me on to reply. "Just do it, get your phone out and –"

She stops speaking. Her eyes are focused on the space behind me, where I can hear that a gaggle of girls have entered the room.

I glance at Matt, but he's staring behind me too, and his face has turned white.

I turn.

There, stood in the centre of the common room with Soraya and two other girls I only know from them being popular, is Lily.

"Fuck her," I hear Matt say, under his breath. "She stops hanging round with us because she has a crush on you, and starts going round with the group who've made our lives a misery for the last seven years."

"Hey! They're okay," Nima cuts in, though her voice is flat and she sounds fractured, hurt. "They just associate with the popular kids. Rosie, Soraya and Jaye are quite nice, really."

But that's not the point.

Lily isn't really *talking* to them, just hovering in her baggy overalls, curls falling over her face to hide the blush. She's significantly smaller than the rest – she's always been short – and is the only one not caked in makeup and false nails, but is picking at her own bitten ones awkwardly, struggling to butt in.

"She won't be coming to Hull Fair with us then, I guess," Nima says, wrinkling her nose. "I'll message her later, but we should probably stop staring. She'll only be stood with them because Soraya's in her English class, and you have English next, right, Remy?"

I nod.

"It's not like she's replacing us, or anything," Nima continues, but she doesn't sound so sure. "She just needs some space."

That's not what it feels like, though.

It feels like everything's falling to pieces.

"Are you going to message her, then?" Matt prompts, turning his back on Lily with a determined whoosh. He prods my phone closer to me and nods at it, gesturing for me to pick it up. "Carmel! We're inviting her to the fair, right?"

"I don't know." There's a sick feeling in my stomach, churning round and round. There has been ever since I turned to see Lily stood with Soraya and the other girls, trying her best not to glance over at us. "If this is hurting Lily so much, maybe we shouldn't invite Carmel, ask Lily to come instead?"

That's not really how I feel, obviously. I want Lily to just get over this silly crush and see me for what I am, her best friend. Then I can carry on getting with Carmel, and everything will be okay again.

"Don't be stupid. Lily won't come. She's made her choice. Now, invite Carmel!" Nima insists. The four of them are staring at me as I pick up the phone. I start to type in Carmel's name, clicking on her contact. It's a photo I took of her in the aquarium last night, the back of her head. She looks… well.

She looks perfect, curls outlined by deep blue, a shoal of fish swimming above her silhouette. The others watch me as I tap out the message, eyebrows knitted.

hey – hope you got home safely yesterday. i was wondering whether you'd like to come to hull fair with me and my friends this weekend?

"There," Matt says, grinning. "Easy."

Nima nods. We all take a deep breath, phone in the centre of the table between us, as Mike and Steph say in unison, "And now, we wait."

carmel

When I got home on Sunday morning, Mum wasn't even awake. She barely spoke to me the entire day, refusing breakfast, saying no to tomato soup at lunch, a usual favourite. She wouldn't let me wash her wig, wouldn't drink the smoothie I insisted on making, hoping it'd provide her with some nutrition.

Around one, she cracked open her eyes and peered over to where I was curled on the armchair opposite. I was sketching her, of course, getting in another simple pen drawing for one of my college assignments.

"Ravi," was all she said.

Ravi.

Mum hasn't had a phone in years, so neither of us have his number. The shop would still be open, but he usually has people helping him on weekends, which are always busy. I was sure he could leave for a few hours to talk to her, to make sure she was okay.

I ran all the way there in some of my old trainers, not caring that the soles were worn and had no laces, feet battering the pavement. She'd been doing so well, acting chirpy, trying hard to get up in the mornings and make her own breakfast, even if it was just heating up some beans or emptying some soup powder into a mug. I didn't understand why she'd relapsed, not so quickly, so out of the blue. It wasn't as though she was complaining of any *pain*.

The shop was empty, a teenage girl stood behind the counter. Remy only works on weekdays, he explained at the aquarium, and even then, he only does three or four nights a week. Ravi glanced up from where he was stacking shelves with chutney and little cheese biscuits, and my throat was hoarse as I croaked: "It's Mum."

He insisted we hurry back in his car. It'd be quicker, and she was clearly desperate. He hadn't seen her since he'd visited the previous weekend, but she'd been on a high ever since. We didn't talk much as he drove, twisting down the backstreets to reach her. It probably took longer than it would've on foot, and there was this uncomfortable tension between us, something that had never been present before. Something must have shifted in their relationship when he'd visited last weekend.

He insisted on closing the door behind him as soon as he entered the living room, leaving me stranded in the front hall. I stood there for a few minutes, straining to listen to what he was saying to her, but all I could hear was the low buzz of his voice, that rough Hull slur, trailing under the door.

They stayed together in there all day, long after the shop closed and Ravi was due to go home to his two dogs and tabby cat. He made them a packet couscous each with some onion and mushroom he found in our freezer, which he fried with the paprika. I made myself beans on toast while he milled around the kitchen behind me – our kitchen, *my* kitchen. We didn't speak, apart from when he asked me where we kept the chopping boards. I told him we didn't have one, that we usually just used the worktops.

"Your mother's a very special lady, Carmel," he said then, and I smiled and nodded. I couldn't let on that I was jealous, that I was acting irrationally and being so, so selfish. It didn't make sense, not even in my own head. I should be happy that he was helping her, lifting her spirits.

But I wasn't. I just felt this numb uselessness, like Ravi was doing what I'd struggled to do for the last year.

Like I wasn't good enough, not for my Mum, not for anyone.

I carried my beans on toast upstairs, where I got on with my art. I couldn't draw Mum, not now. Instead, I drew Remy, the aquarium, our night there together. I worked off the photographs I'd taken, creating jellyfish and seahorses and starfish and sharks and penguins and anemones and stingrays, Remy in the centre of each drawing, eyes wide and blue, skin marked with acne scars and a little rash, moles on his neck and nails long, perfectly manicured.

I kept thinking about that night in the aquarium, his arm around me, both of us asleep under the blanket. How it felt to kiss him. How it felt to have his flesh against mine, bodies pressed together, his chewing in my car as we watched the movie.

But all the while, those two words wouldn't stop dancing through my mind in stark purple and grey, green and black and white…

Asexual. Aromantic. *A person who has little to no sexual feelings or desires, or who is not sexually attracted to anyone. A person who has little to no interest in or desire for romantic relationships.*

Asexual, aromantic, asexual, aromantic –

It's evening now. Ravi has only just left. I watched his car pull away through the foggy glass of my bedroom window, but I didn't have the heart to go downstairs and talk to Mum, say goodnight. I'm sat on my bed, staring at my phone, heart pounding beneath my chest as I gaze at the keyboard so hard that the letters blur.

How can you tell if you're asexual?

Google is full of answers, none of them very helpful. There are countless quizzes, too many guides, but I don't want to find out for definite, not really, not like that. The thought makes me feel sick, all shivery, filled from head to toe with dread.

It's not like it matters. But it does. It does, and I know that, and so does the rest of the world.

It matters, because it's not the norm. I'm not the norm.

There's no other explanation, but actually accepting it makes everything seem so much more… real, like it's cemented into place, no way out. Surely I could change, grow out of it, learn to want relationships the way normal people do, the way normal humans *should*?

It's always been in the back of my mind, having a family. Mum is my only real friend, my only person, and our extended relations haven't exactly been helpful since she got ill. We're not close to anyone else, not really. I always assumed that once she went, taken by the cancer that's still ravishing her, I'd find a man, get married, have kids, a family of my own. It was the only other option, other than ending up alone… which nobody really wants, do they?

What if that's not possible, though? What if I just… can't like people? I'm almost nineteen, and I've never so much as had a crush, even a little one. What if I can't like people, can't have sex?

What if I really am asexual, and destined to stay that way?

How can you have a family if you're asexual?

Adoption is the clear answer, but that's still so much more complicated than just that. You have to show that you're stable, financially or otherwise, and I have no family, won't have a husband to support me, will probably be relying on modelling or art for an income. There are sperm donors if I want to have kids myself, but it's all so... bleak, cold. It's not the way I expected to live my life, not in the slightest.

I swallow, dropping my phone onto my bed beside me. My throat is dry, scratchy. I close my eyes, leaning back so that my head hits the headboard.

Why can't I just be like everybody else?

Why can't I just like boys, or even girls, desire romantic relationships, asexual or otherwise? I don't understand why I'm losing my mum, the only person who's ever been there for me, only to embark on a life of loneliness, a life of being single, by myself, forever.

Why? Why do I have to be like this?

I know it's possible I might just have not found the right person yet, that it's not my time. But I also know myself, know my heart. I like being alone. I don't see other people like that.

I don't think I ever will.

***

Remy asks me to Hull Fair at the weekend, with all his friends. If I'm honest, that throws me a little. It doesn't sound like a date, though I assumed that was how Remy viewed our relationship after the kiss. It sounds like I'm a friend, and I'm meeting his other friends, and we're going to the funfair together, like normal people do.

I'm sat in one of the college cafeterias, nursing a sandwich I made this morning. It's cheese and beetroot; I made the same for Mum, when we woke up. The message has been waiting for me all morning, but I couldn't check my phone during the pottery workshop I had to attend. I'm sat alone, Boy 1 and Boy 2 busy with some extra work they're doing as they resit their maths GCSE, three years later.

hey – hope you got home safely yesterday. i was wondering whether you'd like to come to hull fair with me and my friends this weekend?

I'm not sure. The thought of having to spend the day with those friends of Remy's – Matt and Nima, I think they were called – makes me a little nervous, causes my skin to crawl.

They seemed lovely, but having one new friend feels like enough. I don't cope well in group situations, he knows that. I don't like talking to people. I'm too awkward, stilted, and it makes me come across as rude, like I don't want to be friendly, like I'm incapable.

And yet… Hull Fair. It's the highlight of our city's life each October, when it unfolds across the wasteland and spills stalls and rides and rubbish everywhere, attracting visitors from right across Yorkshire. I remember going with Mum and some of her crazy friends when I was a kid, eating brandy snaps and candyfloss and cones filled with sweets. The whole place reeked of frying onions and smoke, of sweat and grease and too much hair gel worn by those operating the rides. It's beautiful, though, some sort of LSD-created land. Lights, flashing yellow and red and orange and green, and screaming music, shrieking children, couples walking hand in hand, trainers caked in mud.

Of *course* I want to go.

It's the perfect place to take photos, to gather inspiration, to transfer into paintings and drawings and collages of colour. It's the perfect place to just *live*, to breathe in the sticky, onion-scented air, slip on ketchup and tumble over hotdogs, travel round and round on the Ferris Wheel.

I want to go, that's a no-brainer.

I'm just apprehensive about the *people*.

I would love to. Let me know what time to meet you, and where.

It only takes a second for his reply to come through.

aw great, can't wait! it'll just be me, you, nima, matt, mike and steph. mike and steph don't say much because they're constantly sucking face, but you've met nima and matt. shall we meet on saturday outside the mcdonald's near st stephens at five? we can grab a bite to eat, then get the bus to the fair! x

He's enthusiastic, evidently. But… Mike and Steph? Who the hell are Mike and Steph? I assumed it'd just be the four of us. I didn't realise Remy had quite so many friends.

That's when it hits me.

Maybe it's a triple date? Matt and Nima spent the afternoon together while Remy and I went to Paula's Puddings that afternoon, so could well be a couple, and Mike and Steph clearly are. And Remy sent a kiss. A kiss, alluding to the one we shared on Saturday night, next to the poor penguins who really, really did *not* need to see that.

I don't even know how Remy is feeling now. I assumed he realised it was a mistake when he didn't say anything afterwards, twisting his head back towards the tank and staring at the penguins as they slid through the water before us. There was no chemistry, no buzz of electricity in the air between us. I didn't even kiss him back. He didn't try anything for the rest of the night, either, which suggests it was just a spur of the moment thing, a simple mistake.

But what if it wasn't?

What if this evening at the fair, this… event, is actually another date?

It's too late to take back my reply. It's swirling through the universe with every other text anyone has ever regretted sending, spinning out of control, further and further away from my grasp. Remy sounds so excited, too, looking forward to the evening, to seeing me again.

The sandwich is soggy in my hand, beetroot juice seeping through the white bread. Even the cheese is wet. I I've chopped the beetroot too thickly, and the whole thing strong with that vinegary aftertaste.

If I was an ordinary girl, I wouldn't feel so uncomfortable about going on a triple date with a group of nice, non-judgemental people. I'd probably like Remy back, would've *wanted* to kiss him back, would be feeling excited for what he might try on Saturday at the fair.

Remy deserves someone who loves him, who wants to be with him. He's so kind, so innocent and pure and loving. He took me to the aquarium, the whole building empty for just us two to spend the evening together. It should've been romantic, falling asleep inside a tank full of sharks and stingrays, in a glass tunnel. We watched a film, huddled in a blanket with snacks and dip, and I felt… nothing.

You can't cry at college, you can't cry at college –

A girl on a nearby table is staring at me, one eyebrow raised, so I try to swallow my tears, dissolve the lump in my throat. I'm fine, totally fine. It's not a big deal.

But it *is* a big deal. Of course it is.

I don't want to hurt him, but I think it's already gone too far for that.

I never thought a kiss could affect me so much. An innocent touch of lips, huddled beside the penguin tank, knees touching as I leant forward to reach her… but it has.

I can barely think of anything else all week. I go to bed with that tingly feeling, dream of Carmel's lips against mine, my hand grazing the smooth skin of her cheeks, the freckles dotted across her nose, her jaw. Those long lashes, dusted with mascara, and her tongue, stuck out over her bottom lip as she concentrates on taking photos, gazing into the depths of a tank.

Now that my Oxford application is away and gone, I can focus on me, on my relationship, my studies. Mr O'Flannel comments on the concentration I've regained in English, telling me it's a pleasure to note my eyes actually staring at the board, instead of into space like they have been as of recent. He puts that down to me having sent off my application, but I think it's more the fact that I now feel comfortable, safe. I no longer feel like I have to conquer Carmel's affections, or even worry whether she feels the same.

In my eyes, it's a no-brainer.

"And what's going on with you and Lily?" Mr O'Flannel asks as I'm packing away on Wednesday, getting ready to leave. The rest of the class is long gone, scurrying away for lunch. It's chicken naan day, a Vibbington favourite. "I never expected to see a day when you two wouldn't sit together."

"She just wanted to concentrate for once," I explain, though my cheeks are burning. "You know… I tend to talk a bit too much, distract her from working."

"Lily's the chatterbox," he counters. "Poor Soraya can't seem to get a word in edgeways."

I shrug, unsure of what to say. I can't admit to Mr O'Flannel that Lily won't speak to me, that I don't even think we're friends anymore. I can't even admit that to *myself.*

Ravi notices the difference, too, as I turn up for my evening shifts. I have a "glow" – which, in his words, means I have a woman, and she's making me a very happy boy. It's not a lie. I don't tell him who it is, but a part of me wonders whether he knows, whether he noted my interaction with Carmel in the shop that night and realised how completely infatuated with her I am.

I'm happy, content, now that Carmel and I are almost an item. Matt insists I can't call her my girlfriend until I've officially asked, so we all agree I should do so on Saturday night, at the fair. Take her away from the hubbub of the fairground and ask her, under the stars, perhaps over a brandy snap or a cloud of candyfloss. Ask her, my hands in hers, to be my girlfriend, to make this thing between us something permanent, something that's going to last.

"She'll say yes," Nima assures me, passing me a bauble of chicken from her naan bread and an extra sachet of ketchup. "You've been on two dates, and you've kissed her. She's clearly ready to be with you."

But it's more complicated than that. Carmel is independent, doesn't do friends. She'll stick to her art, her family, herself – she never looks happier than when she's sketching or taking photos or scribbling away in that sketchbook. Carmel might like me – *must* like me – but that doesn't mean she wants to be my girlfriend, my person.

I've seen people on TV shows have partners just for casual sex, for a hook-up or two, without wanting to put a label on it. Maybe that's what Carmel wants? To go on dates, to kiss by the penguin tank, without the pressures and loyalties demanded of a boyfriend-girlfriend relationship. Maybe she just doesn't want to be Remy Evan's girlfriend.

As I plan what I'm going to say, the worries won't stop churning. I've always been an overthinker, but this is veering on dangerous, brain spiralling out of control.

But at the forefront of my doubts, Lily still prances about in her overalls, shaking her head and frowning. Making Carmel my girlfriend puts a death sentence on our friendship, and there's no way around that.

We see her each lunchtime now, sat with Soraya and her friends, Rosie Abara and the muscular girl, Jaye. She seems more in with the crowd, joining in with their conversations and eating some of the traditional Indian sweets Soraya's mum makes. They huddle together in English and share jokes about Shakespeare, the kind Lily and I would've once come up with together, Soraya laughing politely with a long-nailed hand over her mouth.

I catch Lily's eye as we're leaving the classroom on Friday, the day before my big date. She's been watching me pack away my *Othello* textbooks with an expression that's almost unreadable, and holds my gaze steady as my eyes meet hers.

I miss you, I try to tell her, sending a telepathic message with my face contorted, as though I can somehow tap into her mind. *I really, really miss you.*

But Lily just turns away.

carmel

Asexual. Aromantic. The two words follow me round all week like a bad smell, unable to shake. It's so much more serious when I think about it properly, about the consequences and how I'm going to deal with it going forward, how it'll affect my life, my family… Mum, her legacy, all of it.

I want to tell her, of course… but I can't, not yet. I need to be sure, need to have concrete evidence, before breaking such huge news to her. It feels almost like the hardest thing I could ever admit, worse than if I were gay, or pregnant, or anything along those lines. Mum's so accepting and chilled out, very progressive, especially because she had me so young. She was only eighteen, used to be big in the Hull Pride scene before she got ill, but this is different. It's something that will actually affect us, something permanent, something I'm taking away from her.

She's always wanted grandchildren. That's maybe the thing she's found hardest in all her illness, dealing with the fact she may not live to see me get married, have kids, a family of my own. It's what she wants, though, more than anything. She won't be there for me, so she wants to make sure I have people around me, a husband, children, who love me and are there for me. Her biggest fear in dying is leaving me all alone.

It's what I want, too, but Mum needs it in a different way.

She doesn't want to feel like she's letting me down when she leaves. She wants me to be happy.

And now, in a way, I feel like *I'm* the one letting *her* down.

I decide to do one of the tests on Thursday night, the ones which determine your sexuality, whether you truly are… asexual, or whatever it may be. I know they're not one hundred percent accurate, but it's the only way to know the truth, to feel like I'm not just going crazy.

And – in a way – I'm hoping that taking it will prove I'm not actually asexual or aromantic or anything other than normal, and that I can just get on with my life and never once think about it again.

The one I pick is high up in the search results, on a reputable website that's full of information and resources, should I need them. I'm sat on my bed, curled up with my duvet around me, Mum tucking into Cup a Soup downstairs with another cooking show on TV. My laptop is resting on my knees. It's a second-hand one Mum bought me for my GCSEs and the screen is severely cracked from where I dropped it last year, but it'll do the job.

Mr and Mrs Acharya next door are still trying for a baby. I know that because the thumping is back, hitting our thin walls, over and over and over. I don't know how their three kids get any sleep, not when our houses are so hollow, airtight shells amplifying each and every sound.

I try to push them out of my head, and focus on the screen.

The first question is multiple choice, and completely undermines the purpose of a sexuality test. It asks me to state what I currently identify as, whether I'm asexual, aromantic, or neither, which I can't really answer, because I don't *know*, don't have a single clue. That's what I'm taking this bloody test for.

I select "neither" as it's the only option that makes sense, and swallow as the answer goes blue.

The next question is fairly simple, so much so that I don't think it should even be a question.

You see a person who would be sexually attractive to most people. How do you feel?

None of the options really apply to me, I don't think – aside from the last one, which states that I'd feel nothing, perhaps just notice that they're attractive, that's it. Surely most people are the same, though? You can appreciate the fact that someone has an aesthetically pleasing face, the kind you want to paint, without wanting to do "sexual things" with them. Who even thinks like that?

You start seeing someone you like. However, this person claims to be asexual. They don't want a sexual relationship, and would much rather be romantic without sex. How do you react?

The third question makes even less sense. I've never liked anyone, so I can't really respond, not using any of the options listed below. The whole quiz is about how I'm unsure of my sexuality, so I don't know how to answer this, either.

I skim the options one last time before selecting "other" and moving onto the next. I select similar answers for the next few questions, all of which are pretty much the same.

How do you feel when you watch porn?

I've never seen it, nor have I ever desired to in any way – it grosses me out completely, makes me feel so uncomfortable just *thinking* about it. I know there's a stigma around females doing this stuff, but it's not just that I feel. It's a horror, an innate repulsion.

How comfortable are you with being naked around other people?

Far too comfortable. It's my job, and it makes me money, and that's all I need to know. That's not what the question is asking, though.

How often do you think about sex?

Never. Literally never. My mum is dying of terminal cancer; I have six hundred things going on with work and school and now Remy… and sex isn't high up on my list of priorities.

How well do you relate to this statement: "I don't feel sexually attracted to anyone, ever – regardless of gender or circumstance."

This final question makes phlegm rise up to my mouth, and I swallow it down with a shiver.

It's… accurate. Too accurate. Is asexuality really so… simple? Other people feel sexually attracted to people, and I don't?

It's not, I know that, but that's how it feels.

I can go and stand in a room full of men, completely naked, and not think about sex. Remy can kiss me – a nice, fairly attractive guy – and I don't feel anything, nothing at all, not even a tiny spark, a thrill. Girls do nothing for me, boys do nothing for me. Sex, romance, the thought of being close to someone... it just doesn't interest me, not even a little bit.

I've never even been interested in friendship, but having Remy makes me feel safe, wanted, comfortable. It's nice being able to tell him things, unload my worries to him, discuss my mum's illness and my fears of never leaving Hull, of being stuck in this city forever. That's all I want it to be, though – a friendship. Platonic, not romantic. I want all the feelings of a close relationship, but not the kissing, the holding hands, the hugs, the sex.

The very thought makes me nauseous.

You're likely asexual, and possibly aromantic.

I know the quiz can't be fully correct and can't determine what my sexuality is, but it's right, I know it is.

I'm asexual.

I'm aromantic.

Asexual.

Aromantic.

I'm never going to fall in love, have kids, a family, a wedding, carry on my Mum's legacy, give her the grandchildren she so wants.

I'm never going to experience all the things people say make life worth living. And if by some miracle I do, it won't be any time soon, that's for sure.

I've failed her, completely. I've failed *myself.* My life stretches out ahead of me in a mess of loneliness and singularity, Carmel Reeves, artist and spinster, destined to die alone.

I have one friend, and I'm about to lose him too by rejecting his advances. I have my mum, but she's going to die.

And then there'll just be me, Carmel, alone.

Me, Carmel.

Alone.

I get ready at Matt's house on Saturday afternoon, pulling on a pair of dark jeans and the yellow jumper Lily once bought me, from an online shop which makes unofficial merch. I spray a bit of "stuff" in my hair, this liquid Mum says gives you volume and lift, and spritz far too much Lynx under each armpit. Matt is wearing normal skinny jeans and a plain shirt. He seems to have grown three inches overnight, towering in the doorway.

"You look good," I say, raising an eyebrow. "I don't know how you do it."

"I'm just naturally gorgeous," he quips, reaching for a piece of gum on his bedside table. "But you're the one getting all the girls, Remy. You must be doing *something* right."

I frown, turning to gaze in the mirror. I look hideous, even with my hair gaining twice as much height from Mum's spray, and my epic jumper. I know Carmel won't be able to see me properly under the lights of the fairground, but tonight is supposed to be *the night*. The night I ask her out, the night she becomes my girlfriend.

Unless she says no, of course.

I swallow, wrinkling my nose and turning away from my reflection. I don't want to stare at him for any longer.

Matt and I head out to the train station just after four, trundling along the back streets of Vibbington, making small talk about the state of the government, picking at my hands, the skin around my nails. I listen to Matt list a spiel of nonsense about foreign policies and harbouring missiles as I try to control my breathing.

One in, one out, one in, one out –

"You'll be okay, dude," he says, interrupting himself. "Just chill."

But chilling is a lot easier said than done.

Nima, Mike and Steph are waiting at the ticket machine. They're all wrapped up warm against the October chill, and Nima is wearing fluffy boots and a thick fur coat, ever the extravagant one. I stay quiet as Matt greets them, too nervous to try and speak. All my Remy buttons have been pressed to mute. I purchase my ticket, but my heart is still pounding beneath my chest and I feel like I'm going to throw up, spew everywhere –

We board the train, squashing five bodies onto four seats. I don't really concentrate on what my friends are saying; it's all white noise to me. I stare out of the window at the countryside rolling by, all hazy brown fields and hedgerows and houses decked out with early pumpkins and tiny ghosts. It's cold, and wind whips through the trees as our train bursts over the tracks and into Hull.

We stop at a few stations along the way. Passengers are decked in typical fair-going outfits, bright colours and wellies and thick trainers, and the carriage is filling up, people spilling out into the corridor. Children, teens, middle-aged couples clinging desperately to their youth…

We all gather together, ready to take Hull Fair by the horns.

"You excited?" Nima asks, dragging me from my daydream. "Or nervous?"

I'm everything, every emotion under the sun, excited and scared and apprehensive and fearful, trembling under my yellow jumper and too-big hairstyle. I give her an anxious smile and my friends all laugh, understanding completely.

The platform is empty as our train spills onto it; nobody wants to be leaving Hull tonight, not when the whole city is caught up in funfair fever. We follow Nima, who leads the way in her furry coat and boots, pushing through the crowds to step out into the sunshine. It's weak, just poking through gaps in the overcast sky, but it's clear that tonight will be cold, bitingly cold, the kind of cold you only experience in autumn. I can sense a real chill in the air, but it won't rain, that's for sure. The air is so dry it pricks my skin.

Carmel is meeting us at McDonald's. Nima actually did most of the arranging for this evening, insisting she take Carmel's number and contact her herself, the two of them bonding over A-level art and someone called Hockney. She leads the way now, stomping down Hull's main street towards the big yellow M.

"Keep your cool, Remy," she instructs me, squeezing my arm so tight I can't help but cry out. "Carmel is going to be your girlfriend, okay? You're going to ask her out, and she's going to say yes."

"And if she doesn't?"

"We don't think about that, okay?"

Nima's right. It won't help to think of the worst.

But that doesn't stop me from doing so anyway.

Carmel is stood outside McDonald's with a wistful, faraway look on her face, hands tucked into the pockets of her signature yellow raincoat. She doesn't notice us until we're right beside her, close enough to notice the wintery plum lipstick she's acquired, and the huge earrings hanging from her lobes – which, on further inspection, are made from circular cut-outs of a Fanta can, and have little pumpkin faces painted across them. Just when I thought she couldn't be more perfect…

"Carmel?" Nima says, waving a hand in front of her face with a grin. "We're here!"

We trek inside to the big ordering screens, two by two. Carmel is instantly swept up in a flurry of Nima goodness, while Matt and I follow behind with our heads down and his eyes trained to his phone, Mike and Steph in front. It's ridiculously busy for a Tuesday night, everyone out for junk food before the fair begins later.

I order chicken nuggets and a small fries, keeping it simple, not wanting to seem too greedy in front of Carmel. I even pick water, which Nima rolls her eyes at. *Anyone who orders water over coke needs their head checking…* I've heard it one hundred times before.

Carmel, of course, goes for the unusual option. Three mozzarella dippers, a mango and passionfruit iced smoothie, large fries, a spicy veggie wrap. I watch her frowning at the total on the screen as she feeds her card to it, the money draining from her account like rice through a colander.

"You should've offered to pay," Matt mutters, nudging my shoulder, but it's too late now.

We collect our food and take it to sit upstairs and eat, on a table looking out over the city. It's the same table we sat on all those weeks ago, coming to try and find Carmel, the elusive, no-named girl I'd saved from a shitty boy the previous night. Carmel eats delicately, taking rabbit bites as my friends laugh and jostle and steal chips from one another.

It's weird, almost, how aware of my body I am around her. I'm more careful than usual as I take a bite of each chicken nugget, making sure my mouth is completely closed as I chew, conscious of the noises I'm making, that I don't accidentally spit or slurp. We don't make eye contact as we eat, as though there's a brick wall between us that only I have the power to see through, unable to keep my eyes off her.

It's the earrings which get me the most. Made from recycled cans, painted to look like they fit with the Halloween season, brightly-coloured and perfectly shaped. It doesn't surprise me that she's crafty, too. There probably isn't anything she's not good at.

After the table falls quiet, Nima steps in again. She reaches forward to snap the end off of one of Carmel's mozzarella dippers, and Carmel holds out the ketchup for her to dunk it in.

"So," she begins. "What do you think of rides, Carmel?"

Mike and Steph have cut a Big Mac in half and are sharing fries and veggie dippers between them. Even they stop eating to hear her reply.

This is a big question, a *huge* deal within our friendship group. Asking whether you like rides is like asking whether you like *Mario Kart*, or Kings of Leon. You can't say no.

Carmel hesitates, glancing up at the five faces staring back and waiting, expectantly, for her to speak.

"They're… okay," she says eventually, taking another bite from her wrap. "They're just rides, aren't they?"

They're… just rides?

Nima is stunned into silence, eyes crinkled as she tries to interpret what that could mean. Lily is the only person allowed to not like rides, and at least her opinion of them is clear.

But Carmel is indecisive, on the fence.

That's not physically possible in the case of funfair

attractions.

"On a scale of one to ten, how much do you like rides?" Matt joins in, frowning. "Ten being rides-are-absolutely-sick, zero being eh-I-could-live-without."

"A solid four," she responds simply. "Yeah, I'll say four."

Four?

Four is below the line of acceptance – way below. I can see Mike and Steph go back to their meal out of the corner of my eye, and Matt and Nima exchange looks of betrayal. I feel, for the first time tonight, like I've brought the wrong girl into our group.

"Well," I say, and – for the first time since we arrived – Carmel looks up to meet my eye. "We'll just have to change that, won't we?"

carmel

I've been exchanging texts with Nima all week, Remy's close friend. I managed to subtly ask whether she's into Matt, and she assured me she isn't, that she much prefers girls on the whole. It puts my mind at ease, tells me that it definitely isn't a double date after all. She seems nice, too. Kind of intense, and very opinionated, but… nice. Friendly, like she really does want to include me, for me to not feel out of place.

We're sat in McDonald's now, Remy opposite, Nima to my left. Matt seems like a quiet kind of guy, head down, playing a Pac-Man game on his phone, but he's as welcoming as the others. Mike and Steph don't say much. They're couple-y to the extreme, so much it makes me feel uncomfortable. Cuddling and holding hands is one thing, but cutting a Big Mac in half and sharing a portion of veggie dippers, taking bites from each end, is a step too far.

"A solid four," I tell them, when Matt asks how much I like rides, on a scale of one to ten. "Yeah, I'll say four."

A four isn't bad, I wouldn't say. A four is… slightly below average. I've been on a few rides at Bridlington harbour with Mum and her friends, and Mrs Dichre took me on a weird Ferris Wheel thing on a trip to Brighton years and years ago. I had to babysit for Mr and Mrs Acharya's children a few months back, and I took them to a local park, where a kiddie funfair was set up for a few days. We went on a carousel, the oldest two on their own animals, little Arjun squashed onto a weirdly misshapen frog with me.

I like rides, like spinning and whirling, the flash of colour, the tinny music and rough fairground hands with their tattoos and piercings, pushing down the barrier and locking you in tight. I like the aesthetic, the drama, the rush it gives you… Yet the thrill is brought on by whirling you through the sky in a little metal contraption, designed to make you scared, for you to feel something. It's not an authentic experience, not when you only use it to feel. It seems fake, artificial.

Remy and his friends are clearly ride enthusiasts. They gush about how incredible they are as we take the bus from the city centre to Hull Fair's site, a little way out, in a field they completely batter each year. The sky has darkened and the wind is picking up as we trundle through Hull's streets, the city looming around us out of the shadows.

The fair can be heard before it's seen, the shrieking and laughing of over-enthused five-year-olds who've eaten far too much candyfloss and gummy snakes. Buses leading to the fairground snake in a long line down the road, ours right at the back. They're letting out visitors a few hundred metres from the gate, before turning round and passing us like empty tombs, ready to pick up the next surge of teens.

"I smell fried onions," Mike says, nose quivering, and Steph pokes it with a giggle.

We're let out of the bus in ten minutes or so, the wait agonising. Remy bounds ahead with Nima, and Mike and Steph travel behind, arms linked, as Matt waits for me to disembark. He offers to hold my bag as I readjust my coat. I smile at him, grateful that he's trying to make me feel comfortable, welcome. Remy has completely forgotten I'm here.

We join a long line of people heading through the park gates to the fairground itself. It's flanked with stalls, a gentle introduction to the main event, the music getting louder, screams more shrill. Hot dogs, burgers, sausages wrapped in Yorkshire puddings, bacon sarnies, brandy snaps, candyfloss, toffee apples, fudge…

Mike and Steph get a sausage bap each, and Nima, Matt and Remy share a portion of cheesy chips. I don't buy anything. The rides alone will cost a bomb.

"We usually have a go on the stalls when we're leaving," Nima explains, appearing beside me with a grin. "Remy is *sick* at hook-a-duck, aren't you, Rem?"

"No," he replies, flushing, "but you're a dab hand at ball-in-the-bucket."

I take out my phone and start snapping photos as soon as I remember to. They'll be useful for our upcoming art foundation project, which centres around light and colour and immersion, being completely overwhelmed by the senses a place can awaken.

I take photos of the rides as we enter the fairground… of the stalls, the cheese on their chips, the little rubber ducks floating in yellowing water. The brandy snaps we share upon wandering around the first batch of attractions, mud slick underfoot and fair alive with brash music, beeping and bright lights, flashing on and off as visitors whirl through the sky. I take photos of Matt, examining the prices of the dodgems and offering to pay for all of us, and of Nima, trying to decide which car to choose.

I take a photo of Remy, turning to ask me to share a car with him, body blurred in motion. The fairground is lit up behind him in yellow and green and red and blue, and it's by far my favourite picture of the night so far.

I've never been on proper Dodgems before. It's difficult to step into the car and get comfortable, especially when I'm hyper aware of Remy's every movement, of his arm touching mine, his knees outstretched to fit us both into the little car – which is shaped as a penguin, of course. The lights go down, the fairground hand raises his chequered flag, and – in the blowing of a whistle, the dazzling of six hundred LEDs – we're off.

Remy pushes forward in his little car as I cling on for dear life, head spinning and vision all a blur as we erupt out of our safety net.

I can barely see where we're going, holding on blindly as Nima shrieks and Matt yells "tally-ho!" over and over again, and Remy spins us into the centre of the arena. We're being hit from all sides, body jolting up and down, sidewards and back again, head coming loose as we go round and round and round and round –

There's an almighty crash as the car carrying Mike and Steph bumps into us, and Steph cries out in pain. I open my eyes just a crack to see her point a water-gun in my face – I have no idea where she got it from – before she absolutely drenches me, and Remy bursts forward as fast as is physically possible.

"I'm soaked!" I screech, only to hear Steph cackling with laughter in the background. "Go get her, Remy!"

And so we surge forward again, this time hitting Nima and Matt square in the chest of their monkey cart, just as the whistle goes again and the arena slows to a holt.

"Have your opinions of rides changed yet?" Remy asks, wrinkling his nose as he reaches down to help me out of the car.

I grin back at him. "Maybe…"

We decide to enter the Hall of Mirrors next, another classic I've never tried. It's *perfect* for photo opportunities. The man taking our money says we have around seven minutes to complete the maze and get out alive, somehow navigating the two-storey mirrored mansion, which is the trippiest thing I've ever seen. We enter as a six, with a few younger kids and this middle-aged couple who tell us it was their favourite attraction when the fair first came to Hull all those years ago. I get my phone ready, camara poised.

The hall only takes about four minutes to actually navigate our way out of, but it's genuinely the coolest thing ever. It's almost impossible to find your way around when each mirror points in a different direction and insists it knows the way to go, floor beneath us even mirrored, the steps upstairs flanked with reflective plastic panels. There's a ramp going downstairs at the opposite end, and even that is covered in a sheen of mirrored material, all shiny, a few bits chipped here and there.

I take so many confusing photographs that it almost makes me dizzy. Mirror selfies, where my reflection continues in front and behind, on and on and on, hundreds of tiny Carmels all smushed into one. Remy, rushing forwards towards himself, hoping to near the corner and find another tunnel to turn down; Nima, in her fluffy coat and boots, brow creased as she glances round at her reflection; Matt, still clutching a few cold chips, so blasé to the whole maze; Mike and Steph, giggling and pulling each other forward hand in hand.

The Ferris Wheel comes after. It's four to a bubble, so Mike and Steph volunteer to go it alone, while the rest of us get in first. It's cold now that we're stationary, stood beside the giant wheel with coins clutched between our fingers and that metallic, fairground-y taste in our mouths, the taste of old gum and too much sugar.

Nima passes me a gummy snake as the man opens the door to the little metal cage he calls our "bubble". We step inside. Matt and I take one bench, Remy and Nima opposite, as the Ferris Wheel jolts to a start and we take a steady step upwards, into the sky.

The moment we leave the ground, everything changes.

Hull stretches out below us in a mismatch of tacky new-builds, dodgy alleyways and battered vehicles, buses moving to and from, trees darkening corners where no light can penetrate. We're silent as we stare out into the city, my house right at the other side, on the outskirt, huddled between the Acharya family and Mrs Dichre, squashed – front door closed, Mum asleep on the sofa, no doubt content from spending the day with Ravi – on our quiet, suburban street.

And there, in the centre of our eyeline, Hull Fair is laid out in a splattering of bright colours and garish, over-the-top signs, all flashing lights and loud music, drifting towards us in a mismatch of sounds. Something One Direction bursts from just below us, and tacky Justin Bieber floats from across the fairground, where two teens are trying to shoot targets with plastic BB guns.

I take in a deep breath, letting my eyes wander. My phone has been snapping photographs all night, but – after I take a few absentminded ones, barely examining what's in the frame – I let it drop into my pocket and focus on inhaling the scene through my eyes, nose and mouth instead, completely absorbed by the moment. Matt and Nima are pointing out funny bits and laughing to themselves as we rise up, up, up, but Remy and I are silent, fixated on the ground below.

When I feel a hand touch my knee, I instantly flinch. But when it starts to circle, thumb and forefinger moving slowly around my kneecap, I relax a little and focus on the sky, the stars and smoke and wandering fried food smell. All the while, Remy strokes me, hand shifting higher and higher, just like the Ferris Wheel.

carmel

Remy's friends and I spend the rest of the evening whirling round the fairground, taking photos with our arms around each other and shrieking in delight as the rides whirl us round and round and round until we're dizzy. Nima tells me all about the time she threw up on her Hello Kitty t-shirt and brogues, and Matt shows me pictures on his phone of their friend Lily when she accidentally spun too far on the Crazy Mouse and ended up disorientated for the rest of the night.

"It was the only ride we could persuade her to go on, and it completely ruined her!" he explains, snorting with laughter. "We all had to help her get on the bus home, it was that bad…"

It seems Lily is the sixth part of their friendship group, but she isn't here now… I am. I can't help but wonder why. I note their shifty expressions and little coughs when Matt brings her up, tries to show me more pictures of her stumbling around that night, videos from his Snapchat memories.

We go on the Waltzers next, an apparent fairground classic. I've never even heard of them before, but Remy insists they're some of the very best; we watch the next group board and spin so fast I swear their brains are going fly from their nostrils, and I snap a few photos as we watch, entranced by the tiny spinning cars. It's fast – very fast – but Nima tells me that's all part of the fun.

"No more than three to a car, please," the man taking our money says, sniffing as the four of us try to board one. "You – out!"

So I climb into a car with Mike and Steph, sitting tight as the man pushes the bar over our chests and onto our laps.

And then we're off.

The Waltzers truly *are* one of the very best rides, as Remy claimed. We start slowly, whirring back and forth, slipping and sliding as we cling onto the rail… and then it begins, truly begins, racing faster and faster and faster, the tiny car gaining momentum as we whirl around the fairground, colours blurring into one and music getting faster, louder, more hectic, the *Jaws* theme tune at the centre of it all. Mike and Steph are screaming in simultaneous delight, and I can hear Nima yelling, "Let's goooo!" from one of the other cars as they follow us. I'm clutching the rail so tight that my hands go numb, mouth closed against the rush of dusty air hitting my face.

We're still gaining speed, tumbling faster and faster through the air, unstoppable, lightning –

And then we're slowing down again, coming to a stop where we first began.

"Wasn't that cool?" Mike asks me, brown eyes filled with wonder. Beside him, Steph is nodding her head vigorously, and they're both waiting for me to agree.

"It was awesome," I say, because it *was* awesome.

We all stumble off together, dizzy now, hands shaking as we join the circle again. I don't have too many coins left in my pocket, but when Nima offers to buy me a root beer to take away the feeling of disorientation, I can't say no.

"This is the first year any of us are actually eighteen!" she explains as the two of us wander towards the food stalls, leaving the others to pick our next ride. "Remy's birthday was at the beginning of September, and mine is just a few days after… though the root beer stands only sell non-alcoholic stuff. But still. The word "beer" is in the name, you know?"

"I'm nineteen in a few months," I say, for loss of any other reply. "It feels so surreal, like I was only a kid five minutes ago."

Nima observes me from the corner of her eye for a moment, before saying, "You're doing an art foundation course, aren't you? What's the plan after that?"

The plan? Ah, yes. My wonderful, well-thought-out plan. I'm trying not to think about uni, about the upcoming deadline for applications. Johnno is still making remarks about the modelling jobs every other night, telling me I need to make up my mind if I want him to contact those people for me, find a permanent placement. I'll need to work on my portfolio, too, but Mum seems to be getting better, not worse, and everything just seems so confusing, conflicting.

"I don't know," I reply, after a moment's pause. "I'm just going to see what happens, I think."

Nima nods, smiling as she reaches into her pocket for her card, the root beer stall fast approaching. There's an unreadable expression on her face.

"Remy really likes you, you know."

We stop at the end of the queue, where there's a chalkboard listing flavours. I pretend to be preoccupied with squinting up at the words, mouthing them under my breath.

"He's never had much luck with girls before."

I don't know what to say. My cheeks are heating up, but Nima must think it's because I like him too. She lets out a laugh and nudges my arm beneath the starry sky, a breeze nipping at my face as I try to avoid her eyes.

"You two would be so cute together," she adds. "Trust me."

But I don't trust her. The fact that Remy's friends – people I was starting to *like*, starting to feel I could be friends with myself – think we're cute together, makes me feel ill. I can't tell Nima how I really feel, what I suspect my sexuality may be, before I talk to Remy.

Yet the thought of letting Remy down makes me feel even worse.

We buy the root beers and take them back to the group with full hands, letting people pick their favourite flavours and settling for the dregs. We're all having a £1 go on the Helter Skelter, apparently – there's no getting out of it. The only other people lining up are little kiddies and their parents, but Matt won't let me leave, even when I insist I'd rather just take photos of the group.

"You're having a go, Carmel," he says, grabbing my arm and grinning. "Let loose!"

Mike and Steph go first, Steph's chubby legs clutched round his waist as they pose at the top for their photograph. They're an odd pair, as friendly as they may seem. Steph's the kind of girl who would've tried to befriend me in secondary school, another loner, the kind of person who gets bullied just for *existing*. She smells faintly of cheese and has muddy dyed hair and pale blue eyes, set on an acne-ridden face. Her boyfriend is just as unique, but they have that lovely, welcoming aura about them, the kind which insists you can just be yourself around them, even if that means acting different, "strange".

They're definitely the kind of people I would've avoided, had I known them before Remy. In fact, I would've avoided the whole group. The only thing worse than being a loner in school was being a social reject. I was never really that. People avoided me, didn't bother speaking to me, even in passing, didn't bother to learn my name, but they still tolerated me.

I was invisible. And now, I feel weirdly… seen.

I stand at the bottom of the Helter Skelter, shivering, as Remy's friends cheer on Mike and Steph. The pair go tumbling down the slide together, snaking right to the bottom with huge, proud grins and bright eyes, as we all clap in unison for the couple's grand exit.

Remy's friends. That's what they are, still, even in my head. Not my friends, yet… even if part of me may want them to be. There's something freeing about having people to joke with, take weird selfies with atop the crazy mouse, share root beers with, go tumbling through the sky with our hands held tight. It feels good to have friends, even though I never thought it would be, never thought I needed any. It feels… safe. Secure.

A part of me doesn't want to get too comfortable, enjoy the evening too much. Once I tell Remy my secret, he'll probably never want to see me again. They're only being so nice to me because they know how much Remy likes me, and are most likely expecting me to become a permanent fixture in their group, his new girlfriend.

Nima goes next, then Matt. We cheer and clap in the exact same way as they spin down the Helter Skelter's candy-striped slide, October wind biting at their skin as they tumble through the night, the fairground alive around us. Then it's Remy, waving to us from the top, and I take a photograph of him, stood there, hands on his hips, as he prepares himself to slide.

He's slower than the rest, being on the bigger side, and

gets slightly stuck halfway down. It doesn't matter, though. The others don't laugh, don't mock him, don't make rude jokes or try to hurt his feelings. They just clap even louder and holler his name across the fair, as he lands at the bottom with a decisive thump.

"Go, Carmel!" Matt exclaims, slapping me on the back to push me forward. "Go, go!"

I pass my pound coin to the man by the door, disappearing into the Helter Skelter. It's almost pitch-black, a few electric tea lights strung above the stairs, which hit my head as I begin to climb. Up and up and up, inside the structure, hands shaking, sweaty palms against my jeans. Dark room, no wind, just endless, stifling cold.

I walk out onto the platform, before the top of the slide. The fair stretches out all around me. Red and yellow and green, a lilac twinge dancing on my eyeline… Remy and his friends are stood beneath me, cheering, but Remy is stood still, staring at me as I hesitate.

He catches my eye, and we share a smile.

There's a breeze now, shuffling towards me and dousing me in cold air, like I've been drenched head to toe. I lower my backside onto the slide, slick with mud and other people's arse sweat, and push my trainers out before me.

The slide goes on and on and on, snaking around the structure like an eel, the kind which lurk inside the water by Princes Quay.

I swallow.

I can hear the others shouting my name, chanting, "Carmel, Carmel, Carmel!"

A root beer burp, burbling up into my throat; hands, still slick with chip grease, clutching my phone as I take one last photo; the cry of a child as he tugs on his mother's hand, asking impatiently when the silly lady will go down the slide so that he can have a go.

The next project for my art foundation, which centres around light and colour and immersion, being completely overwhelmed by the senses a place can awaken. This is what Mr Leam meant when he first explained it to us, Boy 1 and Boy 2 watching on in confusion, trying to figure out how you could capture all those emotions into a painting, translate a scene, a scene you're fully connected to, a piece of art.

I take a final mental photograph, cementing everything in place. I close my eyes, gripping the edges of the slide with all ten fingers, shifting my bottom so that the only thing holding me back is my arm strength.

I let go.

We always have a go on the game stalls as we're leaving. It's a tradition. I'm a dab hand at hook-a-duck, and the others all have games they're particularly good at, except Steph, who sucks at every game ever. We leave the rides behind as we head towards the entrance, down the winding concrete path flanked by stands and food stalls and little children selling glowsticks and flashing neon glasses for charity.

It's evident that it's the end of the fair. Rubbish spills out over the path and onto the grass beyond, crisp packets and discarded photographs and polystyrene boxes, no doubt still holding a hot dog and a few remaining chips. There are sweets dropped everywhere, sticking to our shoes and the bottoms of our jeans. One kid must've thrown his candyfloss into a tree and it's stayed there all night, suspended atop a branch, as he hurries off to buy something more exciting.

"Ravi always helps clean up after the fair," I tell Carmel. "He's big into the environment, you know?"

I still get flustered just speaking to her, and feel my cheeks turning red as she nods.

"I… I think he's said that, yes."

"Do you… go to the shop often?"

Something shifts in her face then. She shrugs. "Sometimes, I guess. I – I don't know him that well."

I have a go on the hook-a-duck first, which happens to be

the nearest stall. Matt jokes that I should win a stuffed duck for Carmel – to which she promptly blushes – and yet, as I grab the rod and aim the first hook, that's what I'm aiming for. A win, a green and brown duck with a stuffed beak and weedy little legs, for the girl who, if all goes well, is soon to be my girlfriend.

I don't get the first duck, trying to grab it with expert concentration. My heart sinks as it bobs away. This particular stand is set up like a little river; the water flows through a trough, rubber duckies in all shades of lemon. I aim for another, and, though I have to reach right across, jumper riding above my stomach, I get it, hooking it with a satisfied whoop.

"Nine more to go, and you've got the prize," the man says. "Four minutes remaining."

Getting the one duck has given me confidence, and I move at lightning speed now. My friends are all clapping and watching closely as I move my little rod over the sea of floating ducks, aiming for one, two, three ducks, a fourth, two more, then another three.

There's only one left, and thirty seconds remaining. I swallow, reaching my hook out for a final time, trying to catch the last duck, bobbing away across the water…

"Twenty, nineteen, eighteen, seventeen –"

I suck in a breath and lean right over the trough, jumper soaked around the edges. My heart is pounding, Carmel's eyes trained on my back. A chubby boy's nightmare is his trousers falling down, but I can't worry about that now. My only purpose is to get the duck, win the duck, give Carmel the duck.

As though in a sudden change of heart, the little duck stops bobbing away from me. Plastic eyes trained on mine, it swivels, retreating through the water towards my hook.

"Five, four, three, two, one –"

"You've won." The man hands me the duck, and I can barely contain my excitement as he rolls his eyes and takes the hook from me. "Thank you for playing the hook-a-duck today."

"We did it!" Nima exclaims, grabbing me around the waist and – Matt to my other side – lifting me just off the ground, letting out a deafening screech in my ear. "See, Carmel? I told you Remy was great at this!"

Carmel just smiles, raising one eyebrow as I pass her the duck sheepishly.

"That's for you," I tell her, trying for a brazen shrug. "It's kind of cute, I guess…"

"Thanks," she responds, hugging it close to her chest. She's sceptical in her own, cold way, but there's something different in her eyes, too, something genuine, teetering on grateful.

Matt takes on the basketball hoops next, in typical nerdy style. He can't throw for toffee, not even when Nima bribes him with a bag of blackcurrant gummies, because, in his words, "They're Lily's thing."

We watch him win absolutely nothing, creasing with laughter as he has hopeless attempt after hopeless attempt, before Mike steps in to show him how it's done. Goofy, geeky Mike, with his bearded double chin and pot-belly stuffed beneath a checked shirt, actually manages to score at least five hoops, presenting a cheering Steph with a pink teddy bear they name Pickle.

"Shall we get toffee apples?" Nima suggests, and the cries of response strongly indicate a yes.

But as the others are lining up to get their last snacks of

the evening, before heading back on the bus, it hits me.

I haven't asked Carmel out yet. I haven't taken her aside to pop the question, like I've been intending to all evening.

My hands are suddenly shaking, palms wet, upper lip slimy with sweat. Matt is eyeing me in all-knowing insistence. I jerk my head towards Carmel as subtly as I can, trying to tell him with my expression that I need to get her away, need to initiate the next part of the plan.

"Erm, Carmel?" Matt says. "Why don't you get your toffee apple first? Then you, Remy?"

We're almost at the front of the queue now, so the two of us shift ahead of Mike and Steph and head straight up to the counter. The lady has hundreds of apples stuck onto kebab sticks behind her, and is swirling a huge vat of toffee before us, row upon row of sprinkles and nuts and freeze-dried fruit.

Carmel picks a green apple smothered in macadamia nuts and raisins, smiling politely as she hands over her money. I instantly regret my decision of chocolate chips, freeze-dried strawberries and almond butter, as the toffee-apple-lady hands me a stick covered in sticky molten goodness and I realise I'm going to make a complete mess of my face. I try to lick the almond butter and melted chocolate off as we back away, but it only smears across my chin and nose, and I jab Matt for a tissue with the most urgent expression I can muster.

"Just get on with it, man!" Matt mutters, rolling his eyes.

So I do.

"Carmel?" I say, tapping her on the shoulder with my only clean finger. She's stood a little way off, taking photos of the stalls lining the path, as she eats her toffee apple one-handed. "Carmel, can I have a word?"

"What?" She swivels to face me, frowning. "What's wrong?"

"Do you think we could go somewhere more private?" I ask. I can feel my cheeks heating up just looking at her, as my brain starts screaming, *breathe, breathe, breathe!*

"Okay...?" she responds, but it comes out more like a question.

Without saying another word, I gesture towards a nearby chip van, and she follows me as we head behind it.

The back of the van is completely trashed, pink spray paint covering the tin walls and rubbish cascading everywhere. There are two binbags overflowing by the door, which is shut, and burnt chips, wasted oil and bits of rubbery cheese have been flung everywhere by the owners. It's not exactly the place I had in mind for when I ask out my future girlfriend, the love of my life, but it'll have to do. Besides, it's not about where I say it, the surrounding area. It's the sentiment, the heart behind it all. It's how I feel.

How *she* feels.

"Carmel," I repeat, the word getting stuck in my throat, awkward, stilted.

Shit.

This is actually *happening*.

Carmel is stood opposite me, taking tentative bites out of her apple. The toffee is starting to set and her lips are edged in crystallised shards of molten brown, eyebrows knitted as she stares back at me.

"Remy?" she repeats. There it is again, that coldness, the emotional indifference that refuses to give away what she's thinking.

My hands are still trembling, so I push them behind my back.

"I – I want to ask you something," I say. My tongue is dry, stuck inside my mouth like a huge, flabby toad, lodged against my gums like it has swollen to half its size. "It's something I've wanted to ask you for quite some time now…"

Her face shifts then, the cold melting away. I know, then. I know that she knows.

She knows what I'm going to ask her.

I take a deep breath, and say, "Will you be my girlfriend?"

carmel

"I'm asexual."

The words have escaped my mouth before I'm even aware of what's happening. It's a knee-jerk reaction, the only thing I can think to say when Remy asks me to be his girlfriend. That and "I'm aromantic", which just doesn't pack the same punch.

We're stood behind a knackered chip van covered in graffiti, staring at each other, his mouth hung open in shock. His hands are still laced behind his back and he's shaking his head back and forth, back and forth, trying to take it all in.

"You're… what?"

"I'm asexual." It's easier to repeat than to say for the first time, but the confession is still sticky in my mouth, words hung awkwardly between us. "I… I don't have feelings for people. I can't be in relationships."

That's the simple way to describe it. Stating that I don't desire sexual intercourse, that I'm *technically* also aromantic as I don't have feelings of a romantic nature for anybody, either, seems much bolder. Remy seems shocked as it is, and part of me feels awful as his eyes flicker to the ground and he tries to form words.

I'm scared that if he does, he'll start to cry.

"I'm sorry," I say. It's the only other thing I can think of to add, as he continues to shake his head, take it all in. Should I be apologising? For leading him on, sure. But I didn't know for sure that was the case until thirty seconds ago, when he dropped the dreaded question. "I should've said something at the aquarium the other night."

This is going horribly. I'm awful at holding important conversations. I avoid confrontation, emotion; it's a trait that comes with having no friends, the awkward independence I've acquired for so long. I try to shift my facial expression to be a little more sympathetic, but it's impossible when I just want to crawl into a hole in the ground and wither away in a pit of my own awfulness.

I caused this. If I'd realised what Remy was working towards earlier on, I could've shut him down, told him I'd rather just stay friends. It would've hurt him, but not as much as it does now. His whole face is collapsing, eyes filling up as he glances from side to side in order to regain his bearings.

"I don't understand," he finally manages to say, voice wobbling. "You kissed me."

"*You* kissed *me*," I retort, realising too late how harsh that sounds. "Not that it matters, but yeah. I'm sorry. I'm a shitty person, I should've told you earlier…"

"But… the dates." He shakes his head, like he's trying to figure out what went wrong. "We've been on *two* dates, and now this. Why did you say yes if you didn't like me, if you never liked you?"

"Because I do like you," I say, and he glances up hopefully. "Just… as a friend. That's why I said yes. I like hanging out with you."

The first tear breaks. It slips down the side of his face and snakes beneath his chin, dripping into the collar of his jumper, before he has time to reach up and wipe his face.

"I'm sorry if I misled you," I repeat, though my own face is burning now.

I've made him cry.

I've made Remy *cry*.

But his eyes just fill up again, and this time there's no filter as they burst from his eyes and down his cheeks, dropping onto the floor beneath us as we stand there, still facing one another, swamped in awkward silence. His mouth is wobbling and his jaw's agape, and his half-eaten toffee apple – which was clutched behind his back – falls to the floor with a thud.

"I'm so sorry," I repeat. "I really am, Remy."

He just shakes his head for the third time, harder now. "You're not though, are you?"

But I am. I feel for Remy so much that it scares me, makes me feel far too exposed, stripped bare. I like him... I *really* like him. I've never had a proper friend before, and now, on the brink of losing six new people I've started to like, properly like, it hits me how much I don't want to be friendless, how much I want to change.

Remy and the others are lovely, genuinely lovely. They're the kind of people I'd have once judged before bothering to get to know them, the way I did Remy, all those weeks ago. Nerdy, pathetic, childish. He's none of those things, and I'm only realising that now.

But it's too late. Remy isn't just hurt, but angry, fists shaking by his sides. I reach out to try and grab one, hoping a comforting squeeze will help, but he pulls away at once. His eyes are still shining, but there's something else inside of them now, something ablaze behind that warm blue, a hue of anger, of vibrant orange fire.

"I'm sorry," I repeat, but Remy takes a step back, as though disgusted by me. He spits on the dusty ground, the glob landing atop a cold chip, as though proving a point.

"You've just been using us, haven't you?" he says, in such a cold, matter-of-fact way that I can't help but I blink, taken aback by his forwardness. "You've got no friends, so you've been using me to make your social life more exciting, haven't you?"

"That's ridiculous," I reply, though my voice is now shaking too. I'm hurt that he'd even assume that, that he now thinks so lowly of me that he'd accuse me of *being* like that. "If I wanted friends, I'd make friends. You're… different."

"Not different enough, clearly." He stops himself then, as though he was about to say more. We both pause, staring at each other for one final time, eyes locked together. "Thanks a lot, Carmel. Thanks a lot."

Then he turns around and disappears back into the fairground, leaving me alone with an old chip van and a discarded toffee apple, lying on the floor beside me.

remy

Everything hurts. My mind, my head, my hands, my fingertips, my freezing cold feet, tucked into my trainers. Sobs are scratching at my throat, dying to get out. I want to be sick, *need* to be sick, to purge the rush of emotions I've been smacked in the face with.

Carmel doesn't like me.

Carmel *never* liked me.

She's asexual.

She can't like me, ever.

It's that fact that dances through my mind over and over again, stark red and mocking, repeating the fact that I just got rejected, that I'm a massive failure, that I'll never find love –

"Remy?" Nima grabs me as I emerge from behind the chip van. Her face falls as she wraps her arms around me, holding tight. "Remy, what's wrong? What happened?"

"I made a fool of myself, that's what happened." I stop, heart still racing as I steady myself and allow Nima's arms to encompass me, holding me still. "She doesn't like me, she never even did, I've just been so naïve and stupid and –"

"Whoa," Nima holds a hand out to stop me, raising an eyebrow. "You're not stupid! What did she say?"

But I can't repeat it, can't say those treacherous words out loud.

It'll make it all feel real.

"We need to go home," I say instead, shaking my head. "I need to leave, Nima, please."

Matt, Mike and Steph have noticed us now, exchanging worried glances. Matt senses the problem straight away. He's there in a flash, hugging me from my other side, warm and reeking of candyfloss as he and Nima clutch me tight and just stay there, holding me still, before I'm ready to speak again.

"Home," is all I can say.

Home.

We leave the park, hurrying between dwindling fairgoers to catch the next bus. Nima has the timetable up on her phone and Matt is right beside me still, Mike and Steph leading the way, barging through people in order to escape. My friends don't need to ask more, to say anything else. They just know, understand, without having to try.

The buses are still dropping in and out of the space, passengers climbing off with pockets full of loose coins and disposable camaras tucked up their sleeves, excited for the evening to begin, despite ours already ending. We get seats right at the back, piling on top of one another before the bus sets off again. I'm right by the window, face pressed up against it as the vehicle below lets out a steady gasp of smoke and trundles off down the road, slowly gaining speed as we leave the fairground behind. Long gone is the fried onion smell, the tacky Justin Bieber songs and bright lights. Long gone is Carmel, still stood behind that ruined chip van with my toffee apple corpse.

"Just try get some sleep, we'll be back at the station soon."

Sleep? I know Nima means well, but I *can't* sleep, not now, not ever. I feel like my heart has been split in two, shattered by the weight of two words, seemingly simple, holding my entire world up.

I'm asexual.

I've never really heard of the term before, apart from in school biology lessons. Carmel said it means she can't like people, doesn't want a relationship, and that sort of rings a bell. We had to list every sexuality we could think of in a year ten ethics lesson, and I remember one girl, maybe Rosie Abara, someone like that, telling us – in confidence – that her cousin had come out as asexual. I didn't understand what it meant, not really.

Carmel is asexual. She never had even a shred of a crush on me, never entertained the idea of being mine. I remember what she said about the kiss we shared, beside the penguin tank…*You kissed me.*

You kissed me.

I kissed *her*, not the other way round.

Maybe that's why she's never had a boyfriend before, never experienced attraction, is so cold towards affection, refuses to send kisses in messages, instead resorting to full stops and question marks.

She's asexual.

She doesn't like me.

She never *did.*

I'm still facing the window, my friends silent beside me. The bus is pretty empty as we head back into the city centre, most people are still enjoying the fair, tumbling through the sky on dangerous rides and rushing through the Hall of Mirrors with chips still churning around their bellies.

We need to catch the train back.

Carmel, somewhere, needs to get home to her mother.

I squeeze my eyes shut, swallowing back a lump in my throat. The pain in my chest is only getting worse, sending jolts across my body, my mind, my arms and legs and face.

My eyes ache, nose is running, tongue feels swollen and bulbous against my foul-tasting mouth…

And Carmel is still etched across the insides of my eyelids, those brown eyes and long lashes, dusted with mascara, and her tongue, stuck out over her bottom lip.

Why did it have to be her? Why?

Why did I have to fall for a girl who will never like me back, however much I want her to?

Anybody. It could've been *anybody.*

It could've been Lily.

My heart stops beating for a second, then.

Lily.

Lily, who has a crush on me, who has done for years, who – for some weird, weird reason – likes me as more than just a friend.

Lily, who wants me to be her partner, just like I wanted Carmel to be mine.

I should like Lily. She's pretty, friendly, smart, has loads in common with me… and she likes me back.

Lily.

Lily.

remy

I get off the train at Vibbington station and say goodbye to my friends straight away. Nima is watching me carefully as I wave, noticing the glint in my eye, the wistful expression, realising I know something she doesn't, something she probably should've figured out by now.

"See you, mate," Matt says, turning to head in the opposite direction. "Don't let it get you down, okay? There are other fish in the sea."

There are, of course there are. There are fish which are better than Carmel, so much better, and I've just been too blind to see that.

"Remy?"

Matt, Mike and Steph have already started walking off, but Nima calls me back. It's starting to drizzle now, miserly droplets hitting my hair and face and bright yellow jumper, splattering it with shades of ochre.

"Remy?" she repeats, jogging to catch up with me. I turn, eyes meeting hers, as she reaches out to grab my arm. "Don't do anything stupid, yeah? Just… be careful."

Careful? I'm always careful. But I know what Nima's afraid of. She's afraid I'll rush to the outskirts of Vibbington and throw myself off the bridge there, in a way not unsimilar to another girl we once knew, just a month ago. She's afraid this will tip me over the edge and I'll leave her, that this is the last time she'll see me, stood beneath the streetlights on the high street in the fucking freezing cold.

"I'm okay, promise." I move my hand to find hers, and squeeze tight. "I'll message you tomorrow, yeah?"

"Okay," Nima says, nodding. "Okay." Then she cocks her head to one side and adds, "Are you going straight home?"

I can't lie to her.

"I… I have somewhere to stop off first," I explain, letting go of her hand. "Then I'll be going straight home, yeah."

She just watches me for a second longer, not saying anything. Then she nods, taking a step back and holding her hand up in a final, solitary wave. It's a wave which says she's giving up, that she's done enough.

I turn, starting to head down the rain-lined pavements, into the centre of town. Where I'm headed is just a few streets away from here, a street lined with semi-detached new-builds and fancy SUVs, but the rain is pummelling harder, smacking my head, arms, hands, feet. It's ice cold and feels like nasty, sticky stuff, and so I'm running now, faster and faster, trying not to get wet, though I'm hoping it won't matter anyway.

The shops along the high street are closed as I pound past them, feet heavy on the ground. There are a few teens lingering outside the bakery, and a man with a bright purple nose hobbles across the road towards me with a walking stick. I dodge him and continue running, down the side street towards the supermarket.

The house I'm heading towards has a bright red front door and orange curtains in the living room, the epitome of bright and cheerful. There are shoddily carved pumpkins on the doorstep, and a plastic bat hangs above the door. The lights downstairs are all turned low, TV off, but there's a light in the upstairs window, and I can just make out the baby blue cloud blinds, halfway down, and the lightshade shaped as Shakespeare's Globe Theatre, before I press the doorbell and step back.

I'm shivering, soaked to the skin with sticky, ice-cold rain, dripping down my nose and onto my mouth. I push my hands up my sleeves to form balls and huddle into myself as I wait, eyes fixed on the letterbox.

There's a slight movement through the frosted glass, and a body shifts, a sliver of black against the light.

The door handle rattles, rain still falling as I step away from the porch and let it drip, a fair distance from the door.

It opens, and Lily's head appears at the crack.

"Re… Remy."

We just stare at each other for a moment, eyes latched together. I'm numb, frozen. Lily's expression is teetering on shocked, but she steps back and pulls open the door a little more, hands trembling.

"Are you coming in?"

I take my shoes off at the door. Lily's house hasn't changed much in the last few weeks; it's bright and cheery, all colour and light and paintings strung along the stairs on a washing line, no doubt made by Lily's ten-year-old twin sisters, Amy and Daisy, and little Chester, the baby.

Lily herself is dressed for bed, all monkey onesie and fluffy socks, curls sticking from the top. She's shifting from foot to foot, cheeks pink, as I hover in the doorway.

"My parents are out," she says, the words slow, deliberate. "They're at a charity do. I didn't go because I'm looking after the littles."

That's what she calls her siblings – the littles.

"What time will they be back?" It's pointless conversation, conversation for the sake of conversation, just to fill the gaps.

We're skirting round the truth, the thing we're avoiding, the questions which need to be asked, answered.

"Soon," she says. "Shall we go upstairs?"

I follow her up onto the landing, where the doors to her siblings' bedrooms are firmly shut. Amy and Daisy appear to be watching something screechy on YouTube, but there's no sound coming from Chester. He's probably fast asleep by now.

"Come in," she says, pushing open her bedroom door with a fluffy-socked foot. "I need to tidy up a bit…"

In the seven years I've known Lily, her bedroom has never changed. The literature quotes still plaster the walls, and her Shakespeare lampshade has only faded, still the same iconic shape it was on the day she bought it. There are teddies all over her bed and books crammed into the bookcase, of which she's had to make extra using cardboard boxes from the school recycling bins.

She crawls onto her bed in her monkey onesie and pats the space beside her, all blue eyes and blonde curls and pink cheeks, nose quivering. I sit beside her, hands folded atop my lap.

We're silent for a moment longer, the air between us thick with tension.

Then Lily asks, "Why are you here?"

Why am I here? That's what *I* want to know. Why I felt so compelled to come here tonight, to see my best friend, to find out whether she truly does have a crush on me, whether Nima was right.

Instead, I reply with, "To say sorry."

Lily cocks her head, glancing at me for a moment out of those huge eyes, before they flicker down to the duvet between us.

"You don't have to say sorry," she says, shaking her head. "I was the one pushing you out. It just... hurt too much, hearing you talk about her, hearing everyone say how much you liked her, how great you'd be together."

"We should've been more sensitive," I say. My heart is beating faster now, trying to fully absorb the weight of her words. *It hurt too much, hearing you talk about her.* It hurt her because she likes me, because she wants me to be with her, not Carmel.

She likes me.

She really likes me.

"You weren't to know," she replies. Her face is a deep red, positively burgundy. She plays with a loose thread on her fluffy sock as she tries not to look at me, nose all scrunched up. "I... never told you how I felt. And I should've done, before it was too late."

"Too late?" My words are barely audible, just a breath from silent. Lily looks up at me again, and this time I can't shift her gaze.

"Too late," she echoes. "Before you met Carmel, and I lost my chance."

"You haven't lost your chance." I almost think she doesn't hear me. There's no response, no shift in her expression, as we sit there on the bed, eyes locked together. "I said you haven't lost your chance, Lil."

"I heard what you said."

I daren't move. My chest is tight as she tilts her head forward just a little, so that I can feel her warm breath against my face.

Slowly, inch by inch, she leans into me. Her hands are white and slender as they reach out and take hold of the edge of my jumper, the jumper she ordered on Etsy, the jumper with the little cartoon face plastered to the yellow fabric. She gives me a look I immediately recognise, one which asks, innocently, "Is this okay?"

I can only nod as she lifts the jumper upwards, ever so carefully, over my head and onto the duvet beside us. She's even closer now, radiating heat from her monkey onesie.

"You're all wet," she tells me, like it's an excuse.

I can't remember the last time I was this bare around another person. I avoid swimming pools, beaches, family holidays which involve the sun and the sky and any kind of water. I daren't look down, scared of my rolls, of the moles on my belly, the sparse hairs decorating my chest and skirting my belly button –

"But… I'm hideous," I whisper. I don't need to say anything more.

She understands completely.

As though as a response, she presses her lips against mine. Unlike my kiss with Carmel, it doesn't send my heart into overdrive, doesn't cause my heart to palpitate, my whole body to tremble with pleasure. It's just… nice. Warm, and soft, and safe, like – even though she doesn't know what she's doing, neither of us do – it's perfect, because she's my best friend, and she knows me better than anybody.

Her kiss moves down then, onto my chin, my jaw, my neck. I can't help but close my eyes then, unable to keep them open any longer. I'm exhausted, but Lily's kisses are like a spell, wooing me to sleep, unable to even moan as her lips move down to my collarbone and beyond, as light as she can.

My best friend is careful, cautious, as her hands reach up towards the zip of her own onesie. Lily has never had a boyfriend before, hasn't kissed anybody until tonight, as far as I'm aware.

It somehow feels… *right* that it was me, that we've gone through everything together to arrive at this moment, and all of our firsts – first kiss which means something, first moment of intimacy – are with each other, our best friends.

I swallow, heart pounding faster, harder, as she tugs on the zip and lets it slide down towards her knickers. They're pink, patterned with daisies. I can barely breathe as she slips the onesie over her shoulders and onto the bed behind her, landing against the duvet with a thud.

And there she is, my best friend, the girl I've known for seven years, better than anybody else. She's pale and smooth and slender, completely bare before me, just her body and mine, facing one another, so many unanswered questions diving between us.

She takes my hand, still breathing so lightly, and lifts it. Gently, slowly, to press down on her breast. I let out a shuddery sigh, unable to help myself, as I feel her beneath me, Lily, the first girl I've seen this up close. I close my eyes as she moans.

Her hand is once again on mine, leading me down to her knickers, to those daisies and the bow. She wriggles out of them, and then it's just me and her, nothing to separate us, and I don't know how to react, what to say, whether there are even any words on the planet to describe how I'm feeling right now, how fast my heart is beating, how hot I am, boiling from head to toe.

Lily looks perfect. In this moment, I don't understand why I've never noticed that before.

"Your turn," she whispers, breath hot against my nose.

She undoes my belt for me, those tiny fingers nifty and quick, pulling it out of the holders and deserting it on the floor below. She tugs down my trousers, my boxers, eyes not lingering, careful not to make me even more self-conscious, to respect my privacy, even though we've already gone way beyond that now.

We're still upright on her bed, both of us completely bare. It doesn't feel wrong, doesn't feel dirty, but just… special. Intimate. Like this was what was meant to happen all along.

I lie back, just resting my head against the pillow behind me. She's so light, so nimble, as she climbs on top of me. Her face is pressed against my chest and her hands are resting on my thighs, ever so slightly. When she breathes in, my heart, I swear, completely stops beating for a second. My eyes are fully closed against her bedroom, our childhood, and I'm completely focused on the feeling of her body against mine.

I don't know how much time passes, how long Lily's fingers roam across me, finding the nooks and crannies I've always been afraid of, the parts of myself I've always tried to hide. With Lily, there's no need to be ashamed. She makes me feel so comfortable, so safe, the way she has done since the day we first met, in year seven English class.

"I love you, Remykins," she murmurs, cheek hot against my chest. "I love you so much."

"I love you too," I say, voice all breathy, already feeling myself drift, letting sleep take me…

Because I do love Lily.

She's my best friend.

carmel

When Remy leaves me standing behind the chip van, hands latched tight around the stick of my toffee apple, I think a part of me dies. It's hardened completely now, but I don't want to eat it anyway.

He's gone.

He's actually… gone.

I knew telling him the truth wouldn't be fun, but it feels like I've ruined everything. My friendship with Remy, my relationship with his friends, Nima and Matt and Mike and Steph, all of whom seemed to like me. He'll be on the other side of the chip van now, telling them all my secret, admitting that I rejected him, that I didn't say yes to being his girlfriend like he – and they – were expecting.

"She's asexual," I imagine him saying, shaking his head in disgust. "She's been leading me on all along…"

Because that's how he feels. Like I should've told him the truth earlier, should've realised that our little meetings were dates, not just two friends hanging out. Only I couldn't have told him, not when I didn't have a clue myself. I've only recently realised who I am, and he's the first person I've told.

I need to go out there and smooth things over, properly explain, but I can't, not yet. I'm shaking, feet cemented to the floor as I try and process what just happened.

Breathe. Just breathe.

And go.

I stumble out from behind the van, onto the path leading out of the fair. I glance around wildly for Remy and Nima, for Matt and the others, but they're nowhere to be seen. A slow trickle of visitors are still entering from the far gates, but Remy and his friends aren't here.

They've left me.

No, they can't have. Would they have gone, just like that? Taken the bus back to the centre without me? Surely Nima would've insisted on waiting for me, getting me home safe… or even Matt. He seemed to like me, too.

But the path is desolate, the only people stood around me middle-aged people and screaming children, buying candyfloss and gummy snakes for the journey home.

I swallow, rubbing my eyes vigorously, as though to replace my view with one that's more satisfactory. When I open my eyes, it's still the exact same.

They've gone. My new friends, the people I thought liked me, maybe even would stick around… have gone.

***

I take the next bus home, the one which pulls out of Hull Fair presumably after Remy's. It's pretty empty so I sit on the top deck all by myself, knees drawn up to my chin as it pulls away from the park and back down Hull's wide streets to the city centre.

I try not to think, during that time. My sketchbook hasn't been touched, photos on my phone full of Remy, Nima, Matt, Mike and Steph holding hands, me stood in the mirror, grinning with sheer happiness. I'm getting mud all over the seat from my trainers, and my hands are shaking.

It's not a long journey, and I close my eyes for the most part. I fixate on a wide blue sky, dreaming of escape, pretending I'm a solitary seagull, a seagull which doesn't need anybody, anything, but the wings which help it to fly.

When the bus draws to a stop by the Paragon Interchange, I check out the window to make sure Remy and the others are safely inside the station, not still waiting in the cold or getting coffees from Café Nero. They're nowhere to be seen, so I hop off and say goodbye to the driver, though I feel a little sick.

This wasn't how I was expecting the night to end.

I decide to catch another bus home, rather than walk. I really don't feel up to navigating Hull's streets in the dark, and so I wait until the right one pulls up on my timetable, hop aboard. I nap, briefly, too exhausted to sit upright and think.

The bus stop I get off at is the same one I met Remy in front of, all those weeks ago. Superboy. The boy who saved me, who – out of sheer kindness – stepped up to fight off the nasty Finn, with no ulterior motives. There's a lump in my throat as I think about it, taking long strides down the street in order to get home as fast as I can. It's ruined, now. Everything's ruined.

Despite it only being mid-October, Halloween not for another week, the road is already decked out with pumpkins and tiny bats hanging from trees, scrabbling through my hair as I pass. As a whole, Britain is shit at Halloween. It's not at all like you see in American movies, each house decked out with sweets and fake cobwebs, the homeowners eager for trick-or-treaters. Hull's estates are usually only mildly decorated, the odd family putting out a pumpkin or two, indicating that they have sweeties. If there's no pumpkin, you don't knock on the door. That's the rule.

This year, people seem to be making a bit more of an effort. One house has caution tape wrapped round the windows and door, a large spider hung from a string above the doormat, while others have those trick doorbells and carved pumpkins set atop plant pots, garden gnomes wearing witches' hats.

That's the first thing that doesn't feel right.

There's a wind picking up, icy cold, typical autumnal weather. The trees have been malting over the last few weeks and dot the path as I walk through the cut-through, flanked by thick wooden walls, using the flashlight on my phone to navigate the dark. I'm shivering, and let out a squeal as a rat leaps out over the concrete and darts under the fence on the other side.

I leave the cut-through and enter the road just next to ours, where the path opens up onto a brightly lit cul-de-sac, the houses all with lawn-lighting and front rooms glowing yellow. It's a far cry from our row of dirty terraces.

That's when I hear it.

A low beeping. A… hubbub. A hubbub, coming from our road, and beeping, beeping, and a hubbub.

I push my phone away, back into my pocket. My heart is pounding and I feel queasy as I near the end of the street, about to round onto my own. I don't know where the noise is coming from, of course. How could I? But there's a bad feeling curling through my stomach, a feeling of foreboding, a feeling that something bad is happening. Something very bad.

A hubbub, coming from our street.

A beeping.

I see the lights before I properly get a glimpse of what's going on. Blue and white, blue and white, flashing on and off and on and off. Mrs Dichre, stood outside her front door, tears running down her cheeks in black streaks. Mr and Mrs Acharya, taking a break from their baby-making sessions to gawp, shaking their heads back and forth and trying to shield their children's eyes, little Arjun peeking through the gaps.

Patrice, our home nurse, is stood beside the ambulance.

And there, being carried out on a stretcher, moaning and flitting from side to side, completely wigless, is Mum.

No. A roar rips through me, bursting from my mouth and rippling across the street. Mrs Dichre turns to me with her mouth open but I'm already tearing across the road to the ambulance, trainers battering the ground. Patrice spins towards me but I ignore her too, focused entirely on getting to Mum, my mum, my fucking *mum* –

"What's going on?" The words fly out of my mouth before I even register them, eyes wide, desperate. I can't get to her, they won't let me, hands on my waist and a blockade before the ambulance doors, stretcher now hidden inside. They close the doors with a crack as I leap forward again, more urgent this time, the paramedics physically restraining me. "What's happening?"

"Could I have your name please?" one of them – a female – asks.

That's when Patrice steps forward again, putting a meaty hand down on my shoulder and pulling me roughly back.

"This is the daughter, Carmel," she says in that gruff voice of hers, frowning. "She's coming in the car with me."

"I need to get to *Mum*," I say, throwing myself forward again and scrabbling at the ambulance doors, trying to navigate all of the poles and holes and crevices, figure out how to open them. My heart is pounding and I feel like I'm going to be sick, but Patrice grabs my shoulder again and tugs, hard.

"Get in the car, Carmel." Her little blue Beetle is parked next to us. She opens the door before pushing me forwards, and something about her tone of voice makes me comply. "We'll follow the ambulance, and I'll explain everything on the way."

The ambulance pulls out of the street, all guns blazing, as Patrice jogs round to the driver's seat on her huge calves. She turns the engine on with a swift flick of her wrist and the car bursts to life, doing a U-turn and sailing past Mrs Dichre and the gobsmacked Acharya family, right on its tail.

"Your mother's illness has… gotten worse," she says, just as something inside of me cracks.

I knew that was what it must be, of course, but hearing it said out loud, as simply as that, makes everything come crashing down at once. I don't notice the tears rolling down my face until I lift my hands and they come back wet, and Patrice turns to me with the same sympathetic expression she wore two weeks ago, crying in our hallway.

I saw the signs. I should've known something was wrong, but I didn't, because I was so wrapped up in seeing Remy and having fun and being jealous of Ravi, stupid Ravi, who makes Mum happier than she has been in months.

"I've got her wig in the back, and some night things," Patrice continues. Cold, hard Patrice, who Mum and I have never really liked, is somehow now being thoughtful, helpful, and I never even noticed she could be. "I'll drive you back when you need me to, for fresh clothes and snacks. If she's in for a long time, you might need to bring some schoolwork to be getting on with – I think you'll want to be with her."

I know what that means.

This is it. These are her last days.

You'll want to spend time with her, say goodbye properly…

I'm going to be sick, sick everywhere, all over the floor of Patrice's car. My eyes are overflowing and my stomach is churning, all that food from the fair whirring round and round in my stomach.

First my new friends, and now Mum. I'm going to lose my *mum.*

Patrice doesn't say anything, just carries on driving, as I push my head down onto my knees and let myself bawl, bawl until my throat is raw and I feel like it really, truly can't get any worse.

carmel

The hospital corridors are squeaky clean, and reek of disinfectant, old blood. I follow Patrice, who must know the way; she trundles along on those huge, tattooed calves of hers, nurse's tunic wrapped round her like a flag.

"Come on, chop-chop!" she calls briskly. I pick up the pace, trainers leaving a trail of dried mud behind us. "This way, Carmel!"

We turn down another corridor towards a lift, faster and faster. Mum was taken in on the stretcher via the back entrance, an entrance we couldn't get to, so we're confined to chasing them down via the main pathways. It's the ones only the public can use, meaning we're ten times slower than we should be. Patrice presses the correct button and we wait, breaths held, as the lift glides us upwards and onto the correct floor.

"I think I can guess which room they're going to…" Patrice says, beckoning to me. "Come quietly now, we're outside of visiting hours, and this ward is only for the severely ill."

Severely ill.

That's what Mum is, now.

I follow Patrice, properly running to keep up with her. Down another corridor, towards a pair of sage green double doors with those round hospital windows, like portholes.

There are doctors and nurses bustling about just on the other side of it, talking in hushed voices and trying to conceal whatever it is they're discussing. Patrice pushes open the door a little hard, forcing them out of the way.

"Is this where Kelly Reeves is?" she asks in that brisk, dinner-lady tone, no-nonsense style.

One of the nurses nods, then frowns when she spots me lurking just behind.

"No visitors allowed," she says, shaking her head in the opposite direction. "The patients are trying to get back to sleep again –"

"She's the daughter."

Something in the nurse's face shifts then. She beckons to me, and, when I step forward, whispers, "Just a few minutes, then I'll find you somewhere to rest in the waiting room. Pull the curtains round the bed so you won't be disturbed."

"Can I not sleep with Mum?"

The nurse hesitates. "As long as you don't mind the visitor's chair, and you aren't too loud."

I'm grateful… my face is just too numb to show it. But she understands that, of course. It's her job to. She probably has to deal with hundreds of visitors every day acting in exactly the same way, completely overwhelmed, unsure of what the fuck is going on. She'll witness children, grandchildren, partners and siblings, trying to grapple with the fact that this may be their *last day* together, the last few hours they'll spend side by side.

Because this is what it is, isn't it? The end. The last day, hours, or even minutes.

They said another bout of something, anything, would kill her, tip her over the edge.

I swallow, trying to calm my heartrate again. The nurse is

leading me down the middle of the room towards the other end, and my palms are slick with sweat, eyes watering. *Calm. Down.* I need to be relaxed, need to be strong, for Mum. There'll be time to show emotion later.

I try not to look at the other patients as I walk, but it's impossible when they're staring at me from their beds, eyes wide and grey. It's like looking into the faces of the dead. Gaunt expressions, hollow cheeks, black circles around eyelash-less lids.

They're old, every single one of them. Eighty, at the very least, if not ninety.

Old enough to die.

"Come on, ladies, it's time for bed!" the nurse says, clapping her hands together. Behind me, Patrice's shoes squeak against the linoleum floor.

On the bed furthest from the door, a tiny head lies on a white pillow, slightly greying. Mum. Her wig is still stowed in the boot of Patrice's car, and her night things, no doubt just our usual shampoo and perhaps a spare change of nightie. She doesn't wear much else.

She looks so small, so fragile, like the bed is ready to swallow her whole. Her eyes are closed and her face is still covered in makeup, false lashes and cakey mascara and lippy, tattooed arms laid on the duvet before her as she sleeps.

I watch her for a moment, unable to speak. Around us, Patrice is drawing the curtains.

"I'll go and get her bag, then we can remove her makeup." Patrice is acting kind, helpful, a far cry away from the wooden home nurse we've known this past year, the one who was always so distant and cold, who didn't want to get attached. Now – though her tone is the same, and I'm still wary of her tatted calves and monstrous forearms – I can see she just wants to be useful. "Stay here, Carmel, I'll only be two ticks."

And then she bustles away down the ward again, leaving me trapped behind the blue curtains with Mum.

Slowly, I tiptoe to her bedside. I'm careful not to wake her, not to cast shadows over her sleeping face. I sit in that hard, rock-solid visitor's chair and hold my hand out to gently grab hers. Her fingers curl around mine but she doesn't wake, and I squeeze back, my way of communicating with her.

"I love you," I whisper, retracting my hand.

She doesn't look peaceful, sleeping there in the hospital bed, surrounded by wires and blue plastic and sticky linoleum. The muscles in her face are taut, eyelids flickering, and her hands don't look comfortable or natural, laid out like that before her on the bed. She looks like... a body. A greying, bald body, one they've somehow managed to mould to fit the shape of the bed.

She doesn't look like my mum.

When Patrice arrives, she's clutching the black holdall we used to take on weekends away to Filey or Scarborough, stuffed with Mum's blankets, nightie, old perfume bottles, the cheap conditioner I use on her wig. And then the wig itself, in her hand, which she pushes over Mum's head as I start to rouse her.

"Wait a moment, Carmel," Patrice says, just as I go to shake Mum's wrist. "Can I have a word with you, out in the corridor? Before we wake your mother."

She leads me out of the blue curtains, down the centre of the ward, both of us careful to be quiet for the other ladies. Through those sage green double doors, and back into the corridor.

She has her arms crossed and a serious, straight-faced expression, and gestures for me to sit on one of the waiting chairs as she starts to speak.

"I need you to be clear of the details of your mother's illness," she begins, frowning. "You're old enough to understand the facts. Your mother has picked up a bug of kinds – easily done, but virtually untreatable at this stage in the cancer. A minor inconvenience for me and you, but Kelly's immune system is… weakened. Severely weakened. I want you to know that this could just as well finish her off."

I'm silent all through this, focusing on my breathing, my racing heart. Patrice is still focusing on me, and I try my best to stare back with equal conviction.

"Is there any other family you think your mother would like to see, before she goes? Any siblings, your grandparents, perhaps?"

I shake my head. Most of my mum's family disowned her when she fell pregnant, or dropped off throughout the years, disinterested. There's her brother, but he only bothers with us at Christmas, and Mum can't stand him. Her friends, similarly, still send the odd birthday card, but don't care much about us now that we're not party central.

"There is one person," I say, and Patrice cocks her head.

Ravi.

Mum would want Ravi to be here. I know it.

"I don't have his number, though," I continue. "I don't know how we could get hold of him…"

"Do you know his address?" Patrice suggests. "I could go and pick him up."

"You'd do that?" I'm hesitant, eying Patrice warily. But she seems genuine enough, nodding and getting out her little blue notebook to write down where she's going, how to find him.

"Sorted," she says, after I tell her the exact location of his shop, the semi-detached house he inhabits just a street away. "I'll be twenty minutes or so, tops. You go in there and wake your mother, help take off her makeup, try get her to eat something. I'll tell the nurses to bring up a bowl of soup on their way. She hasn't eaten all day, poor thing."

Whose fault is that? Mine, of course, for leaving her while I went gallivanting to Hull Fair. And for what? My mum was at home dying, and there I was, breaking Remy's heart behind a battered chip van.

I make my way back onto the ward, behind those blue plastic curtains. Mum is still asleep, so I grab her by the wrist and give it a little shake, waking her up again, hoping she'll open her eyes and smile at me, that she'll be in a good enough place to talk, help take off the makeup. But she doesn't. Her eyes flitter half open and her mouth twists into a yellow-toothed smile upon noticing me.

"Carmel," she says, voice hoarse. "Get this slop off my face, will you? I can barely open my eyes."

I can't help but grin at that.

I start by peeling off her eyelashes, leaving my fingers rimmed with clumpy mascara and bits of foundation. She won't be needing them again, so I drop them in the wastepaper bin, much to her distress – "They're premium lashes, they are!"

I then take some micellar water, the cheap kind I get from B&M, and start to wipe her face, using the cotton pads from our black holdall. The foundation and thick bronzer comes off in strokes, leaving the white stained with orange and glitzy brown. Lipstick is next, bright red and garish, and still leaves her mouth stained a shade too dark around the edges.

"Where's that bloody Patrice got to?" she asks when I put down the cotton pad and grab a flannel. There's a little sink on the other side of her bed, just a tiny one, and I soak the flannel in ice-cold water, feeling it fall through my hot fingers. Mum is too weak to hold it, and so I wash her face for her. Soft, swirling motions across her skin, cleansing and refreshing, cooling her fever.

"She's gone to pick up Ravi," I say, dropping the flannel back into the washbasin. "I thought you might like to see him?"

"Looking like this? Would I heck!" But she's smiling, despite herself, and I give her hand another squeeze as I sit back down on the hard seat. "You're a wonderful daughter, Carmel. I don't know what I'd do without you."

I want to make some quip, lighten the air, but I can't. My throat has swollen with a lump twice the size of my tongue, and my eyes are glassy as I try for a smile in return.

"You still haven't told me about your evening," she continues, but her voice is weaker now, less certain. "But there'll be time for that tomorrow…"

The sound of the sage green doors opening and closing can be heard at the other end of the ward, alongside the squeaking of Patrice's monstrous feet and a softer, lighter tread behind her. Mum glances up with that hopeful expression dancing across her face, and I give her hand one final squeeze before leaning back and away.

"Kelly!" Ravi's voice sounds the moment he pushes through the curtains, and I hear one of the old ladies on the other beds grumble at his volume. But Ravi doesn't care, and neither does Mum. He takes one look at her and hurries forward, seating himself on the edge of the bed and pressing his lips against hers. He doesn't care about the crusty remnants of makeup still on her grey skin, or the wig, skewwhiff on her bald head. He just kisses her, tongue and two wet lips and rough hands and all, as she kisses him back.

Patrice beckons to me, and I take the hint to leave. Mum murmurs a goodbye through the kissing, but I don't mind; I'll come and see her tomorrow, without fail, and spend the whole day by her side if possible.

But now, it's Ravi's turn.

Patrice fetches me a blanket and cushions from the storeroom at the other end of the corridor, and shows me how the chairs lined up outside the ward can be put together to make a makeshift bed. I arrange everything so that it looks comfy enough before saying goodnight to our home nurse, thanking her with that one word for everything she's done for us.

"Sleep well, Carmel," she says, nodding in her own tough way. "You're being very brave."

Hardly. How can she even say that, compared to what Mum's going through right now?

I lie down, a breath shuddering in my throat.

Patrice barely has time to leave before I burst into tears.

I wake up to a pounding headache and freezing cold feet, stuck out of the bottom of the duvet. I'm groggy, unsure of what's going on, until I register the Shakespeare Globe lampshade and the nakedness of my body, hidden beneath the covers of Lily's childhood bed –

"Oh my God!"

I sit up abruptly, wrapping the duvet around myself to maintain my dignity. I glance around and my eyes land on Lily, laid next to me on the pillow, all bare shoulders and slender collar bone and sleeping expression, blonde curls in disarray.

She opens her eyes just a crack upon hearing my exclamation, and it only takes a second for her expression to mirror mine. Blind panic, then surprise, and finally horror, as she realises she's *naked*, what we did, what the fuck is happening –

"It's fine," she mutters, almost as though she's trying to reassure herself. "It's fine, nothing happened, we didn't sleep together, we're just… naked. I think you fell asleep. Oh, lord, my parents are going to kill me!"

Oh, thank *God*. We didn't sleep together. That was my fear, initially – that I'd taken Lily's virginity, and that I'd lost mine in the process, all because of what Carmel said, how crappy I was feeling. But now it's all coming back to me, thick and hot and heavy, tumbling through my brain at a rate of knots…

Lily, peeling off her monkey onesie, exposing her bare chest and tiny waist, that long expanse of pale skin, going on for miles. Lily, kissing my neck and chest, pulling my boxers and jeans down over my knees and feet, discarding them on the floor, where they no doubt still lie. Lily, her hands on my body, letting her touch me, eyes closed –

"Oh my God!" I repeat, shaking my head back and forth, phlegm rising in my throat. "I'm a shitty person. What the actual *fuck*?"

I can't even look at Lily.

Because I don't love her, not like *that*. I was hurt, and she's my best friend, and it somehow wasn't awkward or weird or wrong, but I still completely took advantage of her, and –

Matt.

Matt, my best friend, who's been in love with her for the last three years, ever since she dressed as Shaun the Sheep on Halloween and looked "beyond adorable". Matt, my childhood best friend, my metaphorical brother, my second platonic soulmate.

Matt, whose heart I've just completely shattered into six million pieces.

"You'll have to get dressed," Lily says urgently, tugging the duvet away from me as I glance up. "Mum comes to wake me up, and we need to make it look like you slept on the floor –"

I can barely comprehend what she's saying. My head feels full of guilt and regrets and there's a horrible, palpitating feeling in my chest, the feeling that I've completely cocked everything up and that this is it, the end, the end of everything, all my friendships and what could've been a relationship with Carmel…

"Remy!" Lily barks, smacking me a little too hard on the shoulder. "Come on, move it!"

"You first!" I retort, perhaps a little too nastily, because she blinks and jerks backwards, away from me. "It's your *room*."

So she bounds out of the duvet, all modesty completely gone. She's pretty, of course – there's no denying that – but seeing her like that does nothing to me. I don't like her, that's so much clearer now. She's more like a sister to me than anything, and what happened last night was just one big mistake.

I watch as she pulls on those bunny knickers again.

I've seen Lily naked. I've seen Lily *naked*.

I'm a terrible, terrible person. Probably one of the very worst, ever.

She dresses in a hoodie and leggings instead of her classic overalls. A brush is tugged through her curls several times before she starts pulling out blankets and tossing them onto the floor in some sort of makeshift bed shape, the kind I'd usually sleep on at sleepovers in the past, though they're few and far between. Then she turns her back and says, "Clothes, Remy!" as I climb gingerly out of the bed.

It's weird, being naked in another person's room. Strangely… invasive. I feel like I'm breaking some kind of law, just my exposing myself to all her teddies and that Globe Theatre lampshade, hung above us and casting golden light over the room. I reach for my boxers and start pulling them up my chubby legs, a sick feeling in my stomach.

How am I ever supposed to look her in the eye again?

I pull on the jumper, which is still slightly damp, and yesterday's jeans. My socks are nowhere to be seen.

"Shall we go down and have breakfast, act like nothing happened?" Lily suggests. "Or I can go get pancakes, bring them back up here with the golden syrup, if Chester hasn't eaten it all –”

But I shake my head. I can't go downstairs and act like nothing happened, like we're completely fine, and never address the elephant in the room again.

That wouldn't be fair on either of us.

“Lil,” I say, stopping her in her tracks. I'm still sat on the bed, and she turns all in a hurry, hand already on the door handle.

“What?” she says. “I'm hungry, Remy. Can we not just talk later?”

“We need to talk *now*,” I say. “We need to get it out of the way, discuss it properly.”

Trying not to look me in the eye, she moves away from the door. I watch as she perches on my makeshift bed in her hoodie and leggings, and starts to pull on her fluffy socks from yesterday, which must've rolled under the bed.

“Here are yours,” she says, handing the socks back to me, as though it'll cut the tension.

It doesn't.

The two of us just continue to stare at the floor.

“Lily,” I begin, but she holds up a hand to stop me.

“No.” Her voice is wavering, unsteady, as she shakes her head. “Let me go first.”

She pulls the socks up around her shins, then opens her mouth and begins to speak.

“I've had a crush on you for years,” she admits, avoiding my eye. “Like, years and years. I think just because you're so nice, and we've always been close, but I never wanted to ruin the friendship by telling you, because I knew you didn't like me back. That's why it was easier to distance myself over the last few weeks, until I got over you. I wanted you to be happy, and I could tell how much you liked Carmel…"

Liked.

Liked Carmel.

As though last night might have changed the fact I'm in love with a girl I barely know.

"But… I don't think it was ever a crush in the way I thought it was." Lily frowns. It's as if she's trying to make sense of what she's saying, knotting her hands together on her lap. "I thought I loved you or something, but I think it was more just this… I don't know, childhood attachment. Because you get me, and I'm not exactly the type of girl most guys like, and I thought maybe I could get you to like me back. I don't think it was really *you* I had a crush on, just… the idea of liking you, how convenient it would be."

And I get that.

I get that, because I feel the same, in a way.

Lily and I should be perfect for one another. We have everything in common, grew up together, have an amazing friendship group we play an equal role in maintaining. If we liked each other, properly liked each other, it would be so easy. We'd become another Mike and Steph, go off to university together, partake in this incredible life which we'd only ever dreamt of before.

But that's not the case.

"I think last night helped me to get Remy Evans out of my system." Lily smiles, and snorts under her breath. "I'm glad it was you I did that with, but… I think once was enough. You're my best friend, nothing more. I think I should've realised that earlier."

She cocks her head then, and asks, so innocently, "You don't have to tell me, but… do you really like me, or did something happen last night? I know it was Hull Fair… I really did consider going, but you guys never asked, so I thought it might be awkward."

That's when I know I have to tell her. She's my best friend, and I can't keep secrets from her. I know that now.

"Carmel rejected me," I admit. "She never actually liked me... not in that way. She's asexual. She just thought we were hanging out as friends, and I guess I interpreted things wrong."

"Oh, Remy," Lily says, pulling a face, as she stands to envelop me in a hug. "I'm really sorry. Really, *really* sorry."

"It's just one of those things," I say, shrugging. And then it dawns on me, how awfully I reacted, how horrible I was when she told me that, how insensitive. "I... I think I was a bit of a dick, to be honest. I said some nasty things in the heat of the moment, then came straight round here to see you thinking that would fix everything." My voice is wobbly, lump in my throat apparent as I try to speak. "I really thought I was in love with her, but I think you're right, Lil. I was in love with the idea of her, the idea of her being my girlfriend, of this big, romantic meet-cute and incredible relationship. I barely even knew her, and I treated her like shit."

"You should message her!" Lily says, reaching for my phone. I can't even remember leaving it on her bedside table. "Go on, say sorry, ask to meet again and explain. The others seem to like her – that's what Nima said, anyway. It sounds like she needs a few more friends."

"You really mean that?"

"You *know* I do, Remy. I'm a good person, remember?"

I glance up at her, still glassy eyed. Lily is so kind, so genuine, and to think over the last few weeks I've been blaming her for acting so rashly, cutting us out. I click to Carmel's profile and begin typing out a message, under my best friend's guidance.

hey, carmel. i'm so, so sorry for how i acted last night – i said some disgusting things to you, and i'm honestly embarrassed by how i acted. i was upset, but that doesn't excuse it. if you're willing to give me another chance at being friends, proper friends, we can meet up this weekend – and this time, i know it's not a date!

"That's perfect," Lily says, smiling as she thumps me on the back. "Hopefully I'll get to meet the famous Carmel soon…"

I shake my head. I'm still stunned by how wonderful she's being, so kind and genuine and accepting of what a fool I've been.

"Are you sure you don't feel awkward about last night, or anything?" I check. "I completely took advantage of you, Lil, and that was a shitty thing to do. I'll never forgive myself – I took your first kiss, and… well, we did other things, and I kind of thought we both wanted our first times to be special."

"I did," she says simply. "I still do. And it *was* special. It was you."

"Why?" I continue. "I don't get it, not when you had a crush on me for so long."

"Because I felt safe, and comfortable, and like I was with someone I trusted, someone who wouldn't judge me. And besides, I think I've been put off being intimate with someone for life, seeing your hairy bum – not something I'll forget in a hurry."

I flinch, but Lily just burst out laughing and thumps me on the arm again, a little too hard.

"Are we not joking about it, yet?" she asks, grinning. "Because in my head, it's kind of just… funny. I mean… I saw you naked, Remy." She's watching me carefully, that playful expression on her face, eyes alight. "You were literally in my bed, naked, Remykins. I almost considered –"

"Hey, hey!" I hold up my hand to stop her, but I can't help laughing now, either, snorting as a burst burbles out of my mouth uncontrollably. In a way, it really is funny – so funny it's almost hard to believe it actually happened, that we actually did that, me and Lily. "One day, we'll laugh about this, but today is *not* that day."

Lily just rolls her eyes, but she's smiling as she throws her arms around me, squeezing tight.

"I love you, Remy," she says, into my chest.

My heart swells a little, hands finding their way around her back as I hug her back, blonde curls all in my face.

"I love you too," I say, into her hair. "Always have, always will."

I spend most of Sunday curled up in bed, nursing my achy legs and scratchy throat from all that screaming at the fair. Mum doesn't realise I didn't spend the night at Nima's with Matt and the others, and waits on me hand and foot, making hot honey and lemon drinks for my throat, letting little Angelique lie in my arms on the sofa as we watch some kid-appropriate daytime TV, the presenters on some Sunday morning cooking show chef-ing up a storm. All the while, I keep Carmel close by me on the phone, should she think to reply.

She doesn't, however. The day passes in a haze of rubbish-y gardening programmes and a huge roast dinner, another one of Dad's famous dishes we haven't eaten since Toby died. His photograph watches us from above the dining room table as we eat, Angelique left in her cot in the next room, a rare occasion. Mum makes us all say grace, a relic from her own childhood, and even brings out a pot of mint jelly from the fridge – homemade, her first attempt.

I sleep easy that night, knowing I've patched things up with Lily and done what I can to help Carmel. I can't do much more until she responds.

The only thing still playing on my mind is Matt.

Matt, my best friend, who is going to be absolutely heartbroken if he ever finds out what Lily and I did on

Saturday night. Matt, who is the most loyal, loving person you ever did meet, who would never think to hurt anyone, who would stop trying to get with Lily in a heartbeat if he thought I liked her.

He's the perfect friend, a total gentleman, and I'm the exact opposite.

I take my time getting ready on Monday morning, hoping, secretly, that Matt might decide to walk alone after enough of my dawdling. I hurry round my room collecting my English books and stationery, scattering my highlighters all over the floor so that I have to pick them up, doing a weird fake-sigh when Mum walks past and spots me on the bedroom floor. She rolls her eyes and kicks one of the scattered pens towards me, which I tactfully deflect with my foot, so that it goes spiralling in the opposite direction.

I don't grab breakfast, too nervous to eat. Matt usually waits on the corner between both of our streets, and he's there when I arrive, glued to his phone. I swallow a long, dry mouthful of saliva, slowing when I start to approach him.

"Morning," he says, glancing up briefly. "You okay now?"

Of course. The last thing he knows is that I was rejected by Carmel, and went "home" in an absolute state. We parted outside Vibbington train station in the rain, where he walked off with Mike and Steph, and I disappeared in the opposite direction – the long way to my house, or the short way to Lily's.

"I'm okay," I reply, shrugging. "I sent her a message, so I think we're just going to be friends now, if she's okay with that."

"That's good," he says, pocketing his phone. My heart sinks a little lower then, knowing that he wants us to talk. *Talk*, instead of just gossip, debate, while he plays his little

Pac-Man game and attempts to multi-task. "At least Lily might want to sit with us again now, instead of those tangerine girls. I should try and speak to her, go find her in the library before maths... I can tell her how much we've missed her."

My cheeks flood with red. It's all I can do not to show how against that idea I am, without him getting suspicious.

"Don't bother," I tell him. "She made her choice. She'll come back when she's ready."

Matt nods, easily persuaded. I don't know whether that means he'll listen to my advice or not, but at least it shuts him up for now.

We spend the rest of the walk reminiscing about Hull Fair, what happened before everything went wrong. Mike and Steph, his hand stuck down her trousers when they thought no one was watching, after we went on the Helter Skelter; how Nima did so well to stay cheerful the whole evening, how she's coping ridiculously well with her heartbreak, and how we're all proud of her; the photos Carmel took, and how we should ask her to email them over, to stick on our pin-board of friendship in Matt's bedroom.

We walk past the smokers, the little year sevens knotting together bracelets made of embroidery thread, the year elevens frantically shuffling flashcards. We make our way through the gates and onto the main playground, down the path which leads to the sixth form block, following tough-guy Tyler Campbell and his new girlfriend Soraya. Through the automatic doors, lanyards swiped, and into the main space.

On the high table in the corner, our friendship group is assembled, as usual.

But there's one difference, one huge difference, the two of us notice straight away.

"Lily's back," Matt breathes, as my heart sinks lower and lower and lower, down towards my stomach. "Nima must've told her, or something." He turns to me, smile a mile wide, as we both take in the scene. "Shit, Lily's back, Remy!"

Lily's back.

I think I'm going to be sick.

We walk over to the table, my hands pressed firmly inside my pockets. Nima's smiling as she talks to Lily, clearly happy to have her sitting with us again, and Matt goes bounding over instantly, over the moon. Mike and Steph are chopping up sausage rolls into bite size chunks. Even they're grinning, on the fringes of our conversation.

I hesitate by the door. A few steps, and it'll be over. I'll have to act like normal, like nothing has happened, welcome Lily back into the friendship group as Nima and the others bombard me with questions about Carmel.

But, just for now, I want a few seconds to myself.

Lily looks animated, as usual, history textbooks spread out before her and an exercise book open on a half-written essay, covered in her neat handwriting. She's smiling, laughing at something Nima says, as she reaches over to steal a chunk of sausage roll. Matt wipes a crumb from the side of her face, rolling his eyes, and she bats his hand away affectionately.

She's still pretty, still the same Lily I was with on Saturday night, but it's obvious now that it really was just the hurt talking. She's my best friend, and she fits into our friendship group like it's meant to be.

And Matt loves her, of course.

He's waited three years to make a move, and he deserves his chance.

I collect my thoughts before breathing out and heading over, trying to replicate that same, animated smile of Lily's, holding up a hand to wave. Something shifts in her expression. The others all greet me, but she just laughs and ducks her blushing head, muttering a half-hearted, "Remy…" under her breath.

"Look who's back!" Nima says, nudging me as I take a seat on one of the stools, adjusting myself opposite Matt. He, Steph and Lily are on the other side of the table, and I can feel Nima and Mike peering at me from my left.

"Are you going to speak, or just ignore her?" Matt asks, frowning. "Lil, apologise to Remy, get it over with, then we can just go back to normal."

I expect Lily to be awkward, but she simply passes me a blackcurrant gummy bear and tilts her head. She's smirking, cheeks still pink. The look we share says everything.

"I've already apologised," she says. "After you guys went to the fair."

I try to play it off, try to act like I'm not getting flustered, and add, "She's right. I went round to say sorry, and we both realised how stupid we were being. It's sorted now."

The others are staring between us, the confusion evident. Even Lily seems baffled, chewing her lip and tip-tapping her pen against the table as she says, "Are we not going to tell them?"

Every bone in my body stills. Matt and Nima have wide eyes as they wait for an explanation, for some drama to unfold, and Mike and Steph go back to their sausage rolls like they don't want to intrude. Lily's smiling in a way which seems uncertain, and adds, "I thought we agreed it was funny, in hindsight? Something we'd look back on and laugh."

I seem to have lost the ability to form words. My mouth opens and closes, like that of a goldfish, as every inch of my body fights to stop my heart from beating too fast and flying right out of my chest.

There's no way she'd tell them, surely? Doesn't she understand that things like that are private, not to share with anyone? Doesn't she see how much Matt likes her, how much she's going to hurt him?

But of *course* she doesn't. Just like I was blind to Lily's affection, she's completely tone-deaf to Matt's.

And as for spilling secrets… I don't think there's anything I don't know about my friends. The day Nima's girlfriend died, before the body was found and her suicide revealed, she came knocking on my door with Matt and Lily in tow to tell us about their steamy make-out session the night before, how the girl had rushed out before they had the chance to go further, and she hadn't heard from her since. When Matt's grandma died, we were all at the funeral; and we were there afterwards, at the wake, when he told us how she'd starved his family of their inheritance for the sake of a donkey sanctuary in Nepal.

We tell each other everything, that's a fact. I suppose, from Lily's perspective, it would be more strange *not* to tell them about what happened.

I want to stop her, want my throat to start working and form some actual, comprehendible words, but I can't. I *can't*.

"I thought Remy would've told you all, to be fair," she says, a small frown playing across her forehead. "Or at least you, Matt. I thought boys had this whole shag-and-tell thing going on."

It only takes two seconds for the light to completely drain from Matt's face. White and gobsmacked, he turns to me, mouth open in a simultaneous goldfish-like fashion, lost for words.

"Not that we actually had *sex*," she says, letting out a short laugh. I think she was expecting something more from Nima and Matt, for them to somehow find it funny, but there's nothing but radio silence. "I mean, we got naked, and I did some pretty nifty hand stuff, but… what?"

Nima is staring at me and slowly shaking her head. Back and forth, back and forth, back and forth. Matt's entire face is lilac, like he's about to throw up, and I'm well aware of how red I've become, cheeks and neck burning as the whole table turns its attention to me.

"How could you?" is the first sentence he tries to spit out, though it sounds all funny, like he's talking through a tube. "How – could – you?"

He just looks so… broken. More than I've ever seen him before.

"It was just a heat of the moment thing," Lily cuts in, frowning. "He was upset when he got rejected by Carmel, so he turned up on my doorstep, and… I don't know, it just happened. And now I'm over him, aren't I, Remykins? I completely got that crush out of my system. I'm ready to move on now, to find a nice hunk to satisfy my needs."

Once again, she's expecting a laugh.

There are no laughs.

"What's the issue?" Lily asks, still baffled. "It's not a big deal. We both laughed about it afterwards, and there are no feelings there. He didn't hurt me, Matt, or take advantage, if that's what's wrong – I promise I knew what I was doing, even if that sounds stupid."

"Just tell her, Matt." I don't know where that comes from. The words are flying out of my mouth before I can stop them, and Nima is nodding to my left. Mike and Steph have ducked down again, out of the firing line.

"Tell me what?" Lily asks, voice significantly smaller.

Matt turns, looks right at her.

Looks at her with the same, wistful expression he's acquired for the last two years, since he saw her in that Shaun the Sheep costume, all blonde curls and big blue eyes and spindly legs in black tights. He looks at her with the kind of admiration you only ever see within a boy who likes a girl, who *loves* a girl, who thinks she's the best thing since sliced bread and would do anything to be with her.

"Tell me what, Matt?" Lily repeats, more panicked now, like she's terrified of what he has to say. "Oh my God, just spit it out!"

"I love you."

The table falls silent.

Lily continues to stare at him, mouth now open in shock.

"I'm in love with you, and he's a dick." Matt turns to me then, pushing back on his stool so sharply that the screech echoes through the whole common room, and several heads turn in our direction. "A dick who thinks it's okay to almost fuck the love of his best friend's fucking life, then try and hide it from me, clearly."

I've lost the ability to speak. The only time I've ever seen Matt this angry was when a bunch of older boys started mocking his Minecraft book in the library, aged twelve, and he completely went for them; aside from that, he's supposed to be the calm one, the one we all know wouldn't say boo to a goose.

Now, his hands are shaking by his sides and a vein is pulsing in his forehead. He looks as though he's about to attack me, leap on my chest and scrape out my eyeballs with his fingers.

"Time out, Matt," Nima says, climbing off her stool and rushing to grab his wrists, holding them behind his back.

"Time out. Come on – let's go to maths, yeah? You're in the classroom next to me."

"It's over," he spits, as Nima starts to lead him from the room. Lily's face is now white, too, eyes watering and bottom lip trembling as Matt is dragged away, still shaking his head at us both, his own eyes glassy. "I never want to speak to either of you again."

Matt doesn't eat with us at lunchtime. Our table is silent, aside from Nima breaking in and stating, calmly, that he's gone to spend the rest of the day with his older brother Leo in town.

"You've completely fucked things up," she says, addressing both Lily and I, like we don't already know that enough.

"I was shitty to Carmel, too," I say, pushing my head into my hands. "I can't seem to do anything right at the moment."

"What did you do to Carmel?" Nima asks sternly.

I flush. "She… she told me she was asexual," I explain, to which Nima lets out gasp. Lily doesn't flinch; she's heard it all before. "I was awful. I didn't react well, and… well, I may have spat at her, just a bit."

"You… spat?" Nima's voice is teetering on incredulous, as I nod and shudder.

"I've messaged her to apologise," I say, but Nima just shakes her head, gobsmacked. "I feel awful about it."

Lily sits with me again in English, though we don't really speak. Mr O'Flannel tells us some anecdote about how he and his old friendship group had a huge blowout in sixth form and haven't spoken since, as though that's supposed to make us feel better, and we're forced to laugh as though it's the funniest thing ever, as though we *totally* can't relate, now that the two of us are back together.

"I never knew about Matt," Lily tells me as we're packing up our stuff. "I wouldn't have said anything otherwise, you know that, Remy."

I do, of course. It's not Lily's fault, not in the slightest, and I think Nima can see that, even if Matt can't. *I'm* in the wrong, the person who ruined our friendship, who betrayed Matt's trust and utterly tore him to shreds. It's me, Remy, the blundering disaster, who needs punishing. Not anybody else, not Lily or Matt… not even Carmel.

Who, on that note, still hasn't responded to my apology message. It went something along the lines of me asking for us to still be friends, of which she clearly has no desire to do.

I'm working that night, so I dash to catch the train as soon as school's out. I can't face the monotony of the bus. I avoid the shop where Matt's brother Leo works, instead taking the backstreets, and arrive to find the train almost ready to leave. I just have time to purchase a ticket and leap on board before the doors shut and I'm trapped in Vibbington for the foreseeable future, destined to dwell on all the mistakes I've made this week.

And where do those mistakes begin? They start with Carmel, of course. With me thinking she might like me, taking all the wrong hints and being so blind, so ridiculously blind, that I cocked up everything. I shouldn't have asked her to be my girlfriend without discussing those things with her first, finding out what she actually wanted.

I shouldn't have asked her, full stop.

Did I ever actually love Carmel, the way I thought I did? That's another question. I told Lily I didn't, that it was just infatuation, and now, three days later, that still seems to ring true.

Carmel was beautiful, talented, mysterious. She was

everything a boy should like, but maybe not everything *I* should like. I accepted her closed-off, ice-queen exterior, because it added to the mystery, to the illusive nature of her personality and image. If I'm being honest, it's those qualities I'd typically avoid when considering what my "type" is. Being open, vulnerable, adventurous, emotional... I love those things about Lily, Nima, the people I attract into my life.

Carmel is wonderful, an interesting person to be friends with, but I'd be lying if I said she was perfect for me. I haven't found perfect yet, still haven't found "The One".

Maybe that's not such a bad thing.

The train pulls out of Vibbington, gliding through the familiar countryside. I check my phone for the six hundredth time, hoping for another message from Carmel, but there's nothing, not a single word. I click onto WhatsApp, then onto Snapchat, heart thumping in my chest. Matt has left the group chats on both apps. He's archived the Instagram posts we were all tagged in, the ones which included Lily in her sheep costume, me and him stood at the beach with a sci-fi battleship moulded into the sand before us.

Matt is gone, *gone*.

The train reaches Hull faster than usual... or maybe I just don't notice the time disappearing, melting away like sand through my fingers. I take the bus to the other side of the city. It's slow, bumpy, and the city is grey and cold around me, made up mildly for Halloween. I spy the odd carved pumpkin or fake spiderweb, a few plastic bats hung from the hedgerow by the bus stop. The driver mutters something about "commercialised shit" as I wave him goodbye.

The walk to Ravi's shop is short, but ten times prettier than usual. It's a shame I can't find it in me to appreciate the autumn colours, the leaves of orange and red and yellow, tumbling across the street like flames. I used to love the feeling of freshly fallen leaves underfoot, the crunch of twigs and seeds.

Today, everything is black and white. The leaves feel like mush beneath my trainers.

Ravi's shop is empty when I arrive, the counter bare. I hear rustling from the backroom and almost expect him to appear with a boxful of chutney held under his arm, but it isn't Ravi who pushes open the door and smiles at me. It's one of his other workers, one who doesn't usually do shifts on a Monday.

"Hey, Remy," the girl says, raising a hand in greeting. "You okay?"

I nod back, dumping my bag just behind the counter. The shop is bare, shelves of fresh produce dwindling, and my own stack of chutneys and jams and speciality products is naked, not a jar in sight.

"What's going on?" I frown, turning back to the girl, who's shaking her head. She's clearly harassed, Ravi nowhere to be seen.

"Ravi has had to take some emergency time off, and I can't organise the stock," she says, pulling a face in an attempt to hide how stressed she's actually feeling. "I asked two of the others to come in later to help, but I just… I don't know where anything goes, and you won't, either, since you usually only work out front, but we're not getting any customers in today anyway, because everyone seems to have heard how much we're slacking…"

"Where is Ravi?"

Ravi – solid, stable Ravi – doesn't do time off. He never lets down the community, even when he's ill. Should he take a day away from the shop, he leaves detailed plans of how to take care of everything, where things go and what needs to be done, which orders are coming in and when. If Ravi has left in a hurry, it must be serious.

"Is he okay?" I add.

The girl nods, then pulls another face, frowning. "He is, yeah, but one of his friends – a local woman, lives a few streets away – has cancer. He usually visits her on the weekends, but she's really ill, apparently, had to be hospitalised and everything. I don't think she's going to make it, so he's gone to spend her last days with her, in the hospital – you know, the main one."

The girl continues to talk, telling me about how Ravi was called away by a nurse on Saturday night and hasn't been back since, has only rung her twice, giving brief, not-very-detailed instructions, but I'm not really listening.

I knew, the minute she said "cancer", who she was talking about.

Carmel's mother.

A local woman, a friend of Ravi's, with terminal cancer.

That's why Carmel hasn't replied to me. She's in hospital, spending the last few days of her mother's life by her bedside.

She hasn't replied because her mum is *dying*.

"Oh no," I whisper, eyes wide. The girl stops talking and frowns at me, cocking her head to one side, as I ask, a little louder, "She's in the main hospital, you said? With Ravi?"

She nods. "Yes, but why? They'll probably want some privacy. If you need to talk to Ravi, just drop him a call."

But it's not Ravi I want to talk to.

"Thank you!" I call, rushing to the door. I grab my bag from where it rests behind the till and the girl frowns, trying to understand what's going on, why I'm not taking in a word she's saying.

"Where are you going?" she asks. "You need to help me with the stock, Remy! The others aren't coming until six, and I told you Ravi wants privacy –"

I'm already out of the door.

Money. I have money for a taxi, I think, twenty pounds or so in my wallet, left over from when Ravi gave me a few notes from the till due to the success of my deal with the local business. I bring up Hull taxi firms on Google and click on the number of the very first on the list.

"I need a taxi on McKing Street, urgently," I say down the line, feet thudding on the pavement beneath me. "I need to be taken to the hospital."

carmel

I spend Sunday by Mum's bedside with Ravi. He strokes her hand and plants kisses on her forehead while she sleeps, still too weak to do much for herself, and we feed her soup together, carrot and coriander, from the hospital's cafeteria. It's a grotty little room and most of the meals are too hearty for Mum, who's been given strict dietary instructions from Patrice. I take a portion of Sunday roast for Ravi and I, while Mum sticks to the soup of the day for lunch and tea, managing a few mouthfuls of cornflakes when she first wakes up.

The pain she's in isn't evident; she's too tired to talk much, to say what's wrong with her, but she throws up twice during the evening, and I think that says enough. My mum is never, ever sick, not even when she eats something dodgy, or smokes too much, or spins around too fast on the rides on Bridlington seafront. This time, it's proper, soul-shaking vomiting, into a little cardboard bucket the nurses provide.

She can't go to the toilet like normal, as she's so weak, but they have a solution for that, too. Ravi and I have to wait outside the curtain while a bowl is placed under her and she's instructed to go as normal, though it must be mortifying to have all those nurses fussing around her, knowing her private business. Mum's a fairly open person, but she's never liked doctors and nurses much. She thinks they're invasive, digging into her private life where they have no business delving.

We eat tea together that night, Ravi and I sat on chairs either side of her bed, taking it in turns to spoon-feed Mum. Patrice has gone home for the evening, but the other nurses on the ward are still bustling around. We're technically not supposed to be here, they tell us. We're not allowed to stay after visiting hours, but they do make exceptions in some cases – like when Patrice has an unexpected soft spot for someone in particular. The relatives of the other ladies on the ward don't want to visit too often, which is why they're still alone at this hour. We, however, are doing a much better job of making Mum's stay bearable.

As the clock strikes half past, my phone starts to ring. I immediately assume it's Remy; he messaged me earlier, saying he was sorry that he hoped he could see me this weekend. I ignored it, didn't have time to listen to his ridiculous apology, not when there are more important things going on.

hey, carmel. i'm so, so sorry for how i acted last night – i said some disgusting things to you, and i'm honestly embarrassed by how i acted. i was upset, but that doesn't excuse it. if you're willing to give me another chance at being friends, proper friends, we can meet up this weekend – and this time, i know it's not a date!

He's right. It *was* disgusting. I don't think I've ever been so insulted in my life, and I'm not likely to be again, not on that level.

Now, however, as I grab my phone, it isn't Remy's name at the top of the screen.

It's Johnno's.

"I'll just take this outside," I say to Ravi, pulling a face. "It's work."

I hurry to the end of the corridor with my phone, getting into the lift for some privacy. I don't press the button yet, instead accepting the call, scared it'll ring off. I've been wary about alerting Johnno to the fact I'll want time off, aware that it's really hard to get models last minute, but he's ringing me anyway, which he never does.

There's pause down the line before he speaks, and I wait, breath held, to hear his voice.

"Carmel?" he says eventually, in that soft, artistic voice of his, one I've grow so used to. "Hey, Carmel, it's Johnno. I was just wondering whether you'd be free to come in tomorrow, work two of the classes? Dolores has a bad bout of diarrhoea, and you're my only hope. It's a class of sixth formers from quite a way off, and they've booked a double session. They're paying a lot of money, and I can't afford to let them down."

Shit.

"I'll give you extra, of course," he says, and I can hear that pleading tone in his voice, begging me to say yes. "If you can't do it, I'll have to hire someone else... and I can't do that without giving your job to another student, Carmel. You do understand that, don't you?"

I do, of course. There are a few girls on the waiting list to become life models like me, and, should I skip one class, he could give my job to one of them in a heartbeat.

Hence my panic about calling in sick this week, while Mum's in hospital. Only with Dolores off sick too, they can't just replace me with one of the other models, not when a double session is booked; they'd have to replace me full-time, sack me from the position, replace me with some fresh-from-college bimbo.

"I'll do it," I say, heart pounding beneath my chest. "I... I'll be there around five tomorrow, if that's okay."

"The class starts at half past," Johnno says, the relief in his voice evident. "I'll see you then, Carmel. Thanks a lot, though. You're really saving my butt."

"It's my job," I tell him, before hanging up.

A few hours of modelling… I can just about manage that. Ravi will be here, looking after Mum, I hope. I'll be okay. I'll be okay.

"I have to work a few hours tomorrow," I tell Ravi, back in the ward. He just nods, understanding completely, and gives my hand a little squeeze.

"I'll look after your Mum," he says, nodding. "I've put some of my part-timers on shift this week, so I can take at least five days off to be here. You can count on me, Carmel."

I can count on Ravi.

I can.

carmel

Monday passes in very much the same way as Sunday. We eat terrible hospital food and feed Mum soup from the plastic bowls they provide, giving her a wash and properly shampooing her wig, setting it straight on her head. I make the most of my time with her, as she's growing weaker by the day, the pain in her body evident, however much she tries to hide it.

"I don't have to go," I tell her, as the classes draw nearer. "I really don't. I could easily find work elsewhere if I pack it in, and then I can stay with you for as long as you need…"

But Mum shakes her head, rolling her eyes in a weak attempt to tell me off, inform me that my suggestion is stupid. "You'll do no such thing, Carmel Reeves. You earn a bomb there, and you love it. No, you need that job – and I'll still be here when you get back."

That's not really the point, though. If Mum's growing more and more ill by the day, she mustn't have long left; that's what Patrice keeps implying, what Ravi was hinting at with his mere five days off. And I should be spending as much time as possible with her in these final days. It's the kind of thing you never stop feeling guilty about, right?

I arrive dead-on half past, once I've navigated the local buses and set things straight with Mum, assuring her that Ravi will stay by her side, keep her safe while I'm gone. I run all the way to the arts centre once I'm off the bus and in the city centre, desperate not to be late, to get the class over with so that I can spend the night with Mum again, clutching her hand as we listen to Ravi's anecdotes.

"You're cutting it fine," the receptionist says to me. It's not my usual, and this woman is thin and sharp, with a face like a knife. "Come in, come in – you're in the first floor studio today. Careful with the students, I think they've had a bit to drink…"

I disappear behind the screen once in the room, as usual. Johnno meets me before I can take any clothes off, shoving a leaflet into my hand and jabbing at the page it's open on.

"Leeds Arts University," he says, waving it at me. "You could do a fine art BA, and I can get you a job as a life model in one of the city's best firms. You just need to tell me *now*, okay."

I swallow, nodding, as I take the leaflet and fold it inside the pocket of my jeans.

"Give me a week," I say, and he can hear the pleading in my voice. "Just a week, until I know whether it's possible to even *apply* to university next year."

"Carmel…" Johnno shakes his head, taking a step backwards, out from behind the screen. "You can't keep putting this off, you know. You have to make a decision, or –"

"I don't think my mum has much time left."

His expression softens to sympathy, mouth opening to say something, perhaps to apologise, say how sorry he is, but I get there first.

"I just want to see her through to the end, then I'll know whether I can leave Hull, okay?"

"Take the week off," Johnno cuts in, holding both his hands in the air. "I'll do the modelling myself, if I can't find a temporary replacement. Take the week off after tonight, and I'll see you back here in a week, okay?"

I can't help but smile as I start unbuttoning my top, and nod, grateful. "Thank you. I promise I'll let you know soon."

"I know you will," he says, turning to leave. "I know."

I strip with ease, eager to just get this session over with. Clothes off, shoes off, pile them up, folded neatly... I remember the receptionist saying some of the students seemed slightly off their faces – sixth formers, she told me they were – so I'm more nervous than usual, but I swallow and shake off the worry, trying to stay calm. I've done this dozens of times before, and I'm going to be okay.

I step out from behind the screen, careful not to look at anyone as I climb up onto the table. There are a few crude wolf whistles and one dick-ish sounding boy telling me I need to shave, but I don't give him the satisfaction of eye contact, instead pulling a pose and keeping it, head straight and eyes unfocused, pointed at the window just behind the central easel.

The class begin to paint, draw, sketch, hands moving and students chuckling as they make the first marks of ink against paper. I'm shivering slightly as I stand there, back arched, and the class begin to create their pieces, blurred bodies moving before my eyes.

There's one body which isn't moving, however. After five minutes of silence, they still haven't put pen to paper, haven't adjusted the easel even a little bit.

I'm curious, I can't lie. I never break my own rules, move my eyes to look at the students, make eye contact. It's something I've gotten good at, practiced hard in the mirror at home, staring at the same spot with those blurry, unfocused eyes, lost in another world.

I move my gaze slightly, just a little.

And my eyes meet those of Nima's.

My panic is evident, as I almost topple right over onto the floor and off the table. Johnno frowns at me, hinting at how unprofessional that was. I'm trying not to look back at Nima, who still hasn't moved an inch, her piece of paper no doubt still bare.

Why is she here?

We stop for a break, and the students start to evacuate the room to get coffee and biscuits in reception or at the Starbucks down the road. I rush back to my clothes, however, wrapping myself in my coat, and call "Nima!" as she starts to follow the others out.

I don't know what compels me to speak to her. It'd be easier if I just didn't, no doubt, but ten times more awkward for the both of us. Aside from the fact they left me at Hull Fair that night, didn't give me a second thought, I want to speak to her. I *need* to speak to her.

"Carmel." Her voice is wobbly. She's unsure of whether to smile or not as she walks over. Johnno, sensing the tone, gives me a little wave as he disappears for his own break. "This is… a surprise."

"I work here." Like that isn't already obvious.

"Yeah, I gathered." There's an awkward silence which lasts a second too long, before she adds, "Remy only told us what happened this morning. He… he was a mess, and if I'd known at the time how he'd treated you, I wouldn't have just left you behind the van like that." She shakes her head, continuing with, "I know it isn't an excuse and you probably shouldn't forgive me, but it's the truth. I'm really sorry, Carmel. Remy is too."

I shrug. She genuinely does seem sorry, too, stood

opposite me with an honest expression and enough eye contact to indicate sincerity.

"I should've realised I was leading him on. I kind of knew he liked me after he kissed me and kept inviting me places, but… I was scared I'd hurt him, I guess. And scared of his reaction." Which was for good reason, clearly.

But Nima is shaking her head, rolling her eyes at me. "You were both just confused, had the wrong end of the stick. Remy is just more sensitive. It's not your sexuality that's the problem, it's him, and the fact he never thinks he's good enough for anyone."

I blush at the mention of my sexuality. Remy must have told her, then. Wonderful.

"I probably didn't help that, though," I say. "After you were all so kind to me, I completely screwed that up."

Nima's eyes open wide as I say this. She starts shaking her head back and forth in disbelief, like she's shocked I'd even suggest that. "Are you bonkers? You haven't screwed it up! We're still your friends, you just need to speak to Remy. He knows he was in the wrong, and he just wants to be a friend to you, like you needed all along."

I flinch. I didn't need a friend – I didn't need anything. I was completely fine by myself.

But I can see that she's just trying to be nice.

"Thanks," I say stiffly. "I do really appreciate it, you know."

"I know." Nima smiles, holding out her arms to me. "Hug it out?"

So I do. I let myself be enveloped in Nima's warm embrace, her soft arms hugging me close, squeezing tight. And it's nice. I'm not much of a hug person, but feeling Nima around me, passing on just a few good vibes from her to me, makes me feel… special. Wanted.

"So you're going to message Remy back, okay?" she checks, giving me a little shake. "And accept his apology? Because he really does mean it, Carmel. He's a good person, even if he can be a little… impulsive, sometimes."

I nod. And I will – once all this is over, and I've focused on Mum, not boys and friendships and drama.

"Good." Nima smiles, giving my shoulder a little squeeze. "I quite liked having Carmel in our friendship group. You slot in well."

And – despite everything – hearing her say that makes me grin, a proper grin, as both of us start to laugh.

∗∗

The hospital is lit up when I get back, the foyer an electric blue against the dark night. It's almost midnight, and I'm shivering as I get inside, making my way up the familiar corridors and into the lift, pressing the button upwards as though in a trance.

Mum's floor is eerily quiet, and I'm far too aware of my squeaky trainers on the floor as I walk past doors leading to staffrooms and storerooms and different wards, all numbered and labelled for easy access. I stop off at the vending machine before realising I left my money in my bag beside Mum's bed, and so I carry on walking, planning to come back later and get something sugary, something to give me a boost.

I'm pretty sure I'm on the right corridor, now. There's a sage green door at the end which I recognise as leading onto Mum's ward, and so I head towards it, sleep almost swallowing me whole.

There's a body on one of the chairs outside, slumped over,

dressed in all black. It looks like Ravi, hunched over, asleep on the little blue chair, but it jerks awake at the sound of my footsteps, head whipping backwards to see me approach.

Remy.

remy

I can see Carmel approaching and stand, feeling myself flush. I've been asleep for the last half an hour, while I waited. She's been gone since four, Ravi informed me, away at work, wherever that may be.

She's still beautiful, of course, all brown eyes and corkscrew curls and angular frown. But it's not a palpitating heart and dry mouth I experience now, as the girl I thought I was in love with comes closer. It's a sense of guilt, of awful disgust at myself, at my actions, as she stops in front of me with her arms crossed.

"What are you doing here?" She doesn't sound *angry*. Perhaps just… forlorn. And I don't blame her.

"I came to apologise," I explain, standing so we're level. I still tower over her when she's stood like that, all tall and proud and confrontational, eyebrows knitted and eyes narrowed at mine. "And… I heard about your Mum, and I thought you'd need some company, maybe someone to cheer you up a bit."

Her face softens as she glances back towards the door, to the ward her mother is on. When I arrived earlier, Ravi introduced me to her, to the tattooed Kelly I'd heard so much about. She looked terrible, all pale grey and exhausted, but still managed a joke with me about Carmel, about me being her *special friend*, whatever that means.

"I… I need to go see Mum, and get some money for the vending machine." She starts walking away, pushing on the door to the ward, and turns back to add, "I'll meet you at the end of the corridor in five, okay?"

It's less than five, more like two, when Carmel arrives at the end of the corridor with me, by the vending machine. She gets a Mars bar and two sherbet dib-dabs each, the kind with pockets of sherbet you stick a saliva-covered lolly into to gather the dust.

"There's nothing better than sherbet dib-dabs," she says, giving me a small smile.

She leads me down the corridor and into a lift, where we glide to the bottom floor. The hospital car park is empty as we find ourselves somewhere to sit and make ourselves comfy, pushing aside someone's neglected hat and scarf to hover above a bench, the floor before us scattered with fallen leaves, sticking to our trainers and the bottom of her jeans.

"It's cold," she says, and we both laugh at what an understatement that is.

We sit in silence for a while, eating our sherbet dib-dabs and watching the road ahead light up with Hull's late-night, music-thumping visitors. I have sherbet all over my mouth and lips, and Carmel's jeans are similarly covered. The streetlights light us up in bright orange as we huddle into our coats and watch the world go round, midnight covering us in that tranquil, evening glow.

"I saw Nima earlier," Carmel starts, and I glance sidewards in surprise. "She was at my work."

"I thought they were at a life drawing class tonight?" I ask, confused. "Did they stop for food or something after?"

"I was the life model." There's a smile on her face as she says this, as though she likes that she surprised me.

And she *did* surprise me. I never thought quiet, reserved Carmel would be a life model, of all jobs – it's so obscure, so random.

"I really don't know you at all, do I?" My voice is a little quiet as I say that, scared that if I talk louder, she'll notice how distraught I sound. It's not heartbreak, that's for sure. Like I said, I don't know her enough for that. It's more guilt, embarrassment, disgust at myself for being so stupid. "I really am sorry, Carmel. I should never have asked you out."

"It was a learning curve," she says, and there's a reassuring smile on her face as she turns to look at me. "For both of us, I think."

I wonder what she means by that.

We carry on eating in silence for a moment, before I ask, "Did Nima tell you the whole story of what happened that night, after we left you at the fair?" I wince, realising how awful that sounds, and add, "I'm sorry about that too, by the way – I was an awful human being that night."

Carmel ignores my apology. "She didn't tell me," she says, "but now I'm intrigued."

It's funny, but talking to Carmel is somehow… easier, now. I don't have to keep up the pretence, act like I'm something I'm not, somebody I'm not, someone better and more interesting and not as weird. I tell her the whole thing, everything which happened with Lily that night, as we sit beneath the stars with sherbet-encrusted mouths. It's maybe just easier to spill secrets in the dark, I don't know, but there's no filter, no holding back. It's like I was talking through a filter before, aware that I wanted to impress her, get her to like me. There's none of that now.

"But you and Lily are fine now?" she checks, frowning. "So *that's* why she didn't go to the fair. I get it. And that's why Matt kept showing photos of her. She's in love with you, and he's in love with her."

"And I thought *I* was in love with *you*." Saying that makes her snort, and I can't help but do the same. "Turns out two of us were wrong."

"So you've ruined your friendship with Matt?" she says, frown deepening. "What are you going to do about that?"

I'm thoughtful for a minute, turning things over in my head. I haven't actually thought about ways to get Matt to forgive me. This feels like the gravest of all sins, the worst of the worst, the crème de la crème of betrayals. There's no way Matt will just want me back in the flick of a wrist, with an apology ice cream or a sci-fi figurine.

"I don't know," I say, eventually. "I really don't know."

Carmel's thoughtful for a moment, crunching on the edge of her lolly. Then her eyes light up, face animated beneath the streetlights.

"See… I've never had friends before," she says, expression still thoughtful. "And I've never had the chance to throw huge romantic gestures. But this needs to be massive, Remy. You've let him down in a way that's greater than anything you ever could have done, and now you need to apologise, but in the greatest, most beautiful way of all time, something that'll completely blow him away."

"Like what?" I ask.

Carmel ponders for a moment longer. It's silent, street before us almost empty now, the odd car flying past every few minutes and pulling to a stop at the petrol station opposite. We're so lost in the dark night, the cold, that I almost forget what we're talking about for a moment.

"Well, Remy," Carmel says, grinning at me through the black. "Luckily, we live on the east coast."

I let her tell me her plan, drawing in the mud before us a tiny diagram with a stick and the torch from her phone, as we huddle closer away from the cold and lick our midnight sherbet.

And everything, for once, seems to be looking up.

remy

Mum drops Nima, Lily and I on the clifftops the next day, on the sweeping hills above a cove. East Yorkshire is blessed with little bays, cut away from the earth and surrounded by white cliffs, the landscape erupting all around us. It's vast and green and luscious, even in October, and the waves crash against the rocks below at a rate of knots, deep teal and frothy.

"It's Halloween next week," Nima says, shivering as she wraps her fur coat further around herself. "You can really tell, can't you?"

And she's right. The scene is like something from *Macbeth*, all jagged chalk cliffs and angry yellowing bracken, the slopes beneath us steep and deadly. It's the kind of place you'd never survive a tumble, destroyed by the tawny plants and branches before you even reach the stone-lined beach below.

It's an overcast day, moody and full of dark grey, and spittle begins to fly as we approach the cliff path. It's narrow and surrounded on either side by thick wildlife, scratching at our jeans and bare hands as we go, following closely in a line. There are metal steps at the bottom, not unlike the fire escape we encountered behind the arts centre that night, and we disembark slowly, one by one.

"Do you think this will work?" Lily asks, pulling a face. I shrug. "I mean, Matt's just so stubborn, and we've really hurt him, that's obvious…"

"We have to try," Nima says, nodding her determination. Matt's even been giving *her* the silent treatment, despite Nima doing nothing wrong. He won't eat with us, won't speak during our mutual classes, goes home for free periods and lunch. It's like he's completely disappeared.

Down on the beach, the sand is soft and wet and cold beneath our feet, like it's been hit by a downpour. It's covered in dogwalkers and families, taking their last few walks of autumn before the winter takes a hold and it's too chilly, too breezy, to get onto the beach.

The waves crash before us, powerful and extreme, a deep turquoise attributed only to the Yorkshire coastline this time of year. There are a good four or five metres of seaweed and rockpools before the sand begins, and we wander over in our trainers and puffer coats, careful not to slip. The sea air is thick with salt. It brushes our cheeks and stains them pink as we shriek and clamber across the rocks, Nima rushing on ahead and standing, hands on her hips, facing the water.

"It's going to work," she says, turning to us with an expression of certainty, nodding. "This place is magical."

We get to work immediately, climbing back through the rockpools and over the slippery strands of seaweed to the main expanse of beach. Lily starts by finding three large sticks, big enough that you can properly draw in the sand with them. The evening is drawing in and thick clouds begin to cross the sky, drawing the dogwalkers and screaming children back up the cliff path and away from our creation. We need to be careful of the tide, Nima says. Careful that it doesn't mess up our sand art, and careful that it doesn't trap us in the cove.

"When's your Mum dropping Matt off?" Lily asks,

frowning, and I check my watch.

"In about half an hour."

We have plenty of time.

We get to work on the next part of the apology, working inside Lily's box with the large sticks. The box is long and thin and helps for accuracy purposes, and I'm in charge of telling everyone which shapes to draw next, how to craft them on the sand.

Nima is the only artist between us. She does it for A-level, hence the trip to Carmel's life drawing class last night, but prefers flowers and portraits, loose watercolour and funny anime sketches. It still surprises me, knowing that's what she does for a job, but at the same time, it… doesn't. I've always known there's more to her, more to her life, than I'll ever know, and that's just one more piece of the mystery.

That and the fact that Ravi is dating her mother, which I still can't quite get my head around.

We work tirelessly for the next fifteen minutes or so, drawing and marking and rubbing the sticks back and forth in the sand, making sure the symbols are clear and thick and deep, readable from high up on the clifftops. The few dogwalkers and elderly couples still walking along the beach avoid our creation, careful not to mess it up with any heavy footprints or wayward puppies.

"What language is that?" one old lady asks, tapping me on the shoulder.

"It's Terminal Partlet."

We're all trying to hide our laughter as she smiles and nods, as though she understands completely, and wanders off with her equally confused husband.

We're finished with five minutes to go, when Mum sends me a text, and I dive into my pocket to read it.

All sorted. Was wary at first but came in the car willingly. No kidnapping was involved. We're in the car park now, am i keeping him here for a bit longer? xxx

"We're all set," I say, and Lily and Nima throw back terrified expressions, faces contorted as we make our way back up the steps, onto the cliff path, towards the car park.

At the top, right on the edge of the cliff, the three of us stop to stare over the edge. There, in clear, blocky lines, are the symbols we spent so long painstakingly drawing and crafting, two lines of apology for our best friend, our Matt.

Across the field, a door slams. And there's Matt, all lanky limbs and brown hair quivering in the wind, as he makes his way over to us. His eyes are all puffy and his hands are pushed firmly into his pockets, and he's frowning, avoiding eye contact with Lily and me.

"All right?" he says to Nima a little gruffly, and she smiles and nods, pulling him in for a quick hug.

"We've missed you," she murmurs, as he pulls back and rolls his eyes.

That's when he sees it.

Spread out across the sand, our message, our two sentences of apology, saying more than any words ever could.

"I…" He frowns again, eyebrows creasing, as he tries to understand what's written. "I don't know how to translate Terminal Partlet."

"Would you like some help?" Lily pipes up, and he looks at her for the first time, expression softening.

"Go on, then."

Lily brings up the Terminal Partlet translator on her phone, tip-tapping with her short, bitten nails. Matt is trying not to smile as he watches her, the corners of his mouth turned up just a little.

She holds out her phone to him, showing the symbols translated directly from the language used in *Back to Terminal Five*, Matt's favourite sci-fi programme, and their meaning when written in English.

WE'RE SORRY. WE LOVE YOU, MATT!

He rolls his eyes again, but it's a less hostile roll now, more of a shrug of the humble eyelid. His eyes flit between the three as we stand there, shivering on the top of the cliff, the message spread beneath us in the sand. I can just see Mum by the car, pulling our bags out, ready to carry over to us. We've planned to stay here all evening, until the tide comes in, but all that depends on Matt's reaction.

We're watching him carefully, Lily's fingers crossed behind her back, Nima and I biting our lips. Matt seems lost for words. He just keeps staring at the message, eyes running over the symbols drawn into the sand, then back up to us, to Lily.

"This doesn't mean you're forgiven," he says slowly, leaning back a little on one foot. "You really fucked me over, Remy, and I don't know if I can ever look past that."

"I know." My voice wobbles a little, and Matt sighs, holding out a hand to give my shoulder a playful push.

"But... I guess we can forget about it for now." He looks at Lily then, cheeks colouring as he tries to think of what to say to her. "And... the same goes for you, I guess, squirt."

I swear she blushes too.

Mum brings over the two carrier bags and tells us she'll be back to collect us in two hours, when the tide gets too much for us to sit on the beach. We have disposable barbecues, sausages and buns, and plenty of ketchup; the four of us, my best friends and I, all make it down to the sand together. One of the symbols has been completely kicked to shreds by a six-year-old with ginger hair and an evil freckled face, but none of us really care. We have Matt back, and that means more than anything.

I don't deserve him, not really, not after the way I acted. I knowingly did things with Lily I never should have done, betrayed him in the worst way possible. I don't regret what happened, necessarily – all of my proper firsts were with my best friend, and I was entirely comfortable around her, perhaps in a way that made me more comfortable with myself, too – but I regret doing that to Matt. As a best mate, there's no greater sin.

I remember the two of us making a pact when we first became friends, all those years ago. A pact to never let a girl come between us, a pact to put mates before dates, always.

I'll be paying a lot more attention to that pact from now on.

We find a little cave to take shelter in, carved into the cliffs on the edge of the cove. We set up across the rocks, setting the disposable barbecue right at the back, away from the wind. Matt is in charge of setting it alight while Nima and Lily cut the buns in half and get out the ketchup. Mum's brought tortilla chips and dip, a little too similar to the snacks of choice at my date at the aquarium, but it's okay. We laugh and joke and take photos as we cook, burning the sausages to a crisp because we're scared of getting food poisoning, making shapes on the rocks with ketchup, playing a makeshift game of Pictionary.

And, in this moment, it's all I want. My best friends, a cove by the coast, drizzle and sea spray and crashing waves, hot dogs and crisps, a too-spicy salsa.

I might not be the most attractive guy in the world, the most desirable. I might be overweight, and single, and spotty. Some might even call me repulsive.

But I'm happy, and I'm loved. I stay true to myself, authentic, and wear my heart on my sleeve.

I'm Remy Evans… and maybe that's not such a bad thing, after all.

carmel

Mum is still getting worse by the day. It starts with the fatigue, creeping over her face like an iron curtain, but that quickly shifts to pain, sharp jabs in her abdomen and legs. She struggles breathing, too, is too exhausted to even cough and sneeze, and sleeps for most of the week, only waking for short bursts.

Ravi and I make sure someone's always with her, of course. He nips back to the shop a few times to check on everything, Remy helping out in between, and I still work each evening, sometimes even doing double shifts as Dolores gets better and is integrated back into the late classes. She and Johnno are subtle, sensitive, as they ask how I'm doing, how Mum's faring in hospital. Once upon a time, I would've preferred for them to just say nothing, but now, it's kind of nice. There are people who genuinely care about Mum's progress, even if they're not the kind of people you'd expect to.

She's still on soup, but her diet is monitored a lot more closely by the hospital staff now. Everything has to have the right level of nutrients, of fibre and different vitamins, of protein and salt and oil. Ravi tries bringing two individually wrapped chocolates, but we have to give them to her with the curtains closed and the nurses are all out of sight, much to Mum's glee.

"You two are saving me, you know," she says, smiling through closed lips.

She knows we're not really saving her.

She knows, deep down, that no matter what she eats, she'll be gone within the week.

We do her makeup some days, on the days she decides she wants to look a bit prettier, perhaps go out into the hospital car park in the wheelchair they let us borrow. She'll insist on me washing her wig and applying her mascara and bronzer, which her hand isn't steady enough to do. I don't mind, of course. It's like art, turning my mother into the version of herself we're all so used to, turning back the clock to a time we were happier, before the cancer took her in its jaws.

I draw her, when she's like this. She never asks me to, but it doesn't seem right to capture the bad parts of her last weeks, the parts when she's asleep, bald and grey and exhausted. My sketchbook is a diary of sorts, a visual one, and we're recording Mum's life as it should be remembered, as she'd want it to be.

I use bright colours and vibrant shades of umber to sketch her in, dulling out the background with black and dark blue. She's swimming in endless caverns of perfect turquoise water, eyelashes thick and long and luscious, red lippy popping against her pale skin, cheekbones defined. Ravi is sometimes next to her, but he's nothing compared to my mum. Nobody is.

It's on one of these dolled-up days that she takes a photo, a selfie of sorts, on my phone. It's in the hospital bed, of course, the backdrop covered in wires and nutrition posters.

But she's smiling. Her eyes are full of life, makeup perfect, wig shiny on her head. She looks beautiful, the kind of person she used to be. The kind of person she still is, despite everything.

I post it to my Facebook page, the one I use for my photography. Mum's face stands out amongst buildings and sea life and pictures from Hull Fair, a rose amid thorns.

None of her old friends follow my photography page, but they're connected to my personal account still. I copy the link to my post and go through my list of friends, clicking on each profile, each woman Mum once knew and loved. I type out the same message, the same four lines of text, as I send them each the link to the photo.

And I wait.

***

It's Friday. Ravi and I are gathered around Mum's bed as she rests, eyelashes pressed against her pale cheeks. Remy, Lily, Matt and Nima just came to visit, and Mike and Steph waited in reception with big bunches of roses for me and Mum, to brighten up the ward.

Mum loved my friends, of course. She was enthusiastic as she greeted them, taking their gifts and trying her best to be polite and engaged and awake, though it was obvious how much she was struggling. Remy was awkward, stilted, and Matt and Lily hung back and didn't say much, but Nima was wonderful. She took Mum's hand and squeezed it as we were talking, a simple gesture which put everyone at ease, and laughed along with all of Ravi's jokes, as though he was the funniest guy around.

And then they left, Remy leaving me with a sherbet dib-dab and a box of chocolates for Mum. They all promised they'd come back to see me in the coming weeks, perhaps go out somewhere next weekend, maybe for food, another trip to the aquarium… yet it was all hypothetical.

I don't know for sure how much longer Mum has left, but there aren't weeks in her.

I don't think she even has the strength left for days.

Her eyelids flutter open now, just a little, bright and watery as she brings herself back from sleep. She smiles as she notes us both sat there, on either side, two hands clutched tight in each of ours.

"A cup of tea," she mumbles, eyes fixed on Ravi. "Go make a brew, will you? I'm bloody parched."

Ravi grins, nodding, but there's a slight shine to his eyes as he gets up to leave, and pushes behind the curtain and out of sight.

Then it's just me and Mum, my mum, together at last, alone for what might be the last time.

"Carmel," she starts, pulling a face at me. "What's going on with you and this Remy bloke, then? I sensed there was more to the situation than your new friends were letting on…"

I can't help but smile at that. It feels nice, being able to discuss these things with Mum again, have a proper gossip. There's so much we haven't talked about these last few weeks, things we haven't had time for, haven't needed to discuss. There isn't time for all that now – but there's enough time for the important stuff, at least.

"He thought maybe we were more than friends, but… that's not happening, now." That's the easiest way to explain it, in simple terms. Remy was confused. I was naïve, and didn't pick up on the signs. And now we're back to normal, the way I like it.

"Why not?" Mum asks, acting distraught. She's watching me carefully, able to read my facial expressions in an instant.

She's also shivering slightly, so I pull the duvet higher around her neck.

"It's complicated," I start. "I… I don't really like guys, not like that."

"You're a lesbian?" The way she says that, in such a matter-of-fact way, makes me snort with laughter. She doesn't look surprised, not angry or hurt and baffled, but interested, like she really does want to know.

"Not exactly," I explain, squeezing my hands together on my lap. I can say it. I can. I know Mum won't judge me – she's my best friend. "I'm… asexual."

She's silent for a moment, taking it in.

And then she reaches to grip my joint hands, using more strength that I've seen from her in days. She just holds them, skin pressed tight against mine, as we both try to figure out where to go now, what the other person's thinking, where this is coming from.

"I also think I'm aromantic," I add, after a minute of quiet. "I don't desire any kind of relationship. This is all very new, and I might change given time, but I… yeah. I don't think I'll ever have a boyfriend, or anything. This is it."

"Why didn't you tell me this earlier?" That's all she says. She's not disgusted by my revelation, filled with horror at the thought of her daughter never getting married, having children, finding love.

She's just hurt that I didn't let her know sooner.

"I was trying to figure it out, and I didn't want to say anything until I was certain." I shudder, squeezing her hand back, by way of apology. "I kind of realised when everything with Remy happened, and I knew I just wasn't interested in that stuff. I'm just… me. I prefer being by myself."

Mum nods, trying to understand what I'm saying. I know

it's not simple for her to get her head around. She's always had a lot of boyfriends, talks openly about sex, loves being surrounded by people. This is new territory for her… and I get that.

"I'm very proud of you, you know," she says, after a pause. "I always have been."

"I know," I say, and the hug she pulls me into is filled with something much more than just affection; a kind of knowing much stronger than just love.

We're silent for a moment, locked in the atmosphere of the ward, when a crash comes out of nowhere. The sound of the sage green doors flying open and hitting the wall backwards, high heels on the tacky lino.

"Kelly!" comes a cry, as five made-up heads poke through the walls of our curtained palace.

Mum's old friends, friends we haven't seen in years.

Our family.

It's January fourteenth, and we go back to sixth form in a few days' time. I've been prepping for our year thirteen mocks all over the Christmas holidays, but today is a cheat day, an excuse to get away from the exam booklets and textbooks and mindmaps strewn across my bedroom floor, covered in Angelique's tiny handprints.

There are new handprints amid hers, now, too – or pawprints, I should say. Mum and Dad decided to get a puppy, Tony, for Christmas, the most docile little darling, a complete sweetheart of a dog. We all agree that there's some of baby Toby in him, a piece of his soul etched into the heart of our new family member.

We're down on the beach with him now. Me, Nima, Matt, Lily, Mike and Steph… and Carmel, our friend and fellow group member, the person we've welcomed with open arms into our lives. The seventh fraction of our gang, one we didn't realise was missing.

She's stood in the sea with Tony, water rushing over the toes of her trainers and gushing through her feet, up the legs of her baggy jeans. Her curls are all awry, Tony's little nose quivering as they stare out into the waves.

Today is symbolic, of course. You don't just join us on a random day in January, months after we last saw you. January fourteenth is when Oxbridge – the universities of Oxford and

Cambridge – announce whether we got in or not, whether our applications were successful. After interviews and tests and tours of the campus, Lily and I received our emails this morning, sat opposite each other in the bed we almost lost our virginities in. She glanced up at me, all big smiles and round eyes and shock, and I just felt... numb.

I didn't get in, of course. It's hardly surprising, not when my mind was so full at the time. I didn't prioritise my future, and that clearly showed in the results of the email.

It's not all bad, though. I'm hoping to go to Durham still, who've offered me a place on their joint English and history course. It's closer to home, to my friends and family, and the course seems even more well-suited for me than the one I originally applied for.

January fourteenth isn't just symbolic for that reason, however.

It's symbolic because it marks two months since Carmel's mum died.

The fourteenth of November, 2019. I was at home, changing Angelique's nappy, while Mum and Dad were changing the upstairs beds and hoovering all the carpets, when the text came through. It was from Ravi. Kelly Reeves had taken her last breath at quarter past five, on the dot. They were already starting to plan the funeral.

We all went, of course. Matt, Lily, Nima and I, huddled into Mum's car as she drove us to the crematorium. Mike and Steph, who met us there, stood with Ravi at the door. And Carmel, walking behind the coffin as it was carried up the hall and pressed onto the table at the very front, where it stayed until it was taken away to be burnt, burnt to a crisp.

I think that was the hardest part for everyone.

It was a well-planned funeral, if that's even a thing. Much,

much better than the one we attended for Nima's ex, who had an expensive, impersonal service at one of the churches in town. This was different. Carmel planned everything to the very last detail, thinking of the flowers and music she loved, making artwork and instructing everybody to wear colourful clothing and bright suits, like her mum would've wanted. And it worked, in a way. It felt like a celebration of Ms Reeves' life rather than a sad event, a time to mourn.

After the funeral, Carmel moved in with Nima. Her parents are away a lot on business, and she has a huge house that's barely occupied, hence us using it so often for sleepovers. It's only temporary, until Carmel gets her student loan and moves off to university. She still travels into college every day, working at the arts centre in the evenings, but she's been offered an unconditional offer at the University of Newcastle to study fine art, and it's clear to everybody that she's ridiculously excited.

Newcastle is only a half hour from Durham, too. And that's part of the reason I'm glad I didn't get into Oxford after all.

I watch as Carmel moves forward, jeans dragging in the water. We're much better friends now than we were before everything happened. Much closer, more open. She spends most of her spare time with our group, when she's not back in Hull or visiting her mum's headstone at the cemetery. I'm practically always at Nima's, revising or baking or lounging about watching TV. Mike and Steph join us occasionally, but they're mostly busy doing couple things... as are Matt and Lily.

I first suspected she might like him back in mid-November, before the funeral. It was inevitable, really – they're made for each other, anybody can see that. It was

Nima who informed me they'd been on a few dates, started hanging out without us all, and now it's a given that they're an item, without either of them having to spill the beans.

Lily's going off to Oxford if her exam results go to plan, and Matt's following her down south, with a place at the University of Reading to study sociology. Their unis are pretty close, which he insisted is purely coincidental. I'm sure all of us would beg to differ.

They're wandering off together now, down the beach, hand in hand, Matt laughing out loud at something Lily's saying. Nima is wading out to join Carmel, splashing through the waves in her wellies to reach our new friend, and Mike and Steph are making out on the picnic blanket, between munching Lily's scotch eggs.

And I'm stood there, staring out at the sea, trainers stuck firmly to the sand. Alone, yet never alone. A little lost, but so, so grounded.

I'm not perfect, still. I'm insecure, conscious of my weight, of my acne and body hair, of the way I smell, the way I act around girls. I get awkward in social situations, struggle to remember to eat healthy, wear nice clothes. I don't have any chance of getting a girlfriend any time soon, not while I'm still living in Vibbington.

But that's okay.

The difference is, I'm now starting to realise that maybe I don't need those things to be happy, fulfilled. Carmel is learning to live again without her mother, and I'm just happy that I'm alive, that I have incredible friends and loving parents and a healthy baby sister and new puppy, that I've gotten into one university and that my best friend is going to Oxford, bloody *Oxford*.

I sometimes feel like my life is far from good, and that I

have the weight of the world on my shoulders. It's easy to get stuck in a hole sometimes, feeling as though nothing will ever improve, like you'll always be depressed and fat and lonely and a tad heartbroken… but that's never really true.

It's an overcast day, but the sky is bright with clouds, and the waves sparkle as they crash against the shore. Lily is shrieking as Matt splashes her with water, kicking it right up the side of her overalls, and she shoves him, hard, so that he falls over into the shallows.

A low breeze tickles my face, my chin. My hands are blue with cold and I can only imagine Carmel and Nima feel the same, frolicking in the sea with ice-cold water rushing up their jeans and covering them in goosebumps, from head to toe.

This is where I belong. Here, on a wintery day, with my best friends in the entire world, new puppy bounding towards me. Here, beneath an overcast sky, staring out into an ocean full of possibilities, of fun and adventure and an exciting future, waiting for me to grab it with both hands. Here, the cold air filling me with contentedness, with joy and love and honesty, sincerity.

I take in a deep breath, closing my eyes to let the day cover me entirely, fill my body with hope.

And when I exhale, I'm smiling.

acknowledgements

This book was formed when I shut myself in my office and wrote all 90,000 glorious words sat on a little wicker chair, the summer before I went to uni. I didn't think much, just poured every emotion in my head into this silly little story. So thank you, Carmel and Remy, for giving me an outlet. An outlet to write something meaningful, and heartfelt, and full of joy.

Secondly, thank you to Wattpad. I uploaded the book there mid-2021, and finished it just in time to enter the Wattys. When I was shortlisted, I don't think I've ever felt so relieved, so grateful, so sure of myself and my writing. It was the validation I needed that this wasn't all for nothing, that maybe I was at least an *okay* writer. UKYA is an underrated genre across the board, but especially online. To see my story in the spotlight, despite its genre, meant so much to me.

Thank you to the UKYA community, however small a fragment I've engaged with so far. There's no community of writers warmer and more supportive, passionate about our genre and the crazy talent coming out of it. UKYA is only getting bigger and better, and I'm excited to be a part of that, to help make a difference to the literary landscape in the UK right now. 'Midnight Sherbet' is quintessentially British in every way, filled with lovely characters and nods to all the things which made my own childhood so… well, British.

Thank you to my favourite author friends, two of the most talented young writers I know. Martha-may and Sana… I honestly don't think I could write these books without you, but you already know that, of course. And to everyone else in the group chat, for listening to my strange voice-note rants about boys and sleep deprivation and plot-holes. This book was made what it is by you and your endless support. The fact you love Remy and the gang as much as I do is all I could ever ask for.

So thank you to Christina and Hannah, and Isobel, Ada, Bridget… Middy Sherb superfans, till the very end.

To my mum, official proof-reader and editor of my second book in a row. It's not what you signed up for in having a child, but I think you quite enjoy pointing out my grammar mistakes. To Driffield Secondary School and Sixth Form, as always, for inspiring the heart of Vibbington and all it's become. To Yorkshire, the county which inspired my story, and continues to make me want to write day after day.

Thank you to Molly, for being so brilliant and kind and supportive of my first book… and to my wonderful Cath, for taking up the position of photographer and making me laugh enough that I could get through the brain-ache of self-publishing this puddle of words.

To the rest of my housemates and friends, for keeping me somewhat sane and taking a dozen more wonderful photos of me and my books.

And to everyone who read and loved 'Guided', to everyone who bought it or read it online, who left a positive review or a message telling me you enjoyed Macey's story. I'm sure she'd be so grateful if she knew how many people out there were routing for her. Thank you for the photos and posts and words of support, because you really did make my dream come true.

NOBODY KNOWS...

GUIDED

BOOK ONE

EMMA SMITH

NOBODY KNOWS WHAT HAPPENED
THAT NIGHT... NOBODY BUT MACEY.

EMMA SMITH

is a young adult author from Yorkshire, England. She wrote and illustrated her first "book" when she was seven-years-old and hasn't stopped writing since. When she's not walking on the beach or drinking an iced coffee with a crumpet and some chocolate, you'll probably find her reading something dark and mysterious… and most certainly YA.

@themmasmith on Instagram

emmasmithbooks.com

Printed in Great Britain
by Amazon